Starman Press, 2050 Russett Way, Carson City NV 89703
or email
rgw@argee.net

Library of Congress Control Number: 2014914648
Williscroft, Robert G.
Operation Ivy Bells / by Robert G. Williscroft
Illustrated by Gary McCluskey & Robert G. Williscroft
Cover design by Gary McCluskey

ISBN 978-0-9821662-6-0
1. Fiction – War and Military. 2. Fiction – Thriller/Technology
First Starman trade paperback edition
September 2014

PRAISE FOR
OPERATION IVY BELLS

OVER THE PAST FEW DECADES ACTION-ADVENTURE STORIES ABOUT SUBMARINES AND DIVING HAVE BECOME A POPULAR GENRE. TOM CLANCY AND CLIVE CUSSLER COME TO MIND AS EXEMPLARS. BUT ROBERT WILLISCROFT REALLY RAISES THE BAR WITH THIS BOOK. NOT ONLY IS HE AN OUTSTANDING WRITER BUT HE IS ALSO A 'DOER,' HAVING PARTICIPATED IN THE EVENTS DESCRIBED IN OPERATION IVY BELLS

> – *Captain Don Walsh USN, PhD*
> *USN Submersible Pilot #1*
> *Officer in Charge* Bathyscaph Trieste, *1959-1962*

MAGNIFICENTLY WRITTEN! A POWERFUL AND RIVETING ACCOUNT OF THE COLD WAR FOUGHT BENEATH THE OCEANS BY THE WORLD'S MOST FAMOUS ENEMIES. BRISTLES WITH THE SAME HAIR-RAISING AUTHENTICITY THAT LAUNCHED "THE HUNT FOR RED OCTOBER" TO WORLD NOTORIETY. THE FACTUAL AND DETAILED DESCRIPTIONS ARE SO REALISTIC THEY SUBMERGE YOU DEEP IN THE OCEAN DEPTHS AND MAKE YOU FEEL A PART OF THE SUB'S CREW ON A REMARKABLE MISSION TOLD BY VETERAN SUBMARINER, ROBERT WILLISCROFT, WHO DETAILS AN ALMOST UNIMAGINABLE WAR OF NERVES UNDER THE MOST TRYING CONDITIONS, AND OF THE MEN WHO POSSESS THE INCREDIBLE CAPABILITIES TO CARRY OUT THIS MISSION.

> *Martin H. Bloom, President*
> *The Adventurers' Club of Los Angeles*

ROBERT WILLISCROFT HAS PRODUCED QUITE A SEA STORY, A COLORFUL AND ENJOYABLE WORK THAT EXPLAINS ONE OF THE LITTLE-KNOWN SUCCESSES OF THE COLD WAR, WITH PLENTY OF FASCINATING DETAIL ABOUT SUBMARINE AND DIVING OPERATIONS.

> – *Tom Bowman*
> *NPR Pentagon reporter*

PRAISE FOR
OPERATION IVY BELLS

COLD WAR VETERANS WILL LOVE THIS EXCITING SUB-
MARINE ADVENTURE! DR. WILLISCROFT BRINGS READ-
ERS ALONG FOR A THRILLING ODYSSEY IN WHICH
ENGAGING CHARACTERS EXPERIENCE THE DANGER,
PASSION AND COMPLEXITY OF THE UNDERWATER WAR-
RIOR'S WORLD!

– Navy Captain Kathleen Hoff
Arctic Explorer

AN EXCITING LOOK INTO COLD WAR SUBMARINE ESPI-
ONAGE...I WAS COMPLETELY RIVETED TO THE BOOK'S
SUSPENSE AND ACTION...AMAZINGLY BASED ON TRUE
EVENTS. IT WAS INCREDIBLE TO READ ABOUT ISO-
LATED, UNDERWATER HAND-TO-HAND BATTLES THAT
TOOK PLACE IN SECRET DURING THE COLD WAR...
HIGHLY RECOMMEND!

– Marc Weitz, Past President
The Adventurers' Club of Los Angeles

A GREAT STORY...THE AUTHOR HAS DONE THE ESSEN-
TIAL, CRAFTING A NARRATIVE THAT YANKED ME OUT
OF MY SEAT LIKE THE BIG SQUID! I WAS GRABBED!!!
THIS IS WHAT THEY CALL A BREAK-OUT BOOK...

– Ed Offley, Author of *Scorpion Down,*
The Burning Shore & *Turning the Tide*

FOR THOSE WHO HAVE AN INTEREST IN COLD WAR
SECRETS THIS IS A MUST READ. SOME MINOR DETAILS
AND NAMES HAVE BEEN CHANGED, BUT MOST OF IT
IS PRETTY CLOSE TO THE REAL DEAL...CLOSE AS YOU
CAN GET WITHOUT GOING TO JAIL. MY SOURCE OF
INFORMATION? MEMORY – I WAS AN IVY BELLS SUBMA-
RINER.

– A *USS Seawolf* Sailor

OPERATION IVY BELLS

BY

ROBERT G. WILLISCROFT

TABLE OF CONTENTS

Disclaimer

Although this is a work of fiction, it is based upon real events and real people. The *USS Halibut* is real, and what she accomplished is real. The captain and crew members of *Halibut*, as depicted in this work, while mirroring many heroic submariners the author was privileged to serve with, are the products of the author's imagination. The other officers, sailors, and civilians as depicted in this work are compilations of individuals with whom the author served during his twenty-three-year career. The characteristics of individuals in the saturation dive team are a compilation of actual team members as personally known to the author, but none of the characters as depicted in this work are real. The places and incidents actually happened, for the most part, but to several teams over a span of years, in multiple locations, and the specific details are the products of the author's imagination. Except for several prominent individuals who appear by name doing things they would normally have done, although their recorded actions within this work are fictional, any resemblance to actual persons, living or dead, is entirely coincidental.

Acknowledgments

Several people contributed to the creation of this book.

Obviously, I owe the saturation divers of the Test Operations Group a huge debt of gratitude, since they supplied the raw material from which I drew the profiles and personalities of the saturation dive team in this book. It was my greatest privilege to have served with them.

My friend Michele patiently listened to me read each chapter, stopping me when my arcane terminology got in the way of the story, and asking clarifying questions when I assumed too much background knowledge for my readers.

My son Jason made some cogent observations from his time as an Officer in the Navy. His personal experience helped me keep the details accurate.

Most significantly, my wonderful wife, Jill, whom I first met just a few years after the events in this book, and who finally consented to marry me nearly thirty years later, pored over each chapter with her discerning engineer's eye. She kept my timeline honest, and made sure that regular readers could understand fully what actually transpired during the course of Operation Ivy Bells.

Jill's daughter, Selena, and twin sons, Arthur and Robert, also read the manuscript, and provided their insights.

Ed Offley, who penned the Foreword, offered to proof the final manuscript. He gave me his insights based on three decades of reporting on, and writing about, the Navy and submarines. Ed's inputs made Operation Ivy Bells a much better read.

A tip of the hat to Gary McCluskey for supplying illustrations where nothing was otherwise available. Gary created these beautiful illustrations from my words and sketches. He also turned the cover from a sketch and several ideas into the breath-taking scene that graces the front of this book.

It goes without saying that any remaining omissions, errors, and mistakes fall directly on my shoulders.

Robert G. Williscroft, PhD
Centennial, Colorado
September, 2014

FOREWORD

For nearly a half-century, one of the greatest sagas of the sea has remained an untold story – until now. At the height of the Cold War, a small and elite group of U.S. Navy nuclear submariners and deep-sea divers pulled off one of the most ambitions clandestine intelligence-gathering operations in history.

Using the converted nuclear submarine *USS Halibut* as an operating platform, a team of Navy divers, sometime in the early 1970s, was able to place a wiretapping pod around a Soviet military communications cable deep inside the Sea of Okhotsk. The pod successfully intercepted critical communications between the Soviet Pacific Fleet base at Petropavlovsk Kamchatskiy and other bases on the mainland including Vladivostok and Magadan. On a second mission, the team was able to deploy a massive six-ton, plutonium-powered replacement pod that sucked up Soviet communications for months at a time. Despite disclosure of that particular operation a decade later by a turncoat inside the National Security Agency, the diver-spies and their nuclear submarine brethren continued to carry out similar missions elsewhere well into the 1990s – and probably beyond.

Operation Ivy Bells, as the initial mission was called, comprised more than a feat of silent stealth beneath the waves. It was also an incredible accomplishment of a daring – and dangerous – submergence technique known as saturation diving. Navy deep-sea divers "pressed" down to depths of several hundred feet in a pressure chamber attached to the *Halibut's* hull, breathing an exotic gas mixture of helium (which replaced nitrogen that would become toxic to the human body at these depths) and a small amount of oxygen (since the normal amount of oxygen would also become toxic at these depths). They were able to operate at depths far beyond the maximum for ordinary deep-sea gear and scuba tanks. The intelligence they gathered played a major part in America's Cold War victory.

News reports since the Cold War ended have occasionally hinted at the barest outlines of Operation Ivy Bells and subsequent missions, but revealed few details of what it was actually like for a Navy diver to risk capture or death while planting a sensor pod or retrieving Soviet missile nosecone fragments literally under the feet of the Cold War adversary. In July 2000, *Puget Soundings*, a newsletter of the United States Submarine Veterans Bremerton Base, inadvertently let slip one new marker of just how important the sailors of *USS Halibut* – another spy sub, *USS Seawolf*, and later spy subs *USS Parche*, and *USS Jimmy Carter* – were to America's Cold War efforts. Two of the guest speakers at the Howard Johnson Motor Lodge in Bremerton, Washington, were former CIA Director Robert Gates, and world-famous techno-thriller novelist Tom Clancy. In remarks to the reunion of *Parche* sailors – the descendants two decades later of the *Halibut* team – Clancy stated, "The point of the (U.S. Navy's) lance killed the (Soviet) dragon ... and you were the point of the lance." Gates went even further, praising the veterans for all their efforts, where "every mission (was) a life-and-death mission.... I know who you are and I know what you did, and I am honored to be here with you tonight."

Thanks to Robert Williscroft, those interested in Cold War history can now relive the missions of the *Halibut* and its dedicated crew as they undertook two daring operations to penetrate Soviet military communications and to retrieve vital physical evidence of the Soviet missile program. While this book is a novel, with composite characters and some events compiled from stories from former colleagues, it is far from a totally fictional account. As a young Navy officer, Williscroft served both as a nuclear submariner and later became involved as a saturation diver with the Navy's Submarine Development Group One, which carried out the daring spy missions deep inside Soviet waters. Much of *Operation Ivy Bells* comes from Williscroft's own experiences, or that of his close comrades.

You won't be able to put this book down!

Ed Offley
Panama City Beach, Florida
August, 2014

Ed Offley is author of *Scorpion Down: Sunk by the Soviets, Buried by the Pentagon – the Untold Story of the USS Scorpion*, and several books about the Battle of the Atlantic, most recently *The Burning Shore: How Hitler's U-boats Brought World War II to America*.

DEDICATION

This book is dedicated to the heroic submariners and saturation divers who participated in Operation Ivy Bells in the Sea of Okhotsk and the Barents Sea from the late 1960s through the mid 1980s, men whose courageous actions materially enhanced America's Cold War stance and significantly shortened the duration of the Cold War.

USS Halibut (SSN-587) Organizational Chart

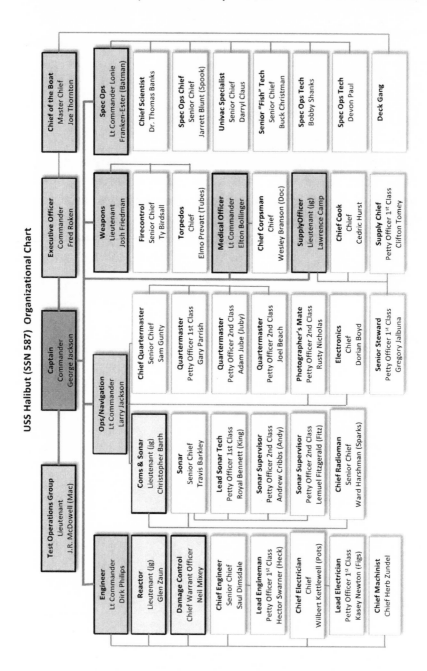

Cast of Characters

Submarine Development Group One (SubDevGruOne)

Commander Dan Richardson – Ex skipper of *USS Pigeon*; Heads Submarine Development Group One activities

Personnelman 1st Class Jerry Peterson (Pete) – SubDev-GruOne staff

John Craven – Brains behind the Project

Marine – Marine guard at SubDevGruOne HQ

Test Operations Group (TOG)

Lieutenant J.R. McDowell (Mac) – Officer-in-Charge (OIC) (Narrator)

Master Chief Hamilton Comstock (Ham) – Master Saturation Diver – Came from Experimental Diving Unit and Man-in-the-Sea Program

Chief Jack Meredith – Master Saturation Diver (Understudy) – Ex SEAL – left to become saturation diver; ex Man-in-the-Sea Program

Petty Officer 1st Class James Tanner (Jimmy) – Saturation Diver; qualified Dive Console operator – Sonar Tech

Petty Officer 1st Class Melvin Ford (Whitey) – Saturation Diver; qualified Dive Console operator – Electronics Tech

Petty Officer 2nd Class William Fisher (Bill) – Saturation Diver; qualified Dive Console operator – Battlefield medic turned saturation diver

Petty Officer 2nd Class Wlodek Cslauski (Ski) – Saturation Diver; qualified Dive Console operator – Quartermaster

Petty Officer 2nd Class Jeremy Romain (Jer) – Saturation Diver; qualified Dive Console operator – Submariner (Engineman) turned saturation diver; Graduate of earlier saturation dive class

Petty Officer 2nd Class Harry Blackwell – Saturation Diver; qualified Dive Console operator – Submariner (Auxiliaryman) turned saturation diver; Graduate of earlier saturation dive class

Cast of Characters (cont.)

USS Elk River

Lieutenant George Franklin (Frankie) – OIC Saturation
Dive Unit
Master Chief Ray Harmon – Master Saturation Diver
Dr. Joseph Lemwell (Doc) – Saturation Doctor
Chief Paul Struthers – Master Saturation Diver
Trainee
Sailor – Deck hand

Horse & Cow

Bartender – At The Horse & Cow
Snorkel Patty – At The Horse & Cow

USS Halibut Deck Gang

Seaman José Roscoe – Topside Watch, Lookout/
Helmsman/Planesman
Seaman Rocky Faust – Topside Watch, Lookout/
Helmsman/Planesman
Seaman Matthew Scott (Scotty) – Topside Watch,
Lookout/Helmsman/Planesman
Seaman Charlie Todd – Topside Watch, Lookout/
Helmsman/Planesman
Seaman Stacy Fisher – Topside Watch, Lookout/
Helmsman/Planesman
Seaman Lyle Dunlap – Topside Watch, Lookout/
Helmsman/Planesman
Seaman Gene Magor – Topside Watch, Lookout/
Helmsman/Planesman

Soviet Whiskey Submarine

Unknown Soviet Officer – Commanding Officer

Soviet Salvage Operation

Sergyi Andreev – The Soviet Diver

USS Richland AFDM-8

Lieutenant Commander Roger Leach – Commanding
Officer
Chief Warrant Officer Tommie Bridger – First
Lieutenant
Lieutenant Junior Grade Odis Weldy – Engineer
Ensign Bennie Poley – Operations Officer

CAST OF CHARACTERS (CONT.)

Halibut Watch Sections

Section One
Deck – Lieutenant J.R. McDowell (Mac)
Dive – Lieutenant (jg) Christopher Barth
COW – Chief Wilbert Kettlewell (Pots)
Nav – Petty Officer 1st Class Gary Parrish
Bow/Helm – Seaman Fred Skidmore
Stern – Seaman José Roscoe
Sonar – Petty Officer 1st Class Royal
Bennett (King)
Maneuvering – Petty Officer 1st Class Hector
Swarner (Heck)

Section Two
Deck – Lieutenant Josh Friedman (Weaps)
Dive – Chief Warrant Officer Neil Mixey
COW – Senior Chief Saul Dimsdale
Nav – Senior Chief Quartermaster Sam
Gunty
Bow/Helm – Seaman Rocky Faust
Stern – Seaman Matthew Scott (Scotty)
Sonar – Senior Chief Sonar Technician
Travis Barkley
Maneuvering – Petty Officer 1st Class Kasey
Newton (Figs)

Section Three
Deck – Lieutenant Commander Larry Jack-
son (Nav)
Dive – Lieutenant (jg) Glen Zaun (RCA)
COW – Chief Elmo Prevatt (Tubes)
Nav – Petty Officer 2nd Class Adam Jube
(Juby)
Bow/Helm – Seaman Charlie Todd
Stern – Seaman Stacy Fisher
Sonar – Petty Officer 2nd Class Andrew
Cribbs (Andy)
Maneuvering – Chief Herb Zundel

Section Four

Deck – Lieutenant Commander Dirk Philips (Eng)

Dive – Senior Chief Ward Harshman (Sparks)

COW – Senior Chief Ty Birdsall

Nav – Petty Officer 2nd Class Joel Beach

Bow/Helm – Seaman Lyle Dunlap

Stern – Seaman Gene Magor

Sonar – Petty Officer 2nd Class Lemuel Fitzgerald (Fitz)

Maneuvering – Chief Dorian Boyd

OPERATION IVY BELLS

BY

ROBERT G. WILLISCROFT

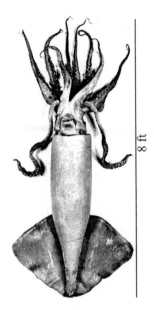

8 ft

Humboldt Squid

CHAPTER ONE

I hung motionless in the frigid water a few yards from the spherical Personnel Transfer Capsule a thousand feet below the surface. It was pitch black, except for two beams of light emanating from the PTC that terminated in white circles on the sandy bottom a hundred feet below. In the crystal clear water there was virtually no diffusion. I felt motion beside me and turned to see a flood of bubbles rising from Harry's plunge through the PTC hatch.

We each had a hundred feet of umbilical snaking back into the PTC, where Bill, the third member of our party, kept the slack out of our umbilicals and stood by to help in the event of an emergency. I put a finger in front of my mask indicating silence. Harry gave me a thumbs-up. We started drifting downward, not paying any attention to our depth. After all, we were saturated to a thousand feet; down was good.

"Red Diver, what are you doing?" Master Chief Ray Harmon was having a conniption topside. As the Sat Dive

Unit's Master Saturation Diver, he was running the dive under Lieutenant George Franklin, the Officer-in-Charge.

"Checking something out, Control, just checking something out." I increased my descent and Harry followed suit. I could hear my distorted voice in my earphones.

"Red Diver!" It was the Master Chief again.

"Red Diver, aye." I needed to delay him for just another twenty seconds.

"Return to one-thousand feet NOW!" He was pissed.

"Say again, Control, say again." I needed just another ten seconds.

"Lieutenant McDowell, get your ass back to the PTC...NOW!" Oops, that was Franklin, and he was really pissed.

"Roger that." I scooped a handful of sand and stuffed it in my leg pocket and looked up at the PTC. It appeared as a lighted jewel against velvet black. Our activities near the bottom had stirred up some detritus, and the water around us sparkled with light flickering off tiny silt particles – an alien, fairytale world.

I gave Harry two thumbs-up, and we slowly ascended, our umbilicals snaking above us, live serpents in the frigid water. Inside the PTC, Bill recoiled the umbilicals to take up the slack. It took us less than two minutes to get back to a thousand feet; our total excursion had lasted no more than four minutes. I pointed to the expanded metal work bin attached to the outside of the PTC. Harry pulled out the make-work project for this training dive, and we started screwing screws and turning bolts.

And that's when it happened!

My first impression was a flashing shadow through one of the light beams, a flicker just below my threshold of awareness – something big and fast.

"What the fuck was that?" Harry squeaked, his voice distorted by helium and electronic descrambling.

"Green Diver, report!" That was the Master Chief.

"Jeezus..." Harry dropped down three feet and grabbed my left fin. I felt him trying to pull me toward him, toward the hatch. "Mac...the hatch!" Harry's desperation came right through his squeak. Then he jerked and let go. "Kee...rist!"

"Red Diver...what's going on down there?" That was Franklin.

Off to my right a green phosphorescent shape flicked into and out of existence. A pink one materialized to my left. Suddenly, from right in front of me, something bright blue hit my faceplate with the force of a sledge hammer.

Everything went black. I don't mean I passed out... everything went black, literally. I reached up and discovered a really large thing covering my entire helmet. It was smooth and spongy, and it was undulating. I heard a scraping, grinding noise against my faceplate. Something wrapped itself around my left arm, jerking my hand away from the pulsing mass. I pulled my arm back, and felt a rush of cold water enter my suit at the wrist. A tear...whatever it was had torn a goddamn hole in my suit! What the hell can tear a hole through compressed, nylon-reinforced neoprene? That shit'll stop a knife!

That's when I noticed that I still held a ten-pound steel wrench in my right hand. You don't move things fast underwater, but I put as much force into my haymaker as possible. The wrench sunk into the mass attached to my helmet, and in a flash it was gone. I could see again. Several feet ahead of me I could make out two elongated hooded shapes arrayed vertically in the water, pulsing green to pink to blue. Large, almost human eyes as big as my hands gazed at me.

"Control, Red Diver...we got some kind of company... three or four giant squid, I think..." I looked down at Harry, backed up warily against the PTC just below me, dive knife glinting in his hand. I could see a big tear in the left shoulder of his hot-water suit. "Harry...you okay?"

"Yeah...what the fuck! Squid? You're shittin' me!" He waved his knife. "One of those fuckers took a chunk outa my suit!"

"You or just the suit?" I asked.

"Just the suit...I think. No blood in the water."

"Mac..." It was Franklin. "You guys get back into the PTC ASAP!"

"Working on it, Control..." One of the creatures hit the top of my helmet hard. Tentacles draped down the entire length of my body. I could distinctly feel razor-sharp sucker teeth dig into my suit. "Harry," I yelled, sounding like a compressed Donald Duck through the helium and electronics, "get this fucker off me!"

I felt Harry come up between me and the PTC and repeatedly stab the creature's carapace. With that, my personal squid apparently had second thoughts, as it unwrapped itself and disappeared. The other two with their changing color patterns continued to hang about ten feet away, large unblinking eyes evaluating me. It seemed as if they were communicating by color and pattern. Suddenly, the right one went dark, dropped its tentacles straight down, and began to undulate. Two thin, suckerless tentacles danced around the creature in a meaningless pattern. I transferred the wrench to my left hand and pulled my knife from its sheath on my right leg. Then, in a blinding white flash, the eight foot squid whipped to horizontal, and propelled itself tentacles first directly at my chest. As it approached, its tentacles rolled back, forming an eight-legged basket filled with a thousand sucker teeth. In the center I could see a mouth as large as my helmet surrounded by a ring of razor teeth reflecting the squid's phosphorescent pulses.

I jammed the wrench as hard as I could directly into the gaping maw and left it there. I grabbed an upper tentacle with my left hand and sliced. It was like cutting tough leather. I sawed frantically while the squid grabbed at my hand and knife with two other tentacles while keeping a grip on me with the rest. After what seemed like an hour, but actually was less than a minute, I held the detached writhing tentacle in my left hand. I tossed it away, still squirming like a snake. With the tentacle out of the way, I could see the large, human-like eye, fully six inches across staring at me malevolently. I plunged my knife into the orb – once, twice, a third time. That did it! The two thin tentacles whipped around frantically, and the giant disappeared into the darkness along with its pulsating companion.

"Harry, where are you?" I was concentrating on the water in front of me, preparing for another attack.

"Right below you, Mac. Let's get the fuck outa here!"

A very long minute later I followed Harry through the hatch opening, and Bill pulled me all the way in.

"Everyone down there okay?" That was Franklin again.

"Control...PTC," Bill responded, "divers are back inside. Everyone seems to be okay."

Just then, the smooth water surface in the circular opening began to boil.

"Shee...it!" Bill shouted, as two thick tentacles darted through the surface and began whipping around the PTC interior. "Fucker's trying to get in the PTC!" Bill's distorted voice in my earphones matched his lip movements. His face registered not so much panic as total shock.

"Or pull us out," Harry added.

Bill and Harry grabbed their knives, slashing into the writhing appendages. I reached over the opening and grasped the hatch in both hands, pushing for all I was worth. I looked down into the six inch eye of the invading monster as I swung the hatch down. I sensed intelligence, driven by pure malevolence. The last thing I saw before I dogged the hatch was a half-sliced-through tapered tentacle tip, as it slipped back into the frigid water around us.

Harry removed his helmet and gave Bill a gloved high-five. From across the dogged hatch I gave them both two thumbs-up, and pulled off my own helmet and gloves. Then I grabbed a Ziploc baggie from my personal kit to fill it with my trophy sand, but when I felt my leg pocket for the sand, it was gone. Chalk up another one to the monsters.

"Control...this is Mac." I was sure they could hear the relief in my distorted voice. "To hell with the rest of this dive. Just bring us home!"

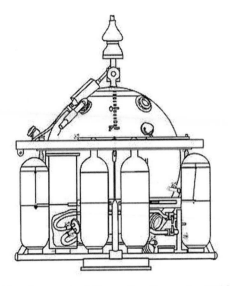

The Personnel Transfer Capsule (PTC)

CHAPTER TWO

About six months earlier I strolled up a hill on the Submarine Base at the foot of Point Loma on San Diego Bay, past a brilliant flower bed of red and purple ice plants toward a row of off-yellow clapboard two story buildings. They were typical government buildings dating from World War II, carefully maintained, but showing their age.

Several uniformed sailors were out and about. One saluted as he stepped into the narrow street to pass me.

"G'morning, Sir!"

I saluted back, and watched him hurry up the street. The warm summer sun glistened off his white trousers and short-sleeved white shirt. He was medium sized, but well built, and he walked with a swagger. Over his left shirt pocket, he sported several ribbons, and above them a silver First-class Divers Pin. He turned toward the building labeled: Submarine Development Group One – Headquarters.

My destination.

I followed him up the broad entrance stairway through the door and paused to let my eyes adjust. He stepped around a desk, passed through a swinging gate in a light oak railing, and flashed his ID to an armed Marine guarding an ordinary looking door in the opposite wall. The Marine punched a code in an unobtrusive keypad mounted to the wall beside the door.

A soft click, and the door swung inward, revealing an office with several desks and a hallway leading back into the building. The sailor stepped through the door, and it swung closed behind him. He obviously was part of the operation behind that door. The Marine resumed his parade-rest stance before the door.

"May I help you, Sir?"

The Yeoman Second Class looked up at me from his desk as the door closed. I removed my sunglasses and handed him my orders.

"Oh, Lieutenant McDowell. We've been expecting you."

I handed him the envelope containing my records. I had just completed forty-eight weeks of deep sea diver training, and was reporting for duty at the U.S. Navy Saturation Diving School.

It was a dream come true. As a boy growing up in Germany, I had thrilled at exploits of the deep-diving bathyscaphe *Trieste* and its successor in plumbing the deepest depths of the world's oceans. The names *Alvin* and *Sea Cliff* were as familiar to me as the Starship *USS Enterprise* (yeah, I was a Trekkie, of sorts). And I practically lived in *Sealab* with Alan Shepard.

So here I was, ex-Sonar Tech, ex-sub sailor, just another surface puke – but I was about to join the ranks of the elite corps of saturation divers. This was heady stuff.

The class work was easy, not so much because I was smart, but because I had covered this material one way or the other either in the previous year in diving school, or while getting my degree in marine physics. My classmates were all enlisted types, but one hell of a group of sharp guys. Without a degree in anything, most of them had no trouble at all keeping up with me.

We spent most mornings in class and most afternoons either working out, gaining hands-on experience with the Mark 2 Mod 0 Deep Diving System on the venerable support vessel *USS Elk River* moored next to the submarine piers, or both.

We had to learn the diving system inside and out; every valve, switch, pipe, and wire. It's not particularly difficult to do, but it does take time. The system consists of a thirty-foot-long pressure chamber called the Deck Decompression Chamber or DDC that contains a lock for entrance and egress, a small lock for passing in food or medical supplies, four bunks, lavatory facilities, and emergency equipment. The Personnel Transfer Capsule or PTC mates to the DDC and can transfer a maximum of four divers to the underwater working site. The umbilical that supports the PTC and supplies communications and power is called the SPCC – Strength-Power-Communications Cable.

I said the guys were able to keep up with me in the classroom work. I should have also noted that I barely kept up with them in physical training. Where did these guys come from? I thought I was in good shape – after all, I had just completed forty-eight weeks of some of the most difficult physical training I had ever undertaken. These guys didn't break a sweat after three miles running with full gear. They got my attention.

Training lasted twelve weeks. I ate, slept, dreamed, talked, thought Mark 2. By the tenth week I had that system nailed. And that's when it – the system, not the giant squid – nearly nailed me.

#

We were out on a local practice site, about eleven-hundred feet deep, basically a hole in the ocean bottom a couple of miles off Point Loma. The idea was that we would anchor over this hole, cinched into a four-point moor. For you landlubbers, you anchor four large buoys to the corners of a rectangle, roughly centered over your spot – in our case the hole. Then you cinch your vessel to each of the buoys, and loosen and tighten the lines until you are directly over the hole. Anyway, we would saturate to one-thousand feet and then lower down near the bottom for some real time experience.

Okay – more details for you non-divers. Even if you're reading this in the International Space Station, the air you're breathing is about twenty-one percent oxygen and seventy-nine percent nitrogen. As you dive, your equipment supplies you with compressed air that matches the pressure of your surroundings, and this increases by about one atmosphere's worth every thirty-three feet. So at a thousand feet, air enters your lungs at about thirty atmospheres or 450 pounds per square inch or psi, as we call it.

It turns out that normal air becomes toxic under too much pressure, because oxygen itself starts becoming toxic when you breathe in more than about twice the amount you would get breathing pure oxygen at the surface. This happens at about two-hundred feet. The other problem is that nitrogen becomes narcotic at about the same depth. This can be a pretty lethal combination: you're breathing potentially poisonous gas and are so narced you don't know what to do about it.

We solved this problem by reducing the total amount of oxygen in the breathing gas mix so that the actual amount is about the equivalent of the twenty-one percent we breathe on the surface, and we replaced the nitrogen with helium. This made us sound funny, but we didn't get narced.

Now back to you non-diver, non-space station types. Sitting there, your body is saturated with all the nitrogen it can hold. Your cells, bones, everything, have all the nitrogen possible. If you dive to say thirty-three feet (one atmosphere, remember), and stay there long enough, you will become saturated at thirty-three feet. If you stay at a hundred feet, five-hundred feet, same thing – stay long enough, and you saturate; you can't take up any more nitrogen, or helium if you are diving deeper than about one-hundred-twenty feet.

Now here's the kicker. If you are saturated to thirty-three feet you can come right to the surface without suffering any consequences. But, if you saturate at forty feet, you cannot come shallower than about seven feet without suffering the bends, when dissolved gases in your body come out of solution to form bubbles; and let me tell you, you don't want the bends. They hurt like hell, and they can kill you! Point is, you can tolerate a one atmosphere difference between your higher body saturation level and the ambient pressure. No more – just one atmosphere, thirty-three feet.

Anyway, the ship was in the moor over the hole, and five of us were in lockdown inside the Mark 2 DDC, pressurizing to one-thousand feet. It took several hours, but we finally "arrived." At this depth, even though we were still inside the DDC, we could only communicate with each other by using a descrambler. You talk into a throat mike, a computer lowers the frequency and does other cool things, and you and everyone else hears you through earplugs. Frankly, we were so tired and our muscles and bones ached so much that we just went to sleep. To hell with talking.

Reveille came early. Since this was the first time for any of us, we were pretty excited. Rank has its privilege, so Harry and Bill, the two senior non-coms, and I climbed into our hot-water suits while we munched on breakfast bars.

We climbed through the overhead hatch into the PTC, while Jimmy and Whitey stood by in the DDC.

"Ready, Mac?" Jimmy's voice sounded distorted and alien through the descrambler, as he prepared to run through his check-off list.

"Yeah." I turned to Harry and checked off his equipment as Jimmy went through his list. We had these things totally memorized, but it wouldn't do to miss something at a thousand feet with a 967-foot ceiling. We did it by the book.

"Suit."

"Check."

"Gloves."

"Check."

"Wrist retainers."

"Check."

"Come-home." He was referring to a small gas bottle that would get a diver back to the PTC in an emergency.

"Check."

"Harness."

"Check."

"Ankle weights."

"Check."

"Fins."

"Check."

And so on for both Harry and Bill, and then Harry did me.

Bill shut and dogged the hatch. "Let's rock and roll!"

"Control, PTC," I said into my throat mike, "we're ready to disconnect."

During our tedious check-off, the topside guys had been busy rigging the crane and SPCC for our descent. The boiler was up and running, to supply our suits with hot water so we wouldn't die of hypothermia. They checked our gas supply and backup, coordinating with the Dive Manifold Complex and Master Chief Harmon. Somewhere along the way, somebody also checked in with Officer-in-Charge (OIC) Lieutenant George Franklin and Doctor Joseph Lemwell.

Franklin was in charge of the operation, but he pretty much let the Master Chief do his thing, although

I suspected he kept totally on top of the situation. The Doc was there just in case.

Oh yeah, I almost forgot about Chief Paul Struthers. He was in training for Master Saturation Diver, the guy who controls the dive. He worked directly for the Master Chief, and this was his final qualification dive. In other words, Chief Struthers would make the life and death decisions for the five of us, backed by the Master Chief and Franklin, of course, and the Doc if something went wrong.

After what seemed like forever, we heard the clanking of the PTC releases and then we swung free on the umbilical, up and away from the DDC. I exchanged high fives with Harry and Bill. Believe it or not, we were sweating up a storm. Even though the PTC was painted bright white, the sun was hot and we were getting more than our share.

Since the PTC has three ports, we each grabbed one. I wished I could have spoken to my buds without being overheard by Control, but without the descrambler we couldn't understand a word. So we said it with raised eyebrows and shoulder punches. This was the real thing; we were on our way.

Things went pretty well. Control lowered us into the water to about ten feet. I turned on the lights, and divers checked us out, looking for telltale bubbles or anything else wrong.

"PTC checks okay," Control announced. "Going down."

"Roger!" I acknowledged.

Harry reached into his tool kit and pulled out a small roll of thread. Bill started to speak, but Harry held a finger to his lips and winked. Then he pulled out his roll of duct tape and taped one end of the thread to the middle of the spherical bulkhead. He stretched it taut across the sphere and taped the other end to the opposite bulkhead.

"Cute." It was the Master Chief, observing on his PTC monitor. But he said nothing else.

"Passing one-hundred-fifty feet," droned Control.

I confirmed on the depth gauge inside the PTC. "Check, one-hundred-fifty feet."

We continued down. It got noticeably dimmer. We passed two-hundred feet.

Three-hundred.

Four-hundred.

At five-hundred feet we stopped.

"PTC, Control, check for leaks."

We did. There were none.

"Okay, guys, undog the hatch." This was no problem, since the internal pressure was much greater than the outside pressure. This way, when we reached a thousand feet, the hatch, located at the bottom of the spherical PTC, would release.

Six-hundred feet. Harry pointed to the thread. It showed a distinct catenary; it looked like it had dipped by at least an inch or so. I shivered as I thought about the immense pressure squeezing the round hull of the PTC.

Nine-hundred feet. We slowed our descent, and crept to the one-thousand foot mark. The thread had dipped nearly a foot.

By now it was pretty cold inside the PTC. Water temperature outside was just over thirty degrees, and it wasn't much warmer inside.

"Harry," I said, "turn on the hot water. It's going to be wet in here anyway."

"PTC, Control." It was Chief Struthers. "That isn't according to procedure..."

"Can it!" I heard Harmon's ringing voice in the background.

"PTC, Control, disregard my last."

We did, and the hot water flowing into my suit felt wonderful – almost as good as...well, you get the point.

Just then there was a slight pop, and the hatch moved off its seal. I reached down and pulled it completely open, assisted by the counter spring. The opening looked like a perfect mirror. Bill stuck his finger into the water.

"Damn! That's cold!" he said, jerking his hand back. Tinny laughter floated from the wall-mounted speaker.

"Can it!" Harmon was a slave driver.

"Okay – Mac and Harry, suit up."

No "PTC, Control," I thought. The Chief's loosening up. I helped Harry with his Mark 14 diver's hat. Shortly I could hear his rasping breathing over the electronic filters in my earplug. Bill assisted me, and a couple minutes later I gave Harry the thumbs-up.

"You ready, Pal?"

"Yeah."

It was much more difficult to understand him through the breathing noise and the helium talk. We donned our fins.

"Control, Red Diver." That was me.

"Control, aye."

"Control, Green Diver." Harry.

"Control, aye."

"Control, Standby." Bill.

Then we cross-checked with each other. Bill made a final check of our come-home bottles, and I stepped through the hatch, blithely unaware of the giant squids that were hanging out just beyond our visibility limit.

\#

Following the coordinated giant squid attack, Master Chief Harmon brought the PTC to the surface in record time, ready to be hoisted aboard *Elk River*. Before we left the water, divers inspected us for any leaks, looking for telltale bubbles. Following their all clear, we were hoisted up and shortly found ourselves inside the chamber, our backs being pounded by Jimmy and Whitey.

Master Chief Harmon came on the circuit. "It looks like you guys were attacked by a group of Humboldt Squid. Pretty unusual. They're normally found off the coast of Baja, 'bout a hundred miles south of here. Never seen 'em here, ever."

Franklin spoke up. "The Doc decided to cancel the second dive for this cycle. You guys get some sleep, and tomorrow Bill will descend with Jimmy and Whitey. We'll winch into a slightly different spot. I don't think the squid will bother you again." He paused. "This was just one of those flukes."

The three of us stripped out of our suits while we tried to explain to Jimmy and Whitey what had happened down there. Harry did most of the talking, backed up by Bill. From time to time, he would look to me for confirmation. He showed them his suit shoulder and my left wrist, while I sipped hot coffee that Control had just sent in through the Medical Lock. It tasted like shit – I mean, it didn't have any taste at all, more like a cup of hot water. At a thousand feet you really can't taste anything except sweet, sour, and very spicy. Might as well eat cardboard and drink water.

"They was coordinating their attack," Harry said. "It was like they was herding us." He grinned at his friends. "Ain't never seen anything like it, that's for damn sure!"

The next morning, Bill climbed back into the PTC followed by Jimmy and Whitey. The dive was routine – they were pretty nervous, but the squid stayed away. They were cold and tired by the time the PTC returned to the surface. It took them about ten microseconds to bed down in the chamber. Struthers had set up a three-hour watch rotation for our three-day decompression, so they had several hours to catch up on their sleep, while Harry and I took the first two watches.

#

We played a lot of cards, watched several movies, and ate more cardboard. You cannot imagine how long three days in a small chamber can seem, when there is absolutely no way to go anywhere. I discovered something interesting during our decompression. Each of us had subconsciously staked out a personal territory. When you were in your territory, the others left you alone. Mine was located so that I had a clear view of the atmosphere monitoring gauges in the chamber. I didn't do this on purpose; I must have done it subconsciously.

We had arrived at a pressure equivalent of 150 feet, which meant that our bodies were at still at 183 feet of pressure, since we were keeping one atmosphere ahead of our saturation level. Harry was in the outer lock brushing his teeth. Normally we kept the lock door completely open, but we had slung it nearly closed in order to set up the viewing screen for a movie.

One of the guys had been producing a lot of methane, if you get my drift. The chamber had become rather... uncomfortable.

"Fer Chrissake," Whitey yelled in his high-pitched helium speech. "Give us a vent! I'm gonna choke to death." He glowered at Jimmy, whom he suspected of being the culprit.

"Roger that." Chief Struthers was back on duty.

Our gas mix at 150 feet normally would be just under five percent oxygen. Do the math; it works out to the same amount of oxygen as twenty-one percent on the surface. I know it sounds screwy, but that's how it works. Anyway, we were on an enriched oxygen mix to facilitate flushing helium from our systems. Chief Struthers opened two valves, one to add gas to the chamber and one to vent gas from the chamber. His job was to make sure the pressure remained the same, and to ensure that our breathing mix percentages didn't change either.

The process was pretty noisy and was supposed to take about ten minutes. Whitey lay down on the deck by the inlet pipe, breathed deeply and smiled with a sigh of relief.

"That's more like it," he squeaked.

At this depth we had removed our mikes and ear plugs since, with a bit of effort, we could understand each other without the descrambling that was necessary at a thousand feet.

Bill was standing in the middle of the sleeping area, elbows on the two upper racks supporting himself. The surveillance camera was aimed at the back of his head, but Struthers wasn't worried since we were about to sit down to watch a movie. Jimmy was sitting on the deck leaning against the bulkhead across from me to my right, and as I said, Harry was brushing his teeth in the outer lock; Whitey was on the deck enjoying the fresh air.

Five minutes passed. That was when I began to notice something funny. I don't mean ha-ha funny, either. The oxygen gauge which had been hovering near twenty percent ever since we reached 150 feet (oxygen enriched – remember), looked like it was near zero. Which explains why I didn't react immediately. I was about to pass out for lack of oxygen.

I got up and crossed over to the gauge and peered at it intensely. Sure 'nough, it read near zero. I stumbled back to my territory, alarms going off in my befuddled brain. Then it hit me. The other guys were unconscious. Struthers couldn't see us because Bill was wedged between the bunks, and his head still blocked the camera. I tried to reach the emergency alarm button, but it seemed to recede away as I reached for it.

The last thing I remember is yelling "Petty Officer Blackwell!" Blackwell was Harry's last name. "This is an order! Hit the emergency alarm!"

I barely heard the raucous Claxton as I slipped into oblivion.

#

A million years later (they told me it actually was less than a minute) I slowly regained consciousness, bleary and befuddled, my head cradled in Harry's arms. I was wearing an Emergency Air Breathing (EAB) mask.

"Come on, Mac, goddammit, wake up! Wake up, dammit!"

I shook my head and struggled to my knees. The chamber was dark except for light streaming through the four ports. The Claxton still bellowed. Harry grabbed another EAB and slapped it on Whitey. I got Jimmy. And then Harry lowered Bill to the deck and I masked him too.

I saw Franklin's worried face peering through one of the ports, and the doc's at the second. I picked up a sound-powered phone handset and held it out toward Franklin. He grabbed the set attached to the outside of the chamber.

"What the fuck!" he yelled.

"You idiots flushed us with pure helium," I squeaked back. "Pure fucking helium!"

I dropped the handset and checked my guys. Whitey was still unconscious, but thank God, he was breathing. Jimmy and Bill were beginning to move about.

I grabbed the sound-powered handset again.

"Get the fucking Doc in here now!" Fuck the protocol. I slammed and dogged the inner lock door. I was pissed. Those bastards had nearly killed us.

Get the whole picture: the inner lock was unsealed. There was no way in hell anybody was coming inside the chamber without full decompression, which would have killed us in an instant. If that door had not been partially shut so that some oxygen remained in the outer lock with Harry...sheese, can you believe it? I heard the lock cycle and the outer door shut behind Doc Lemwell. Then the rush of gas as he pressed down rapidly. I undogged the inner door and glanced at the oxygen gauge. It read thirty percent.

I grabbed the sound-powered handset and spun the ringer. "Our Oh-two is thirty percent!" I squeaked. "I want Struthers off the panel, Now!"

The inner door popped as it swung open.

"Give me the Master Chief," I demanded.

Doc Lemwell ducked into the chamber and went straight to the still unconscious Whitey. He reached up and set the EAB manifold to pure oxygen.

"Careful, Doc," I admonished, pointing to the depth gauge. Lemwell nodded.

"Harmon." The Master Chief's voice was crisp and clear.

"Master Chief," I answered, "Please run the panel until we surface. Check with Franklin, but just do it, okay?"

"Sure thing, Mac." There was a long pause. "We'll talk when you surface."

"Roger that, Master Chief." I hung up the handset and turned my attention to the Doc.

Whitey's eyes were finally open. He didn't look too bright, but then he never did, except when a chick was in his sights.

"We got five more hours, Doc, give or take. You gonna stay with us or go topside?" I wasn't convinced that we were out of trouble yet.

We had gone off our profile and breathed pure helium at 150 feet for two, three minutes at least. The Master Chief and Franklin would get us back on our decompression profile; I wasn't sweating that. But I was worried about one of us bending on the way up – Whitey especially. He had gotten the biggest helium hit.

"I'm a house call kind of Doc. I'll hang around."

Bill whooped and Jimmy laughed. Harry looked at me earnestly and Whitey just stared.

#

Like I said, that old Mark 2 nearly nailed me – us.

Whitey was okay by the time we surfaced. I practically kissed the Master Chief when my feet hit *Elk River*'s deck. It turned out he was the one who got a handle on the situation and saved our asses. We all graduated.

Chief Struthers want back to whatever he did before he nearly killed us. I felt a bit sorry for the guy, but diving to a thousand feet leaves no room for error. You don't get second chances, at least not very often.

Oh yeah. They gave me a medal for my "heroism" in the DDC. Heroism, my ass. I should have figured things out in twenty seconds, not three fucking minutes. The Master Chief should have gotten the medal, but he insisted I was the guy. Turned out they almost fired him for not supervising Struthers closely enough, but I threatened to resign if they did anything to him.

I was the hero, so they did what I asked.

Submarine Development Group One insignia

CHAPTER THREE

My orders read: "TO: LT J.R. MCDOWELL FM: COM-SUBPAC. REPORT TO COMSUBDEVGRUONE FOR DUTY AS OIC TOG."

I knew COMSUBPAC stood for Commander, Submarine Force Pacific Fleet, and COMSUBDEVGRUONE meant Commander, Submarine Development Group One (where I had trained as a saturation diver), and OIC was Officer in Charge. But TOG – what the hell was that?

I had just completed the better part of a year aboard the *USS Pigeon*, the Navy's newest ASR, a catamaran monstrosity of a submarine rescue ship with two saturation diving systems, and mothership to one or both Deep Submergence Rescue Vehicles (DSRVs) – mini-subs used in underwater rescue and other tasks. When I had completed my saturation diving training I was transferred to the *Pigeon* to put into practice what I had learned in school – and to give the Navy sufficient time to vet my background thoroughly. My new orders signaled that the vetting task was complete.

I strolled up the same hill, past the same flower bed, and into the same carefully maintained, nondescript building I had entered a year-and-a-half earlier when I commenced my saturation diving training. This time, however, the Yeoman at the front desk grinned at me and said, "We just got your final security clearance a few days ago, you know," he added. "Looks like you're finally in the system."

I handed him an envelope containing my records. He then pulled out a file folder from the envelope and stamped the outside and the top page on the left-hand side.

I looked at my watch: Nine thirty.

Out the window a large sailboat moved majestically past the submarine tender *USS Hunley* on its way to a day of waterborne pleasure off the San Diego coastline. Maybe whale watching, I thought. I could just make out a golden-maned girl in a bright red bikini. I grinned; deck sailors stopped work on the sub tender to pay her homage.

The Yeoman handed my papers back and gestured toward the Marine guarding the door in the opposite wall that I had only glanced through on my last visit. "They'll take care of you inside."

I showed my orders to the Marine. He wanted to see my ID. I gave it to him, and he actually looked at it and then at me, and then back at the card, and then at me again. I noticed that his sidearm, a standard service .45 semi-auto, was in an open holster. It and the holster were well used. When the Marine asked me to step back, I didn't argue with him. I did, and he checked me up and down.

"You're heavier than it says on the card," he said.

"Yeah, I know. I've been working out." I was pretty proud of the fifteen pounds of muscle bulk I had added during the past two years.

The Marine grudgingly punched in the code and saluted me as I passed through the door. The room was cool and quiet. Its utilitarian gray walls were broken with opaque windows covered with sound absorbing blinds. I suspected they were barred outside as well.

I handed my package to the Personnelman First Class occupying the front desk.

"TOG," he said, pronouncing it like "Dog." "We been expecting you, Lieutenant. Welcome aboard the Test Operations Group!" He stretched out his hand. "I'm Peterson. Everybody calls me Pete."

I shook his hand, and he grinned at me. "I keep you out of trouble," he said, and pointed to a gunmetal gray desk in the corner. "That's yours when you're in town."

Pete punched a number on his desk phone.

"Richardson."

"Lieutenant McDowell's here, Sir."

"Send him in!"

Pete pointed down the hall.

"Door at the end," he said.

As I approached the door, it opened. I recognized the officer holding out his hand. Commander Dan Richardson had been skipper of the *Pigeon* before my tour. He was one hell of a sub-rescue guy. He had worked himself up through the ranks as a diesel submarine Auxiliaryman. Made E-8 and then Limited Duty Officer, or LDO; one of the best. Too old for nukes, they told him, so they surfaced him to the Navy's ASR fleet as the Engineer on the *USS Sparrowhawk*, an aging submarine rescue and salvage ship out of Charleston, South Carolina. He graduated to Executive Officer of the *USS Ortolan*, the Navy's newest catamaran monstrosity – East Coast sister ship to the *Pigeon*. Two years later he assumed command of *Pigeon*.

"Dan!" I shook his hand.

"Mac! Welcome aboard!" He gestured to a thermos on his desk. "Coffee?"

I nodded. "The way I like my women."

"That covers the waterfront," he laughed as he added cream and sugar.

The crusty Commander made himself comfortable in a big well-worn leather chair behind his ancient mahogany desk and gestured to an armchair facing his desk. I sat, sipping my coffee.

"What do you know about Operation Ivy Bells?" he asked, without fanfare.

I shrugged. "Nothing, really, except the married guys tend to get divorced." I sipped my coffee. "And it's Mare Island," I added.

Dan nodded and slid a form across his desk. "Sign your life away," he said.

I looked the form over. He wasn't kidding. It seems that if I didn't destroy the paper I used to wipe my ass, I would face a firing squad, after they hanged and electrocuted me. I signed and shoved it back across his desk. What the hell. I was cleared for Top Secret-SIOP before I got here; how much more secret can you get?

A lot, it turned out.

USS HALIBUT SSN 587

CHAPTER FOUR

Two weeks later I found myself standing at the submarine pier at Mare Island Shipyard. I could spend all day telling you about this place – not just all day, the whole damn week. It's incredible.

Mare Island lies across the harbor from Vallejo (you pronounce this va-**lay**-ho), a few miles north of San Francisco. Most of the piers are parallel to the shore, and when the fleet is in, the sight is magnificent – especially at night. From the piers, the waterfront extends flat for about a quarter mile. Then emerald green hills climb several hundred feet, bejeweled with buildings – some new, and some going all the way back to before World War II. And on the hills, trees everywhere, beautiful, lush, green.

I keep making an issue of green, because except for a couple of months during the winter, the country surrounding Vallejo takes on a golden color, and trees are few and far between. But Mare Island is Green, with a capital G.

All around me I could hear the sound of an active shipyard. The buzz of high-speed saws, drills, and other rotating machinery filled the air. Occasional flashes of high intensity light from welders' arcs momentarily drew my attention away from the view before me.

Anyway, as I said, I was standing on the pier. I had my seabag parked by my feet, and was carrying my orders in a manila envelope. I had picked up the local newspaper from a vending machine at the station gate. I was resting a bit – no sense stepping aboard in a sweat. I braced my foot on the seabag and flipped the paper open to the headline on page two: HALIBUT – MOTHERSHIP FOR NAVY'S FIRST DEEP SUBMERGENCE RESCUE VEHICLE.

I grinned as I glanced through the story. I had to hand it to the Sub Dev Group PR guys. They had really done a job on this one. Mothership for the DSRV...I loved it!

Since I had just come from an assignment on the *USS Pigeon*. I knew the DSRV and her support systems, every friggin' bolt, valve, switch, and rigging. After the nuclear attack sub *USS Thresher* disaster in 1963, there was a lot of public pressure to make submarines safer. The Navy's old submarine rescue ships got a lot of press, and their aging McCann Rescue Bells were featured in papers across the nation. Of course, they were useless below about 300 feet, and the submarine had to be intact to use them at all, but they got press anyway.

The Navy came up with something called SubSafe, which was supposed to limit the number of openings to sea pressure in a submarine, and to make it safer in many different ways. While this was going on, a guy named John Craven, *Doctor* John Craven, came up with a fantastic idea. John had been intimately involved in the search for the *Thresher* and *Scorpion*. In fact, he was personally responsible for finding the *Scorpion*. He was The Man. He had the attention of the Powers-that-Be in D.C. He knew that the Soviets had laid underwater communications cables between their Siberian missile testing facilities through the Sea of Okhotsk due west of the Aleutian Islands to their big naval base at Petropavlovsk Kamchatskiy, and south to Vladivostok. The cables lay in water between 400 and 1,000 feet deep.

Craven's idea was audacious, to say the least. Since Congress and the public had developed such a keen interest in rescuing downed submariners (pronounced submarine-ers for all you non-bubbleheads), he proposed to create a modern submarine rescue program, replete with a couple of new state-of-the-art catamaran motherships that would carry the little DSRVs that could latch onto a downed submarine and rescue the personnel trapped inside. Furthermore, he proposed to modify several nuclear submarines to act as alternative motherships for these little subs. Never mind that most nuclear submarines operated in waters that were deeper than their crush depth. If a sub went down, it would be like *Scorpion*, with the Engine Room imploding right through the sub to the Reactor Compartment amidships. Never mind that the DSRVs could not actually operate to the depths of the waters in which the nukes normally operated.

Here is the brilliance of Craven's idea. All this was an elaborate front. And I do mean elaborate. The guys running the *Pigeon* and *Ortolan*, and the submarine motherships, had no idea what was really happening. They bought into the cover hook, line, and sinker. In fact, so had I until my fateful meeting with Dan.

Anyway, the real purpose for the entire operation was to create a genuine excuse for a submarine to put to sea with a DSRV attached to its rear deck. And this really happened regularly, to the tune of carefully orchestrated PR fanfare. What also happened, however, was that another DSRV-equipped submarine put to sea occasionally, except that this DSRV really was a saturation diving chamber designed to look like a DSRV.

The job of these guys was no more and no less than to retrieve pieces of Soviet missile warheads from the ocean bottom at the splash zone of their test site in the Sea of Okhotsk, and to tap into the Soviet underwater communications cables snaking along the bottom through that area.

It was super secret. Nobody knew about it except for a very select few, including the President, SecDef, SecNav, one admiral, Craven, the very small contingent at SUBDEVGRUONE, part of the submarine crew, and the divers. Let me tell you, that's secret like nothing I had ever experienced.

No wonder I had to wait a year on the *Pigeon* while they checked every day of my life before I joined the program. No wonder Dan made me sign my life away before telling me about it. Hot dang, I thought, this was some scam!

I looked up from the paper. Nestled against the pier, two subs, the *USS Halibut* and a modern fast attack nuke, were just visible as the tide peaked.

The fast attack was moored against the pier just ahead of *Halibut*. It lay low in the water, its bulbous bow dipping below the surface just a few yards forward of its sail structure. Bow planes protruded from the sail, creating two temporary platforms replete with lifelines. Its featureless after-deck disappeared below the water a couple of dozen yards behind the sail, and the rudder and tail structure protruded from the mirrored water surface several yards further back. Nothing on its deck distinguished it in any fashion. It obviously was designed to move sleekly through the ocean realm. It looked like the deadly killer it was.

As submarines go, *Halibut* was nothing to look at. Her forward deck was flat, in contrast to the sleek curved deck of the fast attack moored ahead of her. Her bow was sharply outlined, like that of a destroyer, but a little more soft and rounded – more like World War II subs. Her prow was designed to cut the water instead of push it aside. A line of louvers just above the waterline ran down both sides from the bow two thirds of the way back to where the after deck dipped abruptly into the water. Bow planes were folded against the bow just ahead of the louvers. The sail protruded from the deck amidships as a narrow, featureless slab. About one-third of the way back from the bow, a hump rose from the deck, like a huge shark's mouth, a clam-shell opening into the pressure hull below that could handle large objects like the obsolete air-breathing Regulus guided missiles for which it was designed as the launch platform.

A sailor in dress whites, armed with a regulation .45 cal. semi-automatic pistol stood guard where a brow stretched across the gap between sub and pier. He stood at a small podium that held a logbook. A second armed sailor patrolled the length of the deck. They had noted my presence on the pier, but both paid significantly more attention to the waters on the outboard side of the sub.

Far back on the deck, just ahead of where it dropped into the water, what appeared to be a DSRV, but was actually a double-lock saturation diving chamber, was mounted to the deck, so that it looked to be held in place with clamps. In fact, it was firmly welded to the *Halibut*'s deck. Prominently painted on its side were the letters: DSRV-1. This saturation diving chamber, called the Can by everybody, was forty-nine feet long and eight feet wide. The forward thirty feet, the inner lock, contained two stacked bunks with a total of four beds, a table for eating and recreational activities like cards or chess, and a pressure hatch into the six-and-a-half foot transfer trunk leading to the sub. The transfer trunk had another pressure hatch on the submarine end. It was used to lock into and out of the inner lock from the sub. The inner lock was separated from the outer lock by a bulkhead penetrated by a pressure hatch. The outer lock contained a toilet, sink, and a pressure hatch in the deck to the outside. It also contained the divers' hot-water suits and other equipment, and their coiled umbilicals suspended on hooks.

I folded the paper and tucked it under my arm, swung my seabag over my shoulder, and walked toward *Halibut*. As I approached the brow the guard saluted and challenged me.

"May I help you, Sir?"

"Request permission to come aboard. I'm Lieutenant McDowell." I returned the salute.

I stepped onto the brow and turned right to salute the flag flying on the stern.

"Your papers, Sir."

He made an entry in his log and then stepped back to a comm box temporarily mounted on the side of the sail.

"Control...topside."

"Control...aye."

"I got El-Tee McDowell here, Senior Chief."

"Roger that. COB'll be right up." Meaning Chief of the Boat – the senior enlisted man on the sub – he pronounced the word like corn on the cob.

A head wearing a fore-n-aft cap and sporting a well-groomed red handlebar mustache popped above the forward part of the sail followed by a khakis clad master chief petty officer who stepped over the edge of the sail and climbed down the ladder to the deck. His weathered, craggy face broke into a friendly grin. He saluted and then held out his hand.

"G'mornin' Lieutenant. Joe Thornton."

I saluted back, and we shook hands.

"Morning, COB."

"Follow me, Sir. The Cap'ns waiting." He took my seabag.

He stood aside while I climbed up the ladder to the top of the sail. I dropped down to the hatch level where I stepped through the horizontal hatch onto the ladder, grabbed the smooth handrails and allowed gravity to pull me down the ladder into the submarine control room.

I stepped aside, and my seabag followed, landing with a thud. Then the COB, landing with the finesse of long practice.

The Chief of the Watch was standing by the ladder. He saluted.

"Welcome aboard, Sir. Sam Gunty. Been looking forward to meeting you."

I returned his salute and we shook hands. I removed my hat.

"How's that, Senior Chief?"

"We heard about your exploit on the *Elk River*, Sir. That was some kind of shit!"

"All lies, Senior Chief." I grinned at him, and followed the COB down the ladder, really a narrow staircase, and forward to the Captain's cabin. We passed the Wardroom to our right, a comfortable room paneled with simulated wood Formica, built-in maroon Naugahyde benches around a permanent coffee table, and a dining table that could be converted into an operating slab should one be needed while on patrol. The Captain's cabin was just ahead on the left. The small sign on the door read Commander George Jackson, bracketed by two small gold submarine dolphins.

The COB entered and announced in a clear voice, "Cap'n, Sir, El-Tee McDowell."

I entered the crowded cabin and came to attention. In the Navy we don't salute when uncovered.

"Lieutenant J.R. McDowell, Skipper. They call me Mac."

The Skipper stood and approached me with outstretched hand. He was medium tall, a bit stocky, with a full head of copper red hair and a matching full beard, trimmed to regulation length.

"Welcome aboard, Mac."

We shook hands.

"Take a load off." He indicated a leather-like Naugahyde couch across the cabin.

I handed him my papers and lowered myself to the couch. He nodded to the COB who left, closing the door behind him.

"So...you're the hero of the hour."

He looked me up and down, and I probably blushed a bit.

"We don't want any heroics on board *Halibut*."

I opened my mouth to speak, but he cut me off.

"No explanations needed. I received a full briefing from Dan...I know what you did...and I'm duly impressed." His face broke into a warm smile.

I paused but he went on, "No...really. I mean it. I know what your quick thinking accomplished. In part, that's why you're here."

He opened a humidor on his small built-in desk and removed a big, unwrapped cigar. He paused to sniff it, savoring the smell and texture before putting it to the fire. Pointedly, he did not offer one to me, so I waited patiently while he puffed the cigar to life.

"You've been briefed, of course?"

I nodded.

"Your troops?"

"On their way. I wanted to check out the system before their arrival."

The Skipper got to his feet, so I did the same. It wouldn't do to get off on the wrong foot with this guy. John Craven had hand-picked him for this job. He was clearly one tough customer.

"We sail in three weeks. Keep me informed of your progress."

I came to attention.

"Aye, aye, Sir!"

The Horse and Cow – aka Winnie & Moo

CHAPTER FIVE

The sun was setting as I pulled up to the Winnie and Moo. The weather was balmy and it didn't look like rain, so I left the top of my red Vette down. Since it was Friday, the parking lot was already half full.

The building was nothing to look at: Dirty white vertical clapboard with white trim, low, nearly flat roof, small, blanked windows just under the eaves. A billboard-like sign towered over the establishment, graced along the top edge with a submarine silhouette, and bold letters announcing to the world: HORSE & COW. Below the big sign was another, carrying a caricature of a submarine dolphin pin sporting the features of a horse on one and a cow on the other. The words Horse & Cow curved over the "dolphins," and below "We Service the Fleet." I pushed open the door and entered.

The room was dark and filled with noise and smoke. I glanced around as my eyes adjusted. Every wall was crowded with submarine memorabilia, dating back to World War II. There was a plaque from every submarine that ever passed through Mare Island, and even some from subs that never reached the West Coast.

My eyes were getting used to the dim light, so I started across the room toward an elbow-polished oak bar with a brass foot-rail that nearly filled one wall. On the far end was a swiveling stool that used to be the stern planes seat on an unnamed World War II-era diesel boat. I knew enough not to sit there; it remained empty in memory of lost World War II subs.

I spotted Bill, Jimmy, and Whitey crowded around the stern planes seat at the bar. Jimmy and Bill had copped seats, and Whitey was standing. Hanging behind the bar over their heads I could see the stainless steel submarine urinal that was occasionally used to initiate a newly frocked submariner. The newbie would put his unworn dolphins in the urinal, and then everyone at the bar would dump whatever remained of his or her drink into the urinal. All the newly qualified submariner had to do was fish the dolphins out with his lips. Usually, this meant drinking his way down to the pin. As I approached the bar I passed a complete maneuvering stand, replete with mahogany-colored coxcombing, seizing, and Turk's heads tied at each spoke of the helm. Further over stood a shiny silver bow-planes wheel. Behind the bar a ship's bell hung from a brass yoke, and I spotted several more around the room. The bar was populated by young men and as many women, ranging from young and very pretty to well-worn barflies in the waning years of their short careers. The guys sported jeans, shirts, and trimmed haircuts, many with beards. No freaks here; this was a Navy joint. No, strike that! It was a submarine hangout.

"Hey, El-Tee!" Whitey raised his mug.

"Hush Lad," I said, laughing. "I'm slumming tonight."

Whitey's light hair and pale features caused him to stand out, even in this smoky place. He signaled the bartender, who slid a full mug down the bar at me. I toasted the guys, and Whitey and I leaned back against the bar to watch the action. Across the room the ladies room door cracked, and a silhouette appeared in the opening topped with bright red hair. She was pretty enough, but had obviously been around the block several times.

I grinned and waved.

"Snorkel Patty...over here!"

Snorkel Patty looked in our direction, smiled widely, and elbowed her way through the crowd to our piece of the bar. Bill jumped to his feet.

"Have a seat, Lady."

Silence fell along the bar as all heads turned toward us.

"You dog-loving somobitchin, goat screwin, g'dam arshole. Who the fuck you callin' a lady?"

Bill jumped back, obviously shocked by her display. Patty lifted her skirt.

"These knees look like I been kneelin' in front of an Admiral?"

Bill's jaw dropped as he discovered the raunchy tattoos gracing her thighs. Grins up and down the bar.

"Ain't no g'dam for'd battery whore!"

Patty was nose to nose with Bill when the bartender hit the klaxon button. The ah-oooo-ga, ah-oooo-ga drowned out all the noise in the bar. Patty was good. She nearly convinced me.

"Dive! Dive!" The bartender sounded genuine.

Patty reached up and kissed me on the cheek and patted Bill's ass.

"G'dam brass..." She turned to Bill. "Screwed every bubblehead in the Pacific twice, and startin' over; might even turn YOU inside out. No more lady-crap! Siddown!"

Bill sat, mumbling, to the hoots and whistles of the guys at the bar.

"Sorry ma...," but I slapped my hand over his mouth.

"Don't get her started again, for God's sake!"

"What kind a fresh meat you got here, Mac?" Patty winked at me.

"A couple of my deep-divin' boys, Snorkel. Treat 'em right!" I turned to the three.

"A grain of salt, guys. She hasn't completed the first round yet, cause she missed me."

And to the bartender, "Give Patty whatever she's drinkin'."

Dark rum arrived in a shot glass, and Patty hoisted in the air. "Anybody don't drink straight rum is a friggin' laaaiiidy," she shouted as she tossed the drink down her throat.

The bartender said with a chuckle, "Last week it was gin." He leaned across the bar. "She keeps a hundred dollar bill in her nightstand, says she'll give to the first man who's as good as her dearly departed husband."

"I heard of this place," Bill said, keeping his green eyes on Patty's considerable cleavage.

"You ain't no bubblehead, then?"

I nodded to the bartender, and another shot of rum appeared before Patty. She picked it up and examined Bill's reddish hair and lightly tanned features through the golden liquid.

"You ain't no friggin' bubblehead?"

Bill started to answer, so I kicked him under the bar.

"These guys are special, Patty. They ride submarines, but don't earn dolphins...not even gold ones." I toasted her with my mug.

"No friggin' dolphins?"

I couldn't tell for sure if she was putting us on or not. I reached into my pocket and hauled out the deep-sea diving pin I had brought for just this occasion.

"They wear these," I said as I pinned the emblem to her low-cut blouse, copping a generous feel in the process.

She winked at me.

"Oh," she said, stroking the pin and the top of her ample bosom. "Is it as hard to get as dolphins?"

"Harder," I said, "much harder."

"Harder...I like harder...." Her voice drifted off and she locked eyes with me. I shook my head slightly with a rueful half-smile, and Patty's eyes got wistful and teary. Then she turned to Bill and grabbed his hand.

"C'mon, Billy boy!" Her voice had developed a hard edge. "You gonna earn yo dolphins t'night," and she dragged him out the door to the hoots and hollers of the crowd.

"What the hell was that all about?" Jimmy lifted his half-empty mug. "You got somethin' goin', El-Tee?"

"Easy, Jimmy." Whitey patted him on the back. "Mac here don't trespass."

#

It was the last night before deployment. I had agreed to meet the guys at the Winnie and Moo for a drink or two, partly to keep them out of trouble in this unfamiliar territory, and partly just because it was so much fun. Before the evening got too old, former submariners Ski and Jer showed up, and the Master Chief himself made an appearance. His understudy, Chief Jack Meredith, and Harry had drawn duty, and were keeping an eye on the system.

Whitey was briefing the Master Chief on Bill and Snorkel Patty. "And she literally dragged him out of here, Master Chief."

"Dragged..."

"Yeah, dragged. But he wasn't resisting too hard; he had an eyeful of them melons!"

Master Chief Comstock grinned at me with a lifted eyebrow. He didn't want to lose any of his men on the last night out.

"He'll be okay, Ham," I told him.

Whitey piped in, "Give her another hour, and she'll have cleaned his clock but good."

Everyone laughed, and Ham raised his mug. "To Bill."

"To Bill!" We all clinked glasses, downed our dregs and ordered another round.

That was when the table just across from us burst into flame.

A young sailor in his birthday suit, three sheets to the wind, was attempting to run the length of his table top with the remains of a flaming toilet roll protruding from between his ass cheeks. Someone must have dipped the roll in rum, because it was burning furiously, and the tabletop was covered with blue flames as the fire spread to the spilled rum.

Somebody threw a full pitcher of beer on the flames, but the burning rum just floated to the top of the beer and traveled to the floor, where it quickly spread. The bartender grabbed a fire extinguisher from behind the bar. I reached out, and he handed it to me. Guys were beginning to run in all directions, and several women started to scream.

"Belay that!" I shouted. "Stand still! Stop moving!" And I hosed down the flames with purple-k from the dry chemical extinguisher.

Jimmy, who in another life was a battlefield hospital corpsman, examined the singed behind of the "flaming arsehole" initiate, and announced no serious damage.

"What the fuck was that all about?" Whitey demanded.

"*Halibut* crew – last night out," answered Ski.

"You're shittin' me. Those guys'r driving our sub?" Jer and Ski nodded. They'd seen this before, of course, since they had been around longer than Whitey and Jimmy.

"They'll be good as new by morning," Ham added, "or I don't know their Division Chief."

"I knew they was fuckin' nuts," said Whitey. "No wonder you took up diving, El-Tee."

I laughed and glanced at my watch.

"It's nearly twenty-two-hundred, guys." I looked at Ham. "You gonna stay around a while, Master Chief?"

"I reckon. A while, anyway." He glanced around the room. "I guess we'll wait for Patty to bring Bill back."

I nodded.

"I'll get the guys back. Safe and sound, Sir."

"Roger that," I responded, and wended my way through the tables to the door.

It was fresh and cool outside, and the air didn't smell like spilled beer and flaming rum and toilet paper. I jumped over the door into my Vette, and started the engine. The moon was out, the stars were clear. A light breeze carried the odors of lilac and sea salt to the tarmac in front of the Winnie and Moo. The combination triggered special memories as I slowly cruised across the narrow bridge to Mare Island, memories filled with softness and pleasure, memories of touch and scent that would remain just that – memories – until we returned from our uncertain quest into the unknown.

*Computer rendering of USS Scorpion debris field
(Courtesy JMS Naval Architects)*

CHAPTER SIX

Morning came early. The Master Chief and I had already completed a last-minute inspection of our system the day before, and since Chief Meredith and Harry had kept things copasetic overnight, I wasn't worried. I knew I could rely on those guys – let's face it, my life and theirs depended on it. Besides, I suspected the Master Chief had already gone over the system one final time this morning. It's not that he didn't trust me; it's just how he is.

I left my Vette at the base car storage facility. Mare Island was different than any other facility I had ever known. Everywhere else you made your own arrangements for cars and personal effects, but Mare Island, at least the part I knew, took good care of the guys. While I had to clear out my room at the BOQ, since we would be gone for so long, my stuff was placed in secure storage nearby, and my Vette was inside under lock and key, and covered. The only thing I had to do was make provisions in case I didn't come back.

Yeah, it may seem bizarre, but it was pretty standard, not just for we the few, the proud, the crazy, but for sailors in general – I mean the arrangements, just in case. So far as the rest of the world knew anyway, we were just another submarine going out on patrol. They always came back...most of the time.

I paused to reminisce about the *Thresher* and *Scorpion*. The *Thresher* happened about the time I was in sub school as a young Sonar Tech. It was sobering but challenging. No one quit the training, however, no one. *Thresher* was before SubSafe; in fact, it was the cause of Sub Safe.

And *Scorpion*? Well, *Scorpion* just happened. I had played a role in locating her. That's where John Craven made his reputation. We found *Scorpion* because John told us where to look, made us look there despite what the experts said. That was before *he* became the expert. I guess that's how he got there, mostly.

I'll never forget it, seeing *Scorpion* on the Atlantic bottom about 400 miles WSW of the Azores, telescoped together with the Engine Compartment having crushed its way through to the Reactor Compartment. I remembered an incident that happened to my sub a couple of years after I left sub school when I still was a Sonar Tech.

We were exiting the Med below the layer. Basically, the Med is a shallow ocean. The surface water gets heated by the ever-present sun, and evaporates so that it becomes very salty and heavy. It sinks to the bottom, especially in the Eastern Med, off the coast of Israel and Lebanon. This heavier water then moves westward along the bottom, and flows out of the Med over the lip at the Strait of Gibraltar into the Atlantic. As the warm, heavy water passes the lip at the Strait, immediately it begins to drop like an undersea waterfall to the Atlantic bottom at about 14,000 feet. This "waterfall" isn't vertical like on land, but slants to the west at about 45 or 50 degrees. The actual location of the "edge" of the "waterfall" moves back and forth depending on a host of complex variables. Oceanographers can actually identify this distinct Med water in deep spots all over the world's oceans. This heavy water is replaced by much lighter Atlantic water that flows into the Med on the surface.

So the inflowing layer of light Atlantic water is about 500 feet thick, and the outflowing heavy, dense Med water occupies the next 500 feet below that. The interface between these layers is very distinct.

Submarines use Archimedes' Principle to operate beneath the water. In order to remain at a specific depth, a sub must weigh exactly as much as the water it displaces. As a sub moves from water of one density to that of another, it must pump water in or out depending on whether the new water is more or less dense.

The Soviets wanted to know about American submarine activity in the Med. To accomplish this, they stationed specially-equipped spy trawlers across the Strait of Gibraltar. These disguised vessels maintained sonar listening posts by dipping hydrophones to various depths in the Strait. In principle, they could hear any sub entering or departing the Med.

In fact, we placed our subs in the appropriate layer, powered down, and drifted in or out with the strong currents. Depending on the need for absolute security, sometimes we would shut things down completely, relying on the currents only to get us in or out. More frequently, however, we simply made turns for about six knots where we were virtually silent. Once we departed the Strait, typically we maintained our depth and powered up to normal cruising turns.

On the occasion I am describing, we had been submerged for over two months, and we wanted to get back to Holy Loch. We were trimmed to neutral buoyancy for the deep, heavy layer, and once we were a few miles past the Strait, we cranked our turns to maximum. In fact, the Maneuvering Room guys added a couple of "coming home turns." So picture a large sub, trimmed heavy to compensate for the dense Med water, cruising at high speed through the deep, dense layer. At some point, our bow poked through the "face" of the "waterfall" into the much lighter water on the other side. Because the sub was so heavy, our bow immediately dropped, and as we passed through the angled layer, we started sliding along the interface toward the bottom nearly 13,000 feet below. As we already were traveling at high speed, we quickly accelerated and rapidly approached test depth – the maximum depth the sub could tolerate. I was in the Sonar Shack at the time, and watched the depth recorder bottom out past the sub's design depth limit. Unless something happened immediately, we were going to implode like a light bulb.

Fortunately, the Exec had the conn, and he was our most experienced submariner next to the Skipper. In fact, he was in line for his own command. I heard him give the order: "Emergency blow all main ballast!" We were immediately surrounded by a deafening rush of high pressure air as it blasted into the saddle tanks surrounding the sub. A few seconds later our descent slowed, came to a stop, and we began a slow upward rise. As we rose, the pressurized air in the ballast tanks expanded, displacing more and more water, so that within a minute or so, we were rocketing uncontrolled toward the surface. But that didn't matter, because we were no longer dead men walking, driving toward the bottom, but were on our way toward the surface.

Once on the surface, we collected our wits, verified that the sub was okay, and got back under the waves before we could be spotted by one of the ever-present Soviet trawlers.

I had suspected that this is what happened to the *Scorpion*. Except that we subsequently discovered damage near her stern that could only have been caused by a torpedo. No one knows for sure, but after further investigation, it appears that *Scorpion* was sunk by the Soviets, probably in retaliation for their belief that we had taken out their Golf-II missile submarine *K-129* off Hawaii – but that's another story[1].

#

I had chosen to walk to the *Halibut* this morning. I wanted one last hour of fresh air, morning breeze, singing birds, and the occasional pretty secretary on her way to an early work assignment. It was about to be a long dry spell.

As I had already delivered my gear aboard, my hands were empty. It was early. The sky was blue and the sun was out, but the air was still chilly. I was dressed in summer khakis and was wearing a fore-n-aft cap. I liked it so much better than my peaked cap, because I could fold it into my belt, and never have to look for it when I needed to go topside. And it gave me unrestricted vision. Caps with bills made me feel like I was wearing blinders.

I finally arrived at the gangway, requested permission to board, saluted the stern and stepped aboard the dark gray surface covered with an anti-slip compound. Our newest attack subs avoided using anti-skid because the turbulence it caused added a measurable level of noise to the sub's underwater signature. In our case, however, we were already so noisy that any additional noise created by non-skid paint was way below our baseline profile.

By now the topside guys knew me, and the watch waved me aboard with a cheerful "'Morning, El-Tee!"

"'Morning, Skidmore." I had most of their names down pat, too.

It had been a long haul, getting the equipment ready and keeping my crew razor sharp. I couldn't have done it without Master Chief Ham Comstock. Ham was an

---

[1] See *Red Star Rogue* by Kenneth Sewell with Clint Richmond, Simon & Schuster, New York, NY, 2005, for the story of *K-127*; and *Scorpion Down* by Ed Offley, Basic Books, New York, NY, 2007,

amazing guy, having punched his ticket at the Navy Experimental Diving Unit and then the Man-in-the-Sea Program. At forty, with his sharp blue eyes and thinning, short-cropped dark hair, Ham was a father figure to the guys, and had become my friend. But we were a team, and it really took all of us to get it done.

I mentally reviewed my dive team. Chief Boatswains Mate Jack Meredith, Ham's thirty-five-year-old understudy, had left the SEAL Teams to become a saturation diver. He compensated for his bald pate with a trimmed, brown beard flecked with gray. His weathered face rarely smiled, and his stocky, five-foot-eight muscular frame was deeply tanned. Sonar Tech 1st Class William Fisher – Bill to all of us – had reddish hair and a ruddy complexion like me. He appeared younger than his twenty-five years, and not even Snorkel Patty could rid him of his shyness. Electronics Tech 1st Class Harry Blackwell was an electronics whiz. He could fix anything with electrons – and I mean anything. At twenty-six, he was tall, slender, and athletic with short-cropped brown hair and brown eyes. Hospital Corpsman 2nd Class James Tanner – we called him Jimmy – was a battlefield medic with the Marines in Nam. He was tall, athletic, and wore his light brown hair like a Jarhead. He was twenty-five, and smart as a whip – maybe even smarter than Harry. Quartermaster 2nd Class Melvin Ford – Whitey, because of his light blond hair – was a muscular five-nine. At twenty-three, he boasted more female conquests than the rest of the team combined. His trademark was a small silver bell on a ring pierced through his foreskin – it seemed to fascinate the ladies. Finally were Engineman 2nd Class Wlodek Cslauski – Ski, for obvious reasons, and Auxiliaryman 2nd Class Jeremy Romain – Jer to the rest of us, because he promised to kick ass on anyone who called him Jeremy or Romain. Ski and Jer were former submariners, both having served on the USS Skipjack, the first "modern" fast attack. They were twenty-six and twenty-five respectively, and almost like peas in a pod – stocky and tough, and deeply tanned. Ski's eyes were blue while Jer's were dark. Ski wore his dark hair as long as regulation allowed; Jer cropped his short. Both had graduated from a class before us, and had accumulated some real-world saturation diving experience before joining us.

These seven guys under Ham's leadership were my responsibility for the months ahead. We were a close-knit team. Our individual lives depended on the knowledge, ability, and judgment of each team member. To an outside observer they might have appeared a motley crew, but these guys were hand-picked for the task ahead; they were the best of the best, way smarter than your average bear, and in tip-top physical condition.

Today we started what the Navy calls a "fast cruise." Since we were going to be out for an indeterminate length of time, but certainly longer than a month, we needed to be certain that everything was running as perfectly as humanly possible. For forty-eight hours, we would operate alongside the pier as if we were out to sea. We would operate every piece of equipment onboard, trying to break it before we left, so that when we left, everything would work.

I dropped through the hatch into the Control Room.

Gary E Flynn on the Halibut planes
Photo courtesy Gary E Flynn

CHAPTER SEVEN

In many ways fast cruise is tougher than being out to sea. When you're out, you just do your job, and take in stride what comes along. During fast cruise you deliberately push everything to the limit. If it's going to break, better alongside the pier than 2,000 miles away from nowhere, or on the bottom in the Soviets' back yard.

So we pushed it. Ham and I came up with every angle we could devise, including the one that nearly broke my butt on *Elk River* – but we simulated it, of course. The guys had been working the system for weeks. Ham and Jack were on "port and starboard" watch (alternating duty days), and had done a virtual fast cruise every night watch since we came aboard. The system was as tight as a virgin's...well, anyway.... Try as hard as we could, during the real fast cruise we couldn't break anything. So we drilled.

And I mean drilled! Sat systems are complex, and because they operate under continuously varying high pressures, things can go wrong in a thousand and one ways. Not too long before, during the experimental work-up stage for the Navy's saturation diving program there was an incident.

A bit of background. When you're saturated at any depth inside a DDC, you have to eat, drink, and eliminate. Eating and drinking are not difficult. The outside crew passes food and drink through the medical lock – a small airlock through the chamber hull just big enough to pass medical supplies and a pot of food or a cold drink. Forget that under pressure any food tastes like cardboard – you still have to eat. And then you have to get rid of it.

In smaller chambers you use a bucket and pass it out the lock. But when you have four to six guys living tightly packed in a DDC, the last thing you want to do is spend your time passing shit and pee through the main lock. For long duration dives, it was obvious that we needed a built-in sanitary system. It's pretty simple, really, a lot like an airliner toilet – basically a holding tank with a seat. Actually, it's much more like a submarine toilet. It has a big ball valve between the toilet bowl and the holding tank. Once the tank gets nearly full, you close the ball valve, and open an outside valve in the waste line. Internal gas pressure in the tank blows the waste out. When you're done, you close the outer valve, and then crack open the inner valve slowly so you don't pressurize the entire holding tank in a flash. Because the holding tank is quite small, the gas it uses barely changes the DDC pressure at all.

This differs from a submarine in that the inside of the sub is at one atmosphere and the outside is at ambient pressure – the depth of the submarine. In the DDC, it's the other way around. The inside of the DDC and holding tank is at ambient pressure of the dive, while outside is one atmosphere. So the last stage of the operation in a sub has the holding tank at ambient pressure – high pressure compared to the inside of the sub, whereas in a DDC, the holding tank ends up at one atmosphere, way below the DDC pressure. On a sub this can lead to the situation where a sailor has just completed doing his business into the bowl. Forgetting that the holding tank is pressurized, he leans over the bowl and cracks the ball valve to flush. He is instantly covered with shit and pee as the pressurized gas blasts through his business! It makes a mess, but you can clean it up.

Unfortunately, in a DDC, the equivalent action can turn out disastrously. On one occasion, as I mentioned, a diver had just completed his business, and instead of standing up to flush, he cracked the ball valve while still sitting on the commode. The pressure inside the DDC instantly tried to flush him through the ball valve. What actually happened, of course, was that some of the parts of him that could be sucked through the valve actually were – sucked through, that is. His butt made a seal on the seat, and most of his large intestine was sucked out through his anus before the system could be stabilized. He nearly died, and it almost caused a shut-down of the entire program.

So, like I said, shit (literally) happens, and we were determined to reach a peak of tuned response so we could handle anything Mr. Murphy tried to throw at us.

Since Jack was Ham's understudy, he assumed the role of Saturation Dive Master for most of the drills, while Ham and I threw at them anything and everything we could think of. I even had Ham cross-connect the helium and oxygen valves once, to see how long it would take the team to discover the problem, modify their procedures to accommodate the change, and get the system repaired and back on line. They caught it at once. Not bad, really.

Jack was flushing the empty chamber with four simulated occupants pressurized to 200 feet. This meant he had to keep the pressure constant while adding pure helium, while mixing sufficient oxygen in the stream to maintain the correct percentage of gases. He discovered the oxygen level skyrocketing in about two seconds, and shut down the flush. Then he tweaked in some helium to lower the oxygen percentage. When he saw the oxygen level go even higher, he shut off the valve and grinned at Ham.

"You sonofabitch!" As I mentioned, Jack didn't have much of a sense of humor.

Since a Chief doesn't normally address a Master Chief like that, the whole crew looked up in anticipation. Ham just grinned back.

"That was quick," he said. "Good job."

"So, do I fix it now, or run it cross-connected?"

Ham just shrugged.

"Finish the dive, boys." Jack changed his focus back to the panel. "Stay sharp. We'll fix it after."

#

Half-way through the fast cruise, the Skipper called me to his stateroom. I left the drill in Ham's capable hands and walked forward. We had not spoken but a word or two during the first twenty-four hours of the cruise. He had his hands full making sure that *Halibut* and crew were ready to go, and you know what I was doing. I knocked on his door.

"Enter!"

I did. He was sitting at his small desk puffing a stogie. I came to attention. "Skipper..."

"At ease, Mac. Take a load off." He pointed to his built-in couch.

"How's the cruise going?" His question was casual, but he was dead serious. I know better than to whitewash anything.

"We've wrung out the system – nothing's wrong. It's tight. Ham and the boys did a great job." I leaned forward. "We're running through every operational contingency we can think of. When we get underway tomorrow, the guys will be ready."

"Give me a final report when fast cruise ends."

"Aye, aye, sir." I started to get up.

"Another thing, Mac."

"Sir?" I continued to my feet.

"I've got a good Wardroom, Mac. All my officers are qualified – and you know that's pretty unusual."

I nodded my head.

"I know your submarine background, Mac. You've got a bunch of patrols, a lot of deck time under your belt." He paused, puffing his cigar, looking me over with his steel eyes.

I don't rattle easily, and this guy knew that, but he just stared at me with those penetrating eyes with their slight twinkle.

"Sir..." Where was he going?

"I want you to join my watch list." He paused. "I can't order you, according to Dan, but I need another qualified watch officer. You can be on the step in a couple of weeks..." His voice trailed off.

Interesting! "Be delighted, Skipper! It'll keep me busy on the transit. Of course, I'll have to stand down while on station."

"Of course. I'll inform the SWO.[2]" He turned toward his desk.

"Sir," I said, and left his stateroom.

[2] Senior Watch Officer

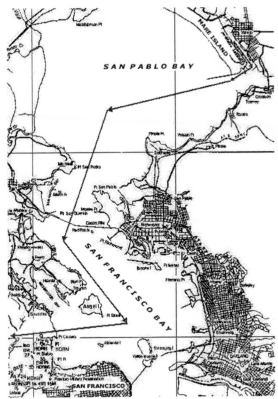

Vallejo to the Golden Gate

CHAPTER EIGHT

"Set the Maneuvering Watch!" Speakers blared throughout the boat. "Set the Maneuvering Watch – underway in thirty minutes!"

My watch read 0730. I dropped my pen, folded up my small stateroom desktop, grabbed a life vest, and headed for Control. I shared the small stateroom with Ops Officer and Navigator Lieutenant Commander Larry Jackson and Chris Barth, Com & Sonar officer. Since I was not part of the regular crew, I ended up with what was left – the bottom bunk in the three-tier. Ops had the center, of course, and I guess Chris just liked to be on top of it all.

So I arrived to the controlled mayhem that is Control as the Maneuvering Watch is being set. I donned my life vest, pulled my fore-n-aft from my belt and put it on, and climbed up the long ladder and through the hatch just below the open Maneuvering Bridge on the top of the sail. Two lookouts were already in place, Skidmore who had Topside Watch when I reported, and a young Hispanic sailor I hadn't met yet.

"Hey, Skidmore."

"El-tee."

"Who's your friend?"

"I'm José Roscoe." He saluted. "Arrived just before fast cruise. They're breakin' me in."

I returned his salute. "Welcome aboard, Roscoe. I'm pretty new myself. The Old Man's breaking me in today, too." I grinned at him and turned my attention to the deck below.

The COB, with handlebar mustache perfectly groomed, was out there directing the linehandling team. Six sailors from the fast attack moored just ahead of us were standing by the lines holding us to the pier. The COB and all his guys were wearing life vests, and were standing by the deck cleats. It had been a while since I had done this, but like riding a bike – you never really forgot. Besides, *Halibut* was equipped with a full set of side thrusters, so moving to or away from a pier was a piece of cake. I had checked the tide tables earlier – there was a slight ebb tide running southeast, so all I had to do was drive us from the pier using the port thrusters, then push the bow out a bit further with the forward port thruster, and then put her in gear, bring her about, and take us out with the tide. Like I said, piece of cake.

The bridge box squawked, "Cap'n to the bridge!" as the Skipper's head appeared through the deck hatch.

"Cap'n on deck!" I announced as I saluted him and stepped back to make room.

"Morning, Mac." He returned my salute and nodded to the outlooks. "Skidmore, Roscoe."

They dropped their salutes.

"Conn, Bridge, what's your status?" I inquired of the Chief of the Watch down in Control.

"Green board, Sir."

I looked at my watch – 0755. "Five minutes to underway, Skipper. We're ready to go."

"Take her away, Mac."

"Aye, aye, Sir." And to the bridge box, "Lieutenant McDowell has the Deck and the Conn."

It squawked back, "El-tee McDowell has the Deck and the Conn, Aye."

"Single up all lines, COB." I used the bullhorn.

Skidmore was wearing a pair of sound-powered phones. 'Single up all lines, Aye; from the COB, Sir."

I watched as the guys on deck loosened the hawsers holding us alongside. The sailors on the pier cast the secondary loops over the bollards as soon as there was sufficient slack, and the deck guys hauled the lines aboard. It was done in less than a minute.

"All lines singled, Sir; from the COB," Skidmore reported.

I turned to the Skipper. "Permission to get underway, Sir."

"Granted."

"Cast off lines one, two, three, five, and six. Hold line four," with the bullhorn. "Fore and aft port thrusters. Ahead slow," over the bridge box, and paralleled over the sound powered phones.

The boat eased from the pier, and then began to pivot slowly to starboard. On the bullhorn: "Give me some slack on four."

The guys eased off on four. "After port thruster stop. All ahead slow." I noted that the stern had plenty of clearance now. "Cast off four," on the bullhorn. "One long blast."

As the ship's whistle sounded, echoing off the nearby sheds and low buildings, I glanced at my watch – 0800. "Underway, Skipper." I grinned at the Captain. "All ahead one-third." I waited for the stern to clear the fast attack moored ahead of us. "Starboard stop. Port bow thruster, ahead full. Right full rudder."

Halibut turned in a tight arc. "Stop thrusters." I lined her up for the center of the channel. "Rudder amidships. All ahead one-third."

"Bridge, Nav – Recommend course one-four-four." Chief Sam Gunty was doing his job.

"Right standard rudder, make your course one-four-four," I said to the bridge box. Slowly, *Halibut* eased onto course down the center of the channel.

"Good job, Mac. Professional. I'll be in my cabin."

"Aye, aye, Sir." And to the bridge box, "Cap'n off the bridge. Secure the Maneuvering Watch."

Control announced the change in status, and finished with, "Set standard watch routine, Section A."

On deck, the COB supervised four guys stowing the hawsers in cages below the deck plates where they were securely tied to the bulkheads so they wouldn't rattle. The other two turned over and secured the cleats. The COB personally checked each hawser and each cleat to make sure they would remain silent. Where we were going, it would not do for some periodic rattle or clunk to be transmitted into the water – that was a sure sign of human presence.

#

The morning was crisp and beautiful. The surrounding hills glowed golden in the bright sunlight. We were heading into a slight breeze that resulted in a twenty-five knot wind from the southwest across the bridge. Roscoe went below while Skidmore waited to be relieved by the duty section. I asked Roscoe to send up a jacket. Stupid of me not to have taken one with me initially. Skidmore's relief arrived with the jacket a few minutes later. It was Seaman Rocky Faust, bundled up for a long, cold bridge watch. He handed me the jacket, and settled down to scan the water ahead of us with his binoculars.

We were the only vessel in Mare Island Strait. I took us down the channel, past the dikes with their end lights marking the entrance to the channel. We turned starboard generally west by southwest, skirting the Naval Anchorage Area 21 and the disposal area just past Pier 35. After about a mile we picked up the Pinole Shoal Channel heading about 260° and then on 240° down into San Pablo Bay. From there we eased to port down through one-and-a-half mile-wide San Pablo Strait, and around the east side of Angel Island into San Francisco Bay.

The Skipper's standing orders required him to be on the bridge when we transited the Golden Gate, so I called him on the analog Centrex, a simple but very reliable dial phone system with appropriate executive overrides located wherever they might be needed.

"We're entering the Golden Gate," I informed him.

"Thanks...be up in a minute."

A few minutes later the Skipper arrived at the bridge hatch and passed up a steaming coffee mug, and then a second and a third, handed up to him by someone in Control. "Blond and sweet, right?" he asked me, winking broadly. I nodded and grinned back. "Skidmore said you liked yours B n' B," he said to Faust.

"Gee, thanks, Cap'n," he said, apparently surprised that the Old Man would actually bring a lowly Seaman coffee.

"Need you bright-eyed and bushy-tailed up here," the Skipper told him, and settled back to scan the horizon, transected by the orange filigree of the Golden Gate Bridge about three and a half miles ahead.

"Take a good look, Mac – you're not going to see this for quite a while."

I didn't respond. No need to acknowledge the obvious.

#

As we sailed beneath the main span of the Golden Gate Bridge, I tilted my head back to watch it pass some

720 feet above me, allowing twenty-six feet for my distance above the water, give or take. From somewhere in the recesses of my memory some figures bubbled up. "One and three-quarter miles from tower to tower," I remarked as the bridge slipped behind us. I turned around to look at it again. "Built in 1937 for $35 million – a lot of money back then," I added to no one in particular.

As we passed Point Bonita to the north and Lands End to the south, Control recommended course 250° as we headed out the main channel. I glanced around at the incoming commercial traffic off our port side and the outgoing traffic both ahead and aft of us. We seemed very small when compared to these giant ships, some longer than a thousand feet, and nearly as wide as we were long.

The seas were picking up, long rolling waves coming right at us out of the Pacific. They'd had several thousand miles to get that way, and we could definitely tell when they hit. Our stubby bow rose high to the incoming wave, and dropped into the wave as it passed, slamming against the leading edge of the sail, and covering us with drenching spray. I slowed our forward speed to let us settle better into the waves' rhythm, keeping a wary eye out for the approaching tanker behind us. From the stern we presented a small silhouette, both visually and on radar.

"You want to dive the boat, Mac?" the Skipper asked, water dripping from his peaked cap.

"Absolutely! Glad you asked," I answered, and sent the lookout below. On the bridge box I ordered, "Lookouts man periscopes one and two." I wanted to be sure we kept abreast of the traffic around us. "Watch that big tanker about four miles astern," I cautioned. "I don't think he can see us in these swells." I looked back. She seemed to be gaining on us.

"I think we should try to raise her on horn," I told the Skipper.

He nodded, so I called Com on the Centrex, and instructed them to raise the tanker behind us. I gave them the name I saw on the bow: *Choja Maru*. She was riding low in the water, obviously with a full load.

Control called me back. "She displaces a hundred twenty-three thousand tons – that's one big sucker!"

The *Choja Maru* was about three miles behind us. I glanced at the Skipper. "See if San Francisco Traffic Control can raise her," I told Control. "And give me her speed."

The *Choja Maru* was doing fifteen knots to our twelve, so she was closing at three knots. "How long 'til we can dive safely?" I asked Control.

"One hour, Sir."

"She'll be on us in an hour," I told the Skipper, and I'm pretty sure she doesn't know we're here."

Our problem was that we were in a traffic-controlled shipping lane. There was some pretty shallow water to the north of us, and incoming traffic, a lot of it, kept us from turning south – plus, turning broadside to the swell was not a good idea. They were pretty big.

"Bridge, Control. Traffic gets no response from *Choja Maru*." Control paused. "Looks like they increased their speed to sixteen – maybe a bit more."

"When the *Choja Maru* closes to a mile, Mac, dive the boat! I'm going to Control."

Now it was just me and *Choja Maru* – at least it felt that way. Time to get ready.

"Rig the ship for dive, Control," I ordered.

"Control Aye." And on the 1MC system: "Now hear this, now hear this. Rig ship for dive! Rig ship for dive!"

I carefully checked the bridge for anything that could rattle. I sent the Centrex and sound-powered phones below. Just me, the bridge box, and the 123,000 ton *Choja Maru* coming up my rear.

"Bridge, Control. One and a half miles, Sir. No way she sees us!"

The bow lifted, and I was drenched by another big one. If I hadn't been clipped to the rail, I might have gone overboard.

"I'm coming below," I told Control. "Put number one scope on *Choja Maru.*" I checked ahead for another swell. "Soon as the next swell passes," I added, and then braced as the bow lifted again.

This one was bigger, but we rode it better, and I only got a little more wet. But soaked is soaked. "Comin' down," I announced, and unplugged the bridge box.

A pair of hands reached up through the deck hatch. I gave them the bridge box, and scrambled through the hatch, slamming it shut above me, and torquing it down with the hand-wheel. I dropped to the deck, and someone clambered up to close the second hatch. The Skipper was on number one scope.

"Where is she, Skipper?"

"Dead astern, about a mile."

"Chief of the Watch – dive status?"

"Green board, Sir."

"Diving Officer," I said to Chris Barth, who had the watch. "Dive the ship! Make your depth two-hundred feet!" I glanced around the Control Room. "Make it snappy, Chris," I added.

The klaxon sounded throughout the sub as the 1MC blared: "Dive! Dive! Dive!"

"Flood all main ballast," Chris ordered. "Full dive on the bow planes, ten degree down bubble. Make your depth two-hundred feet."

Skidmore, on the bow planes, pushed his wheel yoke full forward. Chief Wilbert Kettlewell, on the Ballast Control Panel (BCP), quickly threw switches and the boat was immediately filled with the loud sound of air rushing through the open ballast control valves at the top of each saddle-shaped ballast tank. The boat settled a bit, and then suddenly, the bow lifted high into the coming swell. As it passed, it sucked the stern right back up to the surface, where we wallowed uncertainly between the swells.

"Distance to *Choja Maru*?" I demanded.

"'Bout three-quarter mile," the Skipper said.

"Check," from the Nav table.

Another wave – up went the bow, followed by the stern, and a useless fifteen degree down-bubble.

With an incredible sense of *déjà vu*, I said to the Skipper, "I've been here before on the boomer[3]. I can get us down quick! Please take the Conn, and I'll take the Dive!" And to Chris, "Sorry Chris, no time – no insult intended."

The Skipper: "I've got the Conn."

Me: "I've got the dive."

I turned to the BCP. "Close the forward ballast!"

"Sir?"

"Do it...Now, Pots!"

"Aye, Sir."

"All back full, Pots!"

"All back full, Aye." Pots sent the order to Maneuvering.

"Maintain your planes – hold at ten degree up-bubble."

The ship rumbled with the powerful reverse surge. The stern dropped quickly, and as the next swell hit the bow surged up, dropping the stern even more. Skidmore pulled back on his yoke skillfully. The boat settled into a ten degree up-bubble, settling backward into the deep.

"All stop!" I ordered Pots. Then, "Open forward main ballast! All ahead flank! Full dive all planes. Fifteen degree down-bubble."

Almost like magic, the *Halibut* seemed to pivot down from the stern, the bow dropping rapidly, while the stern remained at depth.

---

[3] Ballistic Missile Submarine

"Down all scopes," the Skipper ordered as he lowered number one to avoid any damage caused by the flank speed.

"Depth one-hundred-fifty feet," I announced in my temporary role as Diving Officer. "Level her out at two-hundred." I looked at the Skipper. He nodded. "I have the deck and the Conn. Lieutenant Barth has the Dive."

As we leveled out at two-hundred feet, we heard a loud roar directly through the hull, and the unmistakable swish, swish, swishing of a giant propeller. The *Choja Maru* was passing directly overhead. She never saw us. She never knew we were there.

"How close was that, Nav?" I asked the Quartermaster, Senior Chief Gunty.

"A sec," he answered, looking at a manual with photos and specs of various shipping. He glanced at the depth gauge, and scribbled on a scrap of paper. "'Bout sixty feet to spare, El-tee." He grinned at me. "That was pretty slick."

The Skipper laid his hand on my shoulder. "Where did you learn that, Mac?"

"I had the Dive on a boomer just off the northern coast of Russia a while back. We were at two-hundred feet with a big storm overhead. One moment we're at two-hundred feet – the next, we're on the surface. The waves were so big we couldn't get her back under. The Old Man was yelling at me to get him down, but nothing worked. For fifteen minutes we tried all the standard ways, but each big wave just sucked the stern up again. We were literally in sight of land. We had to get down. That's when I asked the Old Man if I could try something. He muttered something about what did we have to lose, and told me to go ahead, but he stayed about six inches behind me, breathing down my neck. My trick worked, and it's pretty much standard now on boomers for submerging, except for the high revs, of course. I only needed them in that big storm, and here...the *Choja Maru* was pretty close."

A round of cheers filled the Control Room.

"Piece of cake," I said as the Skipper left the Control Room. "Right twenty degrees rudder. Make your course two-seven-zero!"

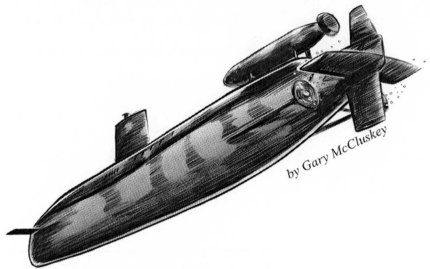

by Gary McCluskey

USS Halibut submerged

CHAPTER NINE

Submarining is generally known as endless hours of tedious boredom, interrupted by moments of sheer panic. I don't intend to spend a lot of time telling you about our month-long submerged trip across the Pacific, and I already told you about our moment of sheer panic at the start of this trip.

Suffice it to say that we drilled a lot, both the ship's crew and my guys. Ham was an absolute evil genius when it came to devising ways to confound the dive team. Like the time he flooded the main lock with Jimmy, Whitey, and Ski inside (simulated, of course), cut off their air into the lock and through the umbilicals, told them the flushing valve was clogged, and then set the team to solve the problem somehow.

When the guys went to use the EABs, Ham shut off that air, too. Now remember, we're talking a chamber full of water, and none of the air sources were working. They had two to three minutes to solve the problem while holding their breaths. Within about thirty seconds Whitey grabbed three come-home bottles, passing them around, which gave them a bit of time to work on the rest of the problem – how to get rid of the water. They tried several things, but Ham kept thwarting their efforts. Jimmy started complaining that he had to take a leak, when Ski suddenly came up with a solution – at least the one Ham was aiming for. He had the outside guys open the sanitary tank drain valve, and then opened the ball valve in the commode.

Sure enough, air started bubbling up through the sanitary drain line, draining the water out of the chamber until it reached the top of the commode. Then they solved the rest of the problem. It turned out, Ham had (hypothetically) clogged the main drain valve with a batch of lithium hydroxide that had gotten mixed with silica gel. Lithium hydroxide is the stuff we normally use to absorb carbon dioxide in our breathing systems, and silica gel is what we use to keep things dry in a moist environment. A spill of both got washed into the deck drain where the wet mix produced insoluble lithium silicate glass that penetrated every part of the valve. The ultimate solution was to replace the valve.

Ham told me he got the idea from when he resurfaced his pool deck. The contractor applied a suspended solution of lithium hydroxide and silica gel that soaked into the prepared concrete surface, and then left behind imbedded lithium silicate which polished up beautifully.

Sure it was a stretch, but it got the guys, including me, to thinking.

#

Everybody knows that submerged nukes are fast. Not so with *Halibut*, however. She was old, with an outmoded nuke plant, and she had accumulated a lot of miles. Furthermore, we were carrying the fake DSRV welded to the stern. We could do fifteen knots at flank for a while, but we were in danger of losing the fake DSRV.

We needed to get to our destination in one piece, so we limped along at ten knots or even slower.

The great circle distance from San Francisco to the tip of the Kamchatka Peninsula is just short of 3,400 nautical miles. This means that if we put pedal to the metal and hauled ass directly to the narrow channel separating Shumshu Island from the southern tip of the Kamchatka Peninsula – ten knots all the way, do not pass Go – it would take us a minimum of fourteen days and change, if everything worked, nothing broke, and nothing went wrong.

Fat chance!

Our route took us just south of the Aleutians. While that may look like a remote part of the world, it lies on a direct path from both Los Angeles and San Francisco and even Seattle to Tokyo. So there is a constant stream of large and not-so-large ships moving in virtual lock-step along the entire route. The three westward paths merge just south of the Aleutians, although some of the shipping passes through the Aleutian Chain into the Bering Sea before crossing back south on its final leg. Did I mention that it's two-way traffic?

To complicate things further, fishing and crabbing fleets from Southeast Alaska swarm up into the Bering Sea, so that at any time – if you are a regular surface ship – you might have between five and fifteen radar contacts to keep track of.

It's different on a submarine, of course. Normally, subs don't deploy any radar, and since subs are supposed to be stealthy, they use sonar only for listening. That's what Sonar Techs do – what I used to do way back in my enlisted days, and the way it was done on this patrol in the early 1970s. So imagine two listening consoles set up at the front of a darkened room, each manned by a Sonar Tech wearing a padded headset. Each has a six-inch hand wheel that drives a pointer around a scale marked off in degrees. Each Sonar Tech is assigned one of the compass halves. A tech moves his pointer slowly from the bow to the stern on his side, covering 180 degrees, listening carefully for any sound over the all-pervasive background murmur of a living ocean. Each identified sound is designated as contact alpha-one, two, three, etc., and the next day bravo, the next, charlie, and so on, and Control is notified of the designation, its bearing, and the direction it is drifting (left or right). The tech uses a grease pencil to mark the bearing of the target directly on his dial, and Control marks a large clear plastic display. As the target bearings move down the side, the tech keeps track of them, reporting them to Control from time to time. As a target moves across the bow or stern, the tech passes it to the other tech.

If there is time, the Sonar Techs analyze the targets to determine what they are, freighter, tanker, trawler, another sub, and so on. Especially interesting targets are then further analyzed by the Sonar Supervisor, using more sophisticated equipment that breaks the incoming sound down into its component parts. This can often give very specific information about a ship, even – occasionally – its name.

The Skipper had made a command decision to stay away from the direct shipping lanes. This made the Sonar Techs' job a lot less hectic, but it made us easier to find in the quieter water away from the shipping lanes, where our sound would carry farther. So we needed to exercise more caution. The last thing we wanted was to be picked up by a Soviet fast attack and tracked to our destination. To help avoid this, the Skipper ordered that we clear our baffles once an hour. The baffles are that part of the after area of the sub that is shrouded by our own noise, so the Sonar Techs can't hear anything. The Officer of the Deck clears baffles by slowing the sub way down suddenly and turning it first left or right twenty degrees, and then the other way, while Sonar carefully checks to see if anything is back there.

The Skipper's Standing Orders said to clear baffles once an hour at random times, in random directions. This made it virtually impossible for a trailing submarine to anticipate our next move, and so made it very unlikely that such a sub would go undetected. But it sure slowed us down.

Also, we didn't take a direct route. Instead, we varied our course so that on average we would be moving toward our destination, but we drove long legs tandem to our base course. The entire process slowed us down tremendously, so that we were barely making five knots toward our target area.

This stretched our trip out to a full month...of tedious boredom, like I said. But not entirely.

#

One night about fifteen days into the voyage, I had the watch. Somehow we managed to stumble right into the middle of a Japanese fishing fleet. Sonar detected a huge factory ship, the type that stays at sea for months at a time, and a whole lot of small trawlers. Within ten minutes I was completely overwhelmed with targets on my tracking screen, and I could only imagine what Sonar was dealing with in the Sonar shack. Every few seconds Sonar hit me with another contact. In less than ten minutes we had designated over twenty-five contacts. Apparently we had come up on the factory ship to the north, and did not initially detect the rest of the fishing fleet to the south. I turned a bit south to remain fully clear of the factory ship, and almost immediately found myself in the midst of the trawler fleet – and that's significant, because trawlers drag long trawl nets behind them, at depths up to 150 feet or more.

I slowed down to a crawl, and called the Skipper by sound-powered phone to tell him what was going on. He decided to get up and come to Control for a while, since the situation was a bit dicey. Just as he entered the Conn, all hell broke loose.

The first thing was a shudder we all felt throughout the entire sub. Almost immediately, Maneuvering called me on the squawk box, reporting heavy current draw, and a sudden strong resistance on both shafts.

"All stop!" I ordered, to stop the screws from turning, and instructed Ballast Control to put the sub into hover, "Maintain two-hundred feet." And then as an afterthought, "Stand by to use thrusters."

Pots had the BCP. I ordered him to find Senior Chief Gunty to relieve him so he could get back to Maneuvering to help out.

The Skipper sat down in his chair, a padded, raised executive seat at the back of the conning station. He didn't interfere, but I was keenly aware that he was right behind me, ready to jump in if I did anything he didn't like.

"Reactor Scram! Reactor Scram!"

That was all I needed. A reactor scram is when all the control rods drop into the reactor core, effectively shutting the reactor down. It's an automatic safety measure that absolutely protects an overloaded reactor from any damage. But it also shuts it down completely, and that immediately shuts down the turbine's steam supply, which also immediately shuts down the generators, and everything else run directly or indirectly by the reactor. That left me with only the diesel engines and the battery.

For obvious reasons we couldn't run the diesels at 200 feet, and I didn't think the Skipper wanted to surface in the middle of the fishing fleet. Besides, we were clearly hung up on something.

"Shift to emergency power, battery," I ordered, glad that I had already sent Pots back to Maneuvering.

Throughout the sub, most of the lights went out, and emergency lights powered up, driven by the large lead-acid batteries built under the Control Room deck.

"Avoid all unnecessary movement about the ship," I announced over the 1MC loudspeaker system. Gunty was going to have enough trouble maintaining the propulsionless hover without having to compensate for people moving about the sub.

I answered the sound-powered phone's shrill burr. "It's Dirk, Mac. Here's the plant status."

"Hold a moment," I interrupted. Let me get the Skipper on line. I motioned for the Skipper to pick up the sound-powered handset by his chair.

"Captain," he said calmly.

"Here's the plant status, Sir. We pulled a terrific strain on the port shaft, and loaded down the starboard shaft as well. Can't see any inside damage, but don't know for sure yet. Still investigating. The lopsided strain cascaded back through the system, setting off the Scram. There appears to be no damage. I'll give you a follow-on report as soon as we know more."

The Skipper replaced the handset and asked, "Well, what do you think, Mac?"

"The *Von Steuben* caught a deep tow cable coming out of the Med several years ago – right after I got my commission." I paused, reflecting on that event, and comparing it to now. "But this is different. I think we snagged a trawl net. With that Can on our stern, we certainly have enough places it could hang up."

The Skipper nodded in agreement.

"We probably snagged a really deep one. When they realized they were snagged, and they obviously couldn't shake it loose, they probably dropped or cut their tow lines. They had nearly everything out anyway. I think one or both the steel tow cables wrapped around the port shaft, jamming it, and then wrapped around the starboard shaft, but didn't actually bind it." I started to picture the consternation and panic on the Japanese trawler. "If they have any smarts," I added, "they probably figure they caught a sub."

The Engineer called back to tell us that there appeared to be no damage. But he could not test the shafts until he got the reactor back on line, and that was going to take another hour.

"Skipper," I said, "we're not going anywhere. Let's deploy the Basketball to examine what really happened. Then I can send my guys out to cut off anything caught on the Can, and clear the shafts.

The Skipper thought it over for a minute or two.

"Make it so," he said. "Captain has the Deck and the Conn. Batman to Control."

"Batman" was the nickname of Special Operations Officer, Lieutenant Commander Lonie Franken-Ester, so called because he was in charge of the Bat Cave, the forward compartment that had been the cruise missile launch facility in an earlier incarnation of *Halibut*. He was also in charge of deploying and manipulating the Basketball – a basketball-size camera-carrying remotely operated vehicle (ROV). Live images were sent to the Display Room in the Bat Cave, and they could also be seen on the Control monitor and in the Dive Locker.

Lonie got his instructions and went forward to launch the Basketball.

A few minutes later the Control monitor flickered. Shortly, the screen resolved into a moving image of a portion of our starboard hull illuminated by a beam of light from the Basketball as it moved upward from the Aquarium – the double-lock hull penetration in the Bat Cave used to deploy the Basketball, the fish,[4] and to retrieve items from deployed divers.

The Basketball moved up to the deck hanging about twenty feet out, and slid back toward the stern. Senior Chief Buck Christman was driving the Basketball from the Display Room. He had a fine touch. The Basketball moved smoothly, without jerks or hesitation. Its beam picked up the Can.

---

[4] High-resolution sidescan sonar towed device that produces detailed images of the sea floor.

"Look at that, Skipper," I said as the screen filled with the trawl net covered chamber.

Buck brought the Basketball alongside the Can to look under it. It appeared that the net had somehow wrapped itself completely around the Can and then got draped over the rudder, which we could clearly see as Buck panned to the stern. Then he followed the net tow cable from the rudder down to the port screw, where it was intertwined in the screw blades. Then he followed it under the hull and wrapped around the starboard shaft.

"It looks doable," I said to the Skipper, and left to get my guys going.

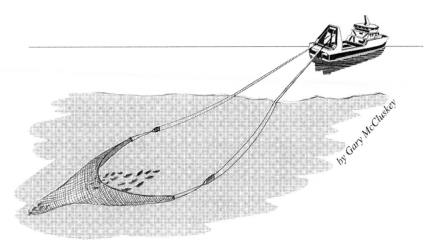

Japanese Trawler towing a pelagic net

CHAPTER TEN

I grabbed Ham and Jack, and sat them down in the Wardroom where I explained the situation. "We caught a Nip trawl net on the Can, and I think they cut their steel tow cables as soon as they discovered their problem. Since the trawl net was a long way out, the cables had a lot of lead, and one got picked up by the port screw as they fell and wrapped around the shaft. The starboard shaft probably picked up the bitter end."

Jack whistled while Ham just looked thoughtful. "We're gonna go fix it," I added. "Give us something to do besides drill."

Ham laughed. "Too bad. I had a good one cooked up for this evening."

"Let's put two guys in the water, and one each in both locks," I said, "Jimmy, Whitey in the water, and Bill and Ski in the locks." I stood and stretched. "I need to stay aboard, 'cause if shit hits the fan while they're out there, I want to make sure Control doesn't do something stupid." I paused. "Besides, I guess I got us into this mess."

"Shit, Mac, give it a rest!" Ham reacted. "The way I see it, you saved the mission – assuming we get this shit off us – and maybe even the boat."

I appreciated the praise, especially coming from Ham, but I was still beating myself up for getting us into the situation in the first place. If I had just given it a bit more thought when Sonar reported the factory ship. I should have given it a much wider berth, so in my book, it was my fault. That's what I told the Old Man. He's still mulling it over.

"Jack, I want you to stick to Ham like stink on shit." I grinned at him. "This is not routine by any means. We're diving over-bottom (that is, the ocean bottom is below the maximum depth we can dive – in this case, way below it, maybe as much as 12,000 feet at our location), and we're hovering in mid column at about two-hundred feet." I stood up again. "Get 'em out, do the job, and get 'em back."

About a half-hour later we were assembled in the Dive Locker tucked into the forward end of the sub's after compartment. Jimmy, Whitey, and Bill were suited up and climbing up the ladder through the lock and into the Can. Ski followed them. Ham was setting in the dive parameters, with Jack double-checking each setting. Jer and Harry were taking up space and getting in the way.

"Harry, you stand by to help Ham," I said; we needed a mobile person around for this. "And Jer, you get some shut-eye in case we need some relief back here." He wouldn't sleep, but we needed some room.

Although I wanted the guys to be on their toes, realistically, this was a pretty routine dive. In fact, under normal circumstances, we could have done it with our regular Scuba gear, although the guys would have been a bit narced. They would have been perfectly fine on Nitrox or Tri-mix, but we didn't have time to mix the gases, and besides, why give up an opportunity to strut our stuff?

Just as the guys settled down in the Can, the lights flickered, and the main lighting came back on. "Looks like the reactor's back on line," I said to Ham. "I'm going to the Conn. You got the watch." As I left, I noticed that Jack made the proper log entry.

The Captain still had the Deck. He asked me if I was ready to take over again. "If it's alright with you, Skipper, I'd rather hang out here to keep on top of the hover, but be available to get back to the dive station if I'm needed there."

"Any problems?"

"No, Sir, but this is an over-bottom dive, and even though we know what's out there, there may be more to it when my guys get on scene."

"I agree." He picked up the 1MC mike. "XO to the Conn."

Commander Fred Roken arrived shortly, and assumed the watch from the Skipper after being briefed on the status. The Skipper remained in his chair, retaining an overview of everything. I stayed near his chair, keeping an eye on the monitor that currently gave me a view of the dive console over Ham's shoulder. I picked up a headset with a boom mike that tied into the dive communication system.

"Dive, Conn, what's your status?"

"Conn, Dive, we're pressing down the Can. We'll be there in five minutes." Ham flipped a switch on the console, and I could see the divers in the Can on the now split screen. Jimmy was squeezing his nose – clearing was always difficult for him on the first dive, Whitey and Ski were yawning – they could clear with no problem, and Bill looked bored – he had Eustachian tubes the size of pencils.

"Conn, Dive, at two-hundred. Designate Petty Officer James Tanner 'Red Diver;' designate Petty Officer Melvin Ford 'Green Diver.' Divers entering outer lock."

"Conn, Aye," I acknowledged. Sometimes, when things are happening really fast, you just don't get around to acknowledging every call, but you're supposed to do it, and if something ever goes wrong, the log had better show that you did acknowledge. Otherwise the big red finger may be pointing right at you.

Actually, we really did do things by the book. What we did was dangerous, even under the best of circumstances. The guys in harm's way were my responsibility; but even more, they were my friends.

"Dive Control, Outer Lock. Permission to crack the lower hatch." Bill was talking, his voice squeaky and distorted by the compressed helium. He didn't need any electronic unscrambling because we were only at 200 feet, but you still had to listen closely to understand him.

"Outer Lock, this is Dive Control. Wait on that."

This meant that Jimmy, Whitey, and Bill had entered the outer lock, and sealed the hatch. I turned to the Skipper. It was his boat, and Ham was about to breach watertight integrity. The Skipper nodded his permission.

"Dive, Conn. Permission granted."

Ham immediately said, "Outer Lock, Dive Control. Crack the lower hatch."

On the screen the Skipper and I watched as Bill leaned over the lower hatch and turned the locking wheel to the left. After a few seconds he looked up and gave a thumbs-up.

"Hatch unlocked," Bill announced to no one in particular.

"Dive Control, Aye."

We all could see that the hatch didn't lift off its seat. "Open the interlock bleed valve from both sides," Ham ordered. The divers would need to equalize the lock pressure to the outside, and Ham wanted both locks to be at the same pressure. Opening this small valve would maintain the same pressure in both locks, so long as the pressure in either lock didn't change too rapidly. Bill and Ski complied, although I couldn't see Ski in the main lock because the split screen showed

Dive Control and the outer lock. "Bleed the pressure," Ham then ordered.

"Roger." Bill reached for a ball-valve handle near the top of the lock, and turned it slightly.

Buck was monitoring our conversation, and lifted the Basketball to get a view of the top of the Can. A steady stream of bubbles began to rise from the outside of the Can where the outside bleed valve was located. I glanced over at the BCP and the depth gauge. We were at 195 feet. I caught the XO's attention and glanced at the depth gauge.

"Mind your depth, Diving Officer," the XO ordered.

"Aye, Sir." Chris was mildly embarrassed, but it is not easy maintaining an exact depth in the open ocean, especially when you have zero forward speed. Chris was doing okay.

A boomer has automatic hover equipment that sucks water in and out of a specially designed hover tank so efficiently that the boat can remain within about six inches of desired depth. But we were in an aging nuke that never was designed to do any of the things we were demanding of her. On balance, she was holding up pretty well. The hover kept Gunty busy as hell. I saw what he had done. He was running water into one tank and out of another simultaneously, while partially opening and shutting the flow control valves to give him the required momentum. Just before we hit 195 feet, one of his tanks had reached capacity while he was still emptying the other – so we got a bit light. By the time Chris received his admonition, Gunty had it back under control. What they were doing was actually pretty slick – especially since none of us had ever done it before.

As we settled back down, the lower hatch in the outer lock suddenly popped up a couple of inches, and Bill closed the external bleed valve before the lock could flood. Jimmy lifted the hatch back on its springs. The hatch was cocked halfway back, and would remain open.

"Securing the hatch," Jimmy announced as he fastened the hook that prevented the hatch from swinging shut accidentally during an unexpected ship's movement.

"Roger that. Suit up," Ham ordered.

Each diver donned his bright yellow Mark 11 backpack with its bulky canister, bottles, gauges, and connectors, attached the hot water hose to the suit connector; and then each slipped the Kirby-Morgan helmets over their heads, and hooked them up to the gas hoses from the backpack and umbilical.

"Outer Lock and Dive Control, Red Diver. Comm check."

"Dive Control, Aye."

"Outer Lock, Aye."

"Outer Lock and Dive Control, Green Diver. Comm check."

"Dive Control, Aye."

"Outer Lock, Aye."

It takes a while to tell the story, but it happened quickly. Remember, we were in a hurry.

"Divers go!" Ham ordered.

With Bill feeding umbilical, Jimmy lowered himself through the open hatch, followed immediately by Whitey. Buck brought the Basketball down, so we watched the divers enter the water on the split screen.

"Red and Green Diver, Comm check." Ham was just making sure, and I understood. We were hovering at 200 feet with divers tethered to our ass. It was dicey, to say the least.

"Red Diver, Aye." Jimmy's voice sounded squeaky and muffled, and his breathing noise made it even more difficult to understand him.

"Green Diver, Aye." Same for Whitey.

"Dive Control, Red Diver, we confirm the problem. The Can's completely covered with a trawl net, and it's draped completely around, and then back across the rudder." He paused. "Whitey – your light..."

On the split screen I could see the beam of brightness barely visible in the darkened water column as Buck focused in on Whitey.

"Look, Whitey...see!" We could sense his excitement, even through the distorted helium speech. "Dive Control, Red Diver, there's one tow cable wrapped in the port screw. It extends right from the net caught around the Can. It passes under the stern and is wrapped around the starboard shaft." And then, "Let's go, Whitey. We can cut this sucker loose."

For the next ten minutes all we heard was heavy breathing mixed in with gas bubbling sounds as we watched the divers struggle with their knives and the tough fiber of the trawl net. Then, suddenly, the net slid out of the view of the Basketball.

"That does it, Dive Control." It wasn't exactly according to the book, but Jimmy had earned the right. "The net's on its way to the bottom, Dive Control."

"Sheeeit!" Whitey suddenly squeaked, sounding like nothing so much as one of the Christmas chipmunks. "Down, Jimmy!" There was no mistaking his intent. "Right now!"

Buck rotated the Basketball upward toward Whitey just in time to see a dark shadow sweep past the divers.

"Dive Control, Green Diver. Can you take us down about another fifty feet or so? We nearly got snagged by another trawl net."

The XO looked to me, and I nodded emphatically. "Make your depth two-hundred fifty feet – take her down slow and easy," he ordered.

"Two-hundred fifty feet slow and easy, Aye," Chris said, as Gunty adjusted his flow valves.

"We're going to two-fifty, Ham. Track her down," I ordered through my boom mike.

"Dive Control, Aye."

The sub began a slow, level descent. I kept an eye on the Can depth gauge visible on the monitor, while I watched the effect on the split screen as Buck kept pace with his Basketball. That guy was really good. While we were descending, he went back to the screws for a closer look.

"That was close, Dive Control," Whitey said. "The net actually slid across the sub's sail."

"Dive Control, Red Diver. Can you have Engineering jack the starboard shaft a bit in reverse to loosen up the cable?"

"Hold on that, Red Diver." Then Ham made a formal request. "Conn, Dive Control. Can you jack the starboard shaft back a couple of turns?"

The Skipper nodded and picked up his handset.

"Roger that, Dive Control. Stand by."

The Skipper explained to Dirk what he needed. Dirk had already anticipated the need to do this, and was ready on both shafts. Buck moved in for a closer look, and we could see the shaft rotate to the left in short jerks. Within two minutes we heard a squeaky whoop.

"Hold the starboard shaft...that's great!" Jimmy said. Buck pulled back to give them room, and we watched them struggling with the cable, working the bitter end up and over the shaft once, and then again. We heard a lot of squeaky huffing and puffing. And then the cable disappeared from view. "OK – that did it. The starboard shaft's free. The cable is hanging from the port screw, but it's way too heavy for us to get it off."

Buck moved farther away to get a larger view, but it was dark and difficult to make out.

"Roger, Red Diver." I was sure Ham really wanted a good view of what was happening out there.

"OK, Dive Control." Jimmy sounded a bit winded. "Now we need you to jack the port shaft in reverse – slowly. With a bit of luck, the cable will pull free and snake to the bottom."

Once again, Buck moved in from the stern, behind the screw, which gave us a great view of the action.

"Roger that, Red Diver."

The Skipper started talking on his handset again. He kept it to his ear. The screw started turning very slowly.

"That's it!" squeaked Jimmy. "Slowly...slowly..." And then, "Stop! Stop!"

Even on the monitor we could see that the cable had crossed itself.

The Skipper said something to the handset.

"The cable crossed," Jimmy told us. "Jack forward about a quarter turn."

The Skipper passed it on.

"OK – Stop!" Heavy breathing. On the monitor the cable snapped free from its constraining hold on the other wrap. "Now back slowly..." More heavy breathing, from both divers. "Slow...slow...SLOWER!"

The Skipper stayed with him. And suddenly, the cable started slipping through the screw blades.

"Bingo! That's it! We did it!" Squeak or no, he definitely was excited. "Let's get the fuck outa here!"

Buck stayed with them until they reached the bottom of the Can. Then he headed back for the Aquarium.

Ten minutes later we could see Jimmy and Whitey emerging into the outer lock through the lower hatch. Bill had wrapped their umbilicals on the bulkhead hooks as they swam to the hatch, and now he pulled them into the lock. He unhooked the hatch and swung it closed. Whitey stooped to spin the locking wheel.

"Dive Control, Outer Lock, hatch secured."

"Dive Control, Aye."

"Conn, ROV Ops, we're secured and the hatch is shut." And that was it.

I gave the Skipper a thumbs-up, and he ordered the XO to secure the hover and get the ship underway. I headed back to the dive locker. The guys had been out for about an hour at a maximum depth of 250 feet on standard heliox. Ham or Jack would have already worked out the decompression schedule. I needed to check it, and then we could start bringing the guys back to the "surface."

It would take a while, but that's what we got paid for.

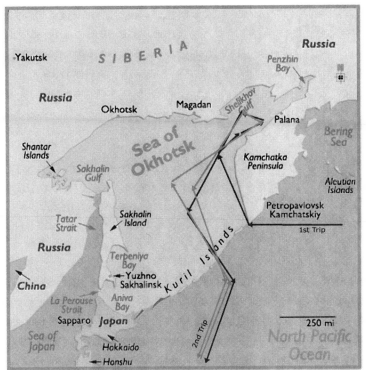

Route from the N. Pacific into the Sea of Okhotsk, Shelikhov Gulf, south to Guam, back again, and finally south to Guam

CHAPTER ELEVEN

"Officers Call! All officers to the Wardroom."

This is a rare occurrence on a submarine. In fact, I can't remember ever hearing it before. I had my suspicions why – we were almost a month underway now, so we had to be close to our secretive destination. I mentioned Kamchatka Peninsula earlier – well, now we were going to learn all about it, mostly.

So I high-tailed it to the Wardroom. My guys and I were the stars of the show, so it wouldn't do to be tardy. The junior officers were already present. Eng and Ops, Lieutenant Commander Dirk Philips and Lieutenant Commander Larry Jackson, were on their way. Special Operations Officer Lieutenant Commander Lonie Franken-Ester and Dr. Thomas Banks followed me into the crowded room. As I explained earlier, Lonie or "Batman" was in charge of the Bat Cave, the specially designed forward compartment that used to be the guided missile bay, and now was the control center for Special Operations. Regular crew needed permission to enter this space. The XO had the Deck and Conn, and Gunty had the Dive, so every ship's officer except the XO was present.

As I sat down opposite the Skipper, he put fire to one of his stogies. As he puffed the cigar to life, we all waited. It was his show, after all. He puffed quietly, looking around the table. His characteristic grin was not present.

"Gentlemen," the Skipper commenced, "in about two and a half hours we will enter the narrow strait between the southwestern tip of Kamchatka and the northern-most of the Kuril Islands, the small island of Shumshu. Shore to shore we're talking about six miles, maybe a bit less. The passage is five miles, give or take, and beyond lies the Sea of Okhotsk. We know very little about this water beyond depth and major currents. We have no information on surface traffic or monitoring." He paused for a puff. "Petropavlovsk Kamchatskiy is the largest Soviet naval facility in the Pacific, except for Vladivostok, and the home of their Pacific submarine fleet. We know the Soviets use an area in the northeastern part of Okhotsk as a test missile splash zone, the Gulf of Shelikhov." He paused again for a couple of puffs, letting the information sink in.

"Earlier this year," he continued, "three fast attacks entered the Gulf and attempted to track incoming cruise missiles. Their gear didn't work, but one of them, the *Swordfish*, was mounted with the same sidescan sonar we installed earlier this year. She got two sweeps of the channel, one going in and one going out, and swept much of the waters off the western slope of Kamchatka." He grinned for the first time. "So, we're not totally blind." The Skipper rolled a chart out on the Wardroom table.

"We're here." He pointed to a spot off the southeastern tip of Kamchatka, still well offshore of Petropavlovsk. Then he put his finger on the tip of the peninsula. "This is the channel."

It looked pretty narrow. On the scale of the chart he was using, his finger completely covered the gap between Kamchatka and Shumshu.

The Skipper moved his finger past the gap and up along the western coast of Kamchatka to an outcropping about halfway up. Across Okhotsk was another outcropping – the two formed the entrance to Shelikhov. "Shelikhov starts here, and the splash zone is about here." He stabbed the middle of the Gulf. "Water depth gets to about twelve-hundred feet in the middle," he pointed to Shelikhov again, "and down to about thirteen-thousand feet here." He pointed to the middle of Okhotsk. "This area," he swept his fingers offshore along the western coast of Kamchatka, "averages three-fifty to four-hundred feet." He looked around the table. "During the late spring and early summer, fishing fleets from around the world ply these waters. They come from as far away as Poland. This means we will have to keep a sharp lookout for ships with nets." A chuckle passed around the table.

The Skipper stood up, but motioned the officers to remain seated. He leaned over the Wardroom table, his hands gripping the edges on either side. "This doesn't leave this room." He paused for a full five seconds. "Is that understood?"

"Yes Sir," from around the table.

"We're going to locate missile parts in this area," he pointed to the north-middle of Shelikhov, "and bring them home with us."

A murmur went around the table. The Skipper held up a hand. "Lonie will brief us on the details later. Following this meeting, I will announce this part of the operation to the crew. So far as they know, that is the extent of our operations here. We don't say exactly where, and we don't say what we got, but they need to understand something about what is going on."

Heads nodded around the table.

The Skipper sat back down and continued. "As important as that is, it's not the real reason for this mission." He held up his hand again at the resulting murmurs. "The Soviets' nearest launch facility is about twelve-hundred-fifty miles due west of here," he stabbed the middle of Shelikhov again. Then he pointed off the chart to the west, "Right here in Yasniy, about two-hundred-fifty miles southwest of Yakutzk. We know they ran a comm Cable all the way to the town of Okhotsk," he indicated a spot on the northwestern coast of Okhotsk, "where it links to another cable from Vladivostok, and from there to Moscow. From Okhotsk it goes to Magadan, here," he pointed to another spot about 280 miles along the coast east of Okhotsk, "with its large port and ship-yards, and then either directly into the water or else to somewhere along here," he pointed to the double peninsula that forms the northern gate to Shelikhov, "and then into the water." He moved his finger to the western coast of Kamchatka on the other side of the bay. "It exits the water somewhere along here, where it probably branches to Palana," he pointed to the northern-most part of western Kamchatka, "but the main section goes to the naval base at Petropavlovsk," he pointed to a spot near the southeastern tip of Kamchatka.

"We believe," he continued, "that the Soviets also have established a cruise launch facility somewhere on the Kamchatka Peninsula, but because we cannot yet track these new bastards, we don't know where the facility is. We also know that they launch them by air from around the region, but they are all aimed to splash down here." He pointed to Shelikhov again.

The Skipper took two long puffs from his cigar. Then he put his elbows on the table, folded his hands with the cigar protruding from his fingers. "Our main mission is to find that cable," he paused and looked around the table, "and place a tap on it."

There was stunned silence in the Wardroom.

"We're talking about all the traffic between the missile base to Petropavlovsk, and everything between Moscow and Vladivostok, and Petropavlovsk." He paused to let this sink in.

"If we find it...if we can attach the tap...if it works... if we get anything...then we go get some missile parts... and then we pack up and head for Guam." The Skipper smiled at his assembled officers. "It's going to be a busy time, Gentlemen. Let's get to work."

#

I had known about this, of course, but it still took my breath away to hear the Skipper lay it out. This had to be the most bodacious thing anybody had ever attempted to do – with the possible exception of the recent Moon landings.

The Skipper wanted to transit the narrow strait during darkness, and as luck would have it, I had the next Deck Watch.

Navy tradition has an incoming watch-stander arrive at the watch station fifteen minutes prior to assuming the watch. Since the watch goes from the top of the hour to the top of the hour, the traditional relieving time has always been fifteen minutes before the hour. But over the years, the watch came to be viewed as starting fifteen minutes before the hour, which has come to mean that an incoming watch stander tries to report to the watch station by half-past the hour. In fact, if you don't show up until quarter 'till, a lot of guys will consider you late. They fully expect to be off watch by then.

I was a guest on *Halibut*, and this meant I needed to play the game as they played it. So I prepared to appear at half-past. Besides, we were about to enter the strait, and I wanted to be sure I had the complete picture.

We still were a half hour or so from our turn to the right. We were down at 200 feet, and running quietly. It wouldn't do for the Soviet listening devices at Petropavlovsk to pick us up out here. The strait had a wide buoy-marked natural channel indicating the shallows on both sides. I intended to remain close to the center of the strait, but somewhat to the right, since Shumshu on the left was low and tapered off slowly into the strait. Shumshu lies just to the northeast of Paramushir, home to four active volcanoes and the second largest of the Kuril Islands. The remnants of a major World War II Japanese naval base spanned the mile-wide channel separating it from Shumshu. The small town of Kuroatovo sits near the northeast tip of low-lying Shumshu, marking the location of a well-camouflaged Soviet air base, complete with underground hangers. Six miles due east across the strait, the village of Cemenovka sits on the southern-most extension of Kamchatka. Cemenovka houses the traffic monitoring facilities headquartered up the coast at Petropavlovsk. The radar we knew about; but we had no intel on possible underwater monitoring.

I assumed the watch, and directed sonar to activate the sidescan. We were at 200 feet.

"Sonar, Conn, what do you have?"

"Nothing, Conn. Everyone's home in bed."

"Make your depth sixty feet," I ordered. The Skipper's Night Orders had specified transiting the strait at periscope depth, with the periscope manned. "Come right to course north."

"Right to course zero-zero-zero, Aye."

I made a mental note that "course north" was not a usual expression on *Halibut*. "Up scope!" I twisted the circular bar near the overhead around scope one.

"Passing one-hundred-fifty feet," Diving Officer Gunty informed me, as the scope slid smoothly into position.

I draped my right arm over the handle, and put my right eye to the eyepiece. I commenced turning the scope to the left, assisted by the scope's hydraulic system. I was just completing my first round when the scope broke surface.

"Holding at sixty feet."

"Roger." I continued turning the scope, looking for any telltale light or surface disturbance. "Clear," I announced, and felt a tap on my shoulder. It was the Skipper, wanting a bit of periscope liberty. It was his boat – I yielded the scope.

I glanced at the fathometer. Two-hundred feet. "Sonar, Conn, put the sidescan on the monitor." The monitor flickered and the strange double lines of a sidescan display appeared.

"Conn, Sonar, it looks deeper to starboard."

"Come right to zero-zero-five." I decided to ease into the deeper water. "Up scope," I said as I raised number two. "Keep an eye on the depth, Sonar," I said as I swept around. Something flashed as I turned the scope. "Mark this bearing," I said as I centered on a faint flash.

Petty Officer Second Class Gary Parrish, Quartermaster of the Watch, had joined me when I raised scope two, ready to record any bearings. "Zero-four-nine," he reported.

He stepped over to the navigation table to check the chart. "Looks like that's the Cemenovka light," he said.

"Conn, Sonar, looks like we're center channel."

"Come left to zero-zero-zero," I ordered. Then I looked up at the monitor. "What're those markings to the port and starboard?" I could see two distinct spots, one off the port bow and one nearly abeam to starboard. I thought I could see faint lines leading outward from the spots.

"We're checking, Conn."

"Could it be the buoys?" I asked.

"We think so, Conn. Most likely, they're buoys." The monitor flickered as Sonar adjusted the resolution. "Definitely, they're buoys."

I did another 360-degree sweep. As I passed the bow, something caught my eye. I swung back, flipped to a higher magnification, and...

"Make your depth one-hundred-fifty feet – fast!" I ordered. "Down scopes." I slapped the overhead control bar as the Skipper lowered his scope. "Watch your depth – don't go below one-hundred-fifty."

I turned to the Skipper. "Did you see it, Skipper?" I asked, as the sub took a distinct down bubble.

"Ahead, about a mile," the Skipper said. "Lights, bow-on aspect."

"Yes sir. We're in a transit lane."

"Conn, Sonar, I have a contact bearing three-five-eight. Designate Bravo-one." It was the first contact of the day.

"Conn, Aye. I saw it. What is it, Sonar?"

"Light fast screws, pair of them – could be a Soviet warship."

"One-hundred-fifty feet," Gunty announced.

"Make turns for three knots," I ordered. "Secure the sidescan, Sonar."

"Bravo-one bears three-one-one. Fast left bearing rate. He's deaf at this speed."

The unmistakable sound of screws began to penetrate the hull.

"Bravo-one two-nine-zero."

"Two-seven-zero."

"Two-six-zero...two-four-five...two-three-zero..."

"I got it, Sonar. Thank you."

"What do you think, Skipper, night ops or are they headed for the barn?" My guess, they were headed for Petropavlovsk.

One ship, at this time. Probably going home." The Skipper sounded thoughtful.

"Sonar, it's the Captain. Why didn't we hear this guy earlier?"

"Light fast screws masked by the sidescan, Cap'n."

"What do you suggest, Mac?" The Skipper was well aware that I had spent a lot of time making sure my sub stayed undetected. But we needed the sidescan to find our way deep in waters that were, for us, virtually uncharted.

"Shut down the sidescan every fifteen minutes for a complete sonar sweep," I suggested. "And clear the baffles during the sweep."

"That often, you think?"

"This is their lake, Skipper. Better safe than sorry. The last thing I want is for my guys to be deployed when they find us." That's the one that gave me nightmares.

"Good point. I'll put it in the Standing Orders." He reached for his Standing Orders notebook and outlined the procedure for shutting down the sidescan and clearing the baffles every fifteen minutes. It would be a bit tedious, but it came with the territory.

"Sonar, Conn, what's your status?"

"Clear board, Conn. No contacts. We lost Bravo-one in our baffles."

"Roger. Activate sidescan."

As the display lit up, I could see the bottom was dropping away. "Right full rudder, I ordered to clear our baffles. "Check the baffles, Sonar."

As the boat swung, Sonar reported nothing. Apparently the warship had turned the corner for home. "Rudder amidships. Make your depth sixty feet."

I raised the scope and checked the landscape as we leveled at sixty feet. "There's a glow in the sky – mark this bearing," I said as I saw an eerie glow low on the horizon.

"Two-six-five," Parrish reported. He went back to his chart table. "I think that's the Alaid Volcano on Atlasova."

"That's a pretty healthy glow," I said as I handed the scope to the Skipper so he could take a look. "How far is it?"

"The base is about fifty-five miles away, but it's over a mile high, so you should be able to see the glow if it's bright enough."

"Sounds like it," the Skipper said as he made a full sweep.

And that was it for the night. We turned toward the west for a stretch to gain a bit of clearance around the tip of Kamchatka, and then set a course just west of north, paralleling the western Kamchatka coast. We moved slow and easy, because the Skipper wanted to start looking for tell-tale coastal signs of a marine cable at dawn, and he didn't want to get too far north before commencing our search.

Soviet Kashin Class Destroyer

CHAPTER TWELVE

As dawn climbed up the eastern slopes of the Kamchatka central ridge, I approached the chart table in Control where the boat's Navigator, Lieutenant Commander Larry Jackson, and the Skipper were poring over the annotated Admiralty chart of the Sea of Okhotsk we had received from NSA – the National Security Agency. Each corner was prominently stamped in red: TOP SECRET – SPECIAL PROJECTS. A couple of temporary curtains shielded the chart table from curious eyes, and draped over the table edge was an opaque cover sheet that could be flipped over the chart when it wasn't in use.

Our track during the night traced back to the strait we had entered on my watch several hours earlier. For the last two hours we had been angling toward the coastline. I could see that the bottom was shallowing. The Skipper wanted to remain outside the three-mile limit – just in case. We were there, three miles from the beach, three miles off the small community of Ozernovskiy. The sidescan was running. It showed the bottom about 300 feet beneath us. We were at 100 feet.

The Skipper had the Conn, while leaving the Deck in Weaps' capable hands – Josh Friedman (Weapons Officer).

"Exactly what are we looking for, Skipper?" I asked, leaning over the chart with them.

The Skipper grinned at me. "We're looking for a sign in Russian that is the equivalent of the signs you see all over Chesapeake Bay that say, "Don't anchor here! Underwater cable!" The Skipper was from Tidewater, Virginia, and knew the bay like the back of his hand. "The only problem is, in the morning we're looking east, and the sun can glint off our optics, giving us away to any observer. Nothing high-tech about it," he said with a smile, and stepped into the Conn.

"Give me a heading, Nav," the Skipper asked.

"Three-five-zero, Conn."

"Contacts, Sonar?"

"We're clean, Conn."

"Make your depth sixty-five feet." The Skipper didn't want any more scope sticking out of the water than necessary.

"Mark your depth"

"Seven-five feet – rising slowly."

"Easy, Diving Officer, easy. Up scope." As the scope came up, the Skipper commenced a full sweep.

"Seventy...sixty-nine...sixty-eight..."

"Easy..."

"Sixty-five feet and holding."

"Sun's still below the peaks. One-foot waves. Bring her up a foot."

"Sixty-four feet, Sir."

"OK – hold that. Go down if you have to, but not above sixty-four." The Skipper made another sweep. "Horizon clear." Then he concentrated on the shore off the boat's starboard side, sweeping slowly from stern to bow. Then he started back. Suddenly he flipped up the

handles. "Down scope!" He stepped back from the scope
as it lowered into the well. "Take her down to a hundred
feet," he ordered, and added, "Sun's up."

"Batman to Control," the Skipper ordered on the
1MC.

"Yes Sir." Lonie arrived in Control slightly winded.

"How quickly can you launch the Fish?"

" 'Bout fifteen minutes, Sir."

"OK – prepare the Fish, and let me know when you're
ready."

#

The Skipper and Nav hunched together over the
chart table. The Skipper was moving his finger parallel to
the coast for several miles, then back. "Five knots," the
Skipper said. Nav picked up his pencil and parallel rule
and laid out a series of courses. Twenty minutes later
Lonie notified Control that they were ready to launch
the Fish.

"Commence Fish ops," the Skipper announced on
the 1MC. "Sonar, secure the sidescan." The *Halibut's*
sidescanning sonar would interfere with the higher definition, more accurate sidescan on the Fish.

As the Fish winched out from the reel in the Aquarium lower lock, an image began to appear on the monitor.
We were looking for a straight line that crossed our path
at right angles. The Fish also contained a video camera
and a high-speed film camera, but there was no need
to use either of these until we knew we had something
to look at.

We sailed several miles north, and then made a slow
turn so the Fish could track behind us, then moved a
mile further out, and headed back south. About noon, as
I was coming on watch, the Skipper ordered the sub to
periscope depth again to check the position of the sun.

"We're good to go," he announced, and turned the
Conn over to me. I had already assumed the Deck from
Josh.

"Make your depth one-hundred-fifty feet," I ordered. As we settled at depth and while the Fish was still reeling back onboard, I said to Gunty, who now had the Nav Watch, "Take me back to where we left off this morning, Nav." As soon as the Fish was aboard, I pointed the sub in the right direction, cranked on a few extra turns, and headed for the point offshore from Ozernovskiy that we had abandoned when the sun came up. I activated the sidescan as a precaution, since we really didn't have good bathymetric information on this area.

As we approached, I checked the contacts with Sonar, and then ordered, "Make your depth sixty-five feet." Since I didn't know the surface conditions, I wanted the scope as low as possible. I swept around as we came up, broke the surface, and saw nothing. I set a course parallel to the coastline and commenced a careful scan of the area from the water to the back of the beach. There was virtually nothing to see. The beach was bare, even close to Ozernovskiy. The plant life beyond the rocky beach was mostly a scrappy tundra bush not unlike sage interspersed with short, spiky green grass. It was a lot greener than I had expected.

But signs announcing an underwater cable...nada...zippo...nothing.

By the end of my watch we had moved some twenty miles up the coast, and seen nothing. We passed the mouth of a small river, but no boats, no people, no animals, no nothing...

I got relieved from watch, decided to have some well-deserved shut-eye, and the next thing I know it was dinner time, a movie in the Wardroom, and then back on watch again. I had gotten into a routine that kept me either in Control, in the Wardroom, in the Dive Locker, or in my rack, not necessarily in that order. During afternoon hours, the Skipper let some of the senior crew members take turns on the scope. No harm done, and maybe one of them would be the hero who spotted the telltale sign.

After dark we towed the Fish, back and forth...back and forth...back and forth...

We kept up this routine for several days, and were making pretty good progress up the coast, especially since the weather had turned, and the skies were cloudy. This meant we could start scanning the beach at daybreak without fear of the sun reflecting off the periscope lens, and could continue all day. By the end of daylight on day five we were 500 miles up the coast as I took over the watch from Josh.

The seas had picked up quite a bit. Josh gave me the boat at sixty feet, because the waves were peaking at five feet or more. He told me the last hour had been pretty difficult for looking ashore, but he was certain he had missed nothing. In any case, it was getting dark, so I prepared to commence Fish runs. I took her down to a hundred feet and ordered the Fish deployed.

It started out routine, a repeat of the last four days. About an hour later I had moved a mile further out and was working on the first reverse leg. I had just commenced clearing baffles in accordance with the Skipper's Standing Orders when Sonar called me.

"Conn, Sonar, I've got a contact bearing two-five-five, zero bearing drift. Designate Golf-one."

That part about bearing drift was important. Normally, there always is some relative motion between two ships at sea. There are only three exceptions: if the two vessels are on a collision course so that their relative bearings don't change until they slam together (or pass under and over if one is a sub); if they are opening one another on a constant bearing, exactly the opposite of a collision course; or if they are paralleling each other with identical course and speed. In every other case, the relative bearing from one to the other will change.

"Sonar, Conn. Is this guy opening or closing?" Sonar can frequently tell because of increasing or decreasing sound intensity.

"Don't know yet, Conn. It's pretty noisy out there with the storm and everything. He just showed up on this bearing."

I stepped over to the chart table and examined the chart, looking at our position and the vector of Golf-one. I traced back along our track to the point where we first heard Golf-one. Sure enough, the bottom shallowed up significantly on that vector. He could have been out there for quite a while, but his sound got lost in the storm noise. The shallower water channeled the sound in our direction, so we picked him up.

"Do you know what he is, Sonar?"

"A trawler, we think, maybe pulling a net."

"How far out, Sonar?"

"Two, three miles, maybe. With no bearing drift, it's kinda hard to tell."

The last thing we needed was to get tangled in a net again. "Make turns for three knots," I ordered. I would give Sonar a bearing drift.

"Golf-one's started to pull ahead, Conn."

"Get me a range as soon as you can."

"Conn, Sonar, he's slowing – zero bearing drift again."

How could that be? I thought about it for a bit. But just for a bit – then I got it. I grabbed the sound-powered handset and called the Bat Cave. "Shut down the Fish now!" I ordered. "Reel it in as fast as you can." Then I called the Skipper to tell him what I was doing. It's his boat, remember?

I checked the depth – 300 feet. That left 200 feet below our keel. I checked the chart table. In the next mile out the bottom dropped another 300 feet. I called the Bat Cave again. "When will the Fish be back on board?" I asked.

The Skipper showed up and handed me a cup of coffee. "The way you like your women," he grinned at me.

"Thanks, Skipper. This guy's tracking our Fish. Sonar says he's a trawler, but I don't know any trawler that can do that."

I answered the high-pitched whir of the sound-powered phone, "Conn."

"The Fish is aboard, Sir."

"Right full rudder," I ordered. "Ten degrees down bubble. Make your depth two-hundred fifty feet." As the sub began to turn I said, "Steer two-seven-zero."

As we headed out and down I told Sonar to check the depth.

"Two-hundred fifty feet, Sir." That was our depth.

"Three-hundred feet below the keel, Sir." That was *the* depth.

"Make your depth five-hundred feet." With all the cold fresh water flowing into the Sea of Okhotsk, there simply had to be a distinct layer down there somewhere. We needed to get below it fast.

"Passing four-hundred feet."

"Conn, Sonar. We're passing through a very distinct layer. We're talking about a ten-degree temperature gradient here."

And that was a good thing. It probably was caused by the river run-off from the Kamchatka coast. The cold fresh water would tend to float on the saline seawater. The temperature and density difference at the interface would act very much like a mirror, reflecting sound back in the direction from which it came. This meant that I could get the *Halibut* under the layer, and our sounds would tend to remain below the layer. Since the other guy was on the surface, the only way he could hear us would be to lower hydrophones below the layer. He could do it, of course, but it would take time. That would allow me to get sufficiently far away that he would be unlikely to hear me, even with hydrophones below the layer.

So I cranked it up a bit, added a few turns, and took her down deep. The skipper arrived in Control as I settled back to evaluate the situation.

"Conn, Sonar, we've got a pinger out there; active sonar, characteristic of a Soviet destroyer. Bearing two-eight-zero."

I turned to the Captain. "He's going to have trouble finding us with this layer, Skipper, if he doesn't get too close." I walked over to the chart table and pointed to the northern end of Kamchatka, just south of the Gulf of She-likhov. "I recommend we high-tail it up here, and work our way back south." I pointed across the narrow neck that separated the Sea of Okhotsk from Shelikhov Bay. "You said the cable probably crosses here, so maybe we can save some time while we get out of this guy's back yard."

The Skipper spent some time at the chart table laying out possible courses with Larry Jackson. After several minutes he returned to his stateroom.

Larry looked up from the chart table. "Recommend a depth of six-hundred feet, and a course of three-two-ze-ro," he said, putting me on the track he and the Skipper had worked out.

We cruised at 600 feet for about a half hour. Suddenly Sonar announced, "Conn, Sonar. We got the pinger again. It's somewhere in the baffles."

"Left twenty degrees rudder," I ordered immediately. "Make turns for five knots." I could feel the boat slowing right through the deck plates.

"I got him, Conn!" The Sonar Tech sounded excited. "Right behind us...I mean, right behind us on our old course. That's one-four-zero, Conn."

"Rudder amidships," I ordered, "What's your heading?"

"Steering two-three-five, Sir," the helmsman said.

"Steer two-three-five," I ordered. "Sonar, Conn, what is this guy? I don't think he's a trawler."

"He's starting to look like a *Kashin*-class destroyer, Sir."

That was good news or bad news, depending on how old he was. Most of these ships had been built about ten years ago, in the early sixties, which made them pretty new and effective by any standards. The older ones are pretty basic, gas turbine powered, missile-firing warships. A couple of years ago, however, the Soviets upgraded about half of this class. The newer ones had the latest towed array sonar and an anti-submarine helicopter with dipping sonar – definitely bad news for us. The towed sonar array is basically a towed cable containing a hydrophone every few yards. It's a passive device, but because of its long baseline and distance from the tow ship's noise, it can get very good range information. The variable depth or dipping sonar allows the ship to place its active transducer below the layer, which would make us a sitting duck.

"Captain to the Conn!" I announced on the 1MC, "Captain to the Conn!"

The Skipper showed up shortly. "What is it, Mac?"

I briefed him on the situation, reminding him that this guy could have towed sonar and an anti-sub chopper.

"Captain has the Conn," he announced. And on the 1MC, "Rig ship for ultra quiet."

This meant that if you didn't have anything important to do, you got in your rack. All work stopped except what was absolutely essential.

"Shift to the battery," the Skipper ordered. "Make turns for bare steerageway."

The Skipper was serious. In less than two minutes steam was no longer driving the turbines, because Maneuvering had shut down the whole steam cycle. The reactor was still critical, but it was in idle, and was no longer making steam. Silent electric motors took over the task of turning the screws, and they were barely turning. Throughout the sub lights dimmed, leaving only essential lights lit.

I told the Skipper, "I'll step into Sonar to check this guy out." He nodded his assent.

The Skipper donned a headset with a boom mike. "Sonar, Conn. What's the status?" he asked, not wanting to make any noise by using the intercom system.

I stepped into the Sonar Shack. Senior Chief Travis Barkley ran the Sonar gang, but he had the Dive this watch. Petty Officer First Class Royal Bennett – "King" to everyone – was the Sonar Supervisor. "What's up, King?" I asked him.

He handed me a headset with an earpiece turned outward. I put it to my ear and listened as the operator on the console centered on the contact. I could hear the relatively faint double screw sound, interrupted by a periodic faint ping. I donned a boom-mounted headset and listened to King brief the Skipper. He explained that the pinger had been masking his screws, in order to sound like a trawler.

Because we had set a course at right angles to our previous course, within a few minutes Sonar was able to calculate the pinger's range. "Conn, Sonar," King announced on the circuit. "Golf-one bears one-zero-four, drifting left, range five thousand yards."

So he hadn't picked up our turn yet, and he may have lost us when we slowed and went ultra-quiet.

"Where is that layer, Sonar?" the Skipper asked.

"About four-hundred feet, Sir."

"Make your depth three-hundred sixty feet, slow and easy," the Skipper ordered. "Give me an intercept course, Nav," he said to Larry.

Shortly thereafter Larry said, "Intercept course is zero-four-four, Cap'n."

"Right full rudder. Activate the thrusters; forward thruster left full, after thruster right full." Almost immediately the sub began a slow turn around its vertical axis.

As the sub turned, the Skipper kept an eye on the heading. When the bow passed 038 degrees he ordered the thrusters to stop and set a course of 044. Golf-one was in our starboard quarter, drifting left as our tracks closed.

"Depth is three-hundred sixty," Chief Barkley announced.

"Mac," the Skipper's voice sounded in my ears, "I need to know if this guy is towing his array, and if he has his variable depth sonar deployed."

"Hang on, Skipper," I replied, "we're looking into it."

I asked King for his book on the *Kashin*-class destroyer. As I paged through the book, I asked what he had found out about this ship. King was standing in front of the BQQ-3 sonar waterfall display, comparing the LOFAR (for low frequency analysis and recording) printout from the contact with several he had pulled from a case.

"I think I got him, Sir." King turned the pages of my book to one displaying the *Ognevoy*, which the book said meant Fiery. I removed my headset and walked out to the Conn, studying it as I went. I showed it to the Skipper.

"This guy has a towed array sonar," I told him, "and a variable depth as well. But in this weather, he probably has the variable stowed, and his bird definitely is tied down. His towed array is pretty good, but he's going to have a devil of a time putting it below the layer. As it is, if we remain quiet, it's more like a sea anchor than a detection device to him."

The Skipper nodded, and studied the book some more. "We're going to slide up alongside him and cozy under his wake," he said. "We'll slip just above the layer right behind him. His wake noise will play havoc with any reception from there, and they'll never suspect."

Now that was an audacious move. I was near the end of my watch, but I decided to hang around to watch it happen. Josh Friedman (Weaps) relieved me, but the Skipper retained the Conn as we sidled close to the *Ognevoy*.

"Sonar, Conn," the Skipper said, "keep a close eye on the layer."

"Sonar, Aye."

"Bring her up slowly, Diving Officer."

"Dive Aye," Chris Barth answered – he had just taken over the Dive watch.

I strained to listen through the hull.

"Conn, Sonar, passing through the layer at two-hundred feet."

"Make your depth one-hundred-ninety feet," the Skipper told Chris.

Suddenly, I could clearly hear *Ognevoy's* screws right through the hull, as if he were on top of us. We were moving three or four knots at the most, perhaps even slower. The *Ognevoy* was about 150 feet above our sail, and maybe a hundred feet ahead of us. The Soviet warship's towed sonar array was somewhere behind us 300 yards or so, probably fifty feet or so below the turbulent surface.

Even at this slow speed, we could clearly hear the *Ognevoy's* screws riding in and out of the water as he bucked the increasingly rough waves.

"Conn, Sonar, we're gaining on him."

I don't have any idea how King figured that out. He stayed in the Sonar Shack to help out, and it looked like he was earning his pay.

"All stop," the Skipper ordered, looking at his watch. After ten seconds he ordered bare steerageway again. From time to time he gave the bow or stern a gentle push with the thrusters to keep us aligned with *Ognevoy's* course.

"Conn, Sonar, it sounds like he's retrieving his array – looks like he's giving up, Sir."

"Let's get down below the layer, Chris," the Skipper said. "Sonar, Conn, let me know when we pass the layer."

Chris dropped us down slowly. We were moving so slowly that we actually settled on the layer for a bit, while he pumped enough water into the boat to overcome the density difference. Suddenly our rate of descent accelerated.

"Make turns for five knots," the Skipper ordered to help Chris with his depth control.

Sonar called, "Through the Layer, Conn, at two-hundred-ten feet."

"Conn Aye," the Skipper acknowledged. "Maneuvering, Conn, shift the plant to the Turbines."

A few minutes later Maneuvering informed us that we were good to go on the turbines. The Skipper turned the watch back over to Josh and left Control after giving Weaps general directions for the transit to the northern end of the Sea of Okhotsk. As he left, he reminded Josh to clear his baffles according to the Standing Orders.

I left Control myself to get some shut-eye, thinking about the resources Ivan had in the Sea of Okhotsk. When we found the cable, and my guys were out there, I really didn't want one of these updated *Kashins* to show up. They obviously had the potential for making things pretty unpleasant out there. I drifted off with that thought on my mind, and dreamed of pitched underwater battles with my guys being deafened by crashing active sonar while fighting off living metal monsters.

Cable running along the sea floor

CHAPTER THIRTEEN

As I came on watch, I stopped to examine the chart. We had moved over 500 miles north, and were inside Shelikhov Bay, about halfway up the coast. We had been working our way slowly down the coast, looking closely for the illusive Do-Not-Anchor-Here sign that would signal the next phase of our little venture. It had now been over thirty days since I brought us around Kamchatka Point into the Sea of Okhotsk. Except for the encounter with *Ognevoy*, we had seen little traffic. It was the classic "endless hours of tedious boredom interrupted by moments of sheer panic," and of those, we had had only *Ognevoy*.

It stormed more than not up here, so in the morning we generally could start as soon as it was sufficiently light to see the shore. My watch rotation had me on mornings as we resumed our coast watch. That gave me the privilege of getting the first look-see each morning, unless the Skipper pulled rank.

Anyway, I got myself positioned, pointed generally southwest, and started to bring her to shallow periscope depth (because of the rough seas). That's when the Skipper showed up in Control. He grabbed the scope and rode it up. Like I keep saying, it's his boat.

He made a couple of sweeps, and then handed the scope to me with a grin. "Go for it, Mac. See if you can find me a sign." He headed for the Wardroom. And me – well I had another four hours of checking out a bunch of bushes and spiky grass...and a rind of ice at the high water line. That's right, ice six inches or so thick, like a rim of salt around a Margarita.

"Sonar, Conn," I called. "What's the salinity?"

"About twenty-five parts per thousand, Conn."

That was interesting, because normal oceanic salinity is between thirty-three and thirty-five parts per thousand. This water was significantly less salty, which meant it would freeze at a higher temperature. Normal freezing temperature for seawater is about 27 degrees Fahrenheit. The water here would freeze at about 28 or 29 degrees, which is why I saw the rind of ice. It also meant there was a hell of a layer not too far below *Halibut*. I intended to keep that in mind. We were definitely way inside Ivan's back yard. No telling what he might do if he caught us.

None of that changed the routine, however – maintain about five knots; sweep left, sweep right, left, right... left.... Dip the scope every second sweep or so to clear off a thin layer of ice that kept skimming over the optics. Sweep the shore line...and then...wait a sec. What was that? Sweep back...

"Nav, mark this bearing...Mark!"

"One-zero-four, Conn."

I kept the scope on whatever it was. "Make turns for three knots," I ordered. Then I cranked up the magnification – we were three miles out. I couldn't really tell what it was.

"Mark our position on the chart, Nav," I ordered. I needed to get back to this exact point, if possible. "Right full rudder. Make turns for five knots. Come about to new course zero-one-four."

I watched the sub come about and steady on the new course. "Left full rudder," I ordered. "Come about to new course one-zero-four." That was the original bearing of the sighting. What I had done was perform a figure eight to pull me away from the beach, and bring me back to the same bearing from the beach as the original sighting, but further out – if it worked as it was supposed to. I called the Skipper to Control.

The Skipper showed up shortly, finishing off the last bite of what looked very much like an English muffin breakfast sandwich. "What'dya got, Mac?" he asked.

We steadied up on one-zero-four as I briefed him.

"Make turns for three knots," I ordered. We were pointed directly at the coast, just over four miles from the beach. That gave me a mile on this heading. The Skipper put up Scope two. Because of the waves, I needed to get a bit higher. "Come up to sixty feet, easy," I ordered. "Make turns for bare steerageway; activate the thrusters." I wanted to maintain control over my heading while moving as slow as possible.

"What did you actually see, Mac?" The Skipper didn't doubt me, but he apparently couldn't see anything yet himself, and wanted to know what to look for.

"Not so much something, as straight lines across the tangle of shrubs," I answered. "I didn't get a good look, but it wasn't natural. It didn't belong there." And that was about it. It wasn't something, so much as a quick flash that was out of place. I was certain something was on the beach in front of us. I dipped my scope to clear the optics – and there it was again, not directly ahead of us, but a bit off the port bow.

"Mark!" I said as I swung back and forth across the shape.

"Zero-nine-seven," Nav said.

The Skipper swung to that bearing. "Mark!" he said.

Nav: "Zero-nine-eight."

"Mark!" I said as I found it again, a square object about three feet off the ground. "Two-foot-square sign with black Cyrillic letters," I said.

"I got it," the Skipper said.

I tilted the optics up to scan what was above the sign. I noticed a distinctive, wind-blown tree directly in line with the sign, and behind that, just an r-c-h to the right was a volcanic cone. I pointed them out to the Skipper. "I'm going to come left just enough to line them up a bit better," I said. The Skipper grunted his assent.

"Left full rudder, bow thruster left full," I ordered. "Come to new course zero-two-zero." As I came on course, I stopped the thruster.

About a minute later the Skipper said, "Mark this bearing!"

"One-zero-one, Con," Nav said.

I swung my scope over to that bearing. There they were, as pretty as you could wish: sign, tree, cone. I snapped a photo through the scope. "Lay that out on the chart, Nav," I said, while taking another photo.

"What's the depth, Sonar?" I asked.

"Three-hundred twenty feet, Sir."

I stepped over to the chart to check the depth. The chart showed us between the sixty- and seventy-fathom curves. That was about right. I turned to the Skipper and asked, "How do you plan to do this, Sir?"

He leaned over the chart and moved his finger back and forth across the vector leading from the beach. "We'll run below the layer, towing the Fish, back and forth like this, five-hundred yards between runs." He paused, in obvious thought. "Once we find it, we'll figure out what to do. We need to know what we are dealing with first." Then he directed Nav to lay out our track starting right at the three-mile line, moving away from the beach.

Chief Gunty and Larry showed up to check the plot. Since this was the real deal, nobody wanted anything to go wrong. While they were doing this, I contacted Lonie so he could get ready to deploy the Fish.

"Nav, what's my course for getting to the start of the search grid?" I asked in the general direction of the chart table. The table was a bit crowded, what with the Navigator, the Chief Quartermaster, the Quartermaster of the Watch, and the Skipper.

"One-seven-three, Conn."

I ordered the course, and about the time Nav gave me the search leg of 191 degrees, Lonie had the Fish deployed, and Bobby Shanks, one of the two civilian Special Operations Technicians working for Lonie, was busy monitoring the feed in the Display Room. I set the Control monitor to display Bobby's feed.

There was not much to see, really. The bottom appeared virtually featureless, which was good, actually, because something like a cable lying on the bottom would tend to stand out. At least, that was the theory.

So our plan was to run below the layer, and to keep the Fish deployed behind us, sweeping back and forth about a mile in each direction. Sooner or later, we simply had to see the cable.

#

We were nearing the end of my watch. I had stopped staring at the monitor. That was Bobby's job, and as far as I was concerned, he could have it. We were on a northern leg, about halfway into it, when Bobby squeaked on the intercom, "Conn, Display, Look! Look!"

I did. And did a double take. There it was, sitting on the bottom like a long black hose.

"Mark this location, Nav!" I ordered. And then I told Bobby to deploy a marker – a small, low-powered sonar transmitter that put out a periodic burst of "white" sound about once a minute that blended into the background noise. Sonar would be able to find this marker using the BQQ-3 frequency analyzing sonar with the waterfall LOFAR display – the same unit we used to identify the *Ognevoy.*

I told the Bat Cave to activate the Fisheye – the video camera on the Fish – and called the Skipper. He called back from the Bat Cave where he had been watching the operation. He directed me to get back on the cable and follow it away from the coast. As soon as we had something definitive, he said, he wanted to start the high-speed camera. I turned left using the rudder and thrusters, but when things cleared up, the bottom was as clean as a baby's ass. Nada...who knows? It was there when we crossed it a few minutes ago, but now it was gone. It could have been a bare spot on the bottom, perhaps some bedrock exposing the cable, but in any case, the cable wasn't there any more. That's why I had dropped the marker.

Apparently, the Skipper wasn't too concerned, though, because he remained in the Bat Cave.

"Sonar, Conn, find me that marker!"

The marker had limited range, for obvious reasons. We could leave and come back into the general area, and its range was sufficient to pick it up. But it only sounded once a minute, and the BQQ-3 needed several pulses to integrate the incoming sound into a recognizable signal. So it wasn't just a case of listening, hearing it, and going there. You had to hang around long enough to generate a bearing to the marker. But we were close, and we had a good idea where it was. I needed to get it in front of us so I could point at the marker and drive the Fish right over it. I made a wide turn to the right since we had been on a northerly leg when we spotted it, and this turn would bring me inshore of our current position, which was about twenty miles off the coast.

As soon as I moved the presumed marker location out of my baffles, Sonar informed me that they had picked it up. I continued the slow turn while ordering

Lonie to haul the Fish in closer. When we finally saw the cable with the Fisheye, I wanted to be as close as possible so we could do a tight survey, and follow it until we spotted a repeater pod.

That was our basic plan. A repeater receives signals in both directions, amplifies them, and injects the amplified signals back into the cable. This means that we would have stronger signals to work with. We had a three-foot long device from NSA that we intended to clamp around the cable. It would pick up the signals using electromagnetic induction – something like the coils inside a transformer. We did not need to cut into the cable, which would certainly alert the cable system to a breach. This way, moreover, the tap would be entirely undetectable.

"Conn, Sonar, marker bears two-six-five, off the starboard bow." That meant the turn had worked, and I was coming up on the correct bearing. When the marker was off the bow, I wanted to be pointed at 281.

"Ease your rudder," I ordered. I didn't want to cut inside the track.

"Conn, Sonar, marker bears two-seven-eight, just off the starboard bow."

"Make your course two-eight-one," I ordered the helmsman, Skidmore.

A moment later Skidmore announced, "Steering two-eight-one, El-tee." I glanced up at the Fisheye monitor.

"Conn, Sonar, marker bearing two-eight-zero, just off the port bow."

I had overshot it. "Ease a bit to the left," I ordered Skidmore, keeping an eye on the monitor. And there it was, a straight line on the Fish sidescan directly beneath us. "Steer two-eight-one."

As we came on course, the bottom showed up clearly on the Fisheye. Running across the bottom was a series of long bumps with occasional black sections peeping through the silt. It was the cable, all right. I shut down the sidescan. No need to advertise our presence.

Now all we had to do was keep the cable in sight as we moved along it, looking for a lump – the repeater. I told the Bat Cave to start the high-speed camera. Then I cranked up a few extra turns, since we probably had about ten miles to go before we would spot the repeater. That would be in two or three hours, at best.

#

Josh relieved me a bit early, so I went to find Ham. I figured we would be locking out pretty soon, and wanted to get the divers in the Can and acclimated. I found him in the Dive Locker, preparing for the dive. As usual, he was one step ahead of me. I gotta tell you, having a guy like Ham in your corner makes all the difference.

Ham had four guys suiting up: Jer and Harry, because they didn't dive the last time, and Bill, and Ski. Jimmy and Whitey would be available for Dive Console watches. Ham and I would run the dive, and Jack and the other two would alternate in second seat. Ham figured that Jack was ready to run a watch himself, but this first time out, Ham still wanted Jack to understudy. Next time, Ham and Jack would stand port and starboard (alternating watches) with the two non-divers, and I would stand back with the big picture. Occasionally, either Ham, Jack, or myself would suit up and enter the water – just to keep ourselves up to the task, if for no other reason.

"What's our sat depth, Mac?" Ham asked.

"We expect to find the repeater about thirty miles or so from the coast," I told him. "The bottom there is at least four-hundred feet, and slopes down to over five-hundred over the next ten miles. Set sat depth to four-hundred ten feet," I said. "That way, if we settle at four-hundred, we still have a few feet to spare, and can adjust the saturation level without too much excess time for decompression."

"We can even adjust during the dive, if necessary," Ham added.

Our underlying problem was that at whatever depth we saturated, the divers could move below that depth to anything they could reach (within reason), but they were limited to only 33 feet shallower than the designated depth before they ran into decompression problems. The *Halibut* would be hanging off two anchors a few feet above the bottom. If the bottom were at 400 feet, that would put the Can at about 360 feet – our saturation depth. The divers could go to the bottom at 400 feet without any problems, but they could only rise to 327 feet before experiencing decompression problems. Setting the sat depth for 410 feet presumes a bottom at about 450 feet. So if the bottom turned out to be shallower than 417 feet, we would need to adjust the saturation depth before putting the divers in the water – in other words, we would need to decompress the divers by the number of feet the bottom was shallower than 417 feet. That could take up to an hour or more.

We decided to press the divers down as soon as they were ready, and then, as we learned more about the actual depth, commence any adjustments as soon as possible.

While Ham, Jack, and I were discussing this, I felt a rocking of the sub, a sort of nauseating feeling as she commenced a slow roll from side to side, a roll that seemed to be increasing in intensity.

"Excuse me, guys," I said. "I'm going to Control to see what's happening."

As I stepped into Control a minute later, I asked Josh, "What's happening up there?"

"Growing storm," he said. "Long waves setting from the south. Looks like they're fifteen to twenty high, and growing."

I whistled. "Can we hold station and depth in that?"

"Shouldn't be a problem," Josh said. "Those mushrooms are pretty big." He was referring to two large mushroom anchors, one in the bow and one in the stern, that we would deploy once we were on station. The anchors were shaped such that when they were fully retracted, they faired in smoothly with the hull. We intended to lower the anchors to the bottom rapidly so they would imbed themselves into the silt. Then we would trim the sub to slight positive buoyancy so she would ride up against the anchors. It would take a pretty big storm to have any effect on us down there.

I went back and explained the situation to Ham and the guys.

"How soon can you press down, Ham?" I asked.

"Another five minutes, Mac."

"Okay – I'm on my way to the Skipper." I left for the Bat Cave.

#

In the Bat Cave, the Skipper was standing back from the action with his arms folded across his chest, silently watching. I briefed him on our intentions so he would understand the need to determine the anchor depth as soon as feasible. He listened intently, without interrupting.

When I completed explaining the complexities of setting the saturation depth correctly, he acknowledged, and added, "Don't forget to let me know before you open the Can to ambient sea pressure." That was it – nothing more. He got it, he trusted me, and would let me conduct the dive as I saw fit. He just wanted to know when the watertight integrity of his sub was breached.

I stopped by Control on my way back to the Dive Locker.

"How long till we hit the thirty mile mark?" I asked Josh.

"An hour or so," he answered. "I'll call you when we get close, or if we spot the repeater sooner."

I asked him about the storm.

"Appears to be getting worse," he said. "The waves are growing, but they look like long rollers." He glanced up at the high-frequency wave sonar, basically a box with a horizontal series of indicator lights in columns. In a perfectly flat sea, only the bottommost lights would be lit. The columns showed dramatic wave movement, but in a regular pattern from left to right. "Probably means the storm is big, but way south. We're getting only the wave action, and it's had time to consolidate. These buggers will be with us for some time – a couple of days or more, I think."

Well, that was "good" news. I headed aft.

#

Back at the Dive Console, I briefed Ham on the current status. Ski had gone to take a dump – "So I won't stink up the Can," he had said – and the other guys were about ready to climb into the Can.

"Be sure the guys understand the wave problem," I told him.

Ham acknowledged, and sealed the guys into the Can. He looked at me for permission; I nodded, and he commenced pressurizing the Can. Jack kept the log, and I noted that Ham's look and my nod were recorded as "Request permission to commence the dive," and "Permission granted," respectively.

By the book.

Ham stopped at a depth of fifty feet and checked with the divers, ensuring that everything was okay. Then he continued pressing down.

As usual, Bill just sat there, letting his large Eustachian tubes do the work of equalizing his inner ears. Ski and Jer were yawning, and Harry was pinching his nose and blowing, but nobody was in trouble. They were all equalizing without significant problems. When they were about to hit 150 feet, Harry raised his hand, and Ham stopped the descent. Harry puffed against his pinched nose a couple of times, and then signaled with a thumb to rise a few feet. Ham complied, while Harry puffed hard. Suddenly he grinned and gave the okay sign, a circle formed with the thumb and index finger of his right hand. Ham continued the descent.

Once they had passed 150 feet, there were no more ear-clearing stops. Ham stopped briefly at 200 feet, 300 feet, and at 400 feet. And then he took the Can down another ten feet to the agreed-upon sat depth of 410 feet.

"Okay, guys," Ham said over the intercom. "Don your headsets, and get up and move about." After a minute or so he said, "Talk to me, Harry."

"I'm fine, Ham." Distorted by the helium descrambler, Harry sounded a bit like a slow-speaking chipmunk.

"Talk to me, Ski."

"Roger, Dive Control."

"Talk to me, Jer."

"Watdyawant?"

"Talk to me, Bill."

"Yeah, Ham. We're fine."

I picked up the mike. "Okay, fellows, you've got some time. Get some rest while you acclimate. One man awake at all times. We got an eye on ya." I handed the mike to Ham.

"Okay, Bill, you got the first watch. The rest of you hit the sack and get some rest!" Then he turned to me. "If it's okay with you, El-tee, I'll take the first six with Jimmy. Then you and Jack can take over.

"No problem, Ham. I'll get some shut-eye for this first leg."

Doc entering the Can

CHAPTER FOURTEEN

I've said several times how submarining is endless hours of boredom interrupted by moments of sheer panic. Well, saturation diving is all that – in spades!

The Can measured about thirty by seven feet inside. The main lock took up twenty-two, and was filled with eight feet of two two-tier bunks at the front end and fourteen feet of table, several built-in seats, gauges, lockers, etc. toward the rear. The entry lock was about eight feet of toilet, sink, shower head, and both the entry hatch from the sub and the exit hatch to the water. For four people it was not bad, all things considered.

Entertainment consisted of cards, books, and movies projected on a small screen at the Dive Console, and picked up with a black-and-white video camera for display on the inside monitor. We also had a small collection of videotapes, some of regular movies, and other strictly off-the-record "special" tapes to keep the guys happy on long dives. Officially, I didn't know about these special tapes.

The routine consisted of several guys living under great atmospheric pressure in very cramped quarters, with virtually nothing to do between dives except read, play cards, or watch movies. It gets old very quickly. Of course, when something does happen, like the helium flush mistake back during my training, all hell breaks loose in a hurry.

But this one promised to be routine, and I was going to do everything to keep it that way.

Josh had promised a couple of hours or so, and we were getting there. I was hanging around Control, hoping to be there when we found the repeater. Like I explained earlier, the process was actually pretty routine. The cable was plainly visible, and keeping over it presented no serious problem for Josh and his team. Bobby was pumping out high-speed film at a furious rate. We only had a few minutes left before we ran out of film.

Just then Bobby's voice sounded over the intercom. "Conn, Display, we're out of high-speed film. We need to haul in the Fish to replace the film canister."

"All stop," Josh ordered.

I glanced up at the monitor as the sub coasted to a halt. The Fish drifted toward us as the guys in the Bat Cave hauled it in. By the time we were DIW (dead in the water), the Fish was in its rack in the Bat Cave, and the ship's photographer, Petty Officer Rusty Nicholas, had already replaced the film canister with a fresh one.

I joined the crew in the Bat Cave, but things were getting pretty crowded, so I went to the Wardroom to grab a sandwich. Petty Officer Gregory Jalbuna, Chief Steward for the Wardroom, had whipped up a batch of fresh tuna salad – spiced with paprika, garlic, and celery seed, he once told me. It was pretty good when spread on the Chief Commissaryman's freshly baked bread. Chief Cedric Hurst had a way with things baked. When in port his guys would trade several of his famous loaves for all kinds of things that were otherwise unavailable – relishes, pickles, special treats that didn't exist in the Navy food chain. He was a real asset.

Since food normally is not allowed in the Control Room, I wolfed down my sandwich before passing through Control. On my way back to Dive, I stopped again to check on the waves above. They certainly weren't getting any smaller – as everyone aboard could tell by the gentle roll we were experiencing. Since we were down about 400 feet, getting that kind of action from surface waves meant they were really large, deep, powerful rolling piles of water.

When I arrived back at Dive, Ham informed me, "Ski's seasick."

"Seasick? What do you mean?"

"Plain old seasick, Mac. He's puking in a bucket."

I had a decision to make. I wouldn't put him in the water in his present shape. But on the other hand, if we were delayed at all by the storm, he would have plenty of time to recover.

"Put him in his rack, and hang in there for a bit," I told Ham. I needed to check with Josh again about the waves. And see Doc.

#

As I came into Control, things were getting pretty exciting. It seems that Bobby had just spotted what he believed was the repeater. Josh had just killed the sub's forward motion; the Bat Cave was busy hauling in the Fish and getting ready to deploy the Basketball. Josh told me that they were going to pull the film from the Fish, and take a batch with the high-speed camera in the Basketball. Then we had to go to periscope depth so Rusty could develop all the film we had taken for the past however long it was. His chemicals were far too toxic to be used in the closed atmosphere of the *Halibut*. It was going to be a while – several hours at least.

It looked like I had missed out on all the excitement. I left them to their tasks and went to find Doc.

I found him in his tiny cubicle, Sickbay, processing radiation badges. Everybody wears one on a nuke sub, and nobody ever receives any exposure. In fact, during my nine patrols I actually accumulated considerably less exposure than any surface pukes. Basically, I got nothing, while they got cosmic rays and your basic background radiation. So once a week, everybody turned in his badge, was issued a new one, and Doc processed them to see if anyone had picked up anything.

Anyway, I interrupted Doc. He didn't mind. It wasn't his most enjoyable task, by a long shot. "You ever pressed down in a lockout chamber, Doc?" I asked.

"Not really," he responded. "Been down in a regular chamber. You know, the dry kind."

"How deep?" I asked.

" 'Bout two-fifty," he said, "on air. Narced out of my mind."

I nodded. "I got a bit of a problem," I said. "Well, not really me. It's Ski." I grinned at Doc. "He's puking his guts out in a bucket. Can you lock in, give him a shot to settle his stomach so he can get his sea legs back, and then lock back out?"

"Don't see why not," Doc said. "How deep are you?"

"Four-hundred feet or so," I said, "Heliox. You won't be down for more than five minutes after you get there. We'll bring you right back up to about sixty feet for a few minutes on pure oh-two, and then another couple of minutes at thirty feet on oh-two, and then back out." I grinned at him with a shrug. "Piece of cake," I said.

Doc raised an eyebrow. "Why not," he said, sweeping the badges into an open drawer. He grabbed his "road kit," basically first-aid stuff and several ampules of promethazine.

#

When we arrived at the Dive Locker, I briefed Ham on my intent. "We've got several hours," I told him. "Ski will sleep it off and be good to go by the time we're ready to deploy. We'll keep him in the Can for this one."

Ham handed Doc some slippers. "Wear these in the Can," he said.

Doc removed everything from his pockets. Ham pointed to his watch. "Don't want it to blow the crystal on the way up," he told Doc.

While we were standing there, Doc pinched his nose and swallowed. Then he did it again.

"Do you have trouble clearing?" Ham asked him.

"Sometimes," Doc answered. I could tell he was a bit nervous.

Ham handed him a pseudoephedrine nose sprayer. "Squirt each nostril, Doc. That'll take care of you just fine." Ham guided him to the ladder, and Doc entered the outer lock.

"Put your headset on, Doc," Ham told him over the intercom. On the monitor we could see Doc comply. "Sit down and relax, Doc. We'll take you down in stages."

I eased the hatch shut and cranked it tight.

"If you have any difficulty," Ham said, "just raise your hand."

Doc nodded and grinned at us. Then he put his hand to his nose, ready to pinch at the first hint of inner ear pressure.

"Pressing down," Ham announced, and cranked the helium valve open.

The rush of gas sounded loud through Doc's mike. His eyes got big, and he pinched his nose and puffed out his cheeks. Ham stopped the descent at about 25 feet.

"Everything alright in there?" he asked. Doc nodded and gave the universal diver "I'm okay" sign, a circled thumb and forefinger with the remaining fingers pointed straight. "Relax, Doc. Don't blow so hard. This is helium. Clearing is easy in this stuff."

Ham continued the descent. He stopped at 100 feet, but Doc just grinned. He no longer was pinching his nose, and seemed to be enjoying himself. After all, how many times does a guy get to be the corpsman on a nuclear sub *and* get pressed down in a lockout chamber to 400 feet just off the coast of the other superpower? I think the Doc was getting his jollies!

#

Doc was at 410 feet in virtually no time. The guys in the Can welcomed him with "chipmunk" glee, and he immediately gave Ski an injection between Ski's dry heaves. While there, Doc gave him a quick once-over, checking his temperature, pulse, and blood pressure.

When he was done, Doc looked at the camera. "He's fine. He'll go to sleep now, and when he wakes, he should be good to go. Don't let him in the water, though."

"We won't," Ham said. "Now get back in the outer lock so I can bring you up."

This was an unusual profile, so we took it slowly. We got Doc to 100 feet in about fifteen minutes, and to sixty a couple of minutes later. I had calculated a decompression stop of five minutes on oxygen at sixty feet, but just to be sure, we gave him ten minutes. Then we brought him to thirty feet, and kept him there for another five minutes on oxygen, and then we surfaced him. Total time for the ascent was about thirty-five minutes.

"Great job, Doc! Thanks," I said as he put on his regular steel-toe shoes. "Let's do it again sometime."

"So, do I get dive pay for this?" Doc asked with a grin. That was worth about $150 bucks.

"Sure, I said. I'll clear it with the Ex-Oh."

#

As I walked back through Control to check on the state of things I heard Josh order, "Make your depth sixty feet. Mind your depth in this shit, Diving Officer!"

Chief Warrant Officer Neil Mixey had the Dive. "Aye, aye, Sir. Sixty feet, and mind my depth."

This was going to be a lot of fun.

Painting of roiling ocean with ship for scale by the late 19th century Armenian-Russian painter Ivan Konstantinovich Aivazovsky

CHAPTER FIFTEEN

As Neil brought us up, the *Halibut* began to rock big time. By the time we hit 100 feet, we were taking thirty degree rolls. I could hear things falling everywhere – cups, saucers, dishes, eating utensils, tools, books, charts, you name it. That's a problem on a sub. When you are taking it easy for a while – like we were for the past several weeks – people forget that subs move... in all dimensions. Control was a mess – cups, charts, pencils, shit galore. Don't even ask about the rest of the boat.

And we were not even at periscope depth yet...

Josh brought the sub around to a southern heading, pointing into the running sea. That stopped the rolling – but now we were pitching...twenty degrees, thirty degrees...who knows...I was just hanging on.

"Keep her down by the stern, Josh," I suggested while hanging on to the conning station railing. "Bring her up to decks awash, get some speed on, and push through the rollers." I grinned at him. "Trust me, it works."

Josh glanced at the Skipper, who had strapped himself into his chair at the back of the conning station. The Skipper nodded, and so Josh gave the appropriate orders, and Neil and his BCP operator, Senior Chief Saul Dimsdale went to work. I don't know if I mentioned it, but Neil Mixey was the Damage Control Assistant – the DCA – onboard *Halibut*, the guy who knew more about keeping a sub alive than anybody else. And Saul Dimsdale was the *Halibut's* senior enlisted engineer; you could fairly argue that if Saul didn't know it about the plant, then nobody did.

So we had the strongest possible engineering team managing our depth control. No disrespect intended – these guys knew everything there is to know about the plant, but when it came to depth control, they were better engineers, if you get my drift.

I stepped over to Neil's station right behind the planesmen, and stood to his left behind Scotty, the stern planesman.

"I'll give Scotty and Rocky some help," I said quietly to Neil, and laid my hands on Scotty's shoulders.

I squatted down between the planesmen just in front of Neil and whispered to Scotty, "When I squeeze like this," I placed my left hand on his right shoulder and pressed my thumb into his back, pushing him slightly forward, "ease her forward; like this," I pulled back gently against his shoulder, "pull her back." Then I squeezed his shoulder. "Like this, hold your planes."

I looked over to Rocky, who had the bow and helm. "Your job is not to let the bow get away from you. Keep her pointed into the sea – follow Lieutenant Friedman's course orders, and force the nose down, always down." I placed my right hand on his left shoulder and pressed my thumb into his back like I had done with Scotty. I pushed him gently forward. "When I do this, put the planes down, and when I do this," I pulled back, "bring the planes up. Remember, you'll be fighting Scotty, so don't let it get ahead of you. Warrant Officer Mixey here will be keeping us honest."

I grinned up at Neil. "Remember, keep the stern heavy, keep her pointed into the sea, and don't let Saul get ahead of the program."

That was the moment we broached. As the sail broke through the surface, the sub rolled sharply to starboard.

"Left full rudder!" Josh ordered.

I pulled back sharply on both Scotty's and Rocky's shoulders. The following things happened nearly simultaneously. The bow tried to push sharply down from the rudder acting just like stern planes in the full down position as the sub rolled sharply to the left. But Scotty's planes were now full up, countering that, and Rocky's planes were holding the bow up.

"Rudder amidships!" Josh ordered.

I squeezed both planesmen forward, and then brought Rocky's planes neutral, while reversing Scotty's to hold the stern down. "Another thousand pounds aft," I told Neil.

My hands went into automatic, squeezing, pulling, pulling, squeezing...holding.... The pitching settled down, the sub plowed through the towering seas, but the ride was gentle, almost – but not quite – smooth. Scotty, Rocky, and I became one organism. We moved together, we merged our minds and skills, and thirty foot waves towered past us as we slipped through the trough of one and plunged through the face of the next. Neil concentrated on keeping the weight distributed to maintain a heavy stern without pushing the bow into the air. He issued quiet orders to Saul who had virtually no time to think, but only to open and shut valves and throw pump switches. Soon the five of us were as with one mind, working with the soul of the submarine, no longer conscious of passing time or anything but the motion of the sub surrounding us.

Once we had stabilized, Josh extended the snorkel and started up the diesel engines, sucking massive amounts of air into the sub, and exhausting the diesel exhaust and the noxious fumes from Rusty's developing operation in his cramped lab. A rush of fresh air blasted through the interior of the sub, but it didn't last long. As we plunged into the face of the next wave, its thirty foot crest completely covered the top of the snorkel. The valve slammed shut, and immediately, the powerful engines drew a vacuum throughout the boat.

Within seconds, our ears were popping as the vacuum sucked the air from our lungs. Then we broke through the trailing side of the wave, and just as suddenly, the snorkel valve opened again, and with a mighty *swoosh*, air rushed back into the sub.

At the dive station, we hardly noticed – as one with the sub, we were maintaining depth. Down by the stern, towering waves sweeping past us, ears popping with each plunge into a wave face, rush of fresh air, smell of diesel exhaust, a whiff of Rusty's chemicals – but all we noticed was the movement beneath us and around us and in us.

#

It seemed like hours, but in reality, it was just a few minutes, fifteen or so until Rusty was done with his job. Josh shut down the diesels, dropped the snorkel, and ordered us back down to 400 feet.

"Thanks, Mac," Neil said, as I got up from my cramped position.

"It wasn't me, guy. Thank these fellows." I patted Scotty and Rocky on their shoulders. They did it; I just helped a bit. Next time you guys will be able to do it without help. By the time Josh was ready to go back down, these guys were doing it by themselves. I just did a bit of coordinating." I stepped away from the dive stand. "You guys were great," I said as I left Control to see how my guys were doing in the Can.

#

Back at the dive-control panel I asked Ham how things were progressing in the Can.

"A little bit rough inside," he answered. "I had the guys strap themselves into their racks. Believe it or not, Bill actually got some sleep."

I told him we were back down at 400 feet, and that as soon as Rusty had reviewed his films we would be returning to the cable and commencing the dive. As it turned out, I really didn't understand the entire picture at that point.

It didn't take Rusty very long to ensure that we were, indeed, at a repeater junction. It was also fairly obvious that the bottom was nearly level at that point. It sloped down to the west a bit, but there appeared to be no serious obstacles for my guys to do their task.

It was nearing the end of Ham's watch. I had the next six hours with Jack while Ham tried to get some sleep. This meant I was tied to the Dive Console, no matter what happened. I was responsible for the lives of Ski, Jer, Harry, and Bill. Even though, typically, there was nothing to do during an extended dive like this, there still was always the possibility of that interruption by moments of sheer panic. And whatever panic we might experience at the Dive Console, it would be a thousand times greater inside the Can.

I set up one of the monitors to show what was happening outside, so that while we wiled away the hours, I could at least keep up with what was happening. I glanced up at the monitor. Nothing at all, except a silted bottom. There was a sense of motion, sort of, but it could have been an optical illusion. The rocking from the surface waves had not abated one bit, however. If anything, it seemed to be getting worse.

Ski woke up and reported that he had his sea legs back. He asked for something to eat. Since it was about time for the evening meal anyway, I ordered up six meals, four for the divers and two for Jack and me. It was spicy southern fried chicken. That was good, because at 400 feet, breathing helium, food lost most of its flavor. The guys would really enjoy the spicy treat.

The food arrived in about fifteen minutes. On a regular DDC, all we had to do was pass the food through the "medical lock." Here things were different. First we had the guys close the inner lock door. Then we depressurized the outer lock – blowing the helium into a holding tank from which we would later repressurize and reclaim the gas. Once we could open the lower hatch, Jack climbed into the lock, and I passed the food trays up to him. Then we closed the outer lock, and pressurized it back to depth. The entire process took about three minutes, so the guys got a hot meal.

Meanwhile, on the monitor something was happening. It looked like we had relocated the cable, and were following it to the repeater. After about an hour or so, we turned around and headed back. I called Control to see what was happening. It seemed, according to Larry Jackson who was on watch, that the surface action had disoriented our sense of where the repeater was located, so that when we finally relocated the cable, we had turned the wrong direction. When the bottom dropped off to 450 feet, Larry had figured it out and decided to turn around. That made sense to me.

More than anything, at that moment, I was glad Larry had the watch, and not me. I suspected he had followed the recommendation of his own guy, which would have been Adam Jube – Juby – on that watch. The guys would inevitably give him a hard time about it. That's just the way subs are.

As it turned out, events would completely eclipse his *faux pas*.

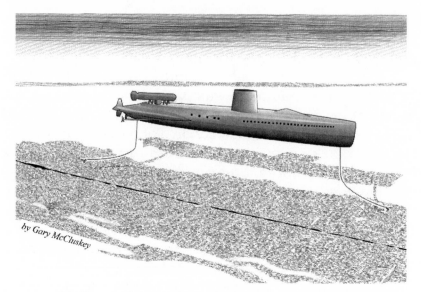

Halibut anchored above the bottom near the cable

CHAPTER SIXTEEN

It took about ninety minutes – an hour and a half. I was still on watch at the Dive Console, and had about an hour or so still to go before Ham would take over again. Jack and I had been having a lively conversation about how we could improve the Can's interface to the *Halibut's* hull, but as time passed, our conversation died down. We each became lost in our own thoughts. I felt a distinct change in the sub's motion and glanced up at the monitor.

There it was, plain as day in the dark depths of Shelikhov Bay. The floodlights on the Fish caused the repeater to stand out clearly. To my eye there was no doubt. It was the repeater. It looked like a long snake that had swallowed a rabbit for supper. It was half-covered with light colored silt.

Suddenly the view shifted radically, so that I was seeing the repeater from the other side. And, the picture was sharper. Then the view moved up and over the repeater, and I realized we were now seeing things through the eye of the Basketball. We watched for a while as the ball moved all around the repeater, looking at it from every aspect. Then the Basketball moved along the cable for several hundred feet, and then back and in the other direction. I guessed that the Skipper was looking at the anchor points, trying to find the absolutely best spot to put down our mushroom anchors.

What was fun during all this was that I could feel the sub being moved around by the surface wave action. We were dealing with one very angry ocean up there.

Now all we had to do was put the anchors down and then get to work.

I was itching to get to Control to see what was happening, but I still had a pesky hour or so before Ham took over. And since we were getting ready to do what we came for, I was in no mood to change any of the rules.

#

Finally, Ham relieved me at the Dive Console, and I high-tailed it to Control. I should have had the Deck Watch, but since I had been at the Dive Console, the XO, Commander Fred Roken, had taken over.

"Want me to take over?" I asked the XO. "I have a significant stake in where we put the anchors down," I reminded him.

The XO turned to the Skipper who was still occupying his Periscope Stand chair, nursing a cup of coffee. "He's got a point, Skipper."

"I agree." The Skipper turned to me. "Take the watch, Mac. I want to be pointed west, ahead of the repeater and just to one side of the cable, with about fifty feet or so between the stern and the pod." He glanced up at the surface wave monitor. "With that mess up there, I don't want your divers under the ship."

Now how could I disagree with that logic?

The XO had put the sub into a general hover mode. We were at all stop with the thrusters activated. Chris and Pots were keeping themselves busy maintaining the fore-to-aft buoyancy by pumping water back and forth, and maintaining the hover by pumping water in and out. Devon Paul, the other civilian Special Ops Technician, was busy with the Basketball, comparing what he saw with the photos Bobby had taken. He wanted to find the best way to attach the pod.

So that was the situation into which I stepped. "I have the Deck and the Conn," I announced to the Control Room. And now it was my baby.

The close-up photos of the anchor spots were scattered on the shelf at the front of the Periscope Stand. I laid them out in order and examined them. The bottom was smooth and virtually featureless. With all the glaciated runoff from Kamchatka Peninsula, I was probably looking at fine glacial silt – soft, but not very sticky. This meant that our mushroom anchors were not likely to get any kind of a bite on the bottom. And this meant that the only thing holding us down would be the weight of the anchors. I wasn't particularly happy about that, but there was nothing I could do about it either.

From the photos, I selected a spot to the west for the bow anchor, and another to the east for the stern anchor – four photos in all. I showed them to the Skipper, and he told me to check the spots out, and then call him. He said he would be in his stateroom.

I figured it wouldn't hurt to take another close look at the two spots I intended to anchor, and so I eased the sub a bit to the west so Devon could have the longest possible tether on the Basketball to examine the bow anchor spot.

I called him to Control on the intercom, and when he arrived, I showed him the photos for the bow and stern anchor locations.

"I want you to go over these spots with a fine tooth comb," I told Devon. "Let's do our best to put the anchors on silt, and not on rock."

"Sure thing," Devon said as he turned with the photos and went back to his cubicle.

I swung the sub around to a northern heading as we hit the bow anchor spot, and reestablished the hover with the spot just to the starboard side of the Can. On the monitor the bottom loomed and then everything went hazy as Devon purposefully drove the Basketball into the silt with a slow, even tempo. Then he backed out and moved to one side. As the silt cleared, mostly carried away by a slow bottom current, I could clearly see a crater in the silt left by the Basketball.

Devon then swept back and forth across the crater, very close to the bottom. The turbulence generated by his passing caused the bottom silt to lift and hover just above the bottom, where it then got picked up by the current and slowly swept away. The edges of the crater eroded quickly from the turbulence of his passage, and – in fact – seemed not entirely substantial, but a bit like a fluffy mixture of silt and water that was just sufficiently dense to retain a shape. Within a couple of minutes, the crater had almost entirely disappeared.

I would like to have had a couple of external manipulators right about then to set a visible marker in the bottom. I thought about dropping a pinger that the guys could retrieve while they were out there, but I couldn't place it accurately enough to make any difference.

"Maintain the best track you can," I told my watch navigator, Gary Parrish.

He grinned at me and said, "We're here, El-Tee," stabbing the chart with his finger. "That's about the best I can do with what we've got."

He was right, of course. It would take a boomer with precise bottom navigation capability to give us the kind of accuracy I wanted. I felt the sub moving vertically. I glanced at the surface wave monitor. It presented such a chaotic picture that I really couldn't make out what the wave height was.

I used the thrusters to push the sub sideways to the right. Devon had the Basketball out ahead of my crab-like path, looking for the repeater.

"Can't see the cable any more, Conn," Devon reported over the intercom. "Can you move ahead a couple hundred feet?"

"Stand by," I said, and cranked on minimum turns – just enough to give her a bit of forward momentum. I could see the bottom begin to slip from top to bottom on the monitor, but there was no real way to distinguish our motion from the motion of the Basketball. All I could see was the combined effect of both motions.

"Okay, Conn, I can see it," Devon reported. "I'm stretched way out ahead of you. I think if you bring it to a halt about now, we will be okay."

I took off the forward turns, popped a quick set of back bells, and then returned to all stop.

"Bring the Basketball up against my keel," I told Devon, "with the eye pointed straight down." I wanted to get a sense of our motion over the bottom.

"You got it, El-Tee," Devon reported, "but you're going to have to get a lot closer to the bottom to see anything."

I looked up at the monitor and saw that he was right. Nothing...nada, just grey haze.

"Bring her down slowly, Diving Officer," I told Chris. "Don't build up any momentum." I pressed the intercom button. "If I get too close for comfort, Devon, get the hell out of there."

"Roger that," Devon said deadpan. I probably didn't have to tell him that, but it didn't hurt to do so, and now my ass was covered.

As Chris eased her down, I began to see the beginnings of the bottom. In about fifteen seconds, I said, "Okay, stop the descent. Mark your depth."

"Four-hundred and one feet," Chris said.

"Do not exceed four-hundred feet," I ordered.

From the monitor, I could tell that we obviously were still moving forward. I rang up back bells again for about five seconds. The forward motion nearly stopped. I figured the current would do the rest.

"Okay, Devon," I said over the intercom, "check out the stern anchor spot."

The bottom on the monitor started moving around, and then the cable appeared flowing from the top to the bottom of the screen as the Basketball moved along it. Then the Basketball stopped over the repeater. Carefully, then, Devon retraced his path for about a hundred feet, and then the cable disappeared off the left side of the monitor as he veered to the south to find the anchor spot. About fifty feet or so from the cable, he drove the Basketball into the silt once again. The results were virtually the same.

I called the Skipper to Control. The XO and Nav showed up with him. Obviously, they had been having a powwow when I called.

"Here's the plan, Skipper," I said. "I'm pointed north into the current right now. I'll drive left on the thrusters until we reach the bow anchor point. Then I'll position the bow using the Basketball, lift her to twenty feet above the bottom, and let go the bow anchor. Then I'll crank down on the anchor cable until I'm about fifteen feet off the bottom. I'll place the Basketball on the keel under the Can looking down, and bring the stern around to the cable using the stern thruster with the anchor cable as a pivot. Then I'll back along the cable with short back bells, letting out anchor cable as I move. When I reach the stern anchor point, I'll let her drift south with a bit of help from the thrusters, and when the stern is over the point, I'll let go the stern anchor." I took a deep breath, and sketched the position on a piece of paper on the shelf, then continued.

"Then I'll set a couple of thousand pounds of positive buoyancy, and haul the anchor cables in and out until we are properly located about fifteen feet over the bottom with about equal amounts of cable fore and aft." I indicated this in my sketch. "The current will push us off the cable so the divers won't have to work under the sub."

"Why to the south of the cable?" Larry asked. "Looks like it's pushing you away from your site."

"No chance of dragging the anchors over the cable," I answered.

Larry pursed his lips and nodded. "Good point."

The XO had no comment.

"It's a good plan, Mac," the Skipper said. "Let me know when you're ready to set the bow anchor."

"Aye, Sir." And they left the Control Room.

#

Working together with Devon and his Basketball, we inched back down the cable, trying to take a measure of our progress. After a few minutes, Devon called to say that he had completely lost his orientation. I glanced at the monitor, and saw only confusion. Something had hit the Basketball, Devon told me. A large fish, perhaps. In any case, he no longer knew where we were on our track from the repeater to the bow anchor spot.

I reversed the thrusters, gave her a bit of forward momentum with the screws, and we set off to the east once again. Fifteen minutes or so later we found the repeater.

"Can you measure your track along the cable?" I asked Devon.

"Indirectly," he answered.

"In real time?"

"Yeah."

"You know where the point is, right?"

"Yeah – yes Sir!" I had to grin at that. Senior Chief Buck Christman, the guy in charge of the Fish and Basketball, had probably slapped Devon alongside the head, and told him to stop being such a civilian puke. I didn't mind, though. Submariners and divers hang pretty loose.

So we worked our way back west for about a half hour. Then Devin told me that we were there. I called the Skipper, and he came to the Periscope Stand and reviewed where we had been, where we were, and our exact current orientation. We were drifting slowly south, while Devon kept the Basketball on the cable.

"Okay, Conn," Devon said. "You're there."

I glanced at the Skipper (it's his boat, remember?). He nodded, and I told the Bat Cave to let go the anchor.

There was a rush of sound, and then Devon said, "Wow...shit! Look at that!" And a cloud of silt blocked out the monitor.

A minute or so later, the current had cleared the cloud, and was pivoting the sub around the bow anchor. I activated the stern thrusters to counter the current, and brought us back to a west-east orientation – along the cable.

"Well done, Mac," the Skipper said as he settled into his chair at the back of the Periscope Stand, lighting up a cigar. He didn't offer me one, but the smoke smelled sweet.

I had Devon place the Basketball on the keel under the Can as before, and I dropped to about fifteen feet or so from the bottom. I gave a brief back bell.

"Stay nimble," I told Chris, and ordered another brief back bell.

Up in the Bat Cave, the guys were letting the anchor cable have its lead, but keeping it taut.

"Conn, Forward Anchor, the cable is tending a bit to starboard." Which meant that we were being pushed to port by the current.

"Conn, Aye," I said, and used the forward thruster to push us back.

The idea was to keep the anchor tending a bit to port from the bow. With the Basketball keeping track of the cable under the stern, I could "pivot" around the Basketball to keep the sub on track. We worked our way slowly back, periodically adjusting bow and stern position to keep over the cable.

Finally, Devon announced, "I've got it. There's the repeater." And sure enough, there it was off to one side of the monitor.

"Okay, Devon, now bring me back along the cable to the anchor point."

After a few minutes, Devon said, "We're there, Conn."

I told the guys manning the anchor in the Engine Room to stand by.

"Mark your depth," I said.

"Four-hundred feet, Sir," Chris answered.

"Make your depth three-hundred and eighty feet," I ordered. "Count your way up so I know where you are."

I applied just a bit of thrust to the starboard bow, and let the current carry us for about fifty feet, while in the background Chris counted the decreasing depth.

When I heard "three-hundred eighty," I ordered the anchor released. As soon as the stern anchor hit the bottom, I ordered both cables held.

"Make us a thousand pounds light, Chris," I ordered, and waited for things to settle down.

Devon ran the Basketball fore and aft to examine the anchor cables. Within a few minutes he reported that the bow cable was about a third longer than the stern cable, and that the sub had reached equilibrium against both of them. We were in a slight starboard roll, and reacting with an up-and-down motion to every passing wave.

I had the Bat Cave winch the forward anchor cable in until both cables were about even. Then, with Devon's help through the Basketball, I had both anchor cables winched in until we were about fifteen feet over the bottom, with the anchor cables tending nearly straight down beneath the keel.

Such a maneuver would have been difficult under the best of circumstances, but we were being thrust about by the surface waves with a strange action that was almost like the moving cylinder of an internal combustion engine – up and down, with distinct sideways thrusts that came up short against the two anchor cables. Each time this happened, I could hear a distinct twang that rang throughout the sub.

The Skipper sat through all this, not saying a word, but I was keenly aware that he was watching my actions with an eagle eye. Any mistake, and he would have reacted instantly with correcting orders. But he let me have my head of steam. I think he was enjoying himself.

He reached over to the mike and paged the XO to Control. "Time to do your thing, Mac," he said as the XO arrived. "Take over for Mac, Fred." The Skipper grinned at me. "He's got a job to do."

Bill grabbed by a large fish

CHAPTER SEVENTEEN

The time had finally come. This was why we were here. This was the payoff. Ham, Jack and I stood around the Dive Consol discussing the forthcoming excursion. I laid out for them how the *Halibut* was placed.

"We're anchored parallel to the cable pointing west, and about fifty feet south – down-current," I explained. "The repeater is about sixty feet or so aft of the Can." I looked at Ham.

He said, "Everybody suits up, but Ski will remain dry. He says he's okay, but I want more time for his stomach to stabilize before he gets in the water." Ham checked his clipboard. Let's keep Harry in the outer lock, which puts Bill and Jer in the water."

"We're going to observe with the Basketball," I added, "but I want to make sure the guys stay to the sub's starboard – up-current. Should something go wrong, I don't want them under the hull if it comes down." As if to emphasize my comment, the sub took a particularly strong roll to starboard, and then dropped down several feet with a sickening surge that left all our stomachs in the lurch.

"Jeeezus!" Jack muttered. "I should be out there with those guys." He looked directly at me. "This is a bunch of shit, Mac. You know that."

"Easy, Jack," Ham said. "Bill and Jer have a lot of water time. They know what they're doing. We're in here because we know how to save them IF something goes wrong."

Ham was right, but I completely understood Jack's sentiment. If the truth be known, I would have much rather been in the Can ready to go out there myself. I let it ride.

The Skipper approached us with the science guys in tow – Lonie (Special Ops – Batman), Dr. Thomas Banks (Chief Scientist), and Senior Chief Jarrett Blunt, known to one and all as Spook.

As they arrived, the sub took another quasi-roll to starboard followed by the same sickening drop as before. We all grabbed onto something to maintain our balance.

Spook was carrying a three-by-one foot cylinder with a fist-size hole running its length. The cylinder was split down its length with a hinge on one side so it could be laid open. Dr. Banks described it.

"This is a Styrofoam mock-up of the real pod out in the pod bay." He was referring to an external compartment that held the pod and its connecting cables. "We have estimated that the comm cable is about this thick." He closed the cylinder and pushed his fist into the cylindrical hole through the middle. "Basically, this is an inductive pick-up device. The inside surface," he opened the cylinder and stroked the inner surface of the "hole" almost lovingly, "needs to be as close to the cable as possible. We designed this using our best intelligence about the size of the cable, but we could be wrong." He pointed to the surfaces that were in contact when the cylinder was closed. These surfaces can be trimmed down if necessary. You have just over a half-inch you can remove at the site to make a snug fit against the cable." He closed the cylinder again. "Hopefully, that won't be a problem. We expect it to fit exactly, but if the cable is larger, that's no problem, up to a point. Just snug it around the cable as tightly as possible."

Lonie handed him a roll of plain old duct tape. "You'll secure it with this," Dr. Banks said with a grin. "Since half this sub seems to be held together with this stuff, I'm sure your guys are familiar with it." Everybody chuckled. "Seriously, though," he added, "this tape works fine underwater, and a couple of wraps at each end should do it. Just be sure you have the best possible contact between the cable and the inner surface of the pod."

"If it's okay with you," Lonie said, "we would like to let the guys in the Can examine this mock-up before they go out."

Ham started to say something, but I interrupted him. "Why didn't you guys give this to us earlier, while my guys were out here instead of in the Can?" I asked.

The science guys looked at each other. "Security reasons, I guess," Lonie said a bit lamely.

"I don't think it's a good idea," I said. I glanced at both Ham and Jack, indicating with a raised eyebrow that they should keep quiet. "Let's just get the show on the road."

Dr. Banks looked at the Skipper. "We really want the divers to have held the mock-up, and looked at it closely before doing the actual operation, Captain."

"But...," I started to say.

"It'll only take a few minutes, Skipper," Lonie interjected.

"Is there any danger, Mac?" the Skipper asked me.

"No, Sir, but..." I really wanted to add a comment, but things were moving quickly, and I could see that the Skipper was in no mood for dissension.

"How long will it take, Mac?" the Skipper asked.

"Five or six minutes, Sir," I said.

"Okay, send it in, Mac. We'll stand by here."

With a wink, I told Ham to surface the outer lock and load the mock-up. The Skipper stood back, taking it all in. I noticed that he had an unusual twinkle in his eye, as if he were enjoying an inner joke.

Well, I had one for them, too.

About three minutes later the outer lock was back down at depth, and the guys opened the inner hatch to retrieve the mock-up.

"What the fuck is this?" Ski squeaked through the descrambler. He held up to the camera a twisted and distorted mess that had been the mock-up before we pressurized it. "Who sent this shit down?"

"I did," I said, "under orders." I glanced at the Skipper. He was grinning broadly. I immediately understood that he had known what would happen, and had deliberately cut me off. I think he wanted the science guys to understand that it was his boat, and even though they were the reason we were at this god-forsaken spot, he made the rules. Obviously, my guys should have seen the mock-up before entering the Can. This security shit was getting out of hand.

What had happened is that the Styrofoam, which consists of a rigid foam of plastic and air, had collapsed under the pressure of twelve atmospheres. Some cells had collapsed more than others, causing the entire mock-up to twist into an almost unrecognizable hard sculpture-like object.

Shock followed by recognition of what had happened crossed the faces of all three of the spooks. Blunt was grinning widely, obviously enjoying the embarrassment of his superiors. Dr. Banks attempted to stammer an apology, but Lonie interrupted him.

"Sorry about that, Captain. We should have briefed the guys earlier," Lonie said.

The Skipper nodded his acceptance. "Let's leave the security decisions to me in the future," he said.

Then he turned to me. "Take her away, Mac. I'll be in Control."

As they left, the sub took another snap roll to starboard. The screeching of the bow anchor cable echoed throughout the sub.

#

Ham briefed the guys in the Can, explaining in detail how they were to attach the pod to the underwater cable. He also told them how the Skipper had put the spooks in their place, and got two high-fives and two thumbs-up.

"You want this piece of shit back?" Ski asked, holding up the twisted mock-up.

"Naw," Ham answered. "Just keep it 'til you surface."

Ham looked at me for permission to continue. I nodded.

"Okay, everybody, suit up," Ham ordered. "Ski, you'll stay dry. Harry, you'll remain in the Outer Lock. Bill and Jer, you got the load. Bill, you carry the air gun, Jer, you got the pod. Remember, guys, I got my eye on you – the Basketball will be looking over your shoulder. No need to give me a running commentary, but speak up for anything unusual." Ham leaned back in his chair and looked up at me, standing behind him. "Give me a heads-up when you're ready to open the outer lock."

We sat there quietly watching the monitors. We had three, each able to show any available data stream. I had set them up so the right monitor displayed the inner or main lock – the inside of the Can. The middle monitor displayed the Outer Lock, and the left monitor was set to show the Basketball eye as soon as it came up. The connecting hatch was open, and Harry was assisting Bill and Jer with their equipment.

The dive rigs consisted of an inner insulating suit that really served more to prevent chafing than anything else; an outer suit that resembled a loose drysuit with a water hose connection at the waist that distributed warm water through perforated tubes along the spine, up over the head in the hood, across the chest, down both arms, in the groin, and down both legs; a modified Kirby-Morgan band-mask rig with a hard helmet with a mounted headlamp, an internal cup that fit over the nose and mouth, and waterproof mike and earphones; inner and outer booties and gloves that received warm water from the suit; a Mark 11 breathing apparatus that removed carbon dioxide from the exhaled gas and ensured that the diver received the proper amount of oxygen; the umbilical that connected the breathing apparatus (and diver) to the Can, and carried hot water, communications, breathing gas, and served as a safety line that could be used to retrieve a stranded diver; and a come-home bottle, a small reserve of compressed gas mixed to the depth at which the diver would be diving. At our depth of 400 feet, a diver would have up to ten breaths before running out of gas in this bottle. As necessary the diver would also don fins or wear weighted boots to keep upright while walking on the bottom, and they also carried lead weights in pockets on the Mark 11 harness to establish proper initial neutral buoyancy. Divers also carried a sharp diver's knife and indicating gauges for monitoring the depth, the breathing gas, and hot water. As necessary divers also carried needed tools, and even occasionally special carrying harnesses and bags.

In this case, Bill would wear weighted shoes to give him more stability when using the air jet to clean the repeater and nearby cable. Jer would wear fins to aid his maneuverability when installing the pod with Bill, who would be firmly "anchored" to the bottom by his heavy shoes.

We could see that both divers were ready.

"Dive, Red Diver, comm check" That was Bill.

"Dive aye."

"Dive, Green Diver, comm check."

"Dive aye."

They were ready to go. Ham checked his panel to see if any pressure difference existed between the Outer Lock and the ocean outside.

"Stand by for equalization blow," Ham informed the Can, and opened a valve on the Dive Console while carefully watching a differential gauge.

I glanced up at the left monitor to see that the Basketball had just arrived and was hovering off the starboard side about three feet away. We had a fairly good view through the murky water.

"Crack the outer hatch Harry," Ham ordered.

Harry cranked the handle to the left on the hatch cover. Shortly he announced, "Hatch cracked."

On the monitor I saw a ring of light appear around the hatch.

Ham secured the blow, and Harry opened the hatch all the way and latched the cover so it wouldn't crash down during one of the powerful lurches the sub was experiencing every few minutes. Then he fed Bill's umbilical out the hatch until he felt it hit the sea floor some thirty-five feet or so below them.

I watched the umbilical slide down and disappear into the haze below. Visibility was too poor to see the bottom from there.

Using his umbilical as a down-line, Bill exited the hatch followed by Jer, trailing his umbilical. On the monitor their headlamp beams cut sharp bright swaths through the murky water, but were swallowed up within several feet. The guys oriented themselves at the base of the Can, adjusting their buoyancy. Jer handed one of his weights to Bill, who inserted it into a pocket on his harness, and a couple more up to Harry, and then Jer launched himself away from the sub to float between Bill and the Basketball, slowly drifting until he was beside the Basketball – just out of view.

Bobby was driving the Basketball this watch, and he maneuvered it a bit further back and aft so we could see both divers again. Then, holding his umbilical, Bill slid slowly toward the bottom with Jer floating beside him, also drifting down. As they descended, the Basketball descended with them. Except for their breathing, it was eerily quiet.

Just then the sub took another of its sickening lurches. It rolled to starboard, dropping Bill about four feet, and then – as the sub swayed against its anchor cables – it dipped down and rolled to port. The combined action snapped Bill up and then dropped him back. The roll was accompanied by the ominous screeching sound.

Bill emitted a little yelp, and then he shouted, "Fuck this!" He let go of the umbilical and dropped rapidly to the bottom. At least that's where I thought he had gone, because all I could see on the monitor was Jer and the rocking side of the sub with the umbilical flapping against it. Jer immediately dove down, his headlamp piercing the gloom in front of him with the Basketball following.

"Everything okay out there?" Ham asked in a matter-of-fact voice. If something was wrong, he didn't want to add to any panic.

"No sweat," Bill drawled, "but who's driving this rig anyway?"

"Okay, guys. Move over to the pod bay. Red Diver, stay on the bottom; Green Diver, stay with him until you get there, then swim up and get the stuff."

"Red Diver, Aye."

"Green Diver, Aye."

Bobby placed the Basketball in front of them and paced their passage to the pod bay about thirty feet forward on the starboard side..It was marked by a white stripe from the keel to the locker, but all we could see was a portion of the hull with the white stripe. Jer swam up and opened the bay with a key that looked like an Allen wrench, twisting all eight locks, and then swinging it open on its heavy hinge. The Basketball moved in for a closer look.

Jer unstrapped the pneumatic gun from its holder, snapped the air hose to the fitting on the handle and activated the air pressure. He then snapped it with a carabiner to a ring welded on the inner face of the bay door.

Then Jer unstrapped the three-foot-long pod that was connected to a socket in the bay with a long, heavily shielded and insulated neutrally buoyant electrical cable. He reached into the gear bag attached to his harness and extracted a parachute-like bag that he attached with the opening pointing down to a ring fitting on the top of the pod. He released air from the pneumatic gun into the upside-down bag until it supported the pod in the water column. For safety, he clipped the pod to the door ring with a short pigtail fitted with a carabiner. The attached cable floated behind it.

"Heads up," Jer announced to Bill as he then lowered the gun to the sea floor.

Jer then unhooked the pod and floated down, guiding the pod as he descended until he was about eye-level with Bill. The Basketball floated down with him, so that we could now see both divers in the monitor.

"Follow the Basketball, Guys" Ham ordered.

Bobby set the Basketball on an angled course toward the repeater. Because he was blind beyond a few feet, he couldn't steer directly there, but he set a flat angle that brought them to the cable twenty or thirty feet west of the repeater. Bill's feet stirred the bottom up so the path behind them was clouded with silt. Jer swam leisurely alongside Bill's head, gently tugging the bag-supported pod with its floating cable tail disappearing into the cloud behind them. Bill lugged the pneumatic gun, dragging its increasingly heavy hose through the silted bottom.

There was a surprising amount of bottom life, especially a significant number of large crabs ranging in size from a half-foot up to two-and-a-half-feet across. They looked to me for all the world like Alaska King Crabs. Every once in a while a fish would come swimming into view, typically several inches long, lashing in and out of the headlamp beams, and occasionally the shadow of something a lot larger would flash at the limit of vision. I noticed that Jer would turn his head in the direction of these shadows at the same time I thought I could see something.

It took the divers a full twenty-five minutes to reach the repeater. Once there, Jer floated off to the side focusing his headlamp beam on the repeater, while Bill used the pneumatic gun to blow the silt away from it. He worked from the east to the west along the top of the repeater and completely uncovered its two-and-a-half-foot length down to about half-way to its bottom, so it looked like it was floating in the silt, half extended out of the silt surface. Then he worked the western face clean and cleared the cable for about five feet to the west.

Just as Bill got to his knees to loosen some hardened silt from under the cable with his fingers, a flash of silver swept out of the murk, and a large grouper-like fish grabbed Bill's left arm.

"What the fuck!" Bill shouted, as he dropped the pneumatic gun and reached for his leg knife.

Bill's struggle with the big fish stirred up the bottom so that the Basketball lost the picture completely. Bobby maneuvered it around to the north side, up-current, and poked in and out of the cloud to try and see what was happening, twin beams of the Basketball getting sucked into the muck.

I picked up the mike at the Dive Console and said, "Harry, get ready to go to their assistance if they need you." I knew Harry was watching the activity on the monitor in the Outer Lock.

Just then the sub did one of its lurching rolls again. It didn't seem to affect the guys out in the water – at least not Jer, since we still couldn't see Bill. Then the cloud began to clear as the current swept it away. What we saw was incredible. The grouper-like fish was easily six feet long. It wasn't long like a barracuda, instead it was fat and roundish, and it was definitely moving Bill around, flashing his headlamp beam around the murky water. Bill was swinging his eight-inch blade at the giant fish's left eye. As the blade plunged into the fish's unblinking orb, its mighty tail flipped, so that Bill and fish flew five feet south, with the fish thrashing wildly, but not letting go, jerking Bill all over the place, his headlamp beam flashing wildly. Bill stabbed again, aiming for the brain cavity just above and back of the eye socket, but he hit bone, and his knife bounced off.

Jer flew into shocked reaction. He picked up the pneumatic gun and jammed it into the big fish's mouth. He activated the gun, hitting the fish's pallet with gushing high-pressure air, while simultaneously using the steel barrel of the gun as a lever to pry the fish's mouth open.

Bobby maneuvered in as close as he could, but just then the thrashing creature hit the Basketball with its tail, and we temporarily lost the picture while Bobby regained his orientation and relocated the struggling divers and their tormentor. As the image in the monitor cleared, we could see Jer finally prying the fish's mouth open. Bill pulled back, and reached under the fish where he slashed a two-foot gash in its underbelly.

"Jer, the belly!" Bill shouted as he pulled away nursing his arm.

"Bobby," I said over the intercom, "try to distract the fish with the Basketball."

Immediately, the image in the monitor began to swing and sway, and to dart in and out, as Bobby worked to keep the fish's attention with the flashing twin beams from the Basketball. From the flashes I could see, Jer had pushed himself under the big fish and had stuck the tip of the air gun into Bill's slash. As the high-pressure air rushed into the fish's body cavity, the giant fish thrashed once again mightily, and then rose rapidly into the murk above us. The divers and Basketball followed its passage with their beams of light until it disappeared. I would imagine that the fish exploded about halfway to the surface, and joined the food chain significantly earlier than planned.

#

"Okay, everybody, give me your status." Ham was all business again. "Red Diver, describe your injuries."

The Basketball moved in close to Bill's shoulder. Jer swam over and examined closely where the fish had clamped onto his arm.

"No apparent break in the suit," Jer reported.

"Dive, Red Diver...my arm hurts like hell. That thing had a bite like a steel vice, but I don't think anything's broken."

"Do you need to go back to the Can?" Ham asked.

"Naw...I'm okay. Let's get this damn pod attached." Bill sounded like his pride was injured more than his arm.

"Okay," Ham said, "back to work."

Bill got back on his knees and Jer floated over with the pod in trail, his headlamp illuminating the area. As we watched on the monitor, Jer guided the pod down to where Bill pushed the bottom half under the cable. Then Jer detached the lift bag and stowed it back in his gear bag. Bill clamped the top half of the pod over the cable, and it fit just like the spooks said it would – no trimming necessary. Jer handed Bill the duct tape. Bill made a couple wraps around each end and another couple in the middle, and it was all set.

"Let's go home," Jer said.

"Yeah," Bill answered, keeping a wary eye peeled for another hungry fish.

Heading back to the Can was easier. They simply followed the umbilicals and the pod cable until it split for the pod bay. As they approached, Harry took up the slack and coiled it on the hangers in the Outer Lock. It took about ten minutes to get back to the gear locker where Jer stowed the pneumatic gun. It took another five to get back to the lip of the outer hatch. Bill entered first, nursing his left arm a bit. Jer followed, Harry closed but did not dog the hatch, and they sat on the deck to catch their breaths.

#

In the meantime, the spooks were going crazy. Apparently, they were receiving no signal at all. Pre-dive checks had confirmed that the pod was working properly. Current checks seemed to indicate that there was nothing wrong with their equipment; but they were dealing with 400 feet of pressure, an unknown situation, and anything could go wrong. Finally the Skipper called a meeting in the Wardroom and asked me if I could attend for a few minutes. I trusted Ham to handle anything without me, so I put Jack on watch with Ham, and hurried to the Wardroom.

The top three spooks were there, with Nav, Eng, the XO, and myself.

"We've got a problem, folks, and we need to solve it fast," the Skipper said.

Lonie then described what they had done to troubleshoot the problem. Dr. Banks added that if there was no problem, then there was no signal, and that meant the Soviets had compromised our plan, shut down the cable, and we were in imminent danger. While he was talking, the sub rolled again, accompanied by the screech.

Lonie jumped in saying, "I think we need to deploy the divers again to check the pod installation. That's the only place we haven't checked, that and the hull connections. Unless we know, then we can't conclude anything about compromise or sabotage."

"How's the weather holding, Nav?" the Skipper asked Larry.

"The waves are still building, Sir."

"What about that screech, Eng?" the Skipper asked Dirk. "Is that going to be a problem?"

Before Dirk could answer, Lonie interrupted. "We looked at it with the Basketball right after the last dive. So far as we can tell, there was nothing amiss." He spread his hands on the Wardroom table. "You can see the tape if you wish," he added, looking at Dirk.

"Even so," Dirk said, "the problem seems to be outside, Captain. Maybe the divers can take a look at it while they are out there." Both Dirk and the Skipper looked at me.

"That's right under the forward keel," I said. "If the sub drops down while they're under there, we're going to lose two divers." I thought about it for a bit. "Can you put more buoyancy in the bow so she goes up rather than down if something happens?" I asked.

"Sure," Dirk answered, "but that changes the situation so the divers will not be looking at what was, but rather at what is."

"Better than nothing at all," I said, because there was no way I was going to put my guys under the keel in this heaving sea.

"I concur," the Skipper said. "Mac, put your divers back in the water as soon as you can and have them investigate the pod installation. Then, before you bring them in, call Dirk to Dive so he can talk with the divers as they investigate the screech."

"Aye sir." This was going to be one interesting dive.

A nest of large crabs on the sea floor

CHAPTER EIGHTEEN

I rejoined Ham at the Dive Console. "How's Bill's arm?" I asked.

"Bruised a bit, but no worse for wear," Ham said.

I briefed him on what had transpired in the Wardroom, and told him to get set up for the next dive as soon as possible.

"I'll keep Bill in the Can for this dive," Ham said. "Let's send Jer and Harry out with Ski in standby in the Outer Lock."

I agreed, so we set it up that way, and Ham got the guys ready for the next excursion.

The Bat Cave brought the Basketball inside for a new film cassette. We had everything on videotape, but that stuff was pretty grainy. For any real intelligence use, they needed film. By the time the Divers were ready for the next excursion, the Basketball was back in the water, hovering by the Outer Lock hatch.

This was our third excursion from the Can. We were beginning to develop a routine that the guys passed on to each other. The process of moving the divers from the outer Lock into the water went faster than last time. Ham still had to do an equalizing blow, but the entire process only took five minutes. For efficiency, Ham retained Jer as the swimmer, and put boots on Harry.

Our view on the monitor was no better than before. In fact, if anything, it was even worse. There seemed to be more turbidity to the water. Bobby was getting pretty good at keeping the Basketball close in, though, so we could keep an eye on things. Harry chose to adjust his suit buoyancy so that he dropped slowly to the sea floor, guiding his progress with his left hand on the umbilical. Jer dropped beside him, hanging in the water column. Bobby was also there, stationkeeping the Basketball just a foot or so beyond the divers.

Getting to the pod bay, retrieving the air gun, and working their way over to the pod was accomplished fairly quickly. You could still distinguish the return path from earlier, although it had dissipated significantly from the current. But it was there. Harry came up with a terrific idea – without telling anybody before doing it. At the Bay, he pounded an aluminum brace from the crushed Styrofoam mock-up into the bottom, tied a piece of white cord to it, and then pounded four more pieces (all he had, apparently) along the trail, wrapping the string around them, and then he tied the string off on the cable at the pod. Great idea.

With the Basketball looking over their shoulders, Harry and Jer carefully cleared the silt that had already accumulated on the up-current side of the pod, and then inspected the pod itself. There really was nothing wrong with it. There was no break in the surface, and it fit snuggly around the cable.

"Bobby," I said over the intercom, "bring the Basketball as close as possible to the cable exiting the pod."

"Red and Green Divers," I ordered, "move back a bit from the pod so Bobby can get a good look."

Bobby brought the Basketball in very close, just a few inches. I thought I saw what I was looking for, but wasn't willing to put it on the line just yet.

"Red and Green Divers," I said, "I want you to clear the silt around the west end of the repeater down to a foot below the bottom of the repeater and a foot on either side. Use the air gun. It won't hurt anything."

The Basketball pulled back, and then the monitor displayed only a swirling cloud of silt. The invisibility went on for about a minute, and then Jer exclaimed, "Well...I'll be a..."

Harry added, "Kee-riste, will you look at that!"

The Basketball moved in as the water cleared, and there it was as pretty as a picture. A second cable exited the repeater about six inches below the one we had attached the pod to. While they were clearing out the silt, the guys also cleared the silt from the cable for about four feet to the west of the pod, where it ended in what looked like a big ball of dielectric silicone, the same stuff we use to seal our underwater fittings. As I suspected, Bill and Jer had attached the pod to a pigtail.

Since it was totally clear what they had to do, I didn't say anything. About ten minutes later, the pod was snuggly attached to the real cable, and the spooks happily reported a strong signal.

"Okay, guys," I told the divers, "on to the next task. You done good, guys!"

#

I contacted Control and had them put the maximum amount of buoyancy forward, so the forward anchor cable took on a significant strain. This caused the sub to take a five-degree up angle. I called for Dirk to come to Dive. I cautioned Harry and Jer to work their way to the forward anchor, and then to rise up along the anchor cable, keeping to the up-current side of the sub, and prepared to hightail it out of there to the north, if anything broke loose. The Basketball was with them all the way.

I had them follow the underwater cable back to about where the anchor should have been. Then I had Bobby bring the Basketball cable around to them so they could grasp the light cable, and feed it to the Basketball as it looked for the anchor. When the Basketball found the anchor, all the divers had to do was follow the light Basketball line to the anchor.

It worked like a charm. Once I stopped the divers on the underwater cable, they were able to feed the Basketball line with no difficulty, although Bobby said it was as if somebody had him by the tail. A half-hour later the guys were at the forward anchor looking up. The cable disappeared into the gloom, and every once in a while it dropped sharply as an overhead wave did its thing with the sub.

Harry and Jer adjusted their buoyancy and floated up the cable. They arrived at the point where the cable passed through a fairing and a guide to a hydraulic reel located in the superstructure. Just then, the sub lurched again. It whipped to starboard. The divers held on with difficulty. Then it swung over to port, and dropped. The cable actually went slack, and both Harry and Jer dropped the cable. The last thing they wanted was to get caught between the cable and the hull when it snapped back. Since only Jer had fins, he grabbed Harry and swam up-current with him in tow.

Once the sub stabilized – ten to fifteen seconds in all, the guys grabbed the cable again, and pulled themselves up close to the fairing. I glanced at my watch and noted that the lurches were coming fairly regularly, every fifteen minutes or so, now.

"Dive, Red Diver...there's no question what's happening here. The anchor cable is chaffing against the fairing pretty badly, especially when the sub surges. Looks like the anchor is a bit too far forward, running the cable out at too shallow an angle. It looks better at this up-angle, and it'll be much worse at a down-angle."

Dirk, who was standing beside me listening to the conversation, picked up the mike and asked, "Do you see any damage? Do I need to be worried about anything?"

I looked at my watch again, and grabbed the mike. "Red and Green Divers, move away from the cable NOW!" I ordered.

They both dropped down and to starboard just as we lurched again. I pointed out the interval to Ham, who set up a stopwatch with a twelve-minute alarm cycle.

Once the *Halibut* had recovered, divers and Basketball returned to the exit point. Harry focused his headlamp on the spot, and Jer got up close. "Looks like several broken strands, Dive," Jer said as he switched position with Harry so Harry could see for himself.

"I agree," Harry said after looking closely at the point. "This thing could break if we don't do something about it."

Ham's stopwatch alarmed. "Okay, boys," he told the divers. "Time to come home. She's about to lurch again, so get the hell out of there."

The divers and Basketball sank slowly to the sea floor.

#

I think I already mentioned that there was a large number of fairly big crabs crawling all over the bottom. As the guys got ready to come back, they both pulled large nylon net bags from the tool pockets attached to their legs. They began to stuff the bags with crabs, large and small. By the time they returned to the Can, they must have picked up a couple hundred of the critters.

The bags were long and narrow enough to fit through the hatch, although once inside the Outer Lock, there wasn't much room for anything else. Since I would not allow the guys to remain outside with the outer hatch locked, Jer entered the lock first, and then Ski quickly cracked the inner hatch, went inside the Can, and shut the hatch. Then Harry tied both bags off to the outer hatch wheel, and entered the Outer Lock. With both divers in the lock, and the bags securely tied to the outside of the outer hatch, Harry closed the outer hatch, and then they opened the inner hatch and Jer doffed his rig and entered the Can.

"Dive, Can, we're requesting to do something a bit unusual. We want to put Harry in the Outer Lock with the inner hatch closed, open the outer hatch and let Harry retrieve both crab bags. We think the bags and Harry will just fit in the Outer Lock. Once they're in, we'll seal the outer hatch, and Harry will enter the Can and seal the inner hatch. Then you can surface the Outer Lock, and give the dinner fixin's to Chief Hurst."

By the time they had finished their request, the Skipper was standing beside me. He had observed the crab catch on his monitor, and figured we would want to ask permission to bring them aboard.

"Any problem with that, Mac?" he asked.

"Not really," I answered. "We take virtually the same risk every time we exit or enter the water. The only difference is that only one diver will be in the Outer Lock while the crabs get hauled in. If something goes wrong, the guys in the Can will intervene."

"Let's have crab dinner, then," the Skipper said as he left for Control.

To paraphrase Yogi Berra, things are always more difficult than they are. When Harry, in the Outer Lock by himself, opened the outer hatch and tried to pull the first bag into the Outer Lock, crab claws from both bags were tangled across both bags at several points, so that Harry couldn't pull in just one bag. To solve the problem, he securely closed the top of one bag, tied a long line to it, and released it from the hatch wheel. Following about five minutes of pulling and shaking, the bag finally broke loose, and plunged toward the sea floor, coming up sharp about ten feet from the seabed. We caught every nuance through the Basketball.

Cheering sailors surrounded every monitor on the sub that could be hooked to this circuit.

Following that, Harry pulled the second bag into the Outer Lock without any great difficulty, other than dealing with a seventy-five pound bag of squirming, wriggling crabs with powerful claws. During all this, every fifteen minutes or so the sub took one of its powerful lurches with its accompanying screech.

Harry tied the first crab bag to the bulkhead, and then pulled the second bag hand-over-hand up to the hatch. "No need to pump iron tonight," he said, breathing heavily following that exertion. With only about half the space he had before, Harry found it significantly harder to get the second bag into the Outer Lock. It kept hanging on the first bag, claws entangling and groping as he hoisted it up.

Finally with a grunt, he hauled it a final foot and lashed it to the bulkhead, just as the sub took another lurch. "Are these things getting worse or what?" Harry asked as he dogged down the outer hatch. Then he doffed his rig and entered the Can, still dressed in his suit. Ski and Bill shut and dogged the hatch.

"They're all yours, Dive," Ski announced as he made the final turn of the wheel.

Ham acknowledged, and surfaced the Outer Lock, retrieving the helium into the holding tank for recompression and reuse. I turned around to find the Chief Commissaryman standing nearby with a couple of his messcooks.

"Let's give these guys something to do," I said to Ham as I went to the entry lock door and started to undog it.

When the hatch sprang open, I climbed up the ladder and secured the hatch to the bulkhead so it wouldn't come crashing down during the next lurch. One of the messcooks joined me, and we unlashed the second bag and wrestled it to the hatch where Cedric and the other messcook pulled it into the sub. Then we did the other bag.

As they carried the crab-laden bags to the galley, they were accompanied by the cheers of the Control Room watch-standers.

Submariners always had good food, but tonight would be the best ever.

What I didn't know then was how soon the good meal would be forgotten when we entered the water again a couple of days later.

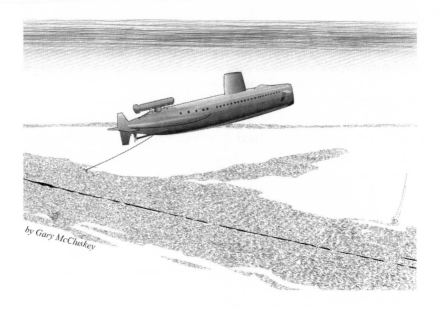

Halibut with forward anchor cable parted

CHAPTER NINETEEN

For the next two days, the spooks recorded some of the most exciting material they had ever received from the Soviets. It was non-stop clear language material that covered the waterfront, from highly sensitive official calls between the Petropavlovsk Commander and Moscow, to unimportant personal calls from a Soviet submariner to his squeeze. Some of these personal conversations were even in English – where the parties apparently were practicing the language. For two days the pod worked flawlessly, proving beyond a doubt that John Craven's idea was not only sound, but entirely achievable. We intercepted over 300 transmissions, of which more than half had real, immediate intelligence value. As a *proof of concept*, we could not have asked for more.

The storm topside continued unabated. In fact, by the end of the second day, the surge interval had shortened to ten minutes, and the depth of the surges was measurably more pronounced.

Based upon the divers' evaluation of the bow anchor cable condition, Dirk and the Skipper had discussed whether to leave things as they were, haul in the cable a bit to bring the broken strands to the reel, or let it out to move the broken strands outside the guide and fairing. The argument for bringing the damaged section to the reel was that less strain would be on that section, but the downside was that the broken strands might prevent letting the cable further out since the broken strands were likely to jam in the guide. There was no real argument for keeping things as they were. The argument for letting the cable out to ensure the damaged section was well outside the fairing was that this would bring an undamaged part of the cable into play. The downside was, of course, that the damaged section was still active, between the *Halibut* and its bow anchor.

They finally decided to let the cable out several feet to get the damaged strands away from the fairing. In an additional attempt to lessen the potential cable damage, the Skipper ordered a five-degree up bubble on the sub. For the first few hours following the dive, these actions actually caused the screeching to disappear, but by the next morning, as the surge interval shortened, it was back. The Skipper put a couple more degrees of up bubble on the sub, but we were reaching the limit of our ability to function normally. It might not seem like much, but a permanent seven-degree up angle on your entire environment really screws things up – things like sinks that don't drain completely, sanitary tanks that have diminished capacity, bilges that need constant monitoring, and little things like pens that roll to the deck and head congestion from sleeping with your head below your feet.

By the end of the second day, the Skipper decided to terminate this phase of our mission, and to send the divers out one more time to retrieve the pod, and then get on with the rest of the deployment.

The divers in the Can were doing pretty well, all things considered. Ski retained his sea legs, and Bill's bruises were fading to a pale green. The crab dinner was a smashing success, and most of the crew members came by the Dive Console at least once to chat with the guys and thank them for such a memorable surprise. It made up a bit for their having to live in such a cramped space, constantly pounded and thrown around by the heaving surges. But it still fit the classic description of endless hours of tedious boredom....

So when I announced that they were going in the water again just as soon as they could be ready, there was no bitching. Anything beat the cramped Can. I told them that the task was simple. Retrieve the pod, stow it and the air gun in the pod bay, and come on home.

"No crabs this time," I told them. "Just stow the gear and get the hell out of here."

I got no argument, and fifteen minutes later Ski and Bill were ready to enter the water, with Jer backing them up and Harry in the Can.

#

Practice makes perfect. Ski and Bill met the Basketball and all three were on the sea floor within fifteen minutes. Harry's marker line was still in place, so getting to the pod was a cakewalk. Ten minutes after they got to the pod, they had completely removed it from the cable, and had it hanging from a lift bag and on its way back to the sub.

The water was more turbid than usual, probably due to the surface storm intensity. Every surge raised silt from the bottom in a visible pattern as the wave swept by overhead. The silt would rise up about a foot or so, hover, and then settle back. During the hover, the current would pull the suspended silt to the south a bit, ripping the visible structure apart, creating streamers of silt that dissolved into the general turbidity of the water. The end result of all this was visibility of no more than about five feet.

The guys were not quite within sight of the sub – not that they could have seen it anyway – when the mother of all surges swept down from the surface. What we saw on the monitor was a swirling that rapidly resolved to a virtually blank screen. What we experienced in the sub was a significantly stronger lurch to starboard, followed by an even stronger roll and drop to port, and then it felt like being on a fast elevator that suddenly started up. A loud screech from the bow anchor cable was immediately followed by a very distinctive twang, and two seconds later we were at a twenty-five degree up-angle, and rapidly going more vertical.

What we heard from outside was the wail of two startled divers....

Larry (Nav) had the deck. I don't care how well prepared you are for something to happen, when it actually does, you still have to take a moment to collect your wits. Fortunately for all of us, Larry's wit-collecting moment was short. Within a heartbeat Larry was sucking water into the forward tanks and moving water forward from the stern and into the ocean from the stern. Within a few seconds the increasing up-bubble stopped, and the bow began to settle back down. This was the tricky part, because if the downward momentum got ahead of him, the bow would smack into the bottom – not a good thing for a nuke. To make sure this didn't happen, Larry popped a bubble into the forward ballast tank, one of the saddle tanks that was open to the sea at the keel, that normally is used to surface a sub and then keep it on the surface. Once he got the momentum under control, he eased the air out of the ballast tank by cracking the vent valve.

In the meantime, I had my hands full.

"Red and Green Divers, status report," I ordered.

"Red Diver okay, but I'm off the bottom. What happened?"

"Green Diver, same-o, same-o...what the fuck happened?"

"Red and Green Divers, check your depths." I didn't want another problem caused by the divers exceeding their depth ceiling. I wanted them back down on the bottom as soon as possible. There was very little room for error here.

"Red Diver, three seventy-five."

"Green Diver, three seven zero."

"In the Can," I said. "Give the divers some slack. They need to get back down ASAP."

"Working on it, guys."

I glanced at the middle monitor. Jer was tangled in a pile of umbilical that had apparently fallen off the hook during the up bubble.

"Harry," I ordered, "open the inner hatch and give Jer a hand."

"We're equalizing right now," Ham said as he cracked a valve on the console.

"Roger that," Harry responded, pulling the inner hatch open.

"Kee-rist Jer," Harry said as he saw the tangle in the Outer Hatch, "what the hell happened to you?"

"Fuck you, Harry, get me out of this mess. We got to give the guys some more slack."

Harry jumped in, and in about thirty seconds, Harry and Jer were passing umbilical through the outer hatch.

"That's more like it," Bill chimed in over the circuit as he dropped to the sea floor. "Ski, where are you?"

"Over here, you dumb ass!" Ski answered, without the slightest hint of where "here" was.

"Red and Green Divers, drop straight down, and maintain your location," Ham ordered.

"Red Diver aye."

"Green Diver aye."

"How do you want to do this, Mac?" Ham asked me.

"Have Red stay put, and have Green follow his own umbilical to the hatch, and then descend Red's umbilical," I suggested.

"Slick, Mac, that'll work."

Devon, who was on the Basketball at this time, was also completely disoriented. He ended up pulling the cable back until the Basketball was just below the Aquarium. Then he meandered back up to the Can and then down to the divers.

"Ham," I said, "get the divers into the Can. Have Jack back you up. I need to see the Skipper about the broken anchor cable and what we can do about it. We really need that anchor for our next task."

I left for the Skipper's cabin.

#

I met Dirk at the Skipper's cabin door. Seaman Magor, the stern planesman for this watch section, also arrived at the door.

"There you are, El-Tee," he said to me, somewhat breathless. The Captain wants to see you. I went to Dive, but you had already left."

"Thanks, Magor. You can tell Commander Jackson you found me."

Dirk and I entered the Skipper's small cabin. He gestured us to sit on his day bed. He was sitting at his built-in desk with his chair turned out to face us.

"We have a problem that we need to solve, Gentlemen," he said without preamble. "Dirk, can you repair the cable?"

"If you mean splice it, Skipper, not really. That would create a thickening that may not pass through the guide, and besides, I wouldn't trust its strength anyway." Dirk's answer was as straight as you can get.

The Skipper looked at me.

"I agree, Skipper, but we have another option." I explained that Dirk would slack the anchor cable so the divers could cut it off above the damage. The divers would attach a pulley to the anchor, and pass a light line from the cut anchor cable, through the pulley to the capstan on the forward deck. Then they would pull the light line with the capstan, drawing the cut anchor cable down and through the pulley. Finally they would attach the cut end of the anchor to itself with a couple of bolt clamps, forming a loop that was attached to the anchor. I spread my hands. "That'll give us the forward anchor back. All you guys have to do is keep the bow from flipping up or crashing down on us while we're out there."

"What do you think, Dirk?" the Skipper asked.

"We've had a lot of bow motion, especially lately," Dirk said.

"That's true," I added. "Perhaps first, we can secure a hawser from a forward topside cleat to the anchor to hold the bow down while we work." As I thought about it, that actually seemed like a better plan.

"I like that better," the Skipper said.

Dirk nodded. "That should give your divers the necessary stability."

"What's your time frame on this, Mac?" the Skipper asked.

"They've taken a beating," I said, "but I think they would rather go now, and rest afterward." I grinned. "I know my guys. They're good for it." Then I added, "One more thing, Skipper, while they're topside, can you keep the sub about ten feet closer to the bottom? Once we have the anchor line back on the anchor, we can bring her back up a bit."

"We'll do that, Mac. Before the divers enter the water, we'll ratchet the stern down, and lower the bow. Don't put them in the water until I tell you." The Skipper swiveled his chair around toward his desk, indicating that Dirk and I were dismissed.

\#

I carefully explained the operation to Ham and the guys in the Can. I wanted Jer and Harry in the water even though they were tired, because this was a time-critical task, and they already were familiar with the territory. Neither had ever worked the deck of a surfaced submarine, so we locked in a diagram of topside forward along with a hot meal.

I pointed out how the capstan could be raised with about twenty turns of a special t-handle wrench they would need to take with them, and how that same wrench could then be used to run the capstan forward and in reverse. I showed them how to use the same wrench to flip a topside cleat and lock it in place. I showed them the location of the hawser locker, and explained that the hawser would be tied to the sides of the locker with short pieces of line. I said to cut the retaining line, and told them to bring several feet of line with them to secure the hawser back in the locker when they were finished. I cautioned them that before they left topside for the last time, they were to ensure everything was properly stowed and secured, and that nothing would rattle or bang when the sub was underway.

The last thing we needed was to make another mid-transit over-the-bottom dive to locate and secure an unintended rattle.

Ham and I debated the value of including a third diver in the water for this job. Ham thought having a diver on the bottom tending the umbilicals of the guys on the *Halibut's* topside deck would make the job easier, and would add to safety. I pointed out that the water was so turbid that the diver on the sea floor would not be able to see the sub above him, let alone the divers on the deck. So, I wondered, would the third diver really add anything to safety, or would we – Ham and I – just have more to worry about with a third deployed diver on our hands?

Ham agreed, so we decided to go with our prior arrangement, and Ham got the team ready to enter the water one more time. Ham pointed out that the surge interval had started to lengthen a bit, which was good news, since we were going to ride the bow very much like a bucking bronco.

I called the Skipper and informed him that we were ready to go as soon as he had reset the sub's depth. Shortly after that the guys in the Engine Room hauled in the stern anchor cable by about twenty feet. Dirk had the Deck Watch, which seemed like a bit of poetic justice. His team brought the bow down so that we were on an even keel about ten feet from the sea floor. Thank goodness, by now the surge was falling off.

While the guys were entering the water from the Can, the engineers had brought the things they would need forward to the Bat Cave, and were loading them into the Aquarium. They brought a small propane cutter with a set of oxygen and propane bottles about the size of a pair of scuba fifties, the t-handle topside wrench, four cable clamps – two for spare, a pulley with a u-clamp to attach it to the anchor, along with a spare, just in case, and a roll of cord for securing the hawser back in the locker.

Within fifteen minutes, Harry and Jer with the Basketball in tow had worked their way to the keel and then along the keel to the Aquarium hatch under the bow. I had them on a hair trigger to move away to starboard should another surge move things about, but the surges seemed to have abated as quickly as they had started several days ago. Just in time, too.

The guys got their equipment and adjusted their buoyancy to rise up the hull to the deck above them. Finding the forward capstan and one of the flipped over cleats is not entirely obvious on the deck of a surfaced sub. Finding them in the turbid water was harder. Jer moved slowly across the forward deck, examining it closely. He located the safety line track down the center of the deck, and followed it forward where he eventually found the capstan head flush with the deck about two-thirds of the way forward to the left of the track. Harry joined him with the t-wrench, and planted himself over the capstan with the t-wrench head firmly inserted in the top of the capstan. He began to twist the handle, and the capstan quickly rose to its operating level. While he did that, Jer moved to the right side of the deck and located one of the flipped-over cleats. Harry brought the t-wrench over and loosened the cleat, which flipped upright with a nudge from Jer. Harry then tightened the clamp holding it in position.

We were following this activity closely on the Basketball monitor. I think Dirk was especially relieved that the surges seemed to have lessened, since he had the watch, and his guys were responsible for maintaining the sub's depth in this critical situation. The fact is, of course, we were almost totally at the mercy of Mother Nature at this juncture – or should I say Papa Neptune. I was just glad for the relatively calm interval, and urged my guys to move as quickly as they could under the circumstances.

The divers next located the line locker, and Harry used the t-wrench to loosen the clamps. The guys opened the cover together, laid it back on the deck against its hinges, and tied it down. Then Jer positioned himself head-down in the locker and slashed the ties with his dive knife. Jer and Harry pulled the looped end of the hawser from the locker and dropped it over the cleat. They let the weight of the hawser pull the rest over the side to the sea floor. Then Jer cut a ten-foot piece of line and secured the t-wrench to the cleat, and he placed it into the drive actuator of the capstan.

The turbidity of the water seemed to be lessening as well, which was a great relief to all of us. The Basketball backed a couple feet away from the divers as they descended down the starboard side of the bow, following the hawser.

The pair took a couple of minutes to untangle the rat's nest that had formed as the hawser tumbled from the deck. Then, with the bitter end in tow, they moved forward to the anchor, which was barely visible in the clearing water. Once there, they pulled the hawser through the eye of the anchor, and tied it off with a large-size bowline knot, which has the advantage that it cannot slip under tension, and yet when the strain is relieved, it is easy to untie. That laid the stage for the next task, pulling the anchor cable out of the winch.

The divers ascended up to the fairing where the anchor cable exited the superstructure, the relatively thin steel skin that covered the pressure-hull and all the various equipment and other things mounted between the pressure-hull and the skin. Using a clamp not unlike a Vise Grip, they clutched hard on the short exposed cable end, and using a come-along braced against the hull, they ratcheted several inches of cable out of the winch. Then they reset the clamp and did it again, and then again. Now they had about two and a half feet of cable clear of the guide with a frayed end that was badly unraveled.

Jer pulled out the torch and a medium lift bag. He tied off the bag and filled it with oxygen from the torch supply. With the torch in his left hand and a spark lighter in his right, he reached up into the bag with both hands and expertly lighted the torch. He pulled it back down, fiercely boiling and sputtering, sending a roiling column of smoke toward the surface.

"Is that shit a problem?" Dirk asked me over the intercom, obviously worried that it would form a large patch on the surface and announcing to any overflight, "Here I am – look here!"

"It's completely absorbed in less than a hundred feet," I told him.

By the time I had turned back to the monitor, Jer was nearly finished cutting through the cable. The torch flared, and the unraveled end fell to the sea floor. He shut down the torch, dumped the lift bag, dropped the torch inside and stowed it with the rest of the stuff they had retrieved from the Aquarium. Using two of the cable clamps, Harry now looped the cable end around a thimble (a tear-drop shaped loop of metal that forms an eyelet at the end of a cable) and clamped it tightly. Then he took the coil of line from their gear bag and tied one end to the thimble with a bowline.

Down the hawser to the anchor, carrying the pulley and the other end of the line, Jer and Harry were on a roll. It took about three minutes to pull the bolt from the pulley, and attach it to the top of the anchor shank. Then they threaded the bitter end of the line through the pulley and headed back to the capstan on the deck with the bitter end of the line in hand. Jer wrapped four turns around the capstan while Harry activated the capstan with the t-wrench. As the capstan turned, it took up the slack in the line, wound around the capstan four times, and then fell in a heap on the deck, guided by Jer.

When the bowline reached the pulley on the shank, the capstan began to slide under the line, indicating the line was hung up. Jer dropped down to the anchor, released the bowline to the thimble, and then wrapped the bitter end of the line around the cable above the thimble with a clove hitch, and told Harry to pull the cable out another foot or so.

"You're kidding, right?" Harry said. "And who's going to take up the slack from the capstan?"

Which was exactly right, because unless someone took up the slack, the capstan would not take a bite, and would just spin beneath the line.

"Shit," Jer answered, as he swam back up to the deck to grab the line and take a strain as it came from the capstan.

Harry took up another two feet before the line stopped moving again. Jer tied his end off, and went back to the anchor where he had sufficient cable hanging free beyond where the clove hitch ran into the pulley to bend the thimble back and attach it to the shank with a u-bolt. Jer looked at the Basketball and gave us a thumbs-up.

"Cast off the line from the capstan, Harry," Jer said, and then he loosened the clove hitch, removed the pulley, and returned to the deck. The anchor was once again connected to its cable.

After stowing the line and pulley, the divers proceeded to the fairing where the cable exited the superstructure and, after getting me to put the engineers on the line, guided the cable onto the winch reel, while they activated it from the Bat Cave. Once the anchor cable took on a bit of strain, Jer loosened the bowline holding the hawser to the anchor, and Harry pulled it hand-over-hand to the topside deck. Jer joined him, and together, they stowed the hawser back in its locker, where Jer tied it down with the lengths of cord that Harry had cut. Then they flipped and secured the cleat, retracted the capstan, secured everything topside, making sure nothing could rattle, dropped down to the Aquarium and stowed their gear, and headed back to the Can.

It had been a tough two hours, but the guys had accomplished a miracle. The bow anchor was back in commission, and the *Halibut* was ready for its next assignment – well, almost ready, as it turned out.

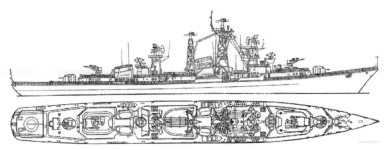

Soviet Kashin Class Destroyer

CHAPTER TWENTY

The Skipper called the officers into the Wardroom, leaving the XO and the COB with the Control Room watch. Dr. Banks and Lonie joined the meeting. The Skipper turned the floor over to the civilian spook.

"That was a very successful operation," Dr. Banks began. "That's quite a team you've got, Lieutenant McDowell. Glad you guys are on our side."

I acknowledged with a nod.

"We've got enough information to keep the NSA boys busy for some time. We'll be shipping all our tapes directly to Washington the moment we arrive in Guam. But first, we have another task." He paused. "The Soviets have developed a missile guidance system that we have been unable to jam. They have a deep-water drop zone just inside Shelikhov Bay. We've had a couple of subs there during splash down, but they have never been able to detect the signal, let alone jam it. We very much need to know how they are doing this."

Dr. Banks looked around the table. "Our next job is to go to the splash zone, find any nosecone pieces, and retrieve everything we can."

"How do we do that?" Josh asked. "Bring stuff back, I mean. Those parts will not likely fit through the Aquarium or in the Can."

"Wouldn't want to bring them into the Can in any case," I interjected. "No way to know what toxins might enter the Can with them – fuel or whatever."

"Don't need to," Lonie said. "We brought along a kind of hanging basket, a sling made of woven steel cable. Your divers will attach it to our underbelly, and then will fill it with whatever the Fish finds out there."

"Basically, that's it," the Skipper added. "Before we leave here, we attach the sling. The NSA boys developed a mechanism for lowering the sling for easy access, and then ratcheting it back tightly against the keel, keeping anything inside secure and rattle free." The Skipper gave me a wry grin. "Unfortunately," he added, "it has to be done from outside."

"What about noise during transit?" Chris Barth asked in his capacity as Sonar Officer.

"The NSA boys supposedly considered that in their design, but we'll just have to feel our way forward." The Skipper didn't seem worried about it.

Lonie showed me photos of how the mechanisms attach. It was relatively simple. The lowering devices bolted into the hull superstructure below the sail area, four per side, each fifteen feet apart. They were identical – a reel with a switchable ratchet controlled by a positive locking mechanism, with a socket centered on the reel. The set came with a couple of crank handles, each with about a foot of leverage.

"Rest your divers, Mac," the Skipper said. "We'll attach the sling in the morning."

#

The following morning, I sat with Ham and went over the dive plan. I had already examined the sling. It was created of fine stainless steel wires twisted into thin flexible strands that were woven into an extremely light-weight, completely permeable mesh that, when folded and tightly rolled, fit completely inside the Aquarium. Ham locked the ratchet mechanisms and crank handles into the Can, and briefed the guys on how to attach the sling.

After they enjoyed a great hot breakfast, with a good dose of hot sauce to make it palatable, we got down to business. We decided to put Ski in the water before we had a mutiny on our hands – Ski and Harry, with Bill in the Outer Lock and Jer in the Can. Like I said before, we had gotten the routine down pat. Getting the divers in the water was becoming routine. A few minutes following the Skipper's okay, the guys were at the Aquarium outer hatch, escorted by Bobby and the Basketball.

"Remember," I reminded them, "the rolled up sling is pretty heavy. You don't want it to fall on you."

The sling was secured to the handle of the inner hatch, but it still posed a significant threat when the guys loosed it.

The storm was completely gone, which made life outside the sub much easier. No more surges, much lower turbidity – visibility was actually a bit over ten feet. But the divers still couldn't see the sea floor from the bottom of the sub.

When Ski and Harry signaled their readiness, the guys in the Bat Cave opened the Aquarium lower hatch with the hydraulic actuator. A light steel cord dropped below the still-attached sling. Keeping to one side of the hatch, Ski pulled the cord, which released a short coil in the piece of cable that secured the sling to the upper hatch. It was supposed to drop the sling out of the Aquarium, but keep it from falling any further. The sling only dropped about two feet – half in and half out of the Aquarium.

"Must be hung up," Ski muttered.

So Ski and Harry began to push and prod the tightly wrapped sling, trying to shake it loose. It was far too massive, however, and neither diver had any leverage.

"What do you think?" I asked Ham.

"No way those boys are going to shake it loose," Ham answered: "No leverage."

"Wait a sec," I said. "They have the six ratchet mechanisms, right?"

Ham nodded.

"Okay, then," I continued, "have them install two of them that are closest to the Aquarium on the side the leading edge of the roll is pointing to. Then tie a strong line as high up as possible on that edge, and use one or both ratchets to pull the leading edge of the roll out of the hatch. That should loosen things up sufficiently for the bastard to fall the rest of the way out."

"Might work," Ham said as he reached for the mike. He started to tell the divers what to do, but on the monitor, it was obvious that they were already on it – with the same idea.

It took about ten minutes to get it set up, and it turned out to be more difficult than I had initially thought, but suddenly, with a distinct zing, the no longer rolled-up sling was hanging from the securing cable on one end and from one of the port ratchets on the other.

Our initial plan had been to arrange the sling on the sea floor, attach as many lift bags as necessary, and hoist it to the sub's belly. Now a different, less elegant but eminently more practical solution presented itself. The forward port ratchet cable was attached, and the after starboard ratchet cable was attached to the hatch cable. First, the divers attached the remaining ratchet mechanisms. Then they attached a line between the after starboard ratchet and the sling corner that was already attached to the hatch cable. When Ski released the hatch cable, the sling swung downward about midway to the sea floor. Then Harry ratcheted the line up until the sling was fairly stretched port to starboard, front to back, across the keel.

Then it was just a matter of stretching six more cables to their ratchet points, doing some minor untwisting, and ratcheting all the cables until the sling was snug against the sub's underbelly. Bobby ran the Basketball along the entire length and width of the sling, getting a good set of photos so the NSA spooks could use them to improve the design for the next time.

Total time in the water – about two and a half hours. The guys were worn out by the time they removed their rigs in the Outer Lock. I told them that they had several days off while we transited to the splash area and attempted to locate the missile parts we were looking for.

"How about some liberty in Okhotsk?" Bill quipped.

"Yeah," Jer chimed in, "we could teach those Russian chicks a thing or two."

"You don't even speak Russian," Ski said.

"Don't need to," Jer said. "All I need is..."

But Bill had unplugged his mike...

#

We got underway almost immediately after we stowed both anchors. We had about 500 miles to go, which was about three and a half days at our maximum sustainable speed of six knots. Then we needed to search the area on a grid about a half-mile per section, so it was going to be a while.

The guys had to remain in the Can, since at their saturation depth it would take about a week to decompress them, and then we would just have to press them down again. It was better and safer to keep them at depth for the duration. I know they weren't looking forward to it, but nobody forced them to volunteer for this duty. If the truth be known, we all loved it. The extra pay and prestige was just a bonus. Most of us would have done it for free.

Because the guys remained in the Can, I remained off the Deck watch list, which was kind of too bad, because I actually liked the change of pace with that duty. Nevertheless, with four lives under our immediate and total control, I didn't begrudge sitting the long hours at the Dive Console. We juggled the watch so that Ham, Jack, or I were at the console, while either Whitey, Jimmy, or one of the three of us was immediately available as backup. This gave us sufficient flexibility for each of us to take in a movie in the mess, or accomplish a personal task, or – in my case – get in a few hours of watch-standing at the Conning Station.

So, I had the Deck even though I was off the watch list at the time, and was cruising at 350 feet, just below the layer, making all of five knots, pointed southwest toward the missile splash zone. On the watch just before mine we had spent some time at periscope depth so Rusty could develop his latest set of photos from our pod listening adventure and from the attaching of the sling.

Intellectually, I knew that the sling was not really affecting the *Halibut* in any significant way, but I could swear that I felt its presence right through the deck plates. It was as if the sling caused a faint vibration that transmitted itself right through my shoes into my gut. Part of me couldn't shake the feeling that we were broadcasting a low-frequency signal that loudly announced our presence. I could imagine the water beneath the layer filled with this low-frequency sound, pointing huge acoustical arrows directly at our position.

The first hour of the watch progressed without significant incident, and I was actually beginning to relax a bit, when Sonar announced, "Conn, Sonar, we've just acquired two surface combatants bearing two-seven-zero, drifting slightly left, designate Mike-one and Mike-two."

I acknowledged and contacted the Skipper. Two warships sufficiently close to pick up through the layer was something he wanted to know about. The Skipper arrived at the Conning Station shortly and took his chair.

"I'd like to rise above the layer long enough to get a better fix," I said to him.

"Do so," he responded.

I informed Sonar what I was doing, and told them to get me course, speed, and distance as soon as they could. Then I slowed down to bare steerageway and gently poked through the layer. As soon as our BQQ-3 hydrophones were above the layer, King, who had the Sonar watch, went to work.

"Conn, Sonar," King said after several minutes, "it's a couple of *Kashins*. They're about ten miles due west, heading south. I'll get you more in a bit."

Gary Parrish, who had the navigation watch, commenced setting up a plot. "Looks like they may be patrolling the splash zone," Gary said.

"Conn, Sonar, Mike-one and Mike-two bear two-seven-five, on a course of one-niner-five at about seven knots or so. It's the *Ognevoy*, Sir, the one we tangled with earlier, and the *Odarenny*, an unmodified type, no array and no helo. Remember that the *Ognevoy* has both – it's a viable ASW combatant."

"Thanks, King. Get me one more update before we descend below the layer again."

In about five minutes, King gave me the update, and I dropped back to safety below the layer, but retained my bare steerageway.

"Keep a sharp lookout for submarines," I told Sonar. "Looks like they're preparing for a missile test," I said to the Skipper. "They've got to know how interested we are in their new guidance system. They've got to know we're out here monitoring the test." I walked over to Gary's chart. "I presume they will patrol the perimeter," I said, "and that they will go active during the test – at least the splash-down."

"I agree," the Skipper said. "Station keep on these guys for the time being. Keep them between the splash zone and us. Rig the sub for ultra-quiet, and get the officers and department chiefs in the Wardroom in ten minutes."

#

Keeping station on two vessels that were moving faster than we were was not realistically possible, so I presumed the Skipper meant not to get inside their patrol zone. It seemed to me that they were relying on their towed sonar; they didn't really appear to be running any kind of pattern. They were about a mile apart, moving along at a leisurely pace that was, however, faster than we were able to go, especially with the sling attached to our belly.

Shortly, the XO came out and relieved me so I could attend the Wardroom meeting. I left, feeling the strange silence of a submarine on ultra-quiet. The turbines were shut down, along with all the associated pumps. The quiet electric motors drove the minimal turns we needed for steerageway. We used hydraulics sparingly to minimize pump use, working off the pressure accumulators. The fans were shut down. No one was walking about. Conversations were subdued – almost whispers.

I entered the Wardroom – the last person to arrive, and took a seat near the end of the table.

"Here's the situation," the Skipper said. "We got lucky. It looks like a launch is imminent." He paused. "The problem is, however, that this puts us in the middle of their observation fleet. The *Ognevoy* and *Odarenny* are just a couple of miles to the west, and I'm certain there is at least one sub out there as well. We're going to stay outside their splash zone until the launch. We anticipate they will go active to track the nose cone to the bottom. We will do everything possible to follow the nosecone from their sonar echo."

The Skipper looked at Larry. "Nav, make sure you and your sonar techs are on top of this. We can save ourselves days of searching if we can track the nosecone to the bottom. Since the bottom is littered with trash, once it hits the sea floor, the *Odarenny* will probably lose it. We're going to move in, right below the *Ognevoy* if possible, because she is towing an array, and will be restricted in her movements. We'll try to lose ourselves inside the debris field. We'll stay on ultra-quiet until they depart the area. It'll be difficult on everybody, but it beats the alternative." The Skipper grinned wryly.

"Watch officers, keep focused. Ivan almost certainly has a sub out there. He's looking for a U.S. fast attack, but he's not going to give his position away if he can help it. Remember, we're twice as quiet. We can hear him at twice the distance he can hear us. In ultra-quiet, he shouldn't hear us at all, even if we're alongside. You department chiefs," he swept the assembled men with a level gaze, "you chiefs need to talk with your men. Tell them what's at stake, and make sure no one drops a wrench or slams a door. Chief Commissaryman," the Skipper looked at Cedric. "We're on paper plates until further notice."

"Aye, Cap'n," Cedric said.

The Skipper rose and departed the Wardroom. The rest of us left quietly – very quietly. I went back to the Can to brief Ham.

#

My guys were pretty much in standby for the time being – until we found something to retrieve. Since it looked like a launch was imminent, it really made no sense for us to go looking until the nosecone found its watery target. Obviously, if we could bring back an intact nosecone from this test – or even pieces – it would be much better than something from an earlier launch.

Being cooped up in the Can made it difficult for the guys to maintain a sense of participation. Ham spent a lot of time answering questions and otherwise handholding. He locked in a complete set of new books, because the guys had read everything they had. One doesn't normally think of rough-and-tumble divers as having an intellectual bent, and I wouldn't argue that they do, but nearly all saturation divers read a lot – what else is there to do during several weeks' long dives, cooped up in the chamber for most of the time? These divers lived for the excursions, but nobody liked the intervening periods. It was just something you had to put up with in order to get to the exciting parts.

I headed back to Control to relieve the XO. He had enough on his platter without having to stand watch while a lowly lieutenant shot the bull with his people. Sonar had a handle on the two *Kashins*, the sub was silent as a tomb, and somewhere out there beneath the waves – I was certain – Ivan lurked. I was reasonably certain that the Soviets would not waste one of their nuke fast attacks on this kind of guard duty, so I expected to find one of their diesel boats, either a relatively ancient *Whiskey* class or a newer *Romeo* class.

Which of these would make a big difference. They both were about 250 feet long. But the *Whiskey* was noisy, carried six torpedo tubes, had a primitive sonar suite, and was limited to just over 600 feet in depth. The *Romeo* class, on the other hand, was a modern, sophisticated diesel submarine with both medium- and high-frequency sonar, eight torpedo tubes, and could operate at a depth of over 1,600 feet. Furthermore, it could do about fourteen knots submerged, which made it a formidable underwater foe.

I directed King to make sure his watch-standers were up on their knowledge of these two submarines, and it's a good thing I did, because another hour into my watch, Sonar announced that it had acquired suppressed cavitation – a sure sign of a submerged submarine – to the northeast. The two *Kashins* were still out there – west and a bit south – apparently cruising north and south on an oval course about ten miles long. Their interest seemed focused inside the splash zone. We were still at ultra-quiet, which meant that we were acoustically virtually invisible to anything Ivan had, but any noise we might be making was completely masked by the background noise of the *Kashins*, since we were situated right between the two destroyers and the sub.

King stayed on top of his sonar techs, and about ten minutes later he informed me that we had an old *Whiskey* on our hands. I was relieved by the good news, and informed the Skipper.

"Keep a close watch on him anyway," the Skipper said. "Remember, he's looking for us."

"Conn, Sonar, Mike-three (as they had designated the *Whiskey*) has a zero bearing drift. He's definitely closing. Based on turn-count, I'd say he's doing about ten knots."

Any submarine doing ten knots submerged, but especially a noisy old submarine, is blind as a bat, unless he goes active. And even then it's a crapshoot.

My guess was this guy was joining his mates – the two *Kashins*. With the noise he was making, there was little chance they would be able to hear us, so this made a great opportunity to get closer to the *Ognevoy*, maybe even under it.

"Sonar, Conn," I said, "what're the contacts doing now?"

"Slowed way down, Conn. Looks like they're on a slow-bell stationkeeping."

I had Gary get me a modified plot on the destroyers' position. We were now about four miles away and closing slowly. I speeded up and set a course to intercept what Gary said was their average position as they tightened their oval to something only a little larger than their turning radius. The *Whiskey* kept coming, and it still appeared that he was coming directly toward us.

The Skipper joined me at the Conning Station, and I briefed him on what I was doing.

"Position yourself right under the *Ognevoy* again," the Skipper said. "Wait 'till he presents his port side, and then slip underneath." He sat down in his chair. "I'll be here," he added, "but do your thing. Take whatever aggressive action you need to take. I'll countermand if I don't like it." The Skipper grinned. "Don't get any closer to his keel than fifteen feet."

"Sonar, Conn," I said on the sound powered phone, "give me your best ranges to the three contacts."

"The *Kashins* are about a mile in front of us. The *Whiskey* is about two miles behind us and closing. Still doing about ten knots."

I checked with Gary. His plot confirmed Sonar's. Gary indicated that about the time we settled beneath *Ognevoy*, the *Whiskey* would be on top of us. Right now he was still blind, with his ten knots. That meant I had about fifteen minutes to get into place.

"Conn, Sonar, the *Kashins* have slowed way down, virtually DIW."

A bit of luck, that. I brought us slowly into *Ognevoy's* wake and eased up to seventy feet. I raised number one scope until I could just squat to look through the eyepiece, and rotated the optics to look straight up.

"Drop down five feet, and bring the scope up another two feet," the Skipper said, as he stepped up to the scope.

I complied, and then raised number two scope and tilted the optics.

"Now ease her up until we can just see the keel," the Skipper said.

About ten seconds later, the Skipper announced, "I got it. We're dropping back. Add one or two turns."

I passed the order to Maneuvering.

"One more turn," the Skipper said. "Okay – now drop back a turn."

"Conn, Sonar, the *Whiskey's* close by, and he's surfacing."

"Conn aye."

Suddenly, we were startled by a loud sonar ping from close by, reverberating right through the hull.

"Sonar, Conn, keep track of these. Try to find an echo."

"We're on top of it, Conn," King answered back. "That was *Odarenny's* sonar. The *Ognevoy* is retrieving the towed array."

P-I-N-G!

Even though I was expecting it, I jumped. A ping through the hull will absolutely get your attention every time.

P-I-N-G!

"I think the missile shot is about to splash," I told the Skipper.

"I agree," he answered.

"Sonar, Conn – keep sharp. We're looking for a transient echo."

P-I-N-G!

The Skipper remained glued to his scope. "A couple more turns, Mac."

P-I-N-G!

"Okay," the Skipper said, "hold it."

P-I-N-G!

"Conn, Sonar, we have an echo..."

P-I-N-G!

"Another one, Conn..."

P-I-N-G!

"Another one..."

P-I-N-G!

"That's it, Conn. No echo this time, but we have the bogey location.

The anticipated ping did not materialize this time.

"Drop down ten feet, Mac," the Skipper said.

"Conn, Sonar, the *Whiskey's* starting up again – cranking on turns. He'll be blind."

And then we heard the rumble of the *Ognevoy's* screws building up speed, and I could hear the distinctive sound of her gas turbines as they revved up. I dropped the sub down to 500 feet as quickly as possible, without using screws. Just a hundred feet off the bottom. I pulled up and held a hover. Overhead the *Kashins* rapidly disappeared from our audible through-the-hull tracking.

"Conn, Sonar, Mike-one and -two are out of here at twenty knots. They're history. Mike-three, the *Whiskey*, just dove. He's on the battery, moving slowly." There was a pregnant pause. "We lost him, Conn. He's out there, but we lost him."

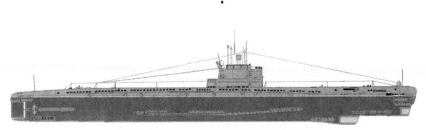

Soviet Whiskey Class Submarine

CHAPTER TWENTY-ONE

A *Whiskey* submarine is old even when it has just been built. It's based on a World War II German submarine model that even the Germans had stopped building. It's noisy, its sonar sucks, and its only good to 600 feet. Having said that, it's still a formidable foe. It has six torpedo tubes, and it shoots the same smart fish as Ivan's nukes. The obvious trick is not to let one find you in the first place.

Well, we had had one in our sights, but we had lost him. And now we were the prey. Fortunately, for him to hear us, he had to be well inside our detection circle on him – unless he shut down completely.

"Skipper," I said, turning around to look at him relaxing in his chair, "this is one smart Russian. He assumes we're out here, but he doesn't know for sure. So he dives and shuts everything down. That equalizes the playing field – we lose our only real advantage, our ability to hear him before he hears us."

I went over to the chart. "He was a mile or so away when he dove, and he was pointed toward the splash zone. If he flooded main ballast, angled her down, and kicked her in the rear before shutting down – well, he could drift right into the middle of the debris field, settle to the bottom, all without making another sound." I paused, looking at the Skipper. "We're at ultra-quiet. He might be able to hear us at several hundred feet, but beyond that – as long as we keep quiet, we're home free." I grinned at him. "Why don't we point toward the nosecone and quietly push in that direction. I think we can get there, find the nosecone with the Basketball, and commence operations without alerting the *Whiskey*." I paused. "We just have to do it silently."

The Skipper appeared to consider my words. "Look, Skipper," I said, "he can't do anything without our hearing him – anything that is but listen, and we listen a lot better than he does. If he actually ends up in our neighborhood, we might even be able to have a bit of fun with him."

"Okay, Mac," the Skipper said after a bit, "we'll follow your plan for the time being; but make sure Sonar is on their toes. There's no cavalry to come to our rescue up here.

The first part was easy. I just dropped the bow to three degrees down angle, and adjusted the heading to point directly at the nosecone on the bottom about two miles away. Then I let physics take over. I called King out to the Control Station to discuss the second part. I explained what we were doing. I told him to keep a close ear to the water landscape. We wanted to know where the *Whiskey* was the very first moment possible. Our cat-and-mouse game was fun, but also potentially very dangerous. The last thing we wanted was an underwater incident.

It's important to understand the big picture here. The water was 600 to 700 feet deep. The *Whiskey* was 250 feet long, and we were 350 feet long. This meant that if either one of us took any kind of angle with any kind of speed, we would be in the bottom or in the air in moments. Speed was not our friend in this venue.

I expected to reach the target in about an hour. I told King to look at the bottom with his secure bottom sounder every minute, but to set it to the lowest possible power setting. Sure it emitted white noise that was supposed to be indistinguishable from surrounding sea noise, but for a smart sub commander specifically looking for us, a periodic burst of white noise on a specific line of bearings was a dead give-away. We were dealing with a wily submariner who knew the ropes. His little trick when the *Kashins* departed was proof enough of that.

For the next hour things were tense but quiet throughout the sub as we crept toward the nosecone somewhere on the bottom ahead in the murky water. Finally, King informed me that we were about fifty feet over the sea floor. I brought us to a stop, and instructed Chris to keep us there with minimal hydraulic noise. I told Lonie to ready and launch the Basketball.

A few minutes later, following a small amount of unfortunate but necessary noise cycling the door hydraulics that we could hear throughout the sub, the Basketball was flying under Bobby's skilled control. I had him search in a thirty-degree arc in front of the sub. He stayed a few feet over the bottom and moved rapidly, looking for the shadow of the nosecone.

We were clearly in a debris field. Everywhere the Basketball looked, we could see missile parts, sections of rocket motor, pieces of siding, clumps that could have been electronics or hydraulics – stuff everywhere. This was a gold mine of an opportunity to get a lot of pretty sensitive stuff from right under Ivan's nose.

"Wait – hold it Bobby, off to your right...there," I said on the sound powered phone. "Go look at that."

Bobby did, and on my monitor appeared a white object that grew as Bobby approached it, until it filled the screen with a black hammer and sickle that turned garish red as the Basketball light illuminated it. It was the nosecone, seemingly fairly intact.

Bobby surveyed it from all angles. No doubt, it clearly had just recently entered the water. The exposed metal exhibited no corrosion at all, and the silt it had pushed out of the way had not yet settled back to a flat surface. The nosecone was sitting in a small crater. We had hit the jackpot.

#

The Skipper called Larry (Ops) and Dirk (Eng) to the Control Station. When they arrived, he explained that we were at the nosecone, and that we needed to put down our anchors in absolute silence. He told them about the *Whiskey*, which Larry knew about, of course, and the very real danger of getting detected.

"Can you lower the anchors soundlessly?" he asked Dirk.

"I don't know for sure, Cap'n," Dirk answered, "but we can give it a try."

"Try's not good enough, Eng," the Skipper snapped. "It must be silent!"

"We've never tried it, Sir..."

"Don't give me that crap, Eng!" The Skipper sounded more than pissed off. "Don't tell me what you can't do," he hissed. "Find a fucking way!" The Skipper stood up and put his hand on Dirk's shoulder. "Look, Dirk," he said quietly, "I know you can do it. Find a way, and make it happen!"

A few minutes later the sound-powered phone by the Skipper's chair whirred softly.

"Yeah," he answered and paused, listening. "Sounds like a plan, Dirk. We'll handle this end."

Then the Skipper turned to me. "Ease the bow down until you're touching bottom, Mac."

I told Chris and Pots to lower the bow by manually cracking the forward sea valve and letting in enough water to accomplish the task. "I want her on the bottom at a ten-degree angle," I said, "so we're resting on the mushroom anchor."

Ten minutes later, with Bobby recording every move on the Basketball camera, we were firmly pressed into the muck forward. Dirk's guys released the hydraulic lock on the bow anchor cable, and then I ordered Chris to move the trim-tank water aft, but to keep the angle at only four degrees. As the bow came up, the cable unspooled silently.

Fifteen minutes later, the stern anchor was also firmly pressed into the mud, and Dirk's boys released the hydraulic lock on the stern anchor line, while Bobby watched closely from outside. Then I ordered Chris to expel enough water to lighten the sub a bit. I also had him trim the bubble so we were on an even keel. I watched on the monitor until I estimated that we were about fifteen feet above the sea floor, and then had Dirk set the hydraulic locks on both anchors.

And there we were, firmly anchored in 650 feet of water ten feet above the sea floor just a few feet from a freshly minted Soviet missile nosecone. And somewhere nearby lurked a suspicious Soviet *Whiskey* with a crafty Skipper who was probably just itching to get into a fight.

#

That's what I told my guys a couple of hours later as they were getting ready to enter the water.

We had spent the preceding two hours listening quietly. That's it – nothing else – just listening. We knew the *Whiskey* was out there, and we were pretty certain he was nearby. Had he operated anything at all, and I do mean anything, Senior Chief Travis Barkley and his guys in Sonar would have heard him. It had been three hours now. That old *Whiskey* did not have our capabilities. Their Skipper had a tough job on his hands. He had fifty-three guys under his command – well some would say fifty-two, since the so-called Zampolit, or Political Officer, really was on independent duty, answerable only to the KGB. The Soviet crewmen were also in far tighter quarters than ours. They had no ready source of fresh oxygen, no water, and under the circumstances, no circulation.

They too were at ultra-quiet, sitting on the bottom somewhere relatively close by. They had two, maybe three more hours of air. I could visualize the scene inside the *Whiskey*: It was dark, the air was thick and clammy, and the Soviet Skipper had certainly promised to cut off the balls of anyone who made a sound. It may not have been the most exciting submarine duty in the Soviet Navy, but this guy, whoever he was, was one of their best, I suspected. He was outclassed, outgunned, and outmaneuvered, and yet we were on an even playing field at this moment, each at the mercy of the other.

We heard nothing. We made certain that he heard nothing, either.

I cautioned my guys to take it easy, and be silent. Three divers were going out this time: Bill, Ski, and Harry, with Jer in standby, and Jimmy in the Can – I had locked Jimmy down in the previous three hours to give us some more latitude in the water on this job. It made it a bit tight inside the Can, but the guys were used to it, and both Ham and I agreed the extra available manpower was worth it.

Bobby and the Basketball were waiting by the lock. During the preceding hours, Devon had been all over the immediate landscape with the Basketball using up a couple of cassettes of film. The Skipper had authorized the activity, but with the proviso that they make absolutely no noise – and somehow they carried it off. Now it was Bobby's turn.

The key to this particular operation was for the three divers to lower the woven mesh sling flat on the seabed, and then wrestle the nosecone on top of it using lift bags. Then, they would pick up the five or six other items Devon had identified and place them on the sling as well. Finally, the divers would raise the sling up as tightly as possible to the keel, and they would adjust things until there was no possibility of a rattle or of anything coming loose.

At least, that was the theory. Once the guys were at the nosecone, they determined that it would be easier to extract the important components from the nosecone rather than retrieve the entire object. They attacked the nosecone skin with old-fashioned tin-snips, and had peeled back a significant portion in short order. There's one thing divers are good at – breaking things. Really good at it, I mean.

Two hours later, every meaningful part of the nosecone was carefully laid out on the sling. The guys had separated and were independently retrieving other pieces of debris under the direction of Ham, who was operating from a list Devon had given him. An hour later, we had a load of Ivan's toys the likes of which no one had ever before collected on any mission, in any place, at any time.

Ham had just signaled the guys to return to the lock, when I received an urgent signal on the sound-powered phone circuit to meet the Skipper in Sonar.

"Call if you need me, Ham," I said, as I left for Sonar.

A couple of minutes later I stood in Sonar with the Skipper listening to Travis describe what had happened.

"I had the watch," Travis said, "and was looking for that *Whiskey*. We had set up compass in three sectors with one guy on each sector. We were doing incremental searches, using the good old mark one mod zero ear." He grinned. "It's still the best thing we've got for initial detection, you know." He stepped over to the BQQ-3 display. "This guy's not much use when we got nothing to analyze." He turned around to face us again. "Anyway, Fitz was scanning off to starboard when he heard something. Just a clang, a single sharp noise. There was nothing else. Total silence followed the clang, but Fitz was certain. The clang came from the starboard side."

"We're certain it didn't come from us, Mac," the Skipper said to me. "It's the *Whiskey*, and he's only a short distance out there." The Skipper motioned me out of Sonar.

At the Conning Station the Skipper asked me how long our umbilicals were.

"Hundred foot sections," I told him. "We can link them together."

The sound-powered phone light blinked. The Skipper took the call. "Yeah, okay, I got it." He turned to me and said, "Bobby found the *Whiskey*."

I looked at him in surprise.

"That's right," he said. "It's just aft of the port beam a bit under five hundred feet away. It's presenting us a starboard beam aspect.

by Gary McCluskey

Ski returning to Halibut from the Whiskey with cut umbilical

CHAPTER TWENTY-TWO

We decided to put Ski in the water for this one. Not because he was best able to do the job, but because we still owed him a dive – sort of. Anyway, Ham and I agreed to put him out there.

I had Bobby and Devon scouring a 500-foot arc to find anything that we could use to disable the *Whiskey*. That's right. You see, we had a problem. We were anchored to the bottom. We had gotten there silently, but there was no way we could leave silently. The *Whiskey* was only 500 feet away. He would be able to hear any sound we made – any sound at all. There was absolutely nothing to prevent him from shooting one of the six torpedoes I was certain were permanently loaded in his tubes.

The *Whiskey* had no reason to leave until he absolutely had to. He was reasonably certain we were somewhere out there. Why leave while he still had breathable air inside the boat? Once he left, he would move from his datum until he was outside what he believed was an American sub's maximum detection range for a silent mover. We would have no idea where he was, and that still would give him the opportunity to get us when we started up.

So what we needed to do was prevent his doing anything but surfacing, because on the surface, he would be virtually blind, and certainly incapable of shooting his fish at us. Unless he had us in his sights, and could keep us there, he wouldn't risk our firing back at him within a second or two of his launching a fish.

That meant that if we could somehow disable his ability to maneuver, then he would really have no choice but to emergency surface. While he did that, we could drop our anchors, leave them there, and get the hell out of Dodge. By the time he got his act back together, we would be outside his detection range and on our way to being home free.

The obvious question, therefore, was how to disable a *Whiskey* submarine on the bottom in 600 feet of water, from the outside, silently, and so that he wouldn't know about it until he had to surface – and do it with one man at the end of a 500-foot saturation diving umbilical.

Piece of cake.

#

"So why not just take a handful of steel crowbars from the Bo's'n Locker?" Ham asked me. "I could jam a couple of those in the bow and stern planes, and that SOB ain't going nowhere."

"And when that Skipper surfaces, and his guys go out and find the crowbars, they might as well have 'Made in the USA' stamped on them," I said. "No, Ham, it's got to be something from out there."

"But they'll know it didn't get there by itself," Ham protested.

"So they know somebody did it to them, but they don't know how, and they have no proof," I said with a grin. "I would love to see the *Whiskey* Old Man's face when he figures out what we did."

So, that was the general plan. While the Bat Cave was searching for our substitute Soviet crowbars, we were busy piecing together a 500-foot umbilical. Although the umbilical was neutrally buoyant, it still had a lot of mass that Ski would have to drag around after himself. That, and whatever Bobby found for him to jam the planes.

We decided to put Ski outside before Bobby was done. It was going to be a long dive, and the sooner Ski got out there, the sooner we could bring him back to safety. Several minutes later, Ski dropped to the sea floor at 600 feet, some fifteen feet below *Halibut's* keel, and a scant 500-feet from a bottomed Soviet *Whiskey*-class diesel submarine armed for bear and running out of air.

I was very much wishing I was out there with him, but we only had sufficient umbilical for one 500-foot length, and there was no way I could have left this critical operation in even Ham's capable hands. This was my baby to make or break, and my guys needed me in charge and on top of the situation at the console, inside the sub.

What we were doing had never been done before. It had never even been contemplated. The dive, the depth, the umbilical stretch, and a live *Whiskey* at the end of the line – the tale would be told in hushed tones long after we were gone.

Ski pulled the complete pile of umbilical from the Outer Lock, laying it out in a snaking pattern leading generally toward the *Whiskey*. We didn't observe this operation because Bobby was still off looking for useable missile pieces. But we had discussed it in detail, and I knew exactly what Ski was doing. As soon as he had laid out his lifeline he called me.

"Dive, Red Diver, I'm ready to go."

"Dive Aye," I answered. "Carry out your orders."

"Red Diver Aye."

I called Bobby to join Ski, and ten minutes later Ski was trudging along the bottom toward the remains of the scavenged missile nosecone, with the Basketball flitting about, looking over first one shoulder, then the other, and then scudding ahead to turn around and watch Ski approaching.

"Dive, Red Diver, take a look at this." Ski pointed at a section of stripped rocket skin, and Bobby moved in close. It was a solid curved piece of aluminum T-bar that served as the nosecone's bottom framework, holding the thin aluminum skin. Using the tin snips he had taken with him, Ski cut away the remaining skin from the frame. Then he pulled a heavy-duty cutter from his leg pocket and proceeded to cut the curved T-bar into three sections.

With a section of line, Ski tied the three T-bars into a bundle that he laid to one side on the sea floor. With the tin snips he next cut away two large sections of aluminum skin, cut a hook in each and secured them to the T-bar bundle.

"Okay, Dive, ready to pay Ivan a visit," Ski announced as he attached a lift bag to the metal pieces, filling it with gas until the bundle lifted off the sea floor to float beside him.

Bobby pulled the Basketball out ahead to guide Ski, and fifteen minutes later Bobby reached the end of his tether, only to find that he was just tantalizingly out of reach of the looming shadow of the grounded *Whiskey*.

"Wheeeeu...look at that!" Ski exclaimed, as he stopped up short to stare through the murky water at the bottomed Soviet sub.

With Bobby watching through the Basketball, Ski dumped the lift bag. Then he untied the line and laid his "tools" out before him on the sea floor: three circular sections of T-bar and two long pieces of foot-wide skin.

"Dive, Red Diver, I'm ready to go. Let's do the bow planes first." Ski picked up two T-bar sections, one in each hand, and started toward the starboard bow plane, tantalizingly out of the view of the Basketball.

"Red Diver, Dive Control, give me a running narrative. We're losing visual on you," I said.

"Right foot...left foot...right foot...."

"Knock it off, Ski!" I snarled.

"Red Diver, aye," with a grunt.

For the next few minutes all we heard was Ski's heavy breathing. Then Ski announced, "Okay Dive, I'm at the starboard bow plane. It's several feet over my head."

"Remember," I reminded him, "the bow planes are virtually flush with the deck."

"Right," Ski said, "I'm lifting to the deck."

I could picture Ski dumping gas into his loose-fitting hot-water suit until he floated gently off the sea floor, rising like a ghost to the deck about thirty feet above the sea floor.

"Okay, I'm on the deck." A long pause. "Be aware they still have their lifeline mounted – along the starboard side."

"Roger that," I responded.

"I got an idea, Dive," Ski said after about five minutes during which he had been closely examining the starboard bow plane where it exited the superstructure. "These planes fold backward into the superstructure, right?" he asked.

"Roger that."

"I think I can cut the lifeline at the back end by the conning tower, pull it out of the stanchions, and use it to secure a piece of T-bar over and under the starboard bow plane, with the end of the T-bar sticking into the superstructure. I think it will lock up the bow plane hydraulics."

"Stand by, Red Diver," I said, and told Ham to get Dirk right away.

Five minutes later, I asked Ski to explain his idea to Dirk. Dirk listened closely, asked Ski some detailed questions about the lifeline, and then turned to me.

"I think it will work, Mac," he said. "Ski should keep the forward end of the lifeline attached to the deck, and should wrap as many turns as possible around the two pieces of T-bar including the bow plane shaft."

I passed this on to Ski, and told him to get to it.

Ski chattered his way through the task. His comments were liberally laced with "diver speak," in several languages. I reminded him that he was on the foredeck of a submerged enemy warship, and that he damn well better be quiet. He started whistling.

Finally, about a half hour later, Ski announced that the *Whiskey's* bow planes were going nowhere fast.

"Heading aft," he said.

"Roger."

The stern planes of a *Whiskey* are down near the keel, right behind each screw. They're hung between two supports, driven from the center. The rudder sits right between them.

Ski chronicled his progress along the deck. As he passed the conning tower, he noted that the after lifeline was strung along the port side. He cut it where it attached to the forward-most stanchion just aft of the conning tower, and unthreaded it as he moved aft. As he reached the sub's stern, we began to see some shadowed motion from the Basketball. Ski dropped to the sea floor at the stern with the coiled lifeline in his hand. Then I could see his silhouette becoming increasingly clear as he approached the Basketball at its extended position. He picked up the two lengths of aluminum skin and the remaining T-bar, and faded into the murk to become a moving shadow at the base of the *Whiskey*.

Since we still couldn't see very well, Ski continued to chronicle his activities.

"I'm at the stern...picking up the lifeline – got to keep the plane from going up, so I lash the T-bar to the top of the plane, and secure it to the stanchions...should lock the hydraulics." He paused while he accomplished the task.

We heard occasional grunts and several swear words, and finally he announced that the stern plane was as secure as it was going to get.

"Dive, I got a bit of lifeline left over, but not enough to wrap the skin around the screws. But there is an antenna line running from the port stern up to the top of the conning tower." There was another pause. "I'm going up there to cut the antenna where it attaches to the tower," Ski announced.

I grabbed the mike. "Red Diver, Hold!" I ordered. I wanted to discuss his going that shallow with Ham

"Red Diver, Aye."

"Ham," I said, "what do you think? The top of the conning tower is more than thirty feet above the sea floor. It's above his ceiling."

"Yeah, I know," Ham said. "If he stretches up as far as possible, he'll keep most of his body closer to the ceiling. He can cut it in a few seconds, and drop back down."

"Sounds like a plan," I said, and picked up the mike. "Red Diver, Dive, here's the situation. The top of the conning tower is above your ceiling. We agree that you should cut the antenna at the top, but we want you to do it this way. Press yourself against the side of the conning tower, and lift yourself just high enough to reach up above your head and cut the antenna wire. Then drop right back down again, and get back to the sea floor ASAP." I paused. "Got that?"

"Roger that."

A few minutes later Ski announced, "I'm on deck and reaching up." Another pause. "Okay...it's cut. I'm on my back down."

All we heard then was heavy breathing, and then, "Oops!"

Immediately, Sonar called me on the sound powered phone. "Dive, Sonar, what was that loud clang?"

"Dive, Red Diver, I dropped the cutter. It hit the deck. I'm back on the bottom by the port screw now. Sorry about that."

I explained the situation to Sonar. "Let me know if there is any activity on the *Whiskey*. Remember, we've got a man right by him."

"Dive Aye. Watch yourself, Ski. Where's your umbilical?" I was concerned that if the *Whiskey* started his screws, Ski might get his umbilical wrapped up in them.

"Up over the stern, Dive," Ski said. "I need to go up and over to clear it."

"Do so," I said, "but make it quick."

A few minutes later Ski informed me that he was in place, and that he was ready to proceed with wrapping the screws. All we could see on the monitor was his shadowy movements in the murk. But I imagined that he was wedging the skin in and out of the blades, wrapping it with the antenna wire as he went along.

"Dive, Sonar," the phone talker sounded excited over the circuit. "Something's going on with the *Whiskey*. We think he's getting ready to start his screws!"

I grabbed the mike. "Red Diver, evacuate now! Evacuate now!" I ordered, putting a bit of urgency into my voice.

"Dive, Red Diver, I've got a little problem," Ski said. "It seems that I wrapped the antenna wire around a section of my umbilical. I can't evacuate until I unwrap the wire and loosen my umbilical."

This presented a real, immediate problem. If Sonar was correct, and the *Whiskey* was about to get underway, Ski was in real trouble, and we had no spare umbilical to send out another diver to help.

"Dive, Sonar, there's no doubt, the *Whiskey* will shortly lift off the bottom."

We had no choice now. "Red Diver, the *Whiskey* is starting up. You need to cut your umbilical and get back here on your come-home bottle immediately. Right now, Ski. Do it right now!" I ordered.

"Roger, Dive. We're going to lose comms in a moment." And suddenly, the circuit went silent.

Bobby had been following the conversation closely. He focused the Basketball on Ski's moving shadow. And then we saw him. He had cut his umbilical on our side of the problem, and then pulled his end from under the antenna wire. He was pulling himself hand over hand along the umbilical, trailing about ten feet of umbilical behind him. Bubbles furiously flowed from the cut end on our side. Five-hundred feet was a long way to go, but Ski had about a minute of breathing gas available in his come-home bottle.

I told the Can to cut the gas and hot water to the umbilical, and I watched as Ski continued to pull himself toward safety. Nearly a minute had passed already, and Ski was still pulling himself through the water. It was going to be close. Ski was burning oxygen faster because of his exertion.

A minute and fifteen seconds had passed. I looked at the Outer Lock monitor. Jimmy was furiously hauling umbilical, doing what he could to hasten Ski's return. A minute and a half – and then the Basketball tumbled away as Ski pushed it aside to scramble into the outer lock, gasping for air.

The first words out of his mouth: "Sheeit! Did that sonofabitch try to lift off yet?"

The crippled Whiskey floundering on the surface

CHAPTER TWENTY-THREE

Ski was safe in the Can, the umbilical was coiled in the Outer Lock, and Bobby was back at full extension with the Basketball. Since Ski cut his umbilical, Sonar had been tracking some unusual activity from the *Whiskey*. Sonar reported the unmistakable sounds of electric motors starting up and hydraulic pumps engaging.

Suddenly a godawful screeching enveloped the *Halibut*. It seemed to be coming from everywhere, but Sonar said it was from the *Whiskey*. The monitor showed a thickening cloud around the Soviet sub's stern. The screeching stopped, and the current swept away the cloud. Through the murk I saw the flash of the missile skin. It was partially torn loose, and in flashes I could see that it was tightly jammed in the starboard propeller shaft. I couldn't see the port shaft, but it was pretty obvious that the starboard shaft wasn't going anywhere soon.

I excused myself, leaving Ham in charge of the dive system, and went to Control. The Skipper and Dirk were already there discussing the situation with Senior Chief Barkley.

"They're revving their hydraulic pumps right now," Travis was saying. He pointed at the monitor. "As you can see, the stern planes aren't moving." He grinned at me. "Nice work, El-Tee."

"Thanks, Senior Chief, but it was Ski. You know that."

"Somebody made it happen, Sir," Travis answered. "We know who we got onboard, Sir," he said as he went back to Sonar.

"No forward motion," Dirk said, "no stern planes and probably no bow planes either. This guy's going no place but up."

"Nav," the Skipper said to Larry, who had the Deck, "cut the two anchor cables immediately!" He turned to Dirk and said, "See to it, Eng. And bring up the plant... right now! When he blows, I want flank speed out of here!"

#

Five minutes later Dirk reported that both anchors were released, just as Sonar reported that the *Whiskey* had commenced blowing main ballast. Seconds before, Maneuvering had reported ready to answer all bells.

"Ahead flank, make your depth two-hundred feet, left full rudder, make your course one-eight-zero," Larry ordered.

Five seconds later we were whipping through the water leaving nothing but cavitation bubbles in our wake.

"Keep it up for ninety seconds," the Skipper told Larry. "Then come to all stop, and coast while Sonar gets their bearings."

A minute and a half later, Larry shut it down, and placed *Halibut* in a shallow dive to let gravity help pull us even further away from a very angry Soviet submarine skipper.

Sonar reported that the *Whiskey* was still on its way to the surface, so Larry kicked it in the ass again for another thirty seconds. When he shut down this time, Sonar reported that the Whiskey had surfaced. That meant we had another minute or so to pour on the power, so Larry hit it one more time, holding it for a full sixty seconds. When he shut down this time, Sonar reported that the *Whiskey* was shutting down on the surface.

I wished I could have seen it – no bow planes, no stern planes, no screws – 250 feet of submarine floundering in the waves. With no way to gain forward momentum, the *Whiskey* couldn't even use his rudder for stability. I could picture the Russian Skipper pissed to the eyeballs, urging his men to solve his triple problems. The bow planes would not have been much of a problem to correct, but the stern planes and screws involved divers in the water, which – on the surface – offered no small danger in a heaving sea. But it had to be done.

Furthermore, the *Whiskey* Skipper was now fairly certain of the presence of another submarine – one with special capabilities. After all, no known fish species can tie knots in lifeline cable. The *Whiskey* commander also knew the probable direction of his quarry, and while he would not be getting underway for some time, he did have sonar. Granted, it was no match with ours, but it still was capable of finding us if the *Whiskey* got close enough.

That's why Larry used every trick in the book to put distance between us and the Soviets. By the time the *Whiskey* was ready to look for us, we were miles away to the south, hundreds of feet below the diesel-powered *Whiskey's* maximum depth. Unless that Skipper was dumber than I thought, he wasn't going to give chase. There were simply too many variables. Besides, he had a more realistic option. Sooner or later his quarry – us – had to leave the Sea of Okhotsk. That meant transiting through one of the several relatively narrow passages between the Kuril Islands.

Ivan wasn't looking for us when we entered Okhotsk at what seemed like ages ago. He sure as hell would be looking for us on our way out. We had a 2,800-nautical-mile trip ahead of us: 700 miles to the middle of the

Kurils, and another 2,100 or so to Guam. That is if we decided to sneak out, which looked like a very good idea right then.

The arithmetic worked out like this: We could do six knots all day with the Can on our stern and the sling holding the missile parts under our belly. That worked out to about five days to reach the sixty-mile wide gap between Shiashkotan and Matua Islands in the middle of the Kuril Chain, and about fifteen days in open ocean from there to Guam.

The *Whiskey* Skipper was in all likelihood all over the radio by now, explaining to his superiors what had happened – or at least what he thought might have happened. I would have loved to be privy to that conversation. But he was still on the surface, probably unable to get underway yet.

If I were the *Whiskey* Skipper, I mused, I would order a load of fuel on an underway replenishment, and hightail it on the surface through the gap the *Halibut* had entered, then down the outside of the Kurils, and station myself just below the layer about a hundred miles to the east. He had to know Guam was our goal. It was the closest U.S. submarine facility.

In any event, by the time we would be ready to lose ourselves in the North Pacific, the whole damn Soviet navy would be out there looking for us.

\#

The Skipper called a Wardroom meeting for all officers and department chiefs. I left Ham at the Dive Console and arrived as the meeting was settling down. Lonie and Spook moved apart to make room for the chair I dragged up. All the officers were present except for the XO and Neil in the Control Room, and all the chiefs were present except Pots on the BCP.

The rest of us were listening to the Skipper talk.

"We need to get to Guam ASAP," he was saying, "but we need to do it without getting caught."

Nods around the table.

"We're limited to six knots. That's slow, but the silver lining is that at that speed we have very long ears. We may not be the quietest fish in the ocean, but we're a lot quieter than Ivan – especially at six knots." He paused and rolled a chart out on the table. I held down one corner, and three of the guys did the same.

"We're here," the skipper pointed to the lower end of Shelikhov Bay, and we're going here." He poked his finger at the southernmost of the Mariana Islands not far from the equator. "Guam." He sat back in his chair and clasped his hands behind his head. "The question is," he continued, "where do we cross these?" He leaned forward and swept his hand along the Kurils.

That's when I piped up with my theory of what I would do if I were the *Whiskey* skipper. I pointed at a spot to the east of the center of the island chain.

"Why there?" The Skipper asked.

"Guam is the odds-on favorite for our destination," I said. "They have no idea of our speed limitation, so they're thinking we do it like they do – balls to the wall, and then disappear for a while, repeat. If they can get out in front of us they might be able to see us coming and head us off."

"Which means maybe we should stay west of the Kurils and head south into Japanese waters," the Skipper added.

"How about this," I said, "we send a quick message in the clear stating our intentions to do just what you said, but then we cut eastward and make our run while they are looking further to the south."

"I don't know…," the Skipper said.

"A broken message," I added, "like we didn't mean to send it. We cut off the transmission in the middle, but after the main information gets out."

"It could work," Dr. Banks said.

And that did it. The Skipper nodded as he rolled up the chart. "Set it up, Nav."

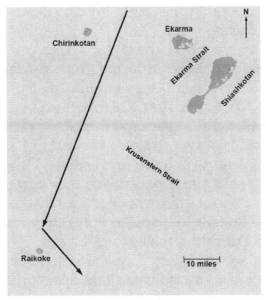

Krusenstern Strait

CHAPTER TWENTY-FOUR

To say the next five days were uneventful would be an understatement. We experienced the epitome of the "endless boredom" part of the classic definition of submarining – endless boredom interrupted by moments of sheer panic. Nothing to tell, really. We stayed deep, and moved as fast as we could.

Basically, we aimed for a small active volcanic island about a third of the way down from Kamchatka named Chirinkotan, located about twenty miles west of Ekarma at the southern end of the Ekarma strait separating Ekarma and Shiashkotan. The island itself is a four-square-mile peak of an underwater mountain that extends about 2,200 feet into the sky – a nearly perfect volcanic cone. Chirinkotan, Ekarma, and another even smaller volcanic island – 1.5-mile wide, 1,800-foot- high Raikoke – together formed a perfect triangular shield spanning Krusenstern Strait between Shiashkotan and Raikoke. This formation was essentially cloaking our approach from the (presumed) lurking Soviet fleet to the east of the Kurils.

As we approached the area, I was on watch with section one, and King reported from Sonar that they could clearly hear rumblings emanating from the volcanic activity. We knew that Raikoke had last erupted in 1924, and thought – perhaps – that it was due again. It turned out, however, that as we entered Krusenstern Strait, the sound was more localized to Ekarma itself.

Regardless, it was a perfect acoustic cover. There was virtually no chance that whoever was out there looking for us would be able to hear anything so quiet as we were against this rumbling background noise.

As luck would have it, the weather turned in our favor as well. The storm wasn't as ferocious as the one that nearly got us caught up along Kamchatka, but it still was a doozy. I looked up at the surface wave monitor. It showed ten- to twenty-foot waves marching out of the Sea of Okhotsk behind us, through the Krusenstern Strait, and out into the Northern Pacific. The wave height, where we were in the Strait was higher than behind us, probably due to the lens focusing effect of the relatively narrow shallow strait. Ahead of us the water certainly would settle down a bit, but for the guys on picket duty looking for us, it was no picnic.

I presumed that they were DIW in order not to alert us to their presence. But in this water they were being tossed all over the place. It was only a question of time before they had to get underway to gain some steerageway and a measure of control over their movement in this chaotic water. Sure enough, as I poked the *Halibut's* nose cautiously around Raikoke, making sure to keep the noisy volcano as a backdrop, King reported that Sonar had acquired a Russian surface contact.

"Make that two Russian surface combatants, Conn, bearing one-six-zero and one-five-three. Designate Kilo-one and two."

I stepped down to check the chart when Sonar called again. "You're not going to believe this, Conn. It's the same two *Kashins* we tangled with up at the missile range, the *Ognevoy* and *Odarenny*. Kilo-one is the *Ognevoy*."

"Damn!" I said to Chris and Pots and to the Control Room in general. "That was some kick-ass transit."

"Conn, Sonar," King announced, "I have a contact with suppressed cavitation bearing one-two-zero, designate Kilo-three. This is a submerged submarine, Sir, at snorkel depth. I can hear his snorkel valve cycling."

Things were pretty unpleasant right then on that diesel sub, because the water really was way too rough for reasonable snorkel ops. The fact that he was using his snorkel meant he was almost certainly not a nuke. Up here that meant probably another *Whiskey* or...

"Conn, Sonar, Kilo-three is the same *Whiskey* we screwed around with up in Shelikhov Bay."

So there it was – a family reunion.

The Skipper joined me in Control and took his place, leaning back in his chair to light one of his cigars.

"How do you want to handle this, Mac?" he asked.

I had known we would have company as we exited Krusenstern Strait, but I really didn't anticipate meeting *Ognevoy* and *Odarenny*. I figured we might run into the *Whiskey* again. That skipper had a bone to pick with us; but the other two? I'm not one to believe in coincidence, but short of someone onboard having informed them where we would cross the Kurils, how else could you explain their presence?

I discussed this with the Skipper, who doesn't believe in coincidence either.

"Look at it this way, Mac," he said. "You figured how to get us here by putting yourself into their Skipper's head. We already know this guy's no dummy. It's a virtual certainty that he has a pretty good idea how his boat got so messed up. He may have trouble believing it, but when he has worked through all the other possibilities, and discarded the ones that are not realistic, what do you think he has left?" The Skipper smiled at me. "What do you think, Mac?"

"When you put it that way, Skipper," I said, "I guess the answer is – if not obvious – then at least in front of your nose. Had to be divers down there. No way they were friendlies. Their only possible purpose would be the missile splashdown, 'cause the cable tap is not even in the radar room, let alone on the screen."

The Skipper nodded.

"So he knows the Yanks are here with lockout capability."

The Skipper continued to nod.

"And we made an ass out of him."

The Skipper's face broke out in a grin as he exhaled pungent smoke.

"So he puts himself in our place without knowing any of the details, but with a general scope of the problem in his mind. He's got to figure we're carrying whatever we took externally on the hull...that means we're speed limited. He can't ignore our intercepted message about heading toward Japan either, but he's one wily sonofabitch." I was starting to enjoy myself. "He gets on a visual conference with his two Kashin buddies and they get themselves placed right where he would cross the Kurils if he were you." I spread my hands and grinned at the Skipper. "So we get here, only to find them waiting. Does that mean he outsmarted us, Skipper?"

"Not really, Mac, it just means we didn't outsmart him."

I certainly could see his reasoning. The bottom line, however, was that two modern *Kashin-class* destroyers and an ancient World War II conventional sub with a world-class skipper were between us and our ticket home. What we had going for us was the storm, and we had at least a day or so of cover left before it passed.

The *Ognevoy's* towed array wasn't worth squat in this weather, and neither *Ognevoy* nor *Odarenny* had hull-mounted sonar that could detect us in this shit. But *Ognevoy* also had a bird with dipping sonar and sonobuoys. If the bird was able to fly in this weather, they could possibly locate us, but there was no certainty.

The *Whiskey*, on the other hand, had several hours of submerged operational capability. Sonar had just determined that they were snorkeling, which meant that they probably had a full battery charge. In this weather the *Whiskey* and the *Ognevoy's* bird would be unlikely to carry out any meaningful coordination of effort – they simply could not speak with one another. In calm water, yeah, maybe, but not in this shit.

So we were faced with a mad-as-hell *Whiskey* and a dipping bird on independent patrol, with a limited *Kashin* in reserve for when the weather abated. Which meant we needed to sneak through before that happened. The Skipper checked the charts, noting that a fairly deep channel cut through the southern half of Krusenstern Strait. We had three advantages: we could operate at more than twice the maximum depth of the *Whiskey*, we didn't need to surface, and we were way quieter.

Having said that, however, our restricted speed was killing us. If any one of them got a bead on us, we would be very challenged to escape the noose. So our job – my job at that moment – was to avoid that fatal bead in the first place.

The Skipper motioned me over to the chart table where he and Larry had been conferring. Larry had laid out a path that followed the deep channel, hugging the north side, leading out into the Pacific in a northeasterly direction.

"So long as the storm gives us cover," the Skipper said, "we'll use the nuke plant to save the battery. As soon as it quiets up above, however, switch to battery power and set ultra-quiet." He looked at me directly.

"Don't wait for my permission. The moment you believe the time is right, make the switch. You have depth and course discretion to keep away from these guys. Stay out of their detection circle no matter what."

I understood his implications. This was not a game. No one knew where we were. If they could sink us before we reached deep open ocean, even our SOSUS network might not have a bead on us. Ivan did not understand how we were able to track him nearly everywhere in the ocean, but he was fairly certain we could. He knew about our SOSUS network, but had no idea how we were able to accomplish such tracking. Bottom line, we really needed to get past these three opponents with alacrity and stealth, or we might not make it home at all.

The Skipper picked up the 1MC mike. "Weaps to the Conn."

Shortly, Josh arrived in Control. The Skipper briefed him on our current situation and then asked, "Is the decoy still in number one tube?"

"Yes Sir – charged and ready to launch."

"Okay. The other three tubes are loaded with Mark thirty-sevens, right?"

"Yes Sir."

Halibut had four torpedo tubes in the Bow Compartment and two in the After Compartment. The two aft tubes, however, had been deactivated when she was converted to her present configuration.

"Good. Set up two, three and four to swim out on very short notice."

There are, basically, two ways to launch a torpedo. The traditional way is to thrust the fish into the water with an impulse of water from the WRT or water round torpedo tank. It is immediate, and allows for quick re-loading of the tube. It's also noisy. There is no mistaking an impulse torpedo launch. The other guy can't miss it. Swimming a fish out, on the other hand, takes longer, but is stealthy. The first time the other guy hears the fish is about the time it's ready to sink him. I didn't know what the Skipper had in mind, but I sure was interested to see where we were going with this setup.

"Sonar, Conn," I said over the intercom, "bearings to the contacts."

"Kilo-one bears one-five-five; he appears to be stationkeeping at about ten miles. Kilo-two bears one-six-five, and also appears to be stationkeeping in synch with Kilo-one. Kilo-three bears one-three-five; he's on a northwesterly course, about ten miles out."

"Conn, Aye," I answered, building a picture in my head of the three-dimensional space we were sharing with these three bad asses.

The basin behind us in the Sea of Okhotsk dropped to several thousand feet, but shallowed up approaching Tschirinkotan to less than six-hundred feet through Krusenstern Strait, except for the channel we were following. It formed sort of a curved slash that cut across the strait, dropping down to over two thousand feet. I was hugging the north wall of this canyon at a depth of about 900 feet, about a thousand yards off the canyon wall. Although I couldn't see it, of course, I could tell from the bathymetric chart that the wall approached near vertical on the north side. We couldn't find ourselves down here. Ivan had no chance at all.

The trench ran for several miles before it petered out, spilling generally into the continental slope to the east of the Kurils, where the entire bottom dropped precipitously to a depth of over 12,000 feet. The *Kashins* were bobbing on the surface about ten miles southeast of the strait, about where the continental slope began its plunge. The *Whiskey* was to the northeast of the two destroyers over deeper water, but squeezed into a relatively thin surface layer that extended down to a bit over 500 feet – just twice its length. It was useless on or near the surface, and could not go deep enough to get below the layer out here. I was certain that the *Whiskey* had his ears extended in our direction, straining to pick up any sound we might make. By the *Whiskey* Skipper's reckoning, right now was about the time we should be making our appearance, IF he was right, IF he had correctly deduced our intentions.

What he didn't know, of course, was that he was dead on.

To complete the picture, our operating layer was about twice the thickness of the *Whiskey's* layer. We really didn't want to go much deeper than a thousand feet, and, in fact, normally did not exceed 900 feet – somewhat less than three times our length. So in practical terms, we had more relative wiggle room in our layer, and the distinct advantage of being able to remain below the thermocline. This fact alone effectively shielded us from the active sonar both *Kashins* would deploy as soon as the storm abated.

The *Whiskey* skipper seemed to understand this situation completely. It was like a Bridge hand; the dummy is exposed to everyone, but there is nothing you can do about it except make the best play. That was where we were, with one big and important exception. They couldn't see our hand. They knew we were there – probably, but didn't know for certain, and had no idea of our actual position. Even there, however, the cagy Soviet submarine skipper would continue to psych out our Skipper's mind and anticipate his next move – which meant that he probably was even now figuring that we were somewhere in the trench, since the numbers worked out that way.

I checked the chart to see how this worked out, and – sure enough – from his present position on his current course, the *Whiskey* was set to intersect with our exit path projected out to the continental shelf edge.

Smart!

The Skipper stayed close to Control, ready to jump in the moment anything cut loose.

"Conn, Sonar, Kilo-three has dramatically changed his aspect. I think he turned radically to his left. I think we have nearly a bow-on aspect."

The Skipper looked up and went to the chart table. I joined him. He was tracing the *Whiskey's* apparent new course, assuming King was right and we had a bow-on aspect.

"Reverse course, Mac," he said, "and go to ultra-quiet on the battery. Move another five-hundred yards toward the trench wall. Get close, but watch yourself. Once you are in position, reduce your speed to bare steerageway; and set the thrusters for immediate activation. Get ready to make us heavy fast."

"Aye, Skipper," I said as I set to the assigned task.

"Sonar, Conn," I said over the sound-powered phone as we settled into ultra-quiet, "did he detect us?"

"Probably not, Conn. We're outside his detection range."

"He's playing a hunch, Mac," the Skipper said. Then he picked up the handset. "Weaps, set the decoy to turn right ninety degrees on launch, five degree up-angle, maximum noise two seconds after launch. Set number two Mark thirty-seven to turn sharp right as soon as it clears the tube, five degree up-angle, and force-arm it at five-hundred feet." The Skipper was telling Weaps to force the torpedo to arm itself at 500 feet. "Set number three the same, except make it turn sharp left. Make absolutely certain the one-eighty cutoff is activated." The Skipper was referring to a safety mechanism that automatically opens the torpedo arming circuit should the fish reverse its course and acquire the firing submarine. It's not cool to be sunk by your own torpedo. "One more, Weaps. Set number four to run straight, five-degree up-angle, same arming sequence. Open the outer doors on all tubes. Let me know as soon as you're ready."

Five minutes later Josh called to say that the Torpedo Room was ready.

"Where are we, Mac?" the Skipper asked.

"About five-hundred yards from the wall to starboard, nine-hundred feet deep, stern to the *Whiskey*, making bare steerageway," I answered.

The Skipper picked up the handset. "Where's the *Whiskey* now, Sonar?"

"Dead astern, coming toward us at twelve knots, at four, maybe five-hundred feet deep, three miles back." King paused. "No way he can hear us, Cap'n, he's deaf and blind at this speed."

"He'll be on us in fifteen minutes at his present speed," I said needlessly to the Skipper.

He nodded. "That won't last."

Five minutes later the sound-powered phone chirped. I picked up the handset. "Conn, Sonar, Kilo-three has slowed way down. He's closer than we thought; 'bout a mile away now, and he's got his ears on."

I acknowledged, and informed the Skipper. Just then a loud screeching sound filled the sub, and the lights dimmed. The Skipper was on the phone instantly and urgently. He grunted a couple of times as the lights came back to full brightness.

"Conn, Sonar!" King was urgently on the intercom, despite being at ultra-quiet. "The *Whiskey* just launched a torpedo! It's running hot and true – eight-hundred yards out! I think it acquired us!"

The Skipper grabbed the 1MC mike: "This is the Captain. Stand by the decoy!" He put down the mike and announced to the Control Room, "I have the Conn. Stand-by thrusters."

And to Sonar: "Distance to incoming?"

"Four-hundred yards, Sir!"

"Count it down, Sonar!"

The Skipper held a stopwatch in his hand, watching it closely.

"Three-fifty...twenty...three..."

The Skipper waited several more seconds and then ordered over the 1MC: "Launch decoy!"

The number one tube cycled as the WRT released its pressurized load. The decoy burst forth, turned right, and headed on its upward slope.

"Right full rudder," the Skipper ordered. "Forward port thruster full; aft starboard thruster full. Take her down to eleven-hundred feet fast – zero bubble!"

Two seconds later the decoy's chattering noise was clearly audible right through the hull. The Skipper held up the stopwatch as...

"Two-fifty..."

"Sound the collision alarm!"

A high-pitched, shrill, slow warble filled the sub as every man not lying down grabbed the nearest firm object for support. As the *Halibut* twisted to the right, the Skipper held up his right hand with the 1MC mike while holding out his left with the stopwatch, his eyes fixed on the heading indicator. He stopped the turn when we were pointed directly at the wall.

"Conn, Sonar, two-hundred fifty yards. It's accelerating on its final approach...two-hundred yards...hold it, Conn, the fish is changing its heading to the right..."

"Passing one-thousand feet," Chris interjected.

The Skipper held up his hand again, and then slowly lowered it. As his hand reached horizontal Sonar announced, "Conn, Sonar, the fish disappeared – it's gone, sir, nothing at all. The decoy's gone too. They both just disappeared."

"Fire Control, shoot four," the Skipper ordered, and punched his stopwatch again.

Although there was no sound, I knew the fish was underway. I ran a quick calculation in my mind. We were less than 500 yards from the wall. The fish swam out with a slight up-angle. It would be at forty knots almost immediately, which meant it was fifteen seconds or less from the wall.

A long, pregnant pause ensued. It seemed to last forever. At the fifteen-second mark, the Skipper slowly dropped his hand, and suddenly the sub was rocked by a huge explosion. The lights blinked as the shockwave passed us from in front and above. The entire submarine shuddered with a lurching, bounce that felt like an elevator suddenly starting down. Loose items like pencils and cups bounced, some falling to the deck, the cups shattering. Unlike submarine movies, however, where streams of water from ruptured pipes inevitably follow nearby explosions, in our real world the lights blinked, the ship rocked, and that was it.

"Absolute silence, Mac," the Skipper said. "Get the word out, if you're not doing something specific and necessary, get in your rack."

I gave the order to the Chief of the Watch, and in seconds he had transmitted it silently throughout the entire sub.

"Find out what happened in the engineering spaces," the Skipper ordered, "but do it silently." He paused. "Not a sound, Mac, not a sound."

I got the point. The Skipper had just pulled off one of the greatest cons in the history of submarining. We were snuggled in close to the trench wall. Whatever had happened back aft had caused the Soviet Skipper to pull his hair trigger – to launch an active fish. At just the right moment our Skipper had launched a noise-making decoy toward the wall, angled upward, and simultaneously dropped us as deep as possible, but in complete silence. The Soviet torpedo picked up the decoy behind us and turned toward it, forgetting about us. Either its tracking electronics went haywire, or its proximity fuse malfunctioned, but apparently both our decoy and their torpedo smacked into the wall, and that was it. No explosion.

This is where our Skipper's brilliance came into play. He didn't count on their torpedo exploding. It was an old *Whiskey*. He figured their armament was at least as old, and thus unreliable. Good for us if it exploded – they would think they got us. But if it didn't, they would simply launch another fish, putting us right back in the same situation again, but less ready to deal with it, because we had already expended the decoy and didn't have another ready to launch. Just in case their ancient torpedo didn't detonate, therefore, the Skipper had set up three alternatives so that no matter what our orientation to the wall, he could run one of our own fish on a short fuse into the wall, where it would explode, giving the Soviet skipper the assurance that he had gotten us.

Like I said, it was a great con.

The event that initiated everything turned out to be a combination of a faulty automatic switch and a propeller shaft brake that worked too well. An automatic switch activated unexpectedly, supplying a lot of power to the electric drive, but the shaft was stopped with a mechanical brake that gripped the shaft like a vice. The screeching was the sound of the shaft under power trying to turn against the vise-like grip of the shaft brake. The damage was local, and Dirk's guys would be able to repair it while we were underway on the plant. In the meantime, we were limited to one screw, which cut our speed down to just over four knots.

Besides, the Skipper wanted to hang around here for at least a day, while Ivan pulled back his hounds, shut down his ears, and went home.

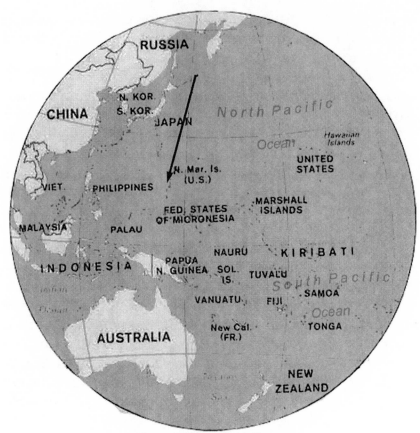

Sea of Okhotsk to Guam

CHAPTER TWENTY-FIVE

Twenty-one-hundred-fifty miles of open ocean lay between us and Guam. There was little chance we would have company, but the Skipper wasn't taking any chances.

The day following our close encounter with the Soviets, we crept silently out of the trench, hugging the north wall and then the bottom until the bottom dropped out from under us as it disappeared into the abyssal deep. The Skipper had Sonar on six-hour port-and-starboard watches. Every piece of sonar equipment was continuously manned, our ears stretched to their maximum. Most of the crew was convinced that we had fooled the wily Soviet submariner, but some of us had reservations.

I, for one, was especially suspicious. The *Whiskey* didn't hang around at all. Instead, he hightailed it north toward Petropavlovsk. The way I figured it, he knew he had a clear speed advantage over us, and he was reasonably sure we were headed for Guam. He could top off his fuel and food, and get out ahead of us before we had covered more than 200 miles.

"Look at it like this," I said to the Skipper, as we set a great circle course for Guam, "he figures us for one-hundred-fifty miles a day at best." I pointed to a spot on the chart where our track intersected the edge of the continental shelf. "He's good for three hundred miles a day at least." I used a pair of dividers to walk 300-mile increments from our encounter datum north to Petropavlovsk, and from there back in our general direction. It was a total of about five days, including a half-day for provisioning. We had traveled about a hundred miles, and were two days out of the confrontation.

"I think the *Whiskey* is refueling right now. In about twelve hours he gets underway," I drew my finger along a path from Petropavlovsk to intersect our projected track ten days out, "to meet us here, five days or so from Guam – in the middle of goddamn nowhere."

The Skipper thought about my analysis for a bit. "So, what do you recommend, Mac?"

That was the conundrum, of course. If we could reach the Northern Mariana Islands before he got there, we could lose ourselves in the island chain, and there was no way he could find us. I measured our distance to the Northern Mariana Islands.

"We've got seven to eight days till we reach safe haven," I said, "on this course, anyway." I slid my finger over to the chain of islands that extended, basically from the southern part of Japan in a curving arc to Guam. It was bordered on the Pacific side by a deep ocean trench, called by various names, depending on where you were, but best known for the Challenger Deep in the Marianas

Trench – the deepest spot on earth, 35,800 feet or 6.8 miles. "What if we headed a bit more south to here?" pointing at the middle of the chain.

"That's still six to seven days," the Skipper answered, "with no guarantees." He looked at me for a few seconds. "What if he thinks that's what we'll do?" he asked.

I thought about it – it was complicated. The Russkie was in the Skipper's head, anticipating what the Skipper would do. But the Skipper knew he was trying to anticipate him, and he was acting with that knowledge, which meant that the Russian would have to take the Skipper's knowledge into account, but the Skipper knew that as well...it was like diving into a fractal diagram. The deeper you go, the more complex it gets.

"We've used island cover at every opportunity," the Skipper mused. "It's our modus operandus. It's what we always do. It's what he'll expect." He stabbed Guam with his pencil. "So this time we'll make a straight run for it. Nav, set a course directly for Guam – shortest route." He turned and left for his stateroom.

#

Two days later I had the watch, balls to the wall at 700 feet – all of six point three knots. Our ears were stretched to their theoretical limit, but we had relaxed back to a three-section sonar watch, much to the Sonar Techs' relief. It was definitely back to boring.

If the Skipper was right, the *Whiskey* would be crossing our path in the next few hours as he headed toward the center of the island arc. He couldn't afford to slow to listen, because he had a lot of ocean to cover. Besides, if he was right, he was in our baffles, coming up on us from astern. We might not even hear him before he nailed us.

There were a lot of ifs...on both sides.

Following the watch, I went back to see how the divers were doing. When we departed the missile splash zone, Ham and I commenced the decompression. It's even more boring than a long, deep transit. It's a slow gradual ascent that takes a relatively focused concentration by the console watch, but nothing spectacular. By now the guys were two-thirds of the way to the surface – at about two-hundred feet.

I relieved Ham for a couple of hours so he could re-fresh himself and take a nap. The divers were in a sleep cycle – actually, Ski was on watch, but the other guys were sound asleep. I let Ski know I was on duty outside.

"Hi ya, El-Tee, heard you been having some fun driv-ing this old tub around. Tangled with Ivan too, I hear." He paused. "So did I, ya know."

His voice sounded strange through the descrambler.

I stayed close while he read and the others slept. How remarkable, I thought, that we were limping along 700 feet below the ocean's surface while my guys were resting peacefully only two-hundred feet down, a full five-hundred feet shallower than we were. And some-where out there a Soviet *Whiskey* was rushing pell-mell toward a date with destiny – or not.

I chuckled as I settled in for another hour of watch.

#

Nothing happened for the next few hours. The divers got closer to the surface, we moved closer to Guam, and the *Whiskey*...the *Whiskey* was the *Whiskey*.

I had just come on watch again with my regular crew. The guys knew me and probably had set up some interesting drills for the late night hours. We settled in, I was on my second cup of coffee, when Sonar announced, "Conn, Sonar, I have a contact bearing three-four-zero, designate Foxtrot-one."

I acknowledged, and then Sonar informed me that Foxtrot-one was doing fifteen knots – at periscope depth. What were the odds?

"Conn, Sonar, Foxtrot-one is on a course of two-two-zero."

I walked over to check the chart. This took the cake: a submerged, snorkeling submarine doing fifteen knots on a course of two-two-zero – right for the middle of the island chain, right where we would be had the Skipper taken that option. That got me to thinking. What if the Soviet skipper had made his decision, but was not 100 percent convinced it was the right decision? His ability to do simple arithmetic was as good as ours. If he was right, we were somewhere ahead of him; but if he was wrong, then we were just about where we actually were right then. I thought about that a bit, and then I did four things.

First, I ordered all stop, and called Maneuvering to shut down the turbine generators, and shift us to battery power. Then I awakened the Skipper to tell him what I was doing, and sounded General Quarters, let the boing-boing-boing sound for only fifteen seconds, and finally shut the ship down to ultra quiet.

As the Skipper came into Control, Sonar announced that Foxtrot-one had slowed dramatically and shut down his snorkeling operation. We were at 700 feet, coasting silently, listening carefully.

I briefed the Skipper completely, and as I finished, Sonar notified me that the Submarine definitely was our old friend, the Soviet *Whiskey* – and he had shut down completely.

"It's his version of the Crazy Ivan," I told the Skipper. He looked at me sharply.

"You may have something there, Mac," he said, and walked into Sonar. I followed, but stayed at the door, so I could keep an eye on Control.

We waited five minutes...another five... No sound... nothing at all. A half hour...still nothing...

And then, finally, Sonar said, "Conn, Sonar, the *Whiskey's* starting up..."

And that simple announcement put an end to the pent-up tension.

"Run on the battery for a couple of hours," the Skipper told me. "Let's make sure he isn't up to one of his tricks again."

#

Two hours later, I ordered Maneuvering to start up the turbines, and I shifted propulsion to the main plant. I remained at 700 feet and kicked her all the way up to six and a half knots as we continued on our course toward Guam. In another ten days or so the *Whiskey* skipper would come to grips with his miscalculation. For the time being, we really didn't care what he would do then. We would be safely tied to the dock surrounded by the might and power of the United States, and – as the southern lady once said, "Tomorrow is another day."

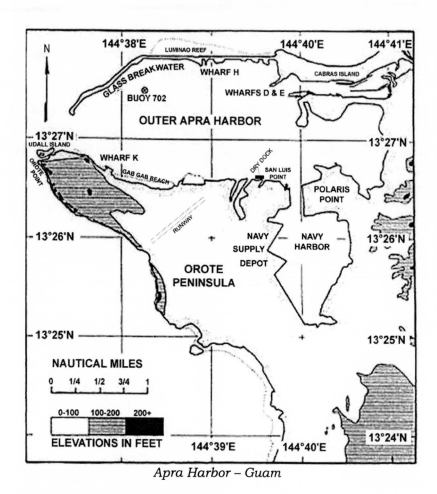

Apra Harbor – Guam

CHAPTER TWENTY-SIX

Apra Harbor is a beautiful natural harbor located midway on the west side of the Island of Guam. To the south it is protected by Orote Point Peninsula, and to the north by an arching reef extending out from Cabras Island three miles to the northeast and by an extended breakwater just inside and south of the reef. At the western tip of the peninsula, the bluffs of Udall Island guard the harbor entrance. About three miles due east from the entrance lies Polaris Point. It forms a narrow north-south channel with the backside of Orote Point Peninsula, the entrance to Navy Harbor. The west side of mile-wide, one-and-a-half mile long Navy Harbor is lined with Naval Supply Depot wharfs.

Right at the entrance to Navy Harbor at the north end of the Navy Supply Depot is San Luis Point, cut by two short inlets on either side of a protected small boat harbor. Immediately to the west of the easternmost cut, a wide wharf juts into the harbor, connecting to a 622 foot long, 124 foot wide blue-gray box-like structure with high slab sides. Emblazoned high on one end, the words *USS Richland AFDM-8* identify the vessel as a floating dry dock ship repair facility. She is run by four officers and 146 enlisted specialists who have the capability of repairing any navy vessel, but who specialize in nuclear submarines.

We timed our arrival at Apra Harbor for dawn, the sun rising ahead of us in a clear sky over the low hills behind the harbor. The Skipper and I were on the bridge with lookouts Skidmore and Roscoe as we sailed past Udall Island, towering above us a scant half-mile to the south. Outside Glass Breakwater, which the Skipper told me was named after Captain Henry Glass, who liberated Guam from the Spanish in 1898 during the Spanish-American War, a rolling swell lifted us by the stern and pushed us forward as the swell passed. Each successive swell caused *Halibut* to rock fore and aft like a giant rocking horse. I suspected some of the guys below were getting seasick. Frankly, I was glad to be on the bridge.

As we sailed through the harbor entrance past the breakwater, the swell diminished and then disappeared. We passed a cruiser docked along Wharf K to the south, and could see some type of supply ship tied off at Buoy 702 to the north just inside the breakwater – probably awaiting room to moor alongside the Supply Depot wharfs inside Navy Harbor. The white sand of Gab Gab Beach sparkled in the morning sun along the north side of Orote Peninsula as we sailed past slowly. Gray-sided

Richland loomed ahead of us on the right, sinking into the water as we approached.

We slowed to just bare steerageway, and a navy tug approached us. I called below for the Deck Gang, and in less than a minute Joe Thornton and his guys appeared topside wearing bright orange life vests. A couple of monkey fists flew through the air, and a minute later the tug was firmly lashed alongside our port quarter.

"We're ready to go, Sir," Joe called up.

"Take her right to the entry, Mac," the Skipper said. "Don't rely on the tug. Keep control at all times with the thrusters. Park her at the entrance and let the line handlers and the capstans on *Richland* do their job."

"Aye, Skipper."

We were doing all of one-half to one knot as I adjusted our heading with the forward thruster. I communicated with the tug by Handi-Talki, the ubiquitous hand-held radios used throughout the Navy. I told him to bring me to about twenty yards from the dry dock, and then to hold me until I told him differently. The tug operator acknowledged as we pulled into position, and sailors on both of *Richland's* walls hurled messenger lines across our bow from both sides.

Joe's guys quickly hauled two hawsers from each dry dock wall and dropped the loops over the sub's deck cleats. Under the watchful eye of the *Richland's* First Lieutenant, Chief Warrant Officer Tommie Bridger, sailors on both dry dock walls wrapped the hawsers from *Halibut* around large capstans, and carefully, slowly hauled the submarine between the walls into the sunken dry dock. On signals from their First Lieutenant, the *Richland* sailors eased off or tightened their hawsers on the capstans to keep *Halibut* perfectly centered.

As our bow entered the dry dock, I officially turned over control of the submarine to Bridger. Should something go wrong now, it was their fault, not ours. As the second set of messengers crossed our deck, and the hawsers dropped over the cleats by the sail, I released the tug.

Thirty minutes later, *Halibut* was firmly moored, centered between the walls, with her stern and rudder just inside the floating dry dock, engines shut down, nuclear power plant secured, silently waiting for the next step.

A group of men in civvies stood in a small cluster across from our sail. They had arrived a day earlier from NSA headquarters at Fort Meade, Maryland. They waited in silence. They would board when the gangway was put over the gap separating the wall from our deck, but that wouldn't happen until we were solidly settled on the blocks and the dock was raised, exposing the sub for servicing. And that wouldn't happen until the *Richland* crew had moved the sub to the back of the dry dock, over the wooden keel blocks waiting for us. And none of this would happen until my guys had safely and surreptitiously dropped the treasures still held snuggly against our belly.

#

Since this dive would not involve saturation, or even decompression, for that matter, I decided to dive with the guys. Getting ready for the dive was simplicity itself. The water was so warm that we would not need temperature protection. Mask, tank and regulator, fins, a tool satchel, and the ever-present diver's knife – that was all we needed; oh yes, and gloves, to keep from getting cut on the sharp edges.

Water entry was basic diving 101. Stand on the forecastle fully dressed for the dive, put regulator in mouth, hold mask and regulator against face with left hand (or right), and jump. Which is exactly what we did.

I hung back, letting the guys do their thing. They had been there before, of course, so I didn't want to get in the way. It took them little more than a half-hour to lower the net entirely. Once it was flat on the dry dock deck, I swam over to examine the haul. Actually looking at the

Russian missile parts was a lot different than watching the operation through the video eyes of the Basketball. I marveled at the haul we had snatched right from under Ivan's nose.

I chuckled. No wonder the *Whiskey* skipper was so pissed.

Together, we pulled a canvas tarp over the haul, so it would be completely concealed from prying eyes when the dry dock was pumped empty. Then we surfaced and I signaled Bridger to move *Halibut* forward to her permanent position.

Bridger's crew had set rolled-up weighted canvas tarps on the dry dock walls at both ends of the *Richland*. They would serve to hide the activity taking place inside the dock from prying eyes once the sub was completely out of the water on large wooden blocks inside the dry dock.

Using a bullhorn, Bridger quickly marshaled his crew, and twenty minutes later the *Halibut* was floating directly over the blocks. Divers from the *Richland* dropped down to monitor how the sub settled onto the blocks as the dry dock was raised to its normal operation float. They communicated directly with Bridger using sound-powered phones hooked to their full facemasks.

We stayed in the water, keeping out of the way of the *Richland* divers. They had their job – we had ours.

The *Richland* rose in fits and starts as Bridger adjusted the sub's position to keep it directly above the blocks. She had only about fifteen feet of clearance, but the fit was exact, and there was no room for error. It took an hour, but suddenly the sub started rising with the dock. We were in the blocks, and rising out of the water.

As we rose out of the warm waters of Apra Harbor, the canvas tarps Bridger had installed at each end of the dry dock stretched downward, completely blocking off the view of the inside of *Richland*, for everyone except an airborne observer almost directly overhead. With *Halibut* firmly sitting on the blocks, the *Richland* crew slid the gangway across the gap and firmly lashed it to the deck and dry dock wall. While we waited for the dry dock to drain completely, a couple of messenger lines flew across the gap between the dry dock walls over the sub. What followed was a lightweight tarp that served two functions, to provide some necessary shade over the deck, and – more importantly – to conceal topside activities from prying eyes.

Halibut maintained her watch routine, modified since the reactor plant was cold, but my guys and I were free to roam the island.

As it turned out, Guam didn't have a Winnie and Moo, or anything like it. It seems the Navy Base commander ran a pretty tight ship. The local city council kept things under control on their end, so it was great for families, but not necessarily for a bunch of sat divers who had just returned from a two-month-plus deployment.

We decided to visit the sights, which meant a mandatory visit to Talofofo Falls, nearly due east on the other side of the island from Apra Harbor. It wasn't Niagara, but given the size of Guam, the falls were pretty spectacular.

While we were there, one of the locals initiated a conversation with Ski. Next thing we knew, over a couple of beers he was telling us about this Japanese soldier who had been hiding out in these hills for 28 years.

"No shit," Ski said. "Twenty-eight years out here?" He pointed over the falls, "Up there...and nobody ever saw him?"

"'Sa fact," our new friend told us. "Me an' other fisherman was upstream when saw dis guy gone total native, if ya ken what I mean." He grinned and took a gulp of beer. "His clothes was, ya know, made of palm fronds 'n other stuff. Look like crazy man." He took another gulp of beer.

My guys said nothing, too astonished to do anything but listen.

" Jan'ry tweny-four, seveny-two," he said. "Name a Corporal Shoichi Yokoi. We chase him down. He live in a cave he dug during the war. Been livin' out here ever since."

"No shit," Ski managed to say, and that just about said it all.

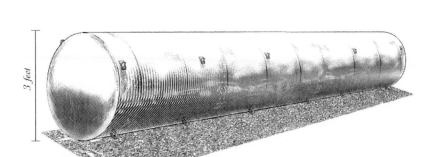

The 12,000 pound Pod

CHAPTER TWENTY-SEVEN

The Skipper had made it perfectly clear that he wasn't going out again without the ability to put *Halibut* firmly on the bottom. No more hanging off mushroom anchors at the mercy of the weather, he had insisted.

I couldn't have agreed more, and Ham was with me a hundred percent. We participated in several meetings that created the skids that finally got installed on our belly – all four of them, two under the bow and two by the stern. They were designed with a flat, broad bottom, a bit like skis. They extended out at a bit of an angle, and sufficiently far to hold the keel off the bottom. Initially, there was a question about the skid's effect on our speed and stealth, but the Skipper quashed that with one – the Can absolutely limited our speed, and two – *Halibut* wasn't known as a particularly stealthy sub anyway.

Installing them was a bit of an operation. The sub was blocked sufficiently high off the dry dock deck to install them, but they could not just be welded to the outer hull. The main problem was that the *Halibut* was encased in saddle ballast tanks with skin that was little more than tin-can thick. The skids had to penetrate to the pressure hull, but they couldn't just be welded to the pressure hull either. The entire weight of the bottomed submarine had to be distributed evenly along a series of distribution matrices, and then down to the skids. It seems the engineering boys had already worked it out, and the skids had arrived a couple of days before we did.

Installing them involved opening the saddle tank skin – peeling it back, so to speak – and then welding the skid matrices to the hull. Finally, the skin was put back, and the penetrations were welded shut against the skid struts connecting to the skid surfaces. The *Halibut* now looked like nothing so much as a big black sausage on Santa's sleigh.

While the skids were being installed, an Air Force transport arrived directly from Washington, D.C., landing on the Navy runway a half-mile to the west on the peninsula. It carried a special package – a twenty-foot-long, three-foot-wide pod recorder. At twelve thousand pounds, this was no little thing. Somehow we had to secure it to the sub, carry it back to the Okhotsk cable, and install it.

The first pod had weighed just a few pounds; this one, on the other hand, was a monster, and somehow, my guys would have to extract it from the sub, float it into position, and secure the cable to the pod. No matter how hard I tried, I simply couldn't see it as a piece of cake.

The first pod was a one-lift-bag-package – this one… my God, this one would need a specially designed lift system just to move it around on the bottom.

Definitely time for another meeting.

I had Ham assemble the guys in the Wardroom, and brought the Spook team in for good measure. We needed to be sure we had a system in place before we departed Guam. There was absolutely no way we would be able to improvise something on the bottom of the Sea of Okhotsk.

By the time everyone was assembled, we had a full house in the Wardroom. With the ship's officers, several of the senior chiefs, the senior members of the Spook group, and all my guys, there was barely standing room.

Once everyone had settled down, the Skipper entered with a guy in a suit carrying a paper roll. I guess no one told him that Guam was near the equator – short sleeves, and even short pants – were more in order than a shirt, tie, and jacket. We had the AC cranked up in the sub, so at least here the DC spook was comfortable.

"Gentlemen," the Skipper said without fanfare, "this is Richard Jenkins from NSA. He brought the pod with him that you all have seen being lowered to the dry dock deck." The Skipper nodded at Jenkins. "Mr. Jenkins..."

Jenkins wasted no time with preliminaries. He unrolled a large drawing and taped it to the bulkhead behind him. He retrieved an extensible pointer from his inner pocket and extended it fully, pointing to the picture of the pod. "This," he said, "is the pod."

Jenkins then explained in detail how NSA had developed the pod. The initial concept, he explained, was to make a pod that could be carried inside the sub and deployed on site. This turned out, however, not to be possible. When you took the required redundancies into account so that the pod could operate unattended for months at a time, added a power source, and made it sufficiently robust and heavy to stay in place at 600 feet, no matter the weather above, what you got was something too big to carry inside *Halibut*.

We still had the webbing we had used to bring back the missile nosecone parts, and would use that rig to hold the larger pod tightly against our keel during the transit.

I knew my guys were itching to find out how they would move the pod from the sub to the cable. I was prepared to ask the right questions, but Jenkins addressed the subject without prompting.

"You divers," he said, addressing the group since he didn't know who was a diver, "normally use air-filled lift bags to support underwater loads. Our engineers have designed special bags that will be filled with helium, giving significant extra lift. They are outfitted with adjustable automatic regulators to maintain a specified height over bottom."

He went on to explain, with the help of an illustration, that each bag came with its own helium supply good for three bag fills. He went into the problem a bit further. Seawater weighs about 64 pounds per cubic foot. Since the pod weighed 12,000 pounds, we needed to support 6,000 pounds at each end, which could be done with a bag containing 93 cubic feet of gas. This is the equivalent of a round balloon about six feet in diameter, or a normally-shaped lift bag about ten feet high.

Jenkins showed an illustration of the twenty-foot long pod suspended by bags at each end that stretched up some twenty feet above the pod, inflated to about the length of the divers swimming alongside the pod.

"Should something go wrong," Jenkins said, "the bags are designed to dump gas quickly to stop an ascent to the surface. The rate of dump is also controlled to prevent the pod from crashing to the sea floor." He paused, anticipating the obvious question. "We tested the mechanisms in every conceivable scenario. They worked flawlessly."

I interrupted the presentation. "Mr. Jenkins, who did these tests, and where were they carried out?"

"The initial testing was done at the Bethesda weapons test tank," he answered.

I knew the tank. It was 100 feet deep and about forty feet wide – sufficient for preliminary testing, but not deep enough to test the system under operational conditions. I told him so.

"You're, correct," Jenkins said. "We shipped a unit to San Diego and tested it from the *Elk River*, using the

open-water training dive for the current class of saturation divers. They worked in six-hundred feet of water
off Point Loma." Jenkins smiled with satisfaction. "They
tried everything, but they couldn't break it."

"Bet we can," Ski muttered under his breath.

Ham glowered at him.

"Did you work with any surface wave action?" I asked
Jenkins, adding, "We experienced twenty-foot waves
while emplacing the first pod."

Jenkins whistled. "Not really," he said candidly. We
chose a mild weather day."

"Those twenty-foot waves," the Skipper said pointedly to Jenkins, "snapped one of my anchor cables.
We're talking about significant vertical surge, even at
six-hundred feet." He paused to let that information sink
in. "Can your automatic system accommodate a vertical
surge of fifteen feet without initiating abort procedures?"

"I don't know," Jenkins said. "We never tested for
that."

The Skipper looked at me. "Mac...?"

I thought while the rest of the room stayed quiet. As
I pictured the situation in my mind I had a glimmering
of an idea.

"The problem is," I said, "that if a deep surge gets
picked up by the sensors, as the bag rises and expands,
the sensor dumps gas. The bag descends, and the sensor
puts more gas in the bag, and before you know it, all
the gas is gone and the pod is stranded on the bottom."
I paused. "The trick is to keep the pod near the bottom
in the first place."

I stood up and approached the drawing with a pencil. I drew a large weight on the bottom under the pod,
and attached it to the center of the pod with a line. "Add
this weight," I said, "and adjust the bag lifts to compensate for the extra weight. Keep the weight inches off the
bottom. Keep the pod oriented in the direction of wave
motion, and adjust the sensitivity of the sensor to the

probable vertical surge. If one end of the pod lifts, the mechanism will dump gas, setting the weight on the bottom. My guys will then manually adjust the gas fills to level the pod and keep it in position until the surge cycle passes."

Jenkins looked at my scribbled modification to his professionally produced illustration. "It might work," he said after several seconds of silence. "It just might work."

"Does anyone else have something to add?" the Skipper asked.

No one spoke up.

"Okay, that's it then." The Skipper stood up and left the Wardroom.

The rest of us milled around for a few minutes, looking at the drawing and talking about the incredible speed with which NSA came up with the pod, and their significant lapse in failing to test under bad weather conditions. My personal take was simple. They had limited time, and something got left out. We discovered it, and seemed to have a working solution. Implement it and move on. I explained my position to Ham, and he concurred.

"We'll set it free," he said, "and keep it under control. We shut that *Whiskey* down. A twelve-thousand-pound sausage will be a piece of cake!"

#

Along with the pod from NSA, SubDevGru sent another umbilical. Not that we expected to use another in the manner of the first that we expended with the *Whiskey*, but I didn't want to be out there without a backup. They also sent us several spare oxygen and helium tanks, and a fresh set of CO_2 absorbent cartridges for our rigs.

We spent the next day stowing the gas and equipment, and running a complete check on the system. Not that we thought anything was wrong, but there were no repair facilities in the Sea of Okhotsk.

The following day the entire crew pitched in loading oxygen candles. As I mentioned earlier, *Halibut* was one of the first generation nukes. All the current models make oxygen by distilling seawater and then electrolyzing the fresh water to produce oxygen. We did it the old fashioned way – with oxygen candles. These are canisters containing a mixture of sodium chlorate and iron pellets. When they are ignited, they produce about 150 man-hours of oxygen each. Do the math. If we're submerged for three months with a crew of 150 men, we need about 240 thousand man-hours of oxygen. That's 2,400 canisters. That's just under thirty candles per day. To be safe, we load out at that number – thirty per day. Then, as an added safety measure, we double that, so we actually load around 5,000 fifty-pound canisters. Do the math again. If we load four candles per minute, the task will take about twenty hours.

Actually, we set up two lines, one into the Bat Cave and one into the Engine Room, and we passed a continuous stream of candles down both lines, so that we loaded about fifteen to twenty candles per minute. That still added up to more than four hours of hard work for the entire crew. You gotta love Treadwell, the company that developed the oxygen generator that has replaced oxygen candles in all our submarines.

While we were in dry dock, we got a fresh coat of paint over our entire exterior, and the crew painted out the entire interior, compartment by compartment. That's a total of about two days work, and a couple of days to get rid of the smell inside. While the paint fumes dissipated, we took on stores, loading every kind of fresh food, fruits, vegetables, tubers – we were in the tropics, after all. And frozen goods – you name it, we probably had at least one crew's meal of it, maybe more if Chief Hurst had his way. Cedric had already bribed every source of special food items on the island with some of his remarkable bread. Part of me could hardly wait to get underway again, just to have some of that good stuff.

We also took aboard a couple of extra decoys, and the Skipper had two loaded in the forward tubes, ready to launch at a moment's notice once we were underway. I certainly had no objections – they had saved our asses once already.

All that remained was to attach the pod to our belly, and then to slip out of Apra Harbor. It turned out that the NSA spooks had actually given some thought to this process. The dry dock deck was still dry, and the spooks had already removed the missile parts we had lovingly deposited on the deck just inside the entrance, before we had moved forward to the blocks where we now rested. The sling still lay where we had left it.

Since this was our baby, the entire dive crew was present on the deck, wearing hard hats and steel-toed shoes, looking to Jack for directions. Ham stood to one side making sure nothing went wrong, and I stood up on the wall keeping an eye on the crane operator – one of the sailors from the *Richland*.

I got a thumbs-up from the crane operator, who had hooked into lift lines attached to a four-wheel dolly about four by six feet. I brought my Handi-Talki up. "She's coming down, Ham. You're in charge once the dolly hits the deck."

One of the things I had learned long ago was that one person should always be in charge of any kind of moving operation – and everyone needed to know who that was. No confusion about orders that way.

"Roger that," Ham said, waving at me. He said something to Jack, and got Jack's thumbs-up.

The crane operator knew his stuff, and a minute later, the first dolly was sitting in-line with the center of the sling, just in front of the sling closest to the sub. Thirty seconds later, Ham passed control back to me, and we hooked up the second dolly. It went like clockwork. A minute later the second dolly was at the other end of the sling.

"Ready for the pod, Ham?" I asked on the radio.

"Roger that," Ham answered, walking over to the twenty-foot-long pod resting on the deck below me near the wall.

The crane operator lowered the hook with four lifting straps, and Harry, Jer, Bill, and Ski each grabbed a snap-hook fitted strap and walked over to a corner of the pod, snapping the hook into a lifting eye. Whitey then made the rounds and checked each hook – not because he mistrusted the guys, but because Jack wouldn't let the lift happen until each hook had been checked. Jimmy was holding a guideline attached to the forward end of the pod and Whitey took the guideline at the other end.

On Jack's signal the pod swung up and over, and gently lowered until it rested in the center of the sling. The guys unhooked the straps from the pod and attached them to the four corners of the sling. On Jack's signal, the crane operator lifted the sling with its 12,000-pound load about five feet above the deck.

Harry and Jer rolled the forward dolly under the sling, while Bill and Ski rolled the after dolly into position. Then Jack lowered the sling and pod onto the dollies. While we were doing all this, another crane on the other wall had lowered a small forklift to the deck. Whitey indicated he would drive it, and since no one argued with him, he started it up and drove it around to the outer end of the loaded dollies. Under Jack's eagle eye, Whitey lowered and extended the forks on the truck, and pushed the entire contraption as far under the sub as he could without hitting the sub with the top of the forklift.

Then, while Bill and Ski attached a steel cable to an eye fixture on the front end of the front dolly, Harry and Jer stretched the cable under the sub to the bow where they were met by Whitey on the forklift. They wrapped a bight of the steel cable around the forklift's tow bar, and Whitey pulled the dolly load about half-way. The guys took another bight, and Whitey pulled it the rest of the way.

Using the same ratchet mechanisms they had used at the missile splash site, the guys then ratcheted the sling with its heavy load tightly against the hull. When they were done, Jack looked it over with a professional eye. I joined Ham, and he and I made a final inspection – just to be sure. Then I called up topside with the radio, had the watch inform the Officer of the Deck that we were ready for the Skipper's inspection.

It wasn't that the Skipper didn't trust us, but it just paid to be absolutely sure with something like this. I was only too glad to have the Skipper give our work his official okay – on one hand, to make certain that everything was as it should be, and beyond that, to transfer responsibility to him if anything went wrong. Not that I wouldn't stand up and take my comeuppance, but it never hurt to share the responsibility.

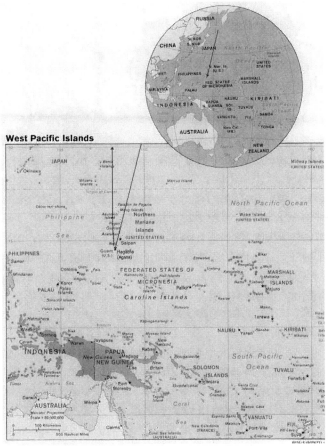

The long trek to and from Guam

CHAPTER TWENTY-EIGHT

One day before our scheduled departure, Dirk and his guys powered up the reactor, running with seawater pumped to the sub through large fire hoses. The rest of the crew settled into an abbreviated fast cruise, wringing out the various ship's systems, and getting themselves back in the groove of regular watch-standing.

Ham and I ran a couple of drills past our guys. Since they had never stepped very far down from their normal operational readiness, the drills were as much for the rest of the crew to see that we were part of the fast cruise as for anything else.

Underway was scheduled for 0100. Sometime before 2300, sailors removed the tarp over our topside, and the crane lifted away the gangway. Promptly at 2300, I joined the Skipper on the Bridge, and with minimum lighting focused onto the dry dock deck, the *Richland* began to submerge. We took it slowly, and a half hour later we were still resting on the blocks, but the water was halfway up our sides. The dry dock stopped flooding while *Richland* divers removed the coolant hoses and made a quick inspection of the hull areas where we had attached the skids. By midnight we were fully afloat, secured to the dry dock walls by four hawsers.

Before we moved out of the dry dock, we spent another thirty minutes running a complete check of our propulsion and power generating systems. Then, with the Skipper watching closely, I ordered shore power removed. At that moment, we became once again our own independent world

In a mirror-image reverse operation of when we arrived, Chief Warrant Officer Bridger pulled us out through the other end of the dry dock, using the capstans to move us and keep us centered. I noticed that he would glance at his watch from time to time as he moved us with deliberate slowness. The tug was standing by, but the Skipper and I had agreed that we would maintain control of our position with the thrusters this time.

Down on our deck, the COB had his guys outfitted with kapok life vests, the kind with the useless little flashlights hooked to them. The team on the afterdeck had already removed the lifelines and stanchions, dropped the cleats, and double-checked the deck openings to make sure they were securely tightened against their rubber seals. They dropped below through the after hatch just as our stern passed the dry dock entrance. The time was exactly 0100.

We didn't sound the ship's whistle as we normally would, because sound carries far over water, and this was a stealthy night departure. Bridger passed control of *Halibut* to the Skipper by radio, and the Skipper turned to me and announced formally, "You have the Deck and the Conn, Mac."

"Aye, aye, Sir," I said, and announced to Control on the comm box, "This is Lieutenant McDowell, I have the Deck and the Conn. Rig for dive, Control. We've got about an hour."

While Thornton's deck crew secured topside forward, I glanced around the sub with my binoculars. We were easing forward alongside the north end of the brightly lit Naval Supply Depot. All I needed to do was let her glide for a couple of minutes, and then ease the bow to port while giving her a little kick in the ass to keep her moving.

"Port back slow, starboard ahead slow" I ordered, while controlling the thrusters myself with the bridge control box, giving the bow an additional sideward vector to port. Once I had a bit of turn momentum, I ordered both screws ahead slow, went to all stop after a half minute, and then eased her forward on a north-by-westerly heading toward the harbor entrance. As I coasted forward, Thornton and his guys made a final topside inspection, and disappeared below.

"Keep a good lookout!" I ordered Skidmore and Roscoe.

They grunted, keeping their binoculars to their eyes, scanning the surface for anything unusual.

The water ahead of me was pitch black, but the lights along the Navy Supply Wharfs in Navy Harbor behind me were brightly lit, and I could clearly see the flashing green buoy marker off the end of Glass Breakwater and the flashing white light marking the end of the breakwater itself. We moved silently through Apra Harbor without navigation lights, and too slowly to leave a wake. The bridge watch of the cruiser tied up to Wharf K probably had no idea we passed within a couple of hundred yards of their position. The red entrance buoy off Udall Island became visible ahead of us to port as we began to feel the Pacific rollers coming in from the west.

It took us a good hour before we had the red and green entrance buoys abeam of our sail. I marked our position with Control, where I was certain that Larry noted the time and location on his chart.

"Right twenty degrees rudder," I ordered, "make your course three-five-zero."

We would hold that course for 200 miles, and then turn due north for 700 miles. That would take us into our seventh day when we would turn a bit eastwardly and head directly toward the Kurils, twelve hundred more miles ahead. With no delays, we were looking at a fifteen-day transit, moving at our enforced leisurely pace of six knots.

"Are you ready, Mac?" the Skipper asked.

"Yes Sir." I turned to the lookouts. "Lay below," I said.

When they dropped out of sight, I made a final scan all around the sub, taking my time. "Control, Bridge, rig for dive status."

"Green board, Sir – except the Bridge Hatch."

I flipped the 1MC switch on the comm box. "This is the Bridge – Dive! Dive!"

Immediately Control sounded the klaxon – Aaoogah... aaoogah... aaoogah....

Just before dropping through the hatch after the Skipper, I glanced fore and aft to make sure the ballast control tank valves were wide open, spouting spray as the deck came awash. As I dropped through the hatch, I sensed Joe Thornton right below me. I grabbed the lanyard and passed it to Joe. He pulled the hatch down solidly, and I reached up and cranked the locking wheel tight.

Joe dropped to the deck before me as Pots announced, "Green board, Sir!"

"Mark your head," I said to the helmsman.

"Three-five-zero, Sir."

"Make turns for six knots."

"Turns for six knots, Aye," Roscoe answered.

"Make your depth two-hundred feet smartly," I ordered.

"Two-hundred feet smartly, aye," Chris said, and I felt the sub take a distinct down angle. A minute later Chris leveled the sub and said, "Two-hundred feet, Sir."

And with that, the boring part commenced.

#

We were about thirty-three hours from our first turn to the north. Aside from periodic clearing of our baffles, the entire leg was without incident. The turn happened on another watch, so I didn't even enjoy that small distraction. The next five days would be no different, except we were pointed ten more degrees to the right of our previous course.

We read, watched movies, exercised, played some poker, and drilled a lot. Even Sonar was quiet. We ran into nobody for the first seven days. We changed depth from time to time to vary the routine, but we remained below a hundred feet. No periscope liberty.

As we reached the end of our seventh day, on my watch, the Skipper took her up to periscope depth and put the snorkel up, not to run the diesels, but to ventilate the ship with the blowers. The fresh air smelled good, and we got another day out of our oxygen candles this way. Up until now the weather had cooperated, and it was nice up there. Most of the crew took a minute or two to gaze out over the calm Pacific waters.

I brought the snorkel down as the last crew member reluctantly gave up his position at the scope. Our blowers were not particularly noisy, but they did have a masking effect on our ears. As soon as I shut the blower down Sonar announced, "Conn, Sonar, I have a contact off the starboard quarter, rapid screw beat, designate Charlie-one."

I acknowledged, and several minutes later Sonar announced, "Charlie-one is actually several contacts, Sir.

I think they're trawlers. They're about ten miles away, heading in our general direction."

"Make your depth five-hundred feet," I ordered. There was no way I was going to risk another entanglement with a trawler net. "Give me your best course resolution as soon as you get it," I told Sonar.

It turned out these guys were headed due west, probably Japanese trawlers on their way home. They would pass well astern of us. I kept the sub at 500 feet and ran a flooding drill that the Skipper had scheduled.

The crew saved the ship from a watery grave in record time. I was actually impressed. Then we reverted to the boring routine that we had to endure for another eight days or so, and settled in for the long haul.

We didn't have a clue about the reception committee awaiting us a week out.

Kuril Trench

CHAPTER TWENTY-NINE

On day fifteen out of Guam, I had just assumed the watch. We were about a hundred miles a bit south-of-east of the Krusenstern Strait, where we had had our close encounter on our way out from the first cable-tapping mission. After careful consideration, the Skipper opted to go back in the way we had come out, if for no other reason, because we already knew a bit about this area – not a great deal, but more than any other passage into the Sea of Okhotsk, except perhaps the narrow gap at the foot of the Kamchatka Peninsula that we transited way back in the dark ages when we first got here.

The Skipper's Night Orders for this transit were very clear on several points. He expected Ivan to be out there looking for us. There was virtually zero chance that our departure had gone unnoticed by the Soviets, despite all our efforts to depart quietly. All they had to do was a bit of arithmetic. How would they determine where we would enter? No way to know, so cover them all – a picket line of Soviet destroyers and cruisers.

The Soviets had a small fleet of *Kashin*-class destroyers at Vladivostok and more at Petropavlovsk Kamchatskiy, with the bulk of their Pacific submarine fleet residing there as well. How difficult would it be, the Skipper reasoned, for Ivan to deploy a string of surface and submerged warships for a few days before and after our most probable arrival date? They would likely designate it a picket exercise with live fire. If we didn't show, the Russkies would still get a bit of sea time and the chance to expend a few old torpedoes; if we did appear, maybe they would get lucky – and get the *Halibut*.

So the Skipper's Night Orders had us stopping at a hundred miles off Krusenstern, dropping down into the Kuril Trench that parallels the island chain – well, maybe not into, since the trench starts at about a mile down, and drops to nearly six miles down, while our max operating depth was less than a quarter of a mile. So it wasn't really down into...more like skimming the surface over the trench at our maximum depth.

But he wanted us deep and quiet. The task was to locate the bad guys, and then to slip past them. I dropped to 900 feet, shifted to the battery, and went to ultra quiet. I set a course that gave me nearly a broadside to whoever might be out there.

The sound-powered phoned squawked. I answered.

"Conn, Sonar, I've got three contacts, one due north – designate Delta-one, one to the northwest – designate Delta-two, and one due west – designate Delta-three, right at the edge of our detection." King was in charge.

Even before these contacts, the crew was running a pool on whether we would find anyone, and if so, whether they would be our old friends. It was a two-by-two matrix, and the guys got five bucks from me, but I had really no idea how it was organized.

I crept along, waiting for more information from Sonar. It was another half hour before we got anything definitive.

King chirped at me. "Delta-one's our old friend *Ognevoy*. Delta-two is a sub, but that's all I got right now. Delta-three is some kind of surface puke. Don't know yet."

There was, of course, no way Ivan could know we would be there, although the *Whiskey* skipper we had previously encountered was probably persuasive in his desire to get a picket in place just in case. And, as before, he was right...here we were.

The sound-powered phone chirped again. "Delta-three is a *Kanin*-class Soviet destroyer, Sir," King said. "I'll bring out the book."

King approached me with his trusty reference book depicting the Soviet fleet. He flipped it open and pointed to a black-and-white photo. "This is the *Gnevnyy*," he said. "It's a converted *Krupny*-class like the other eight *Kanins*."

I looked at him. "Yeah," he added, "that's Delta-three."

The King was earning his keep.

I glanced over the statistics, jotting down some notes for the Skipper.

The *Kanin* was 486 feet long, had a max speed of 35 knots, and was powered by steam turbines driving two shafts – she was an ASW ship, but pre-*Kashin*; she sported two 21-inch torpedo tubes and three RBU-6000 ASW rocket launchers, but she had only a hull-mounted sonar that was not very effective.

The RBU-6000 was essentially World War II stuff. It consisted of twelve ballistic rockets in a circular array that could be range-adjusted by tilting the array. They ranged from about a thousand feet to three miles, and were effective up to about a thousand feet down. To be effective against us, they would virtually have to make a direct hit. By herself, the *Gnevnyy* was no threat. She would never hear us, and even if she did, we could evade her stuff. But with the *Ognevoy* doing the listening, the *Gnevnyy* could present a genuine threat, especially when backed up by the sub.

"What about the sub?" I asked.

"She's still at the limit of our listening range," King said. "Besides, we still got that seismic noise in the background. It's masking a lot of details."

"How do you think that will affect the *Ognevoy's* dipping sonar?" I asked, and then I added, "From their bird."

"It'll cut their range, that's for sure," King said, "but we don't know by how much." King looked thoughtful. "They normally have a twenty-thousand-yard or so range – that's from the bird. Of course, the bird can operate twenty, thirty, even a hundred miles from home, and we got no way of knowing where it is until she pings."

"The layer's about three-hundred feet here, right?" I asked.

"Yep," King answered, "but it dips down to about five-hundred feet just over the trench and for a couple of miles on the shoreward side, because of the south flowing cold water current there."

That worked in our favor. If *Ognevoy's* bird were dipping outside the channel, we could avoid his detecting us on the inside. On ultra-quiet, there was little chance of *Ognevoy* picking us up on her towed array, and no Soviet sub had an effective ranging passive sonar. So we could avoid the sub too. On the other hand, if the bird was dipping shoreward of the trench, it would detect us for sure, if we got within its range. Question is, would he dip below or above the layer? Time to call the Skipper.

I chirped him on the sound-powered phone. I briefed him on what I knew. He said he would be out shortly.

While I waited for him, I continued to think about the problem. When the Skipper showed up five minutes later, I reviewed the Soviets' operational capabilities, and told him what I knew about the layer effect on both sides of the trench.

"What would you do as the Captain of the *Ognevoy*?" the Skipper asked.

"Well, I don't know anything about the sub (us), except that it's a nuke with a depth capability of somewhere between eight-hundred and two thousand feet. It has deep diver lockout capability. I know it's speed limited, but don't know why, but it's possibly due to the mini-sub on its stern. I know it's quiet, too. Of course, I know the layers and currents out here." I paused, deep in thought. The Skipper waited patiently.

"Putting the bird outside the trench is a waste. I think I would put the bird shoreward of the trench, dipping below the layer. I'd place the sub in the middle of the upper layer at a hundred feet or so – Ivan uses meters, so at thirty-five or forty meters. I'd cruise the *Ognevoy* parallel and as close to the islands as possible and still be outside the hundred-fathom curve. I'd park the *Gnevnyy* in the Krusenstern Strait, pointed eastward so she can kick it in the ass should the sub be detected trying another entrance."

The Skipper had listened intently. "Why not place the *Gnevnyy* outside the strait several miles to put it closer to any alternative route?" he asked. He beckoned me over to the chart and pointed at Krusenstern Strait. The current is pretty strong to the west through here – sometimes two, three knots," he said. "The *Gnevnyy* would have to work against that, and certainly give herself away."

I nodded. The Skipper had a point – that's why he was the Skipper.

"So, where do we place ourselves?" he asked.

"Shallow," I answered, "and use the current."

"Good. Make it so," the Skipper said, and went to his chair at the Control Station, lighting up one of his stogies.

#

At six knots, it would take us the rest of my watch plus some to transit the trench. Once the layer shallowed up, we wanted to get above it, and that's what I passed to Larry when he relieved me three hours later.

I got some sleep, grabbed a bite – sandwiches, did a bit of reading, and spent some time with my guys just hanging out and swapping sea stories. There was little else I could do under the circumstances.

As I came back on watch to relieve Dirk, he told me that the batteries were getting low, so we would need to bring up the plant for a while to charge them. I asked when, and he told me we had three or four more hours, so I put that a bit lower on the list. His big announcement really came as no surprise. The sub, Delta-two, was our old adversary, the *Whiskey*. This was the second time he had found us by using guile and submarine sense. This guy was really good, and we couldn't afford to make any wrong assumptions. The Skipper had been on the Control Station for about an hour, Dirk said. Then he left to check the plant and the condition of his guys. Ultra-quiet put them on port and starboard watches, and they were stretched.

We were at 150 feet, maintaining bare steerageway, but Parrish told me that our over-ground speed was nearly four knots. We definitely were riding the inbound current.

Sonar reported the *Ognevoy* underway at six knots, almost off our starboard beam twenty miles to the north, heading toward us. The *Gnevnyy* was eighteen miles to our stern – the Skipper had nailed that one – DIW but the plant was running, so we could hear her just fine. The *Whiskey* was hanging off our port quarter, but he hadn't spotted us, probably because we were outside his sonar range – he was ten miles out. From time to time, the *Ognevoy's* bird would fire off a ping, but Sonar hadn't picked him up for the past two hours.

The bad news was that they had us boxed in; the good news was that they didn't know it.

"Maintain your heading for now, Mac, while we evaluate what is happening," the Skipper said.

"Aye, Sir."

And at that moment a deafening ping rang throughout the entire sub, right through the hull. We had just discovered where the Soviet helicopter was.

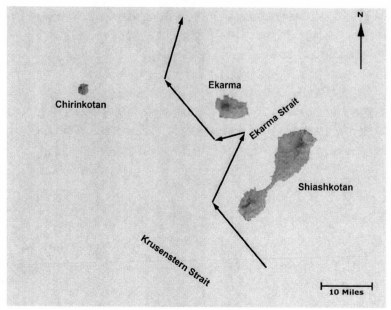

Ekarma Strait

CHAPTER THIRTY

Before the ping reverberations stopped ringing in our ears I issued the order. "Make your depth five-hundred feet – snappy!"

The Skipper stood up and grabbed the 1MC mike. "Open the outer doors on one and two," he said over the 1MC.

"Sonar, how far away is the *Whiskey?*" On the intercom.

"Ten miles, but he's accelerating, Sir."

"Mac, bring up the plant right away. Push with everything you've got straight toward Chirinkotan." He beckoned me over to the chart table and pointed at the westward most island of the nearby group. "As soon as you can clear the tip of Shiashkotan," he pointed to the southern end of a barbell shaped island at the northern side of Krusenstern Strait, cut right into Ekarma Strait."

"I get it," Skipper. "We mask our noise with the background of Ekarma Volcano."

"That's the plan," the Skipper said, puffing on his stogie.

We were about twelve miles southwest of Shiasko-tan, and the *Whiskey* was about ten more miles out. He could easily cover the ten miles in an hour, but would be totally blind while doing it. In the meantime, we would be halfway to Ekarma Strait. He would have to slow down, and perhaps even go to periscope depth to get updated information from *Ognevoy*. Since the bird would have to do several dips in the right location to find us again, they would lose at least another hour screwing around. This would put us in Ekarma's cone of background noise, although they would have a pretty good idea of our plan by connecting the dots. Given the *Whiskey* Skipper's apparent ability to read our mind, we could count on that.

Dirk's guys got the plant up and running in less than five minutes. I goosed it to seven knots – faster than we were supposed to go, but I figured the tech boys had slipped in a safety factor, and right then I needed any advantage I could get. The Skipper didn't question my order, so I guess he agreed.

We weren't going to launch torpedoes against any of these guys unless they launched first. But they had tried once before, so we were definitely ready. I planned to slow for a good look in an hour, since the *Whiskey* was behind us. I wasn't worried about *Gnevnyy*, but I had Sonar keep a close eye on *Ognevoy*, since she definitely had the ability to hear us as she got closer.

An hour later, I went to all stop, and coasted, twisting right with the thrusters to give Sonar a good look to the rear. We couldn't hear anything, so I brought her up above the layer to 150 feet. Sure enough, the *Whiskey* was about where we had been an hour earlier, quietly at periscope depth, just as we figured.

No way the *Whiskey* could hear us, though. He was probably coordinating with another dip from *Ognevoy's* bird.

The sound-powered phone chirped. "Conn, Sonar... Pinging about two miles behind us, below the layer. I don't think he can see us, Sir."

A couple of minutes later, "Conn, Sonar...he's stopped pinging – I think he's bringing the transducer above the layer."

I could picture the chopper pilot simply rising slowly while communicating with his sonar tech.

"Make your depth nine-hundred feet, snappy!" I ordered. "Don't cavitate," I added.

At 180 feet, Sonar informed me that we had passed through the layer. I looked at the Skipper, and he nodded.

"Mark your depth," I said.

"Two-seven-zero feet," Chris answered.

"Make your depth two-fifty feet," I said.

If this guy was going to play yoyo games, I might as well be positioned to move through the layer quickly.

A minute later, Sonar announced: "Pinging from above the layer – still two miles back on our track." Suddenly Sonar announced, "Conn, Sonar, the *Whiskey* is dropping fast. I think he's going to..." King paused for a moment. "Conn, Sonar, make that the *Whiskey* just transmitted a single ping. If his guys are sharp, they might pick us up. If they got anything, we'll get another short burst of pings in a bit."

"Make turns for seven knots," I ordered, "come left to zero-five-five." I turned to the Skipper. "Give him a smaller aspect, and get closer to Ekarma."

The Skipper concurred.

"Three more pings, Sir," King announced. "And he's getting underway again. I think he got a return from us."

"Probably," I said to the Skipper, "but he can't know for sure, so he's coming to investigate."

"Take us above the layer, Mac," the Skipper said.

"Aye, Sir," and I did.

"Conn, Sonar, the bird is pinging continuously below the layer."

No surprise that, since the *Whiskey* might have gotten a whiff of us before he speeded up.

"Conn, Sonar, he's stopped pinging."

I ordered us back below the layer.

"Belay that order!" the Skipper said, and looked at me. "He's going to ping again down there."

"How do you know, Sir?" I asked.

"Because it's what I'd do," he said with a subdued grin.

"Conn, Sonar, pinging again…below the layer."

"Take her down now, Mac," the Skipper said with satisfaction.

We were pointed dead center toward Ekarma Strait. The current was with us. I glanced up at the surface wave monitor.

"Skipper, look at that!" The monitor was indicating a significant increase in wave activity.

"Conn, Sonar, it's getting kinda noisy out there."

During the next fifteen minutes, the surface waves went from a foot or so to over ten feet, and still growing.

I looked at the compass. We were fifteen degrees off course. "Mind your head, Skidmore," I said.

"I'm trying, Sir," he said. "Something's pushing me all over the place."

I turned to the Skipper. "You want to go up and take a look, Sir?"

The Skipper picked up the sound-powered phone. "Sonar, what's the pinger doing?"

"He's packed it in, Skipper. It's useless in these waves."

"Take her up for a quick swing around, Mac," the Skipper ordered.

As we approached periscope depth, the Skipper was already at the raised scope, sweeping around as the scope broached. "Up another two feet," he ordered. "One more." A pause. "One more." Then he stopped sweeping with the scope pointed to port. "Mark," he said, and swept to the starboard side. "Mark." Sweep back to port. "Mark," and to starboard, "Mark. Same landmark each side," he said to Parrish.

"We're not moving, Sir," Parrish said. "We're bucking a seven-knot current."

"Bring her to all stop, Mac, and maintain your heading with the thrusters," the Skipper ordered. "Take the scope." He turned it over to me.

I did a quick sweep around, and could clearly see our drift backward. The Skipper went to the chart table and consulted with Parrish. Then he came back to me.

"When Ekarma is due north, come to three-one-five and set turns for fifteen knots. Hold that for five minutes, and then slow down to six and a half knots. Pass between Chirinkotan and Ekarma. Check your position visually every fifteen minutes." He picked up the 1MC mike. "Close the torpedo tube outer doors. Nav to the Conn." He turned back to me. "Set quiet condition, but relax from ultra-quiet for the time being. I'll be in my stateroom." He squeezed my shoulder as he left. "Good job," he said.

#

As we swept backward, the surface wave activity subsided a bit, but it was clear that bad weather was moving in. On my next sweep around, I tilted the scope up to see the sky. It was dark and angry, and by the time I finished the sweep, I could see rain pelting the water.

In a dramatically short time I was heading three-one-five at fifteen knots. After slowing to six and a half knots five minutes later, I chose to dolphin down below the layer, and come back to periscope depth every fifteen minutes. The current was with us on this side of Ekarma, and much slower, spread out as it was across the much wider passage between Chirinkotan and Ekarma, instead of the scant four miles of Ekarma Strait.

An hour later, we had passed Chirinkotan and were headed toward the open water of the Sea of Okhotsk. Surface waves were a jumbled nasty fifteen feet and growing, so I informed the Skipper, and took her down to quieter water at five-hundred feet.

As I relaxed on the Control Station, I replayed the past four hours. We had slipped the noose once again. But these guys were playing hardball. I could not believe they had any inkling of our actual mission or the location where we would place the tap. They did know of at least one destination we were likely to visit – the missile splash zone. And that is where I suspected they would likely head.

What I didn't know was what they had in store for us.

Pod with lift bags and weights being moved across bottom

CHAPTER THIRTY-ONE

Storms in the Sea of Okhotsk are never your average normal storms. Up here they start at ohmygosh and end up off the normal storm rating scale. The one above us as we crawled toward our destination was over the halfway mark toward off-the-scale. I came on watch to a gently rocking sub, just enough to make it pleasant – except for one thing. We were at 350 feet. For surface action to move us around at this depth would take monster waves. As I arrived at the Control Station, I glanced up at the surface wave monitor. Thirty-five to forty foot waves running in our direction.

Let me put this into perspective. If you were on the typical ocean-going yacht – forty-five to fifty feet long, and if you were sideways to these monsters, they would roll you over in a flash. If you did it right, you'd nearly be standing on your ass one minute, and nearly standing on your nose a minute later. You might survive it – but I wouldn't bet next month's paycheck.

These waves were moving us around at 350 feet, and we were that long and displaced 5,000 tons. What I'm saying is that these monsters were moving 5,000 tons of steel as if it were nothing. In this shit the *Whiskey* was down deep – for him – and getting the crap beaten out of him. He was either going home, or finding shelter in the lee of one of the Kurils. He was no longer a threat to us. For the time being anyway.

The *Ognevoy* and *Gnevnyy* could survive these waves, if their COs were any good, but it was survival time. They had lost all interest in us.

#

It was boring again, except for the potential of being sucked to the surface. The Skipper kept us heavy, so that we had to "fly" using our dive planes to keep us at depth. That meant that we had to be extra alert on watch, because if something went wrong, we would drop quickly if we didn't compensate by immediately pumping water out. But even that got boring as we plodded along at six knots plus a bit, heading for our rendezvous with destiny.

The storm stayed with us as we traversed past the end of Kamchatka Peninsula, and worked our way north to our rendezvous point. As the water shallowed up, the waves beat us up more, but a couple of days later the worst was over, and we began to breathe easier. Our unspoken worry had been that the Soviet trio would tag-team us, keeping us under intermittent surveillance, so that we really could not have approached our actual destination. We were even faced with the possibility that we would have to abort – but as it turned out, they were gone, with virtually no chance that they knew where we were.

I decided to put Whitey, Bill, Ski, Jer, and Harry in the Can. I wanted an extra man available for this task. The pod was 12,000 pounds of delicate equipment, and we wanted to put it in place and get the hell out of there quickly. For that I figured we could stand a bit of crowding in the Can.

I took myself off the watch list when Ham loaded the guys into the Can. Ham and Jack had already done a complete system check, twice over. We were ready to go.

It was always fun to watch the guys press down. As usual, Whitey, Ski, and Jer just yawned their way down. Bill didn't appear to do anything – he just pressed down as his ears equalized in real-time. And Harry, well Harry was always glad when we paused the descent so he could catch up with his nose-squeezing and blowing.

As the topside storm abated, we reached the general vicinity of the Soviet cable. Ham had the divers resting as much as possible, four in the rack and one on watch on a two-hour rotation. Josh had the Deck with Chief Barkley in Sonar, and King was hanging out just in case.

I was at the Control Station giving Josh a personal update on the divers' status when Sonar announced, "Conn, Sonar, we have the transponder, bearing zero-two-zero. It's about five miles away, Sir."

That was my signal. I hurried back to the Can and informed Ham that we were coming up on the set point. Ham held reveille on the guys, and got them ready for the big event.

We had decided to leave Harry in the Can, so the others were getting suited up as we approached the transponder.

The process was a piece of cake when compared with the last time we were here. Josh eased up to the transponder, and went into a hover about fifty feet above it. In the Bat Cave, Bobby Shanks launched the Basketball, and flew it to an observation position off the starboard bow. Using the thrusters and pumps, Josh eased the *Halibut* down and about fifty feet to the south of the transponder, and spun around so we were pointed toward the west. Then he gently settled the sub on the bottom, raising clouds of silt that blocked the Basketball camera's view.

As the current swept the clouds away, the Basketball flew lower, down to the forward skids. The bright shaft of light emanating from the Basketball cut a white swath through the murky water, but as I squinted at the monitor over the dive console, I could see the skid with increasing clarity as the cloud moved away on the current.

I knew that Josh was pumping an extra heavy load of water into the tanks to hold us firmly to the bottom. No rocking on anchor cables this time. With only a relatively small remaining swell from the storm, we probably were not at much risk, but it was good to know that we had this assurance.

Josh called me say the ship was ready for dive ops. It was our show again.

#

Since the guys were already suited up, there was little else to do but equalize the outer lock and put the divers into the water – all four of them this time. Bobby moved the Basketball into position off the starboard quarter a couple of feet from the Can hatch.

"Control, Red Diver, ready to open the hatch." It was Whitey.

"Control aye. Open the hatch." Jack was doing the communicating.

I watched the Basketball monitor as the hatch opened. A rim of light appeared, and then, as the hatch lifted into the lock, a white shaft illuminated the submarine deck just below the opening. The first umbilical snaked its way through the hatch and disappeared down the sub's flank, followed by a second. Then Whitey and Bill (Green Diver) dropped through the hatch and sidled toward the Basketball, floating alongside – I presumed, because I could no longer see them. Two more umbilicals tumbled through the hatch, followed by Jer and Ski, Blue and Yellow Divers, respectively. The breathing of four divers on the circuit created a significant background noise that made it a bit difficult to communicate.

"Proceed to the pod," Jack ordered.

The water was too murky for Bobby to maintain a broad view, so he arbitrarily picked Whitey, who had dropped to the starboard after ratchet. We left the divers alone to get themselves placed and coordinate their actions. It took about fifteen minutes before they were satisfied that they were properly positioned and ready to lower the pod.

While that was happening, I directed Bobby to move the Basketball along the bottom of the sling so I could examine its entirety. I'm not sure what I was expecting, but I could see nothing out of place. By the time the divers were ready to commence lowering the pod, I was satisfied with its apparent external condition. I signaled Jack.

"Commence lowering the pod," he ordered.

Bobby looked over Whitey's shoulder, and I was certain that every available monitor on the sub was tuned to this eerie scene 400 feet below the surface of an enemy super-power's home pond. Four courageous divers worked with apparent unconcern at a crushing water pressure with four feet of visibility and a thirty-foot ceiling above them. With minimum chatter, they lowered the pod inch by inch, until forty minutes later all 12,000 pounds rested on the bottom between the sub's skids.

I ordered the divers to clear the skids and hang off the submarine sides in mid-water, while the sub lifted free of the bottom and moved backward enough to clear the pod. In our initial discussion of this maneuver, we had first considered bringing the divers back into the Can. We rejected that as being too conservative and a significant waste of time. Then we considered putting the divers on the sub's deck near the hatch, but that raised the possible issue of catching an umbilical beneath a skid. We finally opted for the divers hanging alongside the sub with the umbilicals fully off the bottom. Since we were using thrusters and pumps only, the risk seemed minimal.

As we commenced the approximately 150-foot move, Ski's helium distorted vice suddenly squeaked, "Whoa – what was that?"

"Clarify, Yellow Diver, clarify," Jack prompted.

"I just lifted five feet, Control. Jest mindin' my own business, and then I'm five feet shallower." Ski was on the port forward station.

"Red, Green, Blue Divers..." Jack let the question hang.

"Red Diver...nothing." As I said, Whitey was starboard aft.

"Green Diver...nothing." Bill was starboard forward.

"Blue Diver...yeah, I felt something, like a passing wave. Moved me a bit." Jer was port aft.

I called Josh. "Conn, Dive Control, what's the surface doing?"

"Starting to pick up," Dive, "five- to six-foot swells. We may be feeling the edge of a follow-on storm to the last sucker." Josh was the bearer of not-so-good news.

I picked up the mike and spoke to the divers. "Watch yourselves, guys. We've got another storm coming. Let's get this job over with before she hits."

#

Guided by the Basketball, Josh put the *Halibut* on the bottom with just sufficient clearance to move the pod without tangling the lift bags in the props.

Jack sent the divers forward to the Aquarium. They arrived with the Basketball just as the outer hatch was opening. Although it was a bit difficult to observe on the monitor, the guys wrestled the first lift bag to the bottom and pushed it to one side. They lowered the other bag, and then lowered the 500- pound belly weight that I had proposed, using a three-purchase pulley attached to the inner hatch and to the weight. Since the lock had to be completely recycled for each load, and since it took a minimum of ten minutes for each load, the job took three quarters of an hour.

The guys had been working steadily now for about two hours. The work would have been taxing under any conditions, but here, at 400 feet, it was exhausting.

"Ask them how they're holding up, Jack," I said, knowing full well how they would answer.

"Red Diver...never felt better."

"Green Diver...well, I felt better once, but I forget her name...."

"Blue Diver...Once. Shit, Green, that's pathetic..."

"Yellow Diver...I could use a beer, you know...."

Jack looked at me and shrugged. I reached for the mike. "Take five, guys. Relax and work on your suntans."

The chattering stopped – they really were too tired to talk. All we could hear was labored breathing.

"Do you hear any unusual breathing patterns?" I asked Ham.

"Ski seems to be breathing a bit fast, but he's smaller than the others. Still trying to carry an equal load."

"Or more," Jack intoned.

"Boost the heater five degrees," I told Ham. "Let's keep them warm while they rest."

As the warmer water surged through the umbilicals into their suits, Ski muttered, "Ahh...that's better than peeing in a wetsuit."

I actually let nearly fifteen minutes pass before rousing the guys for the next step.

#

"Shake a leg, boys," Jack announced. "Time to move the pod."

"I was just settling in for a snooze," Ski complained. The guy was incorrigible.

With just a small squirt of helium, one lift bag floated nearly weightless as the divers tugged it to its destination at the front of the now-exposed pod on the seafloor just aft of the sub's rudders. The second, Jer attached to the belly weight, added a bit of extra helium and brought it along with equal ease.

"You know the drill, guys," Jack told them. "Let's do it!"

Bobby flitted the Basketball from position to position, trying to give me and the rest of the *Halibut* crew the best possible view of what was happening. First, Jer moved the belly weight alongside the pod on the north. Then the divers set the two lift bag harnesses to the lift rings at each corner of the pod. Coordinating carefully, the divers slowly filled the lift bags until the pod barely rose off the bottom. While they were accomplishing this, another set of large swells passed by 400 feet above them. All four divers and the Basketball lifted and fell about three feet, but the pod stayed put. It didn't appear to lift at all. Probably too much inertia for the short cycle length, I thought. Ski and Bill quickly grabbed the two securing cables for the belly weight and brought them to the top of the pod on either side, while Whitey and Jer gently moved the pod directly over the belly weight.

A minute later the strap was securely attached to the pod, so Ski and Bill returned to their lift bags. Very gently, Bill and Ski inflated their bags until the pod lifted against the belly weight, putting a real strain on the short cable connecting the strap around the pod to the weight itself. Whitey and Jer tested the rig by rocking the pod ends up and down like a seesaw, around the pivot point where the strap was attached. While they did this, Bobby moved the Basketball in closely all around the strap and down to the weight, so I could be sure it was in perfect working order. While we did this, another swell passed overhead, lifting all the divers, the Basketball, and causing the pod to seesaw by itself.

"Let it rock," I told the divers. "Let's see how long it takes to stabilize."

It took about a minute, and that's when I realized that we really needed three weights, with one at each end on a shorter leash than the belly weight. I told the divers to stabilize the pod at minimum float while I sent out some more weights. Then I called Dirk and explained what I needed. He said he'd have them at the Aquarium in ten minutes. I reminded him that I needed a lift bag for each, and he said it would be fifteen minutes. I told the divers what was up, and sent Ski and Bill to get the weights.

Good as his word, Dirk's guys had strapped several anti-corrosion hull zincs together into 200- pound weights, attached short lengths of cable to each, with a set of straps that would reach around the pod. It was one slick fifteen-minute solution. The Bat Cave spooks passed the weights through the Aquarium to Ski and Bill. They attached the lift bags, and twenty minutes after they left, were back, attaching the straps around the front and back of the pod. I had them adjust the short strap to each weight so the weights were just six inches off the bottom with the pod level.

During the half hour the entire operation took, the swells increased from one every five or so minutes to continuously passing swells that were moving everything about, including the silt from the bottom. Visibility was decreasing. The divers inflated the pod bags until the belly weight just remained on the bottom. With the next big swell, they reported to me that the pod commenced a seesaw, but that the fore and aft weights apparently absorbed the momentum when they landed on the bottom, and the seesaw rocking stopped immediately.

Great! The problem was solved and we were good to go.

Visibility made it difficult for the two divers at either end to see each other. In effect, each diver was now isolated in his own cocoon, without the bottom for reference, forced to coordinate his actions by voice alone. I placed two divers on each lift cable, but with the pod visible. Whitey and Ski each had a dump lanyard that would quickly vent helium in the event that end started up. Obviously, the idea was to maintain control, since it would not help to crash one end into the bottom. It would take some finesse, but I had faith in my guys.

Bobby did his best to give us an overall view, but all we really got was a set of snapshots that were difficult to paste into a complete live picture. We had to move the pod only about sixty feet, but it seemed like forever. Whitey announced finally that he could see the cable. Bobby flitted over and showed it to me. As he did, a larger-than-average swell passed overhead.

"Whoa...," Ski shouted, as the back end of the pod lifted sharply, Ski with it.

Bobby quickly moved the Basketball so I could observe the action. By the time he got there, Ski had already gotten control of his own ascent, and had pulled the dump lanyard. The pod's steep up angle quickly diminished, and as the weight crashed into the bottom, the bag automatically inflated under Ski's watchful eye, and kept the pod itself from hitting the bottom.

Although I couldn't see the other end, Whitey reported that the system was working. As their end weight came off the bottom, the bag vented without their having to pull the lanyard, and everything settled down. The divers got themselves organized again, waiting for a short break in the up-and-down moving water. At the peak rise, they injected more helium into the bags, and moved the pod so that it was exactly parallel to the cable and just to the south so that when it bottomed, it would be touching the cable.

"Shit," Whitey said. "We gotta move the weights."

This was going to require more finesse than we had initially figured.

I was about to give some direction when Whitey said, "Let's move the pod south three feet, remove the belly weight, and bring it back to here. Then we can bottom Ski's end, stretch the pod past Ski's weight and bottom his end, and then swing my weight forward by hand and bottom this end."

"Let's do it so the wave bottom'll help us," Jer added.

"Jer, get ready to drop the belly weight," Whitey said. "And Bill, get ready to swing this weight."

I took the mike. "Hold it, guys. Take a moment to make sure your umbilicals are clear of everything. Report back to me before you commence."

It took about a minute.

"Red clear."

"Green clear."

"Blue clear...now," Jer added sheepishly. "Ski's and my umbilicals got tangled."

"Yellow clear."

"Okay, do your thing, guys. Luck," I said.

Since we were virtually blind by now, Bobby hung off to the side and kept out of the way. The divers talked back and forth, coordinating the move to the swell motion. Within five minutes they had dropped the belly weight. In two more minutes Ski's end was grounded, and then Bill swung his weight out of the way and the pod was in place. The divers collapsed the lift bags and set them off to one side. Then they strapped the cable securely against the pod, so that it was directly against a line painted the length of the pod. This was the designated signal pickup strip, especially designed to intercept the cable transmissions by induction.

The final step was to test the rig. While Whitey and Ski were strapping the cable to the pod, Bill and Jer returned to the sub and retrieved the communication cable from the pod bay we had used in our first trip. This time it contained no pod, just the connecting cable with a special fitting designed to make a waterproof connection underwater, and to extrude any water trapped inside when the pins were pushed into the pod socket.

As Whitey and Ski completed their task, Bill and Jer returned with the cable. The water was beginning to show turbulence, even at this depth. I was becoming concerned, and urged the guys to hurry with the systems check and get back aboard the sub.

At their fastest, it was still a slow task. Moving water made it more difficult to hold the connecting cable steady, and the divers had to be extra careful not to bend any of the pins. They ended up putting Ski and Jer on the cable, holding as still as possible, while Whitey inserted it into the pod socket carefully, and screwed the connection tight. While they did this, Bill took the lift bags back to the sub and loaded them into the Aquarium.

Once the connector was attached, the spooks were able to get an immediate signal on all channels. "Loud and clear," Chief Blunt announced.

Removing the test cable was a short, two-minute exercise. Replacing the connector cover likewise. Since it was designed to extrude all water when it closed, and then to open any connection between the connector and the rest of the pod, we didn't have to be concerned about a short between any of the internal elements. Put the cap on and go. That was it.

Meanwhile, we were beginning to feel the surges pass through the entire sub. It looked like we had become the victims of another doozy of an Arctic storm. Josh reported that the surface waves were as big as last week; it was at least as bad as the one a week earlier. And in these enclosed waters, it was much more chaotic and jumbled.

Just as Whitey tightened the cap, we actually felt the sub give a lift off the bottom. Not a big lift, but we all noticed it.

Immediately after the swell swept over the sub, Bill gave a frantic call, "Help me guys! Get over here quick. I'm in trouble!"

Bill trapped under the skid

CHAPTER THIRTY-TWO

I'm not sure who got to Bill first, the Basketball or the other divers. What I do know is that suddenly, the monitor was filled with Bill trapped at his thighs under the forward starboard skid. Right next to him his umbilical passed under the skid as well.

"Green Diver, what's your condition?" Jack was right on it.

"I'm pinned under the skid. I can move my toes. Don't think nothin's broke, but I can't move."

"That's good news." It was the Skipper. "We'll get the sub up off him. Get him onboard ASAP."

"Right, Sir," I said as he left for the Conn. I reached for the mike. "Listen, you guys," I said, "Blue Diver back to the Can right now. Get yourself rigged to get Green into the Can. We're gonna lift the sub gently. You guys get him out, and free his umbilical. Then carry him back – don't let him swim. As soon as you get him in the Can, Red Diver, you go to the pod bay and retrieve the cable. Stow it securely with no rattles, and then return to the Can."

On the 1MC Larry (who had assumed the watch) notified me that they were ready to lift the *Halibut* on my say-so.

"Are you guys ready?" I asked the divers.

"Dive Control, Red Diver, we're standing by."

I gave Larry the go-ahead. Bobby moved the Basketball as close as possible without interfering with the operation. The skid inched off Bill's legs, and two shadowy figures yanked him out from under it.

"Dive Control, Red Diver, we got another problem. When we yanked him out, the umbilical wrapped completely around the skid. We can't pull it out."

That was a shitty situation. We had only two options. We could lift the sub high enough to thread Bill through the skid, and then under it, and then through it again to unwrap the umbilical, or we could cut the umbilical and hustle Bill to the Can on his come-home bottle. I could feel the sub reacting to the surface swells. We had to do something right then. I looked Ham in the eyes and ordered, "Red Diver, Dive Control, cut Bill's umbilical and get him back to the Can immediately. Blue Diver, you jerk the cut umbilical free and then drop it and help Whitey." I took a deep breath. "Go...Now!"

I punched the intercom. "Bobby, pull the Basketball back. I don't want any interference."

"I'll stow it," Bobby answered.

"No, Bobby – we still need to retrieve the sling," I said. "Just stand by."

About thirty seconds later, Bill's gas flow indicator on the console indicated free flow. Jack shut the control valve.

"Dive Control, Blue Diver, I'm in the lock with Harry. We're standing by for Bill."

A minute or so later the lock monitor showed Harry and Ski pulling Bill into the lock. They ripped off his helmet, and he lay on the deck gasping.

"Check him over," I ordered, "especially his legs and back."

I watched as the guys stripped his suit and began to check his legs and back.

"Nothing broken," Ski said, "but his upper thighs are gonna hurt like hell for a while." Ski pointed at marks on his legs. "They're turnin' purple," Ski added.

Bill looked up at the camera. "Thanks, El-Tee."

"Whadya mean, El-Tee? Who you think brought you here, ya dumb ass?" Ski slapped his head. "How the fuck you got stuck, anyway?"

"I don't know," Bill said. "I had just stowed the lift bags when the sub lifted right off the seafloor – me with it. I'm completely blinded by silt, and next thing I know I'm doin' underwater cartwheels. Then nothin', and I can't move. That's when I called for help."

Jer popped up through the hatch and ripped his helmet off. "You okay, Bill?"

"Yeah...where's Whitey?"

"Stowin' the cable," Jer said.

I interrupted them. "We still need to stow the sling."

"Let's keep Bill inside," Ham suggested, "and put Harry in the water with the others."

Within a few minutes, Harry joined his mates, and they spread out on both sides of the sub while Larry nudged it back over the sling, watched over by the Basketball. It took ten minutes, but Larry put it exactly on the dime. On my signal, the divers scattered to the four corners of the sling.

Within a few minutes, the guys had set up the winches, and coordinating between them, raised the sling tight to the sub's belly. Following the final torquing of the winch handles, Whitey swam the entire sling surface, making sure there were no twists or turns, nothing to catch, nothing to rattle. I knew better than to hurry him, even though we were definitely feeling every wave that passed by 400 feet overhead.

Actually, I agreed with Whitey. Making certain now would make it easier to avoid detection later.

We had the routine down pat by this time. The divers got back, stowed their equipment and hoses, grabbed a bite, and hit the rack in record time. Bill took the first watch – he said he was slept out but I figured he was trying to thank the guys for getting him out of his jam.

It had been a close call. If Bill had been pulled just a bit further, his chest would have been crushed. He might have survived that, but if it had gotten his head – well, that depended. Sideways, he might have made it, but front or back – how do you fall?

I was just thankful all he had were bruises.

While the guys slept, I went back on the watch list for a while, since we had about two days, maybe a bit less until the next operation. I brought the *Halibut* up to 200 feet to clear the area.

#

At 200 feet, we were being tossed around like a cork, but I had little choice as I headed due north. I didn't want to be slammed into the seabed, so I had to take the shallower course. We had one final task, to return to the missile test splash zone to see what else we could find. Since we had had no chance on our last visit to plant a beacon, we would have to deploy the Fish once we got into the vicinity to conduct a sidescan sonar area search. It was going to be a fun time.

I figured we would have some kind of company when we got there. For the time being, however, nobody was going to hear anybody in this mess. Sonar was taking it easy, since there really was nothing to hear. Chief Barkley gave them a bit of slack, but he still insisted on one set of ears manned all the time.

There was simply no way that the *Ognevoy* and *Gnevnyy* could do anything but stay alive in this shit. And while the *Whiskey* could be fairly comfortable submerged, a diesel-electric submarine simply didn't have the endurance that the *Halibut* enjoyed. If the Soviets were setting up a welcome party, it seemed likely to me that they would hole up somewhere protected for the duration – somewhere safe but close.

I stepped over to the chart table and examined the coastline due west of our position. The peninsula that defined the Gulf of Shelikhov juts into the Sea of Okhotsk with two prongs at the east and west ends separated by about 120 miles of jagged coastline. The westernmost prong forms the southern border of a 50-mile wide bay bordered to the north by a small peninsula spanned by the port city of Magadan. The main part of Magadan occupies the west side of the peninsula, at the end of a deep natural harbor, but there is a fishing facility and repair shops with several piers on the east side.

If I wanted to be close to the splash zone, but in protected waters, that's where I would go. I called the Skipper on the sound-powered phone and asked him to come to Control. When he arrived, I explained my thoughts to him, pointing to the harbor and its proximity to the splash zone.

"The *Whiskey* certainly could tie up to a fishing pier here," I pointed out. "And the destroyers could anchor safely." I pointed to the area we called the splash zone. "It's only about ten hours to here."

"Makes sense, Mac," the Skipper said. "That's assuming they are still looking for us."

"It's the only destination they're certain of, Skipper," I said.

It turned out that our guess was right, but we didn't know about the other vessel loading out on the same pier where the *Whiskey* was moored.

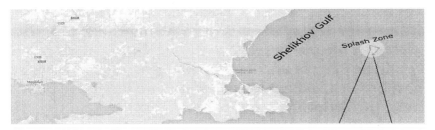

Shelikhov Gulf – Missile splash zone

CHAPTER THIRTY-THREE

It took us less time than the weather. I mean, we were on the bottom in the splash zone, quietly waiting for the weather to cooperate. We stood regular watch rotation, and were on a relaxed alert – just in case.

Actually, when I said we were on the bottom in the zone, I really meant we were somewhere in the vicinity. As soon as it calmed down a bit topside, we were prepared to do a grid search with the Fish. Buck – Senior Chief Buck Christman – was in hot standby with his crew. They really had had nothing to do since the original search for the cable.

I was still on watch rotation, but what that really meant was hanging around in Control, just in case. Once things settled down sufficiently for my guys to go out, I would retire to the dive console while my guys did a bottom clean up, collecting anything that even remotely looked like a rocket part. So we waited.

And finally the surface wave monitor indicated decreasing surface activity. Almost as quickly as it came, the storm left, and the chaotic surface settled into a series of long, shallow rollers heading into the Gulf of Shelikhov.

Josh relieved me before we got underway. That was just as well, because I didn't look forward to the slow back-and-forth search across the featureless bottom, looking for the small humps that indicated the prize pieces we were looking for.

If the Skipper and I were right, in about ten hours we could expect visitors, so the sooner we found the debris field, the better.

#

There really is nothing to tell about the search: one leg after the other with a couple of hundred yards between runs. Six hours into the run we hit pay dirt on Larry's watch. Sonar pulled us into the middle of a debris field with literally thousands of hits. It was time.

Larry put us on the bottom right at the southern edge of the field. Ten minutes later, Bill, Ski, and Harry were clambering out of the Can. Their umbilicals were twice as long as normal, giving them a much larger range, but also making them more vulnerable to any currents. They met at the Aquarium with Devon and the Basketball looking over their shoulders. Well, looking was a bit of an exaggeration, actually, given the turbidity following the storm. Visibility was a couple of feet at the most, so the Basketball concentrated on Harry.

Harry retrieved three mesh bags from the Aquarium, each with its own lift bag. From my perspective, I watched Harry pass each bag into the swirling turbidity. It was almost ghostly. The only way I knew anyone else was there was the chatter from each diver. Ham allocated the divers into three sections, Harry would search out from the port beam halfway to the bow, while Bill took the starboard beam forward, and Ski operated off the bow. They were to fan out, moving left to right and then back, picking up anything of interest.

Devon followed Ski for a couple of minutes, and then traced his umbilical back and picked up Harry. Devon was moving back along Harry's umbilical when Sonar called Control and Dive Control simultaneously.

"This is Sonar – stop everything right now!" It was Chief Barkley, and he sounded worried.

"Take over, Ham," I said, and left for Control. ""Have the divers hold their positions," I added over my shoulder.

I arrived at Control with the Skipper. Chief Barkley was waiting.

"What is it, Chief?" the Skipper asked.

"There's something out there, Sir, in front of us. I'm talking about mechanical sounds that don't belong there."

"The *Whiskey*?" I asked.

"No Sir. No submarine sounds...I don't really know what it is, but it's nearby."

"Go to ultra-quiet, Nav," the Skipper ordered. Then he turned to me.

"Mac, have your divers proceed with caution."

"Yes Sir," I said, and returned to Dive Control.

I explained to the guys that something was out there, but we had no idea what it was, except that it was making mechanical noises. I told the guys to continue their survey, and to continue collecting pieces – no reason not to take treasure just because something was out there somewhere.

The survey was a slow process, since visibility was so bad. Every once in a while, however, the water would clear up for a time – a few seconds to a couple of minutes. As the divers progressed, they were reporting an increasing number of the clear moments. I also noticed that general visibility from the Basketball was improving as well.

Suddenly Ski piped up with, "Whoa...we got company, guys!"

"Green Diver," that was Ski, "say again."

"We got company. I saw a brief flash of a brightly-lighted diving bell suspended over the bottom. I didn't see no divers, but what the fuck they doin' here?"

"Green Diver," I wanted to be sure I had heard correctly, "say again, say again."

"Dive Control, Green Diver, I saw a bell, a diving bell maybe ten feet off the bottom; lights all around, clear as anything. Now it's gone, visibility closed back up."

"How far away, Green Diver?" I asked.

"Hundred, two-hundred feet – hard to tell. Nothing for reference."

"Extinguish your light and proceed with caution, Green Diver," I said. "Red Diver, extinguish your light and swing to your right; Blue Diver, extinguish your light and swing to your left. Both of you join Green Diver. Once you locate him, report to me, and keep together."

On the sound-powered phone I told Devon to douse the light on the Basketball and get about twenty-five feet off the bottom, and then to proceed away from us on our axis. I felt a hand on my shoulder, and turned to see the Skipper standing behind me. I had no idea how long he'd been there. Normally, Ham, Jack, or Jimmy would have alerted me – and everyone else – of his presence, but we were too intently focused on what was out there. None of us noticed his arrival.

"Your thoughts, Mac," the Skipper said to me, ignoring the lapse in protocol.

"They don't have six-hundred-foot lock-out capability on any sub that I know of, Sir. The entire saturation diving concept is pretty new. The French and Swedes are doing it." I paused in thought. "I suppose it's reasonable to assume that Ivan has his own research going." I paused again, scanning the monitor for anything new.

"Red, Blue Divers – anything yet?" I asked generally.

"Red Diver, negative."

"Blue Diver, negative."

I turned back to the Skipper. "The Soviets have a fairly advanced submersible program, but that's one atmosphere, not ambient lock-out. They've got a well-known oceanographer and submersible expert, Anatoly

Sagalevitch, who's working on some state-of-the-art one-atmosphere rigs. No mobile lock-out capability that I know of. But if Ski is right, they got a lock-out bell right here."

The Skipper stood silently, absorbing my information. "They're not looking for us," he said, "that would be totally inefficient. They're cleaning house. They know we were here, and they're removing everything they can before we return."

I had to admit, it made a lot of sense.

The sound-powered phone chirped. "I got something, Dive Control," Devon said. I looked up at the monitor.

At first I didn't see anything. I asked Jack to dim the lighting, and then it began to come into focus, a glowing smudge at the middle of the monitor, near the bottom.

"Move in slowly," I told Devon. "Stay just at the edge of visibility, and see if you can find their SPCC, or whatever they use." The likely answer was that this was a Soviet "Strength-Power-Communications Cable," a combined cable about the thickness of the human wrist that served as a lifting cable while providing electricity to a Personal Transfer Capsule used by hard-hat divers.

The glow moved slowly to the exact center of the monitor, and then moved back and forth, up and down just a bit.

"I got it," Devon said in my ear. "How about if I go up a hundred feet, turn on my light so we can examine it?"

I turned to the Skipper. He nodded, looking intently at the monitor.

"Make it so, Devon, but don't point the light down under any circumstances – got that?"

"Aye, Sir."

The smudge disappeared on the monitor, and we saw nothing at all for a couple of minutes.

"Dive Control, Red Diver, the other guys are with me, and we can just make out a glow ahead of us."

"Roger that, I said. Move back until it just disappears. Then hold your positions."

Suddenly, the Basketball monitor lit up. Right in the center was a shiny cable – probably stainless steel.

"How thick is it?" I asked Devon.

"'Bout as thick as my thumb," he answered.

"That's no SPCC," I said to the Skipper.

The Skipper nodded. "I got it," he said.

"There's another cable-hose bundle out there somewhere," I said to Devon. "But leave it for now. Drop back down to just visible, and hang out with your light off." As an afterthought I added, "Careful that you don't get wrapped around the cable."

"Never happen, Sir." Even over the sound-powered phone, Devon sounded insulted.

"Dive Control, Red Diver, visibility is beginning to clear...whoa – they got divers in the water!"

"Back off, Red Diver. Don't let them see you."

The Skipper picked up another sound-powered phone handset. "Sonar," he said, "any other activity?"

"There's a tender on the surface, Sir. He's station-keeping with thrusters. Too damn much noise to hear anything else, Sir."

"Red Diver," I said, "ascend to twenty feet over bottom." They were at exactly 600 feet. "Watch your ceiling," I added, "don't get shallower than five-hundred seventy-five. Keep that five-foot margin."

"In this visibility they're not going to look up," I said to the Skipper. "I'm going to move the Basketball in closer, so we can watch from above. If they actually glance up, their minds won't interpret what they see as something manmade."

"Okay," the Skipper said, "but be careful."

I gave the appropriate instructions to Devon, and a minute later we had a bird's eye view of two divers about ten feet below the Basketball, trudging along the bottom, dragging mesh bags, partially filled with missile debris.

The visibility moved in and out, but once your mind got the idea, the picture became fairly clear as the brain integrated the flashes of clear with the grainy turbidity.

I instructed our three divers to move over and above the Basketball, and to hang off to one side for the time being. The Soviet divers were emitting bubbles, which meant they were not using closed-cycle rigs. They were burning a lot of helium this way, and the bell displayed no exterior gas bottles, so their breathing supply was being piped down through the cable bundle. I tried to determine if they were using hot water rigs, but couldn't really tell. Their umbilicals were thinner than ours, and dragged on the bottom.

"Red Diver, I said, "are they using hot water?"

"Doesn't look like it, Sir. Umbilicals are too thin, and the suits are too tight. Looks like heavy-weight neoprene."

That was interesting. That meant their bottom time was drastically limited by the cold. Unless they had a way of heating up the bell interior, they would develop hypothermia rather quickly. I looked at their movements. They appeared to move their arms as little as possible, a clear indication that their suits constricted their movement – as heavy-duty wetsuits would do.

The Soviet divers appeared to be using weighted shoes, but they each also had a pair of fins tied to their waists, and seemed to sport a come-home bottle as well. The bell had several large mesh bags attached to the outside that were partially filled with missile parts, large and small. One of the divers dragged his full bag to the bell and began to unload it into the bell's mesh bag.

"What's your bag load right now?" I asked the guys. I had instructed them to retain their bags while investigating the Soviet divers. Visibility was too bad to park the bags on the bottom. They would never have found them again. And the lift bags were to unpredictable to tie them off from the umbilical behind them. So they toted the bags with them. Let's face it. No missile parts, wasted trip.

"Red Diver – half full."

"Green Diver – three-quarters."

"Blue Diver – 'bout two-thirds."

Blue Diver, Dive Control, take control of all three bags and bring them back to Mama," I ordered.

As I gave the order, the Soviet diver at the bell finished emptying his bag and turned to head back to his companion. His mesh bag caught on something on the bell, and as his momentum pulled his feet forward, his torso remained where it was. In two seconds flat, he was on his back looking straight at my divers. At just that moment, the visibility cleared dramatically, and the diver had a full view in the reflected light of three divers hanging a few feet above him, a round tethered ball off to one side, and mesh bags just visible towering above them.

We were unable to see his facial expression, but we did get a glimpse of his eyes. They were wide open with shock. Then, apparently his training took over. He kicked off his weighted boots, stripped his fins from his waist and donned them in one practiced maneuver, and then – to our collective total surprise – grabbed what turned out to be a gas-powered spear gun from a rack on the outside of the bell. In one smooth motion he brought the gun up and fired.

"God damn! The sonovabitch shot me!" Ski yelped. "Right through my fucking arm!"

Bill securing the Russian diver

CHAPTER THIRTY-FOUR

"Skipper?" This was a decision I couldn't make.

"Take them out, Mac!"

"Ski – are you mobile?" I asked.

"I'm fine, I just got a fucking spear in my arm." Ski didn't sound too happy.

"Listen all of you," I said. "First, kill the coms! Cut their main cable bundle. Watch out for spear guns. Move it, Guys!"

We had perhaps a minute or so before someone down there thought to call topside. Perhaps they already had, but we needed to move.

"Dive Control, it's Bill. I'm at the bundle. It's three pieces – gas, comms, and strength member. I'm sawing the comms."

Suddenly the Basketball monitor cleared up and I could see Bill cutting away at the comm cable.

"I'm watching, Bill," I told him.

"I'm through the skin, Dive Control..." Grunting and panting. "Okay – it's cut."

Just then the Basketball monitor went crazy.

"Something jerked the Basketball," Devon said urgently. "I zoomed away, but I think they grabbed the Basketball cable."

"Harry, take care of it!" I ordered. "Devon, try to give me a view."

The monitor swirled, and then a beam of light cut a swath across the monitor. The image swung wildly, and then we were looking into the mask of a stranger. He had a knife in his hand, and was trying to strike the Basketball. Then a hand reached across his mask from behind and ripped it off. The image jerked and went wild again. Then it stabilized.

"I've got control again, Mac," Devon said over the sound-powered phone.

I watched, fascinated. The Soviets were using some pretty basic stuff – plain facemask and a regulator in the mouth. The diver had the presence of mind to keep his eyes open, but he didn't do the next most important thing. He forgot to protect his regulator, and in a heartbeat Harry had ripped it out of his mouth. Instantly, it was a life and death struggle.

The Russian's right hand flashed across the monitor holding a ten-inch serrated blade. But where Harry's hand had been was just empty water, and a moment later Harry's blade sliced across the Russian's neck, and the water turned black.

I turned to the Skipper. "Skipper, we need an explosive cutter fast. With comms gone, they're going to pull the bell up in a bit. They'll get the divers back in the bell somehow, and then bring her up." I gestured to Ham who turned to talk to the guys in the Can.

The Skipper grabbed the 1MC. "Engineer to Control." And he left for Control himself.

Ham had Jer ready to go by the time the explosive cutter arrived at the Dive Console. Ham passed it through the medical lock, and six minutes after I asked the Skipper for the cutter, it was in Jer's leg pocket on its way to the bell.

"Ski, what's your condition?" I asked.

"Hurtin', but I'll live, El-Tee," he answered.

"Then follow your umbilical back. Jer's bringing an explosive cutter to cut the bell cable."

"Right on – I'm on my way," Ski answered.

"Bill," I said, "what's the status of the other bad guy?"

"Back inside the bell, Sir, but I jammed a piece of missile in the hatch. He's got a live spear gun so I can't approach the hatch, but he can't unjam it either. We're at a standoff."

The Basketball monitor lit up with a fairly clear image of the bottom of the bell. I could clearly see a piece of missile T-bar wedged into the opening, bent around the outer lip. Bill was holding it in place from the outside, and although it was wiggling back and forth, so long as Bill kept hold, the hatch wasn't going to close.

I heard Jer and Ski chatting, and shortly thereafter, Jer returned to the Can, and spoke quietly with Ham by sound-powered phone. Ski had a ten-inch spear clear through his upper left arm. He seemed okay, but we had to get him back soon.

"Ski, give the cutter to Harry, and then get your ass back here. Harry," I continued, "clamp the cutter about ten feet above the bell. Let me know when you're ready."

About ten minutes later, just as Whitey was pulling Ski into the Can, Harry announced he was ready.

"Bill, get out of the way now! Cut the cable, Harry," I ordered.

We heard a sharp, muffled crack, and clouds of silt rose as the bell fell ten feet to the seabed. On the Basketball monitor, we clearly saw the T-bar stuck in the sea floor and still jammed through the hatch opening.

The diver inside the bell wasn't going to seal the hatch, that was for sure.

I called the Skipper on the sound-powered phone. I told him that I thought we could use our capstan to pull the bell on its side and force the diver still inside to come out or drown. I told him I thought we could take him captive, and bring him back with us. The Soviets would never know or even suspect we had him, and our guys could probably learn a great deal from him. The Skipper agreed, so I told the divers to relax on station while we set up the plan.

In the meantime, Whitey pulled the spear completely through Ski's arm, and got his hot water suit off. He administered an antibiotic topically and orally, bound the wound and gave Ski a pain reliever, and put him in his rack. Like Ski said, it wasn't serious, but it hurt like hell.

We planned to use the same basic trick we had used on the anchor cable repair that seemed so long ago. The divers would bend a clamp to the bell cable, forming a loop. We would raise the capstan on our foredeck, hook a hawser to the loop and wrap it around the capstan. A steady pull should roll the bell to its side and keep it there. On its side, the bell would quickly fill with water, and the diver inside would have no choice but to surrender or drown.

The air and power lines were still attached to the bell. I wanted to cut them as soon as possible, before the desperate diver inside the bell figured a way to communicate his plight topside. I sent Jer to the foredeck to prepare the hawser and capstan. I sent Bill to finish cutting the gas and power lines. I brought Harry back to get the clamp for the loop and to bring the hawser back to the bell. For that he needed another lift bag, and we had that waiting for him at the Aquarium.

Just as Harry was arriving back at the *Halibut*, the lights on the bell went dark. Apparently, Bill had cut the power. I tried to imaging the stark terror the Russian must be experiencing at that moment. Since he couldn't know we were planning to rescue him, he had to be preparing to die, and if he was anything like my guys, he was holding back the terror, and holding on to the hope of a last-minute miracle.

To Bill I said, "Hold off a bit on cutting the gas. Let's let him experience the full impact of what has happened to him,"

It only took about fifteen minutes for everything to be in place to transport the hawser to the bell. Under the watchful eye of the Basketball, Harry hooked the end of the hawser to his lift bag, squirted sufficient gas into the bag to lift the hawser, and swam it in the direction of the bell. By this time, Bobby had the Basketball again, and he kept close to Harry during the transit.

The water had cleared, so that the visibility was nearly as good as it ever got. I could clearly see the glow from Bill's light as we got underway. Harry ignored Bill, and went directly to the top of the bell. He took the shiny lift cable in his gloved hand and slid along its length until he reached the frayed end. He bent a loose loop and attached the clamp without tightening it. Then he pulled the frayed cable end through the clamp until it extended about a foot. Finally, he tightened the bolts so that the clamp cinched the two cable pieces tightly.

Harry held his handiwork up for the Basketball to examine, and then proceeded to thread the hawser end through the loop. He bent a large bowline, and finished it off with a half hitch. Then he gave Bobby two thumbs-up and announced, "Dive Control, I don't know what the hell diver I am anymore, but your tow's ready."

"First name basis, guys," I announced. Frankly, I didn't know which color Harry was either. The idea of the colors was to keep things simple. We had gone way beyond that.

"Jer," I said, "take a strain until Harry tells you to stop."

On the monitor I watched the hawser stretch out and then take up the slack in the lift cable. As it stretched taut, Harry told Jer to stop. I signaled the Skipper, and a couple of minutes later he was standing beside me at the Dive Console.

"You're in charge, Mac," he said. "Let's see what this guy's made of."

"Okay, Bill," I ordered, "I want you to cut the gas hose the moment the Bell rolls over and begins to fill."

"Roger that, Dive control."

"Bobby," I said on the intercom, "give me the widest view you can, but don't lose the picture."

"Roger that, Dive Control," as the scene widened.

Bobby placed the Basketball so the bell was on the left and Bill was above and a bit left of the bell. The hawser disappeared off the screen to the right. I signaled Jer to begin hauling in the hawser. On the screen the bell did not appear to move at all, but the hawser began to stretch, and even though it was subjected to the pressure of 600 feet, it seemed to vibrate a bit as the tension grew. Then I saw a bit of motion at the top of the bell.

Slowly, the lift ring began to tip toward the hawser. I signaled Jer to hold. Then I said to Bill, "Bill, get ready to cut the gas line...on my mark."

I signaled Jer to continue. We all watched the bell slowly roll to its side – a slow-motion underwater dance. Gas began to bubble from the partially open hatch. I knew what was happening inside. The Soviet diver was scrambling to keep his feet under him, trying to retain his orientation, not knowing whether the roll was a consequence of the broken cable, for which he also did not know the cause, or something the unknown divers outside were doing. I'm sure he had an eye on the light entering through the sprung hatch cover. The bubbling gas turned into a torrent.

"Cut it, Bill!" I ordered.

The topside end of the hose bundle whipped off into the darkness, leaving a rising trail of bubbles behind. We never saw it again. The bell end of the hose bundle whipped around in a figure eight motion for several seconds, and then it dropped to the sea floor, still leaking a trickle of gas.

The torrent of gas pouring from the sprung hatch quickly dwindled to a string of bubbles escaping from the highest point of the opening, and then it stopped. The entire drama played itself out on the monochrome monitor in absolute silence, except for the helium affected breathing of Harry, Bill, and Jer.

"Bill," I said, "place yourself at the top of the sealing ring."

As the bell turned, the hatch sprang inward so that we clearly saw the hatch opening on the monitor.

"Harry," I said, "place yourself by the sealing ring on the hinge-side of the hatch." And I added to both of them, "Remember, he's armed – but he's got no place to go. He probably figures he'll take as many as possible with him."

As I spoke, a spear poked out of the darkened opening. Bill reached down and grabbed it. He pulled out and up, and tossed it to one side, discharging it as he dropped it.

"Look out, Bill!" I nearly shouted, as Bill lifted his legs above him, and started to drop in front of the hatch opening. "That was too easy. He's got another one."

With the grace of a trained athlete, Bill arched his back, bracing his fins against the sealing ring while lifting his upper body back and away from the hatch – just as a flashing metal dart flew out of the hatch, grazing Bill's rebreather pack. Bill lifted his feet above him and reached into the hatch. He came out a moment later with a facemask in one hand and a regulator mouthpiece with two torn hoses in the other. He tossed them aside and pointed at Harry's come-home bottle. Harry pulled it off his harness and handed it to Bill.

Bill moved a couple of feet away from the hatch, and illuminated the bottle with his headlamp, gesturing for the diver to come out, and pointing to the bottle. He stayed there while the rest of us held our collective breaths. Thirty seconds...forty-five seconds...a full minute – and then a neoprene figure appeared and reached for the bottle. Harry came up behind him, knife in hand, and pressed the point through the thick neoprene into the skin to the right of the small of his back, over his liver. The Russian winced, but kept his hands on the bottle.

"We got about five minutes on this bottle," I said on the circuit and to everybody near the Dive Console. "Jer, meet them with your bottle. They'll need it. Watch yourself. We don't know what this guy's intentions are yet. He may just be waiting to take the lot of you out with him."

"Fat chance," Bill muttered.

"Ham," I said, "find some nylon electric ties quick. Pass them into the Can, and get them out to Jer as soon as he comes back. Have another come-home bottle ready for him too."

Ham nodded and sent Jack off to get the ties. In the meantime, we continued to watch the drama on the monitor. Just as Jer joined them, the Russian passed his hand in front of his throat and then pointed to his mouth in the universal diver signal for "give me air." Jer unhooked his bottle and handed it to Bill. Bill held it up in front of the Russian, but out of reach. The distressed diver started to lunge, but Harry jabbed his knife a bit deeper. The Russian stopped immediately and reached back to the knife with his right hand, but Harry pressed a bit more, and the Russian froze. Bill placed the bottle in his left hand, and the Russian took a deep breath.

I sent Jer back for the ties, and by the time they reached the stern of the sub, Jer met them with the ties and another bottle. After a bit of fumbling, Jer securely tied the Russian's gloved hands behind him. I told Jer to pull the ties tight, since he needed to compress the thick neoprene.

"Okay, guys, take a minute to relax and get your acts together." I paused. "It's going to be crowded in the can, and this guy can cause a lot of mischief. When you get him in the outer lock, cut his suit off, with Bill's knife at his throat the entire time. Strip him, get a Nomex jumper on him, and watch him while his hands are free." I paused again to let my words sink in. "Don't be shy about using your knife, Bill," I said.

"I can do anything Harry can," Bill said with a noticeable sneer that came through the Helium speak.

"Any of you guys speak Russian?" I asked.

"You're shittin' me, right El-Tee?" That was Ski.

"Dr. Banks and Senior Chief Blunt both speak Russian," the Skipper interjected.

"I need one of them here ASAP, Skipper," I said.

The Skipper picked up a sound-powered phone handset, and a couple of minutes later Senior Chief Blunt showed up.

"Yes Sir," he said to the Skipper.

The Skipper nodded toward me, and I briefly explained the situation to the Senior Chief. I finished by saying, "We need to get him into the Can, get his suit off, and get him into a dry Nomex. To do this, we need to remove his cuffs. I want you to tell him what we're going to do. Tell him in no uncertain terms that if he so much as blinks wrong, Bill will cut his throat. We'll clean up the mess afterward. Tell him exactly as I said it. You got that, Senior Chief?"

He nodded, wide eyed. "You got it, El-Tee; just like you said."

"I'm serious, Senior Chief," I tried to sound as earnest as possible. "His buddy tried to kill Harry, and this bastard tried to kill Bill, twice. I want him to understand in no uncertain terms that he has no options. He's alive right now because of us. We own his soul, so tell him just like I said, okay?"

This time there was no uncertainty in Blunt's answer. "Aye, aye, sir!"

At that moment the Russian's head poked up through the Outer Lock hatch. Ski grabbed his come-home bottle and ripped it out of his mouth. Before the startled expression disappeared from the Russian's face, Ski had his head pinned back against the deck, hands still tied behind him.

I nudged the Senior Chief, and he began speaking slowly in Russian, clearly detailing the rules as I had outlined them. He finished by asking in Russian if the diver understood.

"Da...yes!" the Russian stammered, probably still disbelieving what he had just seen outside: a nuclear submarine with a lockout chamber attached to the rear deck.

Whitey's head appeared on the monitor. He gestured to the Russian to boost himself into the Outer Lock. As the Russian lifted himself using his fins, Whitey reached across the opening and grabbed the front of his suit with his left hand. One powerful jerk, and the Russian was inside the Outer Lock, facedown on the deck. Bill immediately followed him. With one smooth movement he rid himself of his breathing gear and fins, and straddled the prone Russian, pulling his head back, presenting his blade to the Russian's throat.

Manipulating the Russian diving bell

CHAPTER THIRTY-FIVE

"Whitey," I said, watching the prone Russian diver, "Strip his suit, up the legs to the waist. Then get the rest off – without cutting his hands loose, okay."

"Right, Boss."

Two minutes later the Russian was shivering naked on the deck, trying hard not to cut his Adams apple on Bill's knife. He was well built with very little body fat. At just under six feet tall, he was a fine specimen of Soviet physique, with short-cropped hair and finely honed facial features that presented a slightly different cast than the typical North American of European heritage. Perhaps it was a slight Slavic influence, more pronounced cheekbones, but the effect was subtle.

"Show him the Nomex, Ski," I said.

Ski held up a blue one-piece jumpsuit made of fire-retardant Nomex fabric. The entire front, neck to crotch, sported a Velcro seal.

"Show him how the Velcro works," I said.

We could hear the "ripping sound" of Velcro being pulled apart as Ski closed and opened the Velcro strip down the front of the Nomex.

"Bill, cut him a bit, just enough to get his attention."

The Russian winced.

"Now, cut his hands free, Jer."

The Russian massaged his wrists, and then slipped the Nomex over his legs, and thrust his arms one at a time through the sleeves. He moved slowly and deliberately, not wanting to aggravate Bill.

"Okay, tie him up again," I said, once it was obvious the Russian had settled into the Nomex garment.

Our guest offered no resistance. He seemed overawed by what he was seeing and experiencing. I suspect he was also overwhelmed by the fact that he was still alive.

I looked at Senior Chief Blunt. "Ask him if he's thirsty," I said.

The Russian started speaking, but was incomprehensible. I briefly told Blunt about the helium speech distortion, and he translated for the Russian. Jer installed a throat mike on him, and he was still incomprehensible – to us, but not to Blunt.

#

I arranged with the Skipper and Dr. Banks to have either Senior Chief Blunt or the Dr. himself available on call. Then I motioned Ham over to me.

"We got to stow the hawser and capstan. And we got to undo the loop, and clean up the site out there, Ham. Sooner or later they're going to come back – probably sooner with a submersible. We got to make it look natural. If they figure out for certain that we did this to them, there'll be hell to pay. They'll get even somehow." I looked up to see the Skipper taking in our conversation.

"It's okay, Mac," he said with a smile. I just saved you the task of briefing me."

"I'm going to secure the Russian and leave him with Ski, since his arm is useless," Skipper. "I'm going to send the rest out to clean up the mess."

Ham looked at me a bit startled, and I realized I had forgotten one thing. "Skipper, we need to move closer to the Bell. We only have two long umbilicals."

"Okay, Mac. Get your divers out and float them. Assign one man to guide me. I'll lift the sub a couple of feet and move forward on the thrusters. Give me the word when you are ready." The Skipper paused. "I don't have to remind you that that *Whiskey* is probably out there with the most sensitive ears he's got, trying to find us. So you need to move fast, and keep it quiet. Make sure your men know that!"

"Aye, Skipper," I responded, and turned to Ham again.

"Get the doc on the sound-powered phone, Ham," I said.

A moment later Ham handed me the handset. "Doc," it was Chief Wesley Branson, "I need to knock out my Russian friend for about an hour. It's got to be a shot, not oral. You got something?"

"I got a sleepy shot that will put him out for about three or four hours. Takes effect in about five minutes. That good enough?"

"Bring it to Dive Control, Doc," I said. "Thanks!"

"In the Can, put the Russki in a rack and strap him down," I told the divers.

The Russian continued to cooperate, although he grumbled when he was strapped in. Ham passed the hypo through the medical lock, and when the prisoner saw the needle, he struggled. But when Bill brought his knife in front of the Russian's face, he settled down. Ski jabbed the needle into his arm, and shortly, he was sleeping like a baby.

#

Ham explained to the guys what they needed to do, and in fifteen minutes they were exiting the Can on yet another excursion. Whitey was the mouth, and five minutes after they left the Can, he indicated they were ready to shift the *Halibut*. Jack patched the diver right to Conn. Bobby parked the Basketball just past Whitey, so we could see his hand signals as a backup to his voice.

I could feel the sub lift off the seafloor, but there was no sensation of forward movement. On the Basketball monitor, I saw the bottom slipping by at what amounted to a walking pace. We moved ahead about 200 feet, and then Whitey signaled stop. The Skipper put it down gently – well, actually it probably was Larry, but the Skipper gets credit for everything anyway.

I set Jer and Whitey to stowing the hawser, which was not just a simple stow, because first they had to untie the bowline, and while they were at it, undo the clamp holding the cable loop in place. When the sub moved forward, removing the tension from the hawser, the bell shifted to a more upright position. When I examined it on the monitor, it seemed to be sitting at about a thirty-degree tilt from vertical. Apparently, the base was ballasted, but the open hatch had wedged into the seafloor, preventing the bell from tilting completely upright. The dead diver's body had been partially caught under the bell when it rolled over. The result was a gruesome reminder that the seafloor at 600 feet is a hostile environment. The diver's remains were already being swarmed by dozens of small crabs about the size of a human hand. It was pretty clear that Shelikhov would leave little useable biological evidence for the submersible that was certain to be here in a month or so.

Jer and Whitey could do nothing about the explosively-cut cable and the knife-cut hose bundle, and in a month the sea would do little to soften the evidence. As I thought about it, however, I tried to picture myself on an investigative mission in a small, cramped submersible. Could I connect the dots of the sparse evidence we were leaving behind to construct a clear picture of what had actually happened? Or would I interpret what I saw by assuming that some natural tragedy had befallen the bell? I was sure it would be discussed in hushed tones in quiet corners of distant Russian bars for years to come – until the participants were scattered and no longer had contact with each other in the normal course of business.

And how would our guest fit into this picture, I wondered, and as I thought about that, I began to see some of the astonishing implications the presence of our captive placed on the table. We couldn't return him to the Soviets. That would put an end to our activities in Okhotsk. We couldn't kill him when we were through with him – we just didn't do things that way. At first glance, there seemed only two viable possibilities. Either we kept him an unannounced prisoner virtually forever, or we turned him, and set him up with a new life in America that would totally eclipse anything he had had in the Soviet Union, and that somehow would prevent him from ultimately notifying the Soviets of what had happened. The more I pondered this, the more it became obvious that we had to do some serious talking among ourselves before we got back to port and the problem was no longer ours alone.

It was a full half hour before Jer and Whitey had completely stowed the hawser, and were ready to join Bill and Harry.

In the meantime, Bill and Harry had emptied the baskets on the outside of the bell of the accumulated missile parts the Russian divers had collected. That plus our own haul from before the incident gave us more than sufficient material to justify our treasure-hunting excursion. Jer and Whitey helped them float everything back to the *Halibut*.

We still had to lower the sling, move the sub out of the way, load the sling, move the sub back, and raise the sling with its precious load. That was an hour or more of really hard work, and my guys had been working already

for several hours, which had included a life-and-death struggle.

"Have the guys eaten anything?" I asked Ham.

"I sent in some ham and cheese sandwiches when they brought the Russkie in," Ham said. "And the Doc sent in some energy bars."

"They got an hour left in them?" I asked.

"Is the Pope a Catholic, Sir?" Ham actually sounded insulted.

"I know, Ham, but keep an eye on them anyway," I said.

#

The job actually took an hour and a half. One of the winches jammed halfway up, and the guys had to disassemble it on the spot to make it work. The problem turned out to be grit in the gears – apparently the self-flushing mechanism had failed. But finally the sling was snug, and all the details around the bell had been policed. For the Russians, connecting the dots to come up with us would be most unlikely.

Ham had the guys back safely inside the Can. The Russian was awake, so he and Ski gave up their racks so the other four could get some badly needed rest. Oddly enough, although Ski was the only one who sustained a wound, he seemed to have taken a liking to the Russian, whose name – Ski told us – was Sergyi Andreev. It turned out that Sergyi spoke English fairly well, but he had a bit trouble adapting to the helium speech descrambler, and I began to realize that comms in their system probably was as primitive as their equipment – hand signals and pads of paper.

That was when Sonar announced suppressed cavitation somewhere off our port bow.

Bill and Sergyi playing chess in the Can

CHAPTER THIRTY-SIX

Suppressed cavitation or not, the divers were still my first priority. I had six saturated divers in the Can – one of them a potential saboteur, or at least a possible troublemaker. I thought it best that we treat Sergyi with respect, but hold him at arm's length.

Obviously, he knew about our scavenging activities, and I had little doubt that the Soviet high command was certain an American submarine had been scavenging missile pieces from the Okhotsk seafloor. I was just as certain they had no idea about the pod. I personally cautioned each of the divers in the Can to refrain from any mention of anything but the scavenger hunt. Ham explained to Sergyi as best he could our decompression procedures.

Within a half hour of Sonar's announcement, we commenced the weeklong decompression transit to surface pressure.

\#

I reported to Control to put myself back on the watch list, since the entire decompression process is as routine as things get in the saturation diving business, even with the crowded Can and our Russian visitor. And that brings up something that turned out to be fairly important as this situation developed.

While the rest of the divers were policing the seafloor by the bell, back in the Can Ski had referred to Sergyi as a Russian. Sergyi displayed his first and only genuinely angry response, informing Ski in no uncertain terms that he was *not* a stupid Russian peasant, but a Ukrainian.

The current watch was just about over, and Dirk – who had the Deck – was busy getting the sub underway on the battery, at ultra-quiet, while keeping a wary eye on the *Whiskey*. Yes, Sonar had identified our old adversary once again – not that anyone was surprised by that.

I was up next, so I spent a few minutes in Sonar, getting the big picture, expanding my focus from the limited perspective of the bell and its surrounds. The Tender was still topside, probably trying to ascertain exactly what had happened. Petty Officer Lemuel Fitzgerald – Fitz to one and all – still had the Sonar Supervisory watch, and he briefed me on his best take on the topside picture.

The Tender was still stationkeeping, the *Whiskey* was approaching from the west, and there was some indication that one or more surface combatants were entering the picture as well – probably the *Ognevoy* and *Odarenny* again, since they were apparently the current choices for picket duty up here. There didn't seem to be any other activity, although with the strength of the Soviet submarine fleet stationed at Petropavlovsk Kamchatskiy, they certainly could field just about anything they wanted in their search for us.

That was certainly food for thought. If the Soviets thought we might be a genuine threat – if they connected the dots correctly – we were in serious trouble. That thought was in my mind as I assumed the watch just after we set a southerly course, quietly hugging the seafloor as we crept away from the point that surely would become the datum for an exhaustive Soviet search.

#

On our chosen course of 195 degrees, the *Whiskey* was somewhere in our starboard quarter. In our ultra-quiet mode, running on the battery with virtually everything shut down, there was no way he could hear us. Nevertheless, we still had a bit of a blind spot in our baffles. It was considerably narrower in this mode, but it was still there. Consequently, the Skipper ordered baffle clearing twice each hour, at random times, determined by the roll of two dice, with the numbers rolled multiplied by ten being the points in the hour for the baffle clears.

It wasn't just the *Whiskey,* or even the two surface guys that concerned us. We had to assume that the threat of our potential presence would keep the surface combatants standing guard near the Tender until she finally went back to her home base. The *Whiskey's* wily skipper had to know by now that he was dealing with an out-of-the-ordinary situation. He had to be keenly aware that he had had several near-misses, but he simply didn't have the technology to ascertain which submarine he was dealing with at any given time. Did he believe he was dealing with a series of American subs, or did his instinct tell him that one man had opposed him at every turn of events?

We knew that the Russian (if that's what he was) skipper took chances. We also were pretty sure that he wanted to be the one to bag us, but would that prevent him from calling in reinforcements? Our own submarine service displayed a deep running rivalry between "nukes" and "pigboats." I had no reason not to believe a similar rivalry existed between the Soviet diesel and nuclear submariners. That meant our pigboat skipper would be reluctant to include a nuke puke on his team, but then again, he knew well his limitations, and typically a nuke didn't share his limitations. Bottom line was, we needed to keep our ears peeled for a quieter, more capable foe, one that could go as deep as we could at three times our speed. Our only advantage against one of these nukes was that we were quieter – even counting our age; and the Soviet fast attacks didn't have our sophisticated sonar – better than the *Whiskey's*, but nowhere close to what we could do.

I couldn't get out of my mind that we were right in the middle of the Soviet power triangle, Vladivostok to the southwest, Petropavlovsk Kamchatskiy to the east on the other side of Kamchatka, and Magadan, the closest navy port due west. Most of the Soviet Pacific submarine fleet was at Petropavlovsk, and that included several of their newest – the *Victor I* fast attack.

These guys were a sea change from anything the Soviets had before, but they shared a lot in common with their ballistic missile subs. They were about 300 feet long, with two reactors, one seven-bladed prop, and something really unusual compared to our own fast attacks, a two-bladed screw on each stern plane for slow speed operations. *Victors* could dive to well over a thousand feet, and were capable of speeds in excess of thirty-five knots. Apparently, the Soviets laid little store in sound quieting, because we could hear these subs a hundred miles away with just basic sonar. I could only imagine the signature they left on SOSUS. I guess the psychology was to scare their opponents into submission by sound alone.

Seriously, however, although they outclassed the *Halibut* in every other way – speed, depth, armament – our ability to hear them about five to ten times their ability to hear us more than evened the odds. At least, that was what the Skipper clearly explained in his briefing just before we got underway from the bell site.

Nevertheless, we continued to creep along at 600 feet on the battery, clearing our baffles twice an hour as dictated by the dice. Sonar continued to track the *Whiskey* back behind us, but there was no indication that he was heading in any particular direction – he was obviously looking for us, but had not yet picked up on our departure.

Toward the end of my watch, the Skipper decided to relax ultra-quiet, go back on the plant, and recharge the batteries. Since there didn't appear to be any nearby surface combatants, the *Whisky* was far astern, and no other threat appeared imminent, he wanted to give the crew time to relax, ease the tensions, recharge themselves, so to speak, while we recharged the batteries.

We had about four days of transit to the Kurils. The Skipper and Larry had not yet decided our route through the islands to the open Pacific. The *Whiskey* could hang around the bell site another day or so, and still arrive at the Kurils about the time we would arrive. A *Victor* from Petropavlovsk could get underway and be at our exit point in five or six hours. He would be deaf and blind at that speed, and noisy as hell, but we would not be able to hear him because Kamchatka and then the islands would block the sound. Any number of surface combatants could be out there as well, and we wouldn't know about them until we were within range, if they played their cards right.

Assume they connected the dots correctly, even though it was unlikely. Then it followed that they would probably assume an American nuke, which implied about a day or so to reach the Kurils, best case. So they would need assets spread along the Kurils, concentrated at the northern end. They would be on high alert starting about now, and continue the alert for five days or so. It was a game of decreasing numbers. The longer they went without an intercept, the better the odds were of making that intercept up through day five, as a simple factor of the American sub's speed and path. It would be unlikely for the American intruder to pass later than five days after the bell incident, so if they made no contact by then, they probably would stand down.

During the last hour of my watch, the Skipper joined me at the Control Station, lounging in his chair, enjoying one of his stogies. I had been more quiet than usual, and finally he asked me what was on my mind. I gave him a rundown of my thoughts about what we were likely to face. We discussed the *Victor's* capabilities, and the Skipper told me about a new variety of *Victor*, the *Victor II*, that intelligence said had addressed some of the glaring problems of the original *Victor*. He added that he didn't think the Soviets would use their newest for Okhotsk patrol, since our intel was pretty certain they were designed to track our ballistic missile subs.

"They probably only have three or four of them at the most," the Skipper said, "and they will be on patrol looking for our boomers."

"Do we have squirt capability, Skipper?" I asked. I was referring to a communications mode where we encode a signal and then compress it into a very short burst lasting only a second or two. The transmission is made either from a buoy that sinks after the transmission or is retrieved afterward, or it can be made from a raised antenna at periscope depth. You hope someone is listening. It is nearly impossible to intercept such a message or to locate its point of transmission.

"We have it, Mac," the Skipper answered. "We have several disposable buoys we can load with the transmission, and launch them through a torpedo tube." He paused, obviously waiting for me to continue.

"If I were them," I said, "I would have the whole fleet out there. I'd have my guys bumping into each other. They have to know an American submarine is inside Okhotsk, trying to get out. Realistically, they've got one chance to find us, Skipper – at the Kurils. If they have a dozen surface guys and several subs waiting for us, we're not getting through without some help." I stepped over to the chart table, and the Skipper joined me.

"The way I see it," I said, pointing to the northern group of islands, "they'll bottle this area up tighter than a virgin on her wedding night. They can loiter several nukes here," I pointed just inside the chain, "and place a line of sonobuoys from here to here." I moved my finger along the outside of the Kurils for about 300 miles. "With that kind of coverage, they'll hear us no matter how quiet we are."

"So what do we do about it?" The Skipper's eyes were twinkling. Was I actually lecturing the Old Man? "Sorry, Sir," I said, feeling a bit foolish.

"It's okay, Mac. I like to hear my officers confirm my own analysis. So tell me, how would you solve it?" He folded his arms and leaned back against the steel pole supporting the chart table and overhead.

"A diversion, Skipper. I'd put every available asset right in the middle of their exercise. If we put three or four surface combatants on active sonar cruising the area, there'll be so much noise and confusion that no one will hear us." I paused, tapping the chart with my fingers. "How about this? One of our guys passes a designated position at a specific time on a specific course at a specific speed, and we settle right below him and let him take us out."

"I like that, Mac," the Skipper said, and left for his stateroom.

A few minutes later Josh relieved me, and I went to check on my decompressing divers.

There was literally nothing going on. Ski, Jer, Whitey, and Harry were sleeping, and Sergyi and Bill were playing a game of chess. Sergyi was munching on a sandwich. Ham said it was PBJ – something the Ukrainian had never tasted before.

Ham picked up the mike. "Sergyi, this is Lieutenant McDowell, my boss."

Sergyi popped to attention facing the lens. "Sir," he said with military formality.

"At ease," I responded. "We dispense with protocol inside the Can, and mostly in the submarine. Are you a submariner?"

"Nyet – just diver, special diver, how you call..."

"Saturation," Bill interjected, "sat diver."

"Da...sat diver, Sir." He relaxed and swept his hand around the Can interior. "This good system," he said. "Is real good." He rolled his "r" with a guttural sound.

"Carry on," I said.

Sergyi sat back down and made a move.

"He's eating Bill's lunch," Ham said, glancing at the chess board, "but Whitey gave him a good run for his money." Ham paused, looking for the right words. I looked at him expectantly. "I don't know quite how to tell you this, Mac," Ham said, "but we like this guy. I know it's a bit crazy, Sir, but he was just doing his job, same as we were. He hates the Soviets. Has dreamed of escaping to the West and going to work in the oil industry." Ham grinned sheepishly. "I'm glad we rescued him, Sir. I just hope we can make it work for him, ultimately, if you know what I mean."

"Don't you guys get too close, Ham," I said. "We only got him temporarily. You may never see him again once we turn him over to the spooks." I turned and left to get some sleep. It had been a long, long day, and the next few days promised to be even longer.

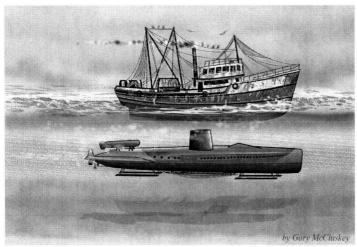

Halibut hiding directly beneath an old trawler

CHAPTER THIRTY-SEVEN

We transited for three days of tranquility. The only interesting events were the launching of the radio buoy with the squirt message, and our subsequent receipt of the confirmation. The Skipper spent a long time composing the message, and I'm certain he was specific as to time and place, with more than one back-up should we miss the rendezvous. The message went out during my sleep period, and I remained blissfully unaware of the event. Not that it really mattered anyway, because it consisted of loading the message into the buoy, setting the flooding mechanism, coming to 300 feet or less, and launching it. Unless you were on watch or in the Torpedo Room, you never knew it happened.

As it turned out, the Skipper also gave several specific times for confirmation, and the first time happened on my watch the following night. The Skipper was in Control as I brought the sub to periscope depth. Although it had been a while, the guys did a professional job. As we hit sixty-five feet, both the Skipper and I rode the scopes up and did quick swing-arounds.

The sea was running a slight swell to the north. The sky was a cloudless, star-studded dome with Polaris, the North Star, dominating the sky behind us. Neither the Skipper nor I saw anything on the surface, so I ordered the whip antenna up, and turned the scope over to a crew member for a bit of periscope liberty. We kept both scopes up for a full five minutes, which allowed about twenty crew members a thirty-second gaze on the gentle swell.

Near the end of our designated slot, Radio announced they had received a Top Secret message. I brought Glen Zaun up to take the Dive from Chris and sent for Sparks since both the Communications Officer and Chief Radioman were required in Radio to decrypt the message. In the meantime, I dove the sub back to 600 feet.

It took about fifteen minutes for Radio to decrypt the message, but not long afterward, Larry and the Skipper had their heads over the Chart Table, measuring, timing, and laying out various tracks. Then the Skipper told me to announce Officer's Call.

We met in the Wardroom as usual, the officers and department Chief Petty Officers. The senior spooks were present as a courtesy as well. The XO took over my watch.

The Skipper wasted no time in preliminaries. He laid out the basic argument I had made to him during my last watch, described the squirt message and then read the response. In a nutshell, headquarters bought into our main argument, but they came up with a different method for getting us out. They agreed with the diversion. Already, a small fleet was approaching the north Kurils. They were confident that they could completely disrupt any Soviet capability to use sonobuoys or active sonar to locate us. They expressed concern, however, with the prospect of a U.S. surface combatant moving through the Kurils at only six knots. I just wasn't normal. So they arranged for an old fishing vessel to rendezvous with us just inside the Fourth Kuril Strait off Antsiferova Island. We would depart beneath this nonentity while the fleet would rendezvous at Krusenstern Strait as a welcoming escort for the returning sub, hopefully drawing off the bulk of the reception committee.

The key word was hopefully.

#

The next evening, about an hour into my watch, Sonar announced, "Conn Sonar, new contact bearing one-four-zero, designate Echo-one."

I acknowledged and stepped over to the chart to see how this contact fit into the larger picture. I laid off a vector in the direction of the contact. It seemed pretty clear that we were dealing with something that had entered the Sea of Okhotsk from the northern end of the Kurils. But we needed more information to say anything more.

"Conn, Sonar, Echo-one is drifting right."

That meant he probably was heading in a generally westerly or southwesterly direction. We needed more information to draw any further conclusions. I was just reaching for the intercom button when Sonar announced, "Conn, Sonar, I got mostly turbine noise on Echo-one. No fisherman sounds like this. Gotta be a warship, Conn."

"Keep an eye on him, Sonar. We got a reception committee out there somewhere." I stepped back to the Control Station. "Let me know the moment you know more," I added unnecessarily.

About ten minutes later: "Conn, Sonar, Echo-one is a *Victor*-class. I'll bring the book out."

I called the Skipper. King arrived with his ship book as the Skipper came into Control with two cups of coffee. He handed one to me with a grin.

"Let's see what you have, King," the Skipper said.

King laid the large book on the chart table, opened to a page with a sleek looking nuke. "The *Victor*," he said. "Been around just a few years, but..."

"They're noisy as hell, right?" I interjected.

"You could say that," King answered. "Apparently, they have no sound isolation."

"I saw some intel before we left," I said, "that indicates they've come out with a *Victor II*, about twenty or so feet longer, room for sound isolation sleds. Quieter, but not by much."

"So this guy, Echo-one," the Skipper said, "you're sure he's a *Victor*, and not a Two?"

"Yes, Sir. Give me a few more minutes and I'll give you his hull number."

I stayed in Control while the Skipper joined King in Sonar. True to King's word, about five minutes later Sonar announced, "Conn Sonar, Echo-one is Kilo four-five-four, Soviet *Victor*-class nuclear fast attack, stationed just around the corner at Petro-whatever its name is."

The Skipper came out of Sonar and joined me on the Control Station. "He can go deeper and faster, but we outclass him in every other respect." He punched Sonar on the intercom. "Where's the *Whiskey* now?"

"Somewhere in our starboard quarter, Cap'n," King said. "No way he can hear us, though."

"How far away is he?" the Skipper asked.

"Twenty, thirty miles, maybe even more, Sir. Hard to tell. We only pick him up intermittently. I think he's just heading for home."

"The *Whiskey* knows we're headed this way," I said. "He's also got to know that the Soviet fleet is picketing the northeast side of the Kurils. He might even know about the four-fifty-four."

"We need to find our escort as soon as possible," the Skipper said with considerable urgency. He went to the chart table. I joined him.

Our track was laid out to a point just west of Antsiferova. If we pushed it a bit, we could get there early, lie low, and look for our escort, while keeping track of both the *Whiskey* and our new friend.

For the next few hours we made a beeline for the island. I slept, took a turn watching our charges inside the Can, had a couple of meals, and then it was my turn in the barrel again.

When I assumed the watch, the situation was this: We were hanging out a few miles to the west of Antsiferova. The *Whiskey* had overhauled us and was passing to the north of the island volcano Atlasova, about fifty miles to the northeast. He was in the island's shadow, so we couldn't hear him at all. Four-fifty-four had cut south between Atlasova and Paramushir islands. He was heading straight toward us about forty miles out. Surrounded by a shroud of noise as he was, he had no idea we were just ahead of him. Better still, when the *Whiskey* passed out of Atlasova's shadow, the *Victor's* noise would shield us from the *Whiskey*.

"Conn, Sonar, I have a new contact bearing zero-niner-zero, designate Foxtrot-one."

That put him between us and Antsiferova. I was pretty sure it was our escort.

"Conn, Sonar, Foxtrot-one is a trawler. It's our guy, Sir."

"You got the bent blade, Sonar?" I asked, referring to a specific characteristic the confirming message had contained. Our escort had a single four-bladed screw, and one of the blades was sufficiently bent to produce a characteristic swishing sound with every fourth blade beat.

"It's him alright, Conn. No doubt."

My instructions were crystal clear. First call the Skipper. Second, move directly beneath the trawler a hundred feet below its keel. Third, transmit a single word on the Gertrude, the venerable underwater telephone: DA. That would be the trawler's signal to come to course one-eight-zero at six knots, and to maintain that course to the middle of the Fourth Kuril Strait exactly twenty miles from Onekotan on a direct line

between Onekotan and Paramushir, and then to head due east.

My task was to creep up until I was just a few feet below the trawler's keel, and to maintain that relative position for the following ten to fifteen hours, depending on the activity around us.

I called the Skipper, and as he arrived in Control I brought us around to face the trawler's position, and drifted up from my 600- foot starting depth. As the *Halibut* passed 300 feet, with a slight up-angle, Sonar announced, "Conn, Sonar, the *Victor's* slowed way down... whoa! He just went active."

"How far to the trawler?" I asked.

"'Bout a half mile, Sir," King said.

"How far is the *Victor?* I asked.

"Ten miles or so, Sir."

I checked the chart. By swinging just a bit to the right, I would put the trawler between us and the *Victor*. I gave the order to come right and explained to the Skipper what I was doing. He nodded, so I continued for another couple of minutes. Then I came hard left, pointing directly at the trawler again, rose to 150 feet, and eased under her, coming back to the right at the same time.

The Skipper picked up the Gertrude mike, depressed the transmit button, and transmitted the single word, "Da."

I ordered a course of one-eight-zero, and as the trawler began to move, I eased our speed up to match the trawler's. We commenced our twenty-mile two-step toward the Fourth Kuril Strait.

We were shrouded in the trawler's noise, and so lost direct contact with the *Victor*, and never regained contact with the *Whiskey* as he emerged from the shadow and turned south to join the *Victor*. All we heard was the steady pinging of the *Victor's* active sonar. He had to be getting a large echo from the combined presence of the trawler and us, but he couldn't know of our presence.

We had about three hours on this heading, and it took everything we had to keep position, a constant checking and rechecking. If our sonar blips separated on the *Victor's* sonar, he would have us.

One and a half hours into this leg, Sonar suddenly announced, "Conn, Sonar, we just got the *Whiskey* back, and he's close, less than a mile off the port bow."

I acknowledged, and then King added with a bit of agitation, "Conn, Sonar, the *Whiskey's* surfacing – right in front of the trawler."

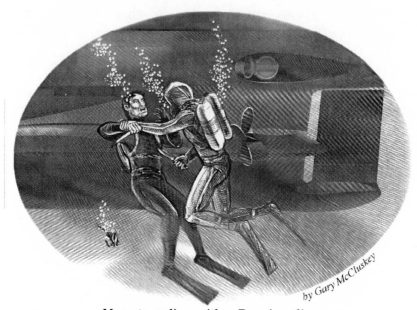

Mac struggling with a Russian diver

CHAPTER THIRTY-EIGHT

"Pots," I said to the Chief of the Watch, "set ultra-quiet ASAP!" I looked to the Skipper for approval.

He nodded. "Keep the plant running," he said.

"The Trawler just stopped," King announced, and then the sound-powered phone chirped. I picked it up. "Sorry about that, Sir, the trawler's DIW."

"All stop," I ordered. "Stand by the thrusters." I trilled the sound-powered phone. "Pinpoint the trawler's engines," I said to King. "I want to stay directly below them."

The Skipper sat down and lit up a stogie. He picked up his sound-powered phone and called the Torpedo Room. "Do we have a decoy loaded?" he asked. "Okay," he said after listening for a moment, "open tube one manually. Try not to make any noise."

The Skipper motioned to Pots. "Get Weaps up here, please."

"Aye, Sir." Pots grabbed his sound-powered phone handset.

"Mac," the Skipper said, "set General Quarters, but not with the alarm. Try to keep the time till ready to five minutes."

I nodded to Pots. People started moving through Control, orderly, but quickly. Normally, Larry had the GQ Deck, but this time the Skipper told me to retain the watch. He said he needed Larry on top of the nav situation. Senior Chief Gunty normally had Nav at GQ, but the Skipper wanted both of them available. That was fine by me. I would much rather be in charge in a critical situation than be an observer. Besides, the Skipper was right there. He wasn't going to let me screw up.

King notified me that the trawler was drifting a bit to the north. I moved us to the left a few yards.

"Skipper," I said as we eased back under the trawler, "we need to give Sonar direct control of the thrusters to minimize our drift."

"How do you propose to do that?" he asked.

"Skipper, look at this," I said, pointing to the thruster controller box. "The installation is not permanent. See this," I indicated a bundle of cable tie-wrapped to the supporting post, "and here…" another bundle right at the overhead, "…and here," a third bundle where the cable joined a larger cable run. The Auxiliaryman standing his GQ roving watch reached into his tool kit for a cutter and snipped the tie-wraps holding the controller and cable to the post, overhead, and cable run. Stretched out on the deck, it reached well into Sonar.

The Skipper went into Sonar and made sure Senior Chief Barkley knew what to do. Then he came back out to Control. "Nice job, Mac," he told me as he settled down in his chair again, relighting his cigar.

Sonar reported that the *Whiskey* had pulled up starboard side too, alongside the trawler's port side. "Looks like they're going to board her, Sir."

That's when it hit me. "Skipper," I said, "we've got a great opportunity here."

I then quickly outlined my still sketchy plan. The Can was at an internal pressure of 130 feet. Jack, Jimmy, and I could suit up in regular scuba, with twin tanks, press down in the escape hatch and exit the sub, carrying a couple of lift bags with us. We could quickly access the hawser stored in the after bin, hang it from the lift bags and swim it over to the *Whiskey's* screws. It would take less than five minutes to entangle the hawser into both screws. If we had any time left, we could even jam one or both bitter ends into the diesel engine cooling water intakes. Then we could secure the bin on our after deck, and the sub could drop down thirty feet or so to equalize the Can pressure with outside, and we could enter the Can. Since our bottom time would be relatively minimal, I could decompress in the lock, and be out in less than an hour. Since there was only about a day and a half left of the decompression anyway, Jack and Jimmy could either decompress one at a time following me, or just stay in the Can for the remaining time. Ham could handle the Dive Console by himself until I decompressed. I said we would work out the details as we progressed.

"We disable the *Whiskey*," I said, "and the *Victor* will have to surface and give him a tow to prevent him from running aground, at least for as long as it will take to get one of their surface ships over here. And before that, they'll have to figure out what happened." I grinned. "We'll be long gone by then."

There was virtually no time to think about the decision. The Skipper had to decide quickly, because we had, at the outmost, forty-five or fifty minutes – more likely thirty or less. He sat quietly for a very long minute, puffing his cigar.

"Let's do it," he said, "but scuttle your equipment as you enter the Can."

"Aye, Sir! We'll hang the weight belts and tanks from the bags, and drop them over the side."

""The Captain has the Deck and the Conn," the Skipper announced as I left for the Dive Console.

#

Time was critical. I arrived at the Dive Console, told Ham to get Jack and Jimmy. Then I outlined to him what we were going to do – at least try to do.

"You're crazy, El–Tee! Mac, fer Chris' sake, you can't do this!"

"Do you have a better solution, Ham?" I asked, not stopping as I ripped my clothing off, climbed into a snug, warmth-preserving wooly undergarment, and then pulled my Poseidon Unisuit over my head – bright orange rip-stop nylon outside, black inside. I forced my head through the tight neck dam. Then I shoved each arm into a black nylon-lined sleeve and forced each hand through the tight, waterproof cuffs. Then the legs, one at a time, into the relatively loose fitting Unisuit legs, down into the attached boots. Reach back and find the pull cord – there it is. Pull the zipper down the back, through the crotch, and up to the middle of the chest. Finally, I rolled the neck dam in so that internal air pressure would seal the soft neoprene to my neck, and slipped the thin black neoprene edged hood over my head, fitting the face seal comfortably. And with that, I was encased in that modern marvel, the Unisuit drysuit.

Next to me, Jack and Jimmy were going through the same contortions, following virtually the same steps. Since the Unisuit came out a couple of years back, divers had tried every possible combination for getting into one. What I just gone through turned out to be the only really practical way.

Somehow, Ham had managed to gather our accessories – if that's what you want to call them. Ankle straps – three-way straps that fit around the ankle and under the arch, so you don't blow your fins off; a set of ankle weights; long, straight, stiff brown rubber fins made by Voit called *Duck Feet*; snug fitting, three-finger gloves that sealed to the cuffs; a buoyancy compensator attached to a contoured backpack carrying twin nineties with two Poseidon regulators and a Unisuit hose, with weight pockets distributed over the entire front and back of the vest, the total weight adjusted to each diver's specific requirements; a facemask chosen by each diver – mine was close fitting, with a soft neoprene seal, sporting a one-way clearing valve in a cup around the nose, with an attached snorkel (mine had a corrugated section connected to the mouthpiece so it dropped away from the mouth); a sharp eight-inch knife with a serrated back edge; a six-inch double-edged dagger mounted horizontally on the BC bottom front; two twenty-four inch bang-sticks in break-away holders on each thigh. That about did it. In five minutes we were ready to go.

The escape hatch was a very snug fit for two of us outfitted as we were. Since time was at a premium, we had to crash down to fifty feet. Jimmy was a blower, pinch the nose and blow all the way down. Me, I just opened my mouth and yawned. We hit fifty feet in just a few seconds, popped the upper hatch, and squeezed out onto the after deck. I immediately pressed the hatch closed, and in less than two minutes, Jack joined us.

The water was cold against my face, but otherwise my suit kept me snug and dry. The water was remarkably clear. I could easily see the keel of the *Whiskey* off to port. I motioned for Jack and Jimmy to get the hawser. They swam forward, opened the hatch, cut the stays and hauled the end of the hawser out on the deck. I attached a lift bag, set the float level, and we pulled the rest out of the bin, attaching a total of four bags.

I felt a real urgency. I had no idea when the *Whiskey* would suddenly start up again, but I hoped I would get some kind of clue a minute or so before it happened. Right then, the rumbling of its diesels created an all-encompassing shroud of sound. There wasn't a lot of clearance between the screw tops and the surface. With the water clarity we really had to be careful the *Whiskey* Bridge watch didn't spot us. The fact was, had they really looked, they couldn't have missed us, bright orange suits and all – but they were concentrating on the trawler.

In two minutes, we had draped the hawser in a figure-eight three times around both screws and shafts. We dumped the air from the bags, and sent them to the bottom. I signaled Jimmy and Jack, and they grabbed the long bitter end of the hawser and swam down to the *Whiskey's* port engine intake. I was standing off about five yards from the side of the *Whiskey*, while they pulled the hawser end toward the opening. It turned out that the opening was blocked by a welded grate. As Jimmy turned around to signal the condition to me, the diesel engines suddenly went from idle to full throttle.

In a split second Jimmy was pulled against the grate, pinned as surely as if had been glued to the *Whiskey's* flank. He flailed his arms, and I could see him strain to pull away from the intake. His suit was sufficiently loose that he could move inside the suit, but his suit's ass was welded to the grate.

We had seconds before the *Whiskey* would put significant turns on the shafts, wrap the hawser tighter than you know what, and who the hell knew what would happen then. I had no time to think. With a powerful dolphin kick, I pushed myself toward Jimmy. I reached out and punched his suit fill valve to put extra air into his suit, and then disconnected the hose. The extra air caused him to rise, stretching the suit material where it was sucked to the grate. I grabbed my leg knife and sliced through two of the three straps holding his tanks. I pulled his regulator from his mouth and handed him my spare. The extra air in his suit caused his feet to rise. The only thing keeping his fins from being blown off was the holding action of his three-way ankle straps. He shrugged the final tank strap off his right shoulder and pushed his tanks away, letting them drop out of sight.

I had seconds left. I jabbed my blade through Jimmy's suit at his waist, releasing a large bubble of air and then sliced rapidly down and across as I rolled him to his right. His lower suit filled with thirty-five degree water, causing his eyes to open with shock as the cold surged across his abdomen, pulling his testicles up into his body. I continued slicing as rapidly as I could, until thirty seconds later, Jimmy ripped free, leaving a ragged patch of heavy black neoprene sealing the grate. His suit was flooded from the waist down, making him heavy. I grabbed a handful of Unisuit, pulled him up, and removed my regulator from my mouth. I shoved it inside the hole in his suit and pressed the button. Air rushed into the upper part of Jimmy's suit. When the downward pull stopped, I put the regulator back into my mouth, grabbed a gulp of air, and signaled Jack to help me. We pulled away, making a wide berth around the screws.

Just as we passed by the propellers, the *Whiskey* set backing turns on the port and forward on the starboard. It was a slow-motion dance of hawser and bronze. Within seconds the hawser wrapped itself tightly around both shafts, jerking them to a stop. I could hear screaming metal right through the sub's hull. We didn't stop to sightsee, however. Jimmy was rapidly approaching hypothermia. We had only a few minutes to get him back to warmth, or we would lose him.

We swam over to the exit hatch of the Can; I could hear shouts and loud clanging from inside the *Whiskey*. I signaled Jack to secure the hawser hatch, which he accomplished in less than a minute. I banged three times sharply on the can with the metal tip of my knife handle – our prearranged signal for the *Halibut* to drop to 130 feet at the deck. Inside the Can, the guys opened the locking wheel as I felt the sub begin to drop.

As we descended I looked up at the *Whiskey's* stern. Motion caught my eye. I signaled Jack to give Jimmy his spare regulator, indicated that he get Jimmy into the Can immediately, and turned to see a diver exiting from one of the *Whiskey's* after torpedo tubes. I grabbed one of my bang sticks and pushed away from the dropping sub. As I did so, another diver emerged from the tube. Their attention was clearly directed at the hawser mess around the propellers, and I don't think they saw me initially, although it would have been pretty difficult not to see the shadow of the sinking *Halibut.*

I swam toward the preoccupied pair, wasting no time with preliminary howdy-dos. Coming from below as I was, I had the disadvantage, since they naturally looked down from their prone positions. That's how one of them saw me approaching with my bang-stick extended in front of me with both hands.

If one of these guys reported back to the *Whiskey* skipper, we were shit out of luck. In that case I had no doubt they would hunt us, overwhelm us, and send us to the bottom. That meant somehow I had to disable both divers and send them to the bottom. An injured or dead diver on the surface would tell the tale as surely as a face-to-face report to their wily skipper.

The diver who spotted me was about five yards from his companion. He signaled frantically, but the other guy was intently studying the mass around the screws. His first indication that I was there was when he heard the small explosion of my bang stick. It worked like this: When I got within striking distance of the diver who saw me, he obviously was intent in getting to me, maybe to pull my mask off or rip out my regulator. I couldn't tell for sure, but he had pulled his knife out and was waving it before him as I approached. I don't think he understood the nature of my bang-stick – essentially a short-barreled, .45 cal. zip gun without a trigger. It's fired by pressure against the end of the barrel. Its two-foot length kept me just outside his knife reach, and he was unable to push the stick away before I jammed it against his stomach. The resulting damage totally disabled him. I dropped the bang-stick, and with one sweep of my own knife, I disgorged the air from his BC. He dropped, trailing a cloud of black blood. I suspect he was dead before he passed 150 feet.

With the sound of the explosion, the other diver turned, saw what had happened, hesitated for a moment, and raced for the open torpedo tube. I reached him just as he got his head and shoulders inside the three-foot opening. I couldn't let him make it inside, so I grabbed my second bang-stick and jammed it against his right leg. The explosion and bullet passing through his calf stopped his forward motion, and I pulled him back out of the tube. This guy wasn't about to go down without trying, though. His tight neoprene wetsuit acted to constrict the wound, and the cold water diminished his pain. He emerged with knife in hand, managing to slice through the back of my left glove and into my hand, causing me to drop my own knife.

I placed myself between him and the open torpedo tube and drew out my dagger. We were three feet apart, and I could see the hesitation in his eyes. Then he decided, and attempted to shoot to the surface about thirty feet above us, kicking with his left leg, trailing his right. I saw his hand reach for the blow button on his BC, as I reached out and stabbed his right fin as hard as I could, penetrating completely through the fin. Using the dagger as a lever, I pulled the surprised diver back down and ripped his regulator from his mouth, while pulling his leg sharply toward me to retrieve my dagger. From the corner of my eye I saw a flash disappear as his knife joined his buddy in the deep, so I stopped worrying about getting stabbed.

This guy was pretty resourceful. Without hesitation, he punched his BC fill button and we both began to rise.

It took me a moment, but I managed to whip my right arm over his shoulder and stab his BC bladder, which immediately belched air, stopping our ascent. Next step, get rid of his mask. A diver doesn't really need a mask, but you can see a lot better with one, and in cold water it's much easier on your face. I fumbled around and managed to pull his mask off just as his hand found mine, pulling it up over my head. At least, that was his intent, but I had donned my mask under my hood, so my mask remained against my forehead, and I still had a regulator in my mouth.

That's when I felt a sharp pain in my upper left arm immediately followed by icy cold as the sleeve filled with water. The son-of-a-bitch had stabbed my left bicep. He had another knife! I should have anticipated it. My screwup – I was tired, but not that tired.

This guy was really beginning to piss me off, though. Every time I did something that should have incapacitated him, he just found another way to get back at me. With a forty-five slug through his leg, he still was with me move-for-move. I locked my legs around him, trying to control his actions, when he ripped the regulator from my mouth. I squinted through my seawater filled eyes, and saw him put my regulator in his mouth. Shit on that!

Cut, stabbed, and now he was breathing my air!

I whipped my right arm around from his back in a wide roundhouse and jammed the needle point of my dagger right through his suit into his belly. I grabbed my mask with my injured left hand and pulled it back over my eyes and nose. Since it was self-clearing, I wasted no time, but reached for my spare regulator attached to the left side of my BC with Velcro. Now, with breathing air and clear vision restored, I saw the Russian's eyes open wide in shock. I pulled my regulator from his mouth with my injured hand, and twisted the dagger with my right. I wasn't looking to hurt the guy, but I needed to put an end to this madness. Only one of us was going home, I swore, and it wouldn't be the Russian. But he still had some fight in him.

A sharp pain pierced my left thigh, and my left suit leg flooded with water. Somehow he had either not dropped his second knife, or he had a third one stashed away. I grabbed his hand with my injured hand and forced him to drop the knife. Should I have anticipated this one as well? I don't really know. That's asking a lot.

He struggled with decreasing energy for another minute, and then he opened his mouth. I watched a stream of bubbles rise to the surface as his lungs filled with water. It was over. I released my hold on the diver and watched as he slowly slipped out of sight.

I didn't know how many more divers the *Whiskey* had available. None, probably, but as a precaution, I jammed the other end of the hawser through the space between the torpedo tube outer door hinges so they wouldn't be able to close the outer door and prepare to deploy a third man. Now, if they had another diver available, they would first have to remove a torpedo before they could put him in the water through a different tube. The alternative was to launch him from topside, and that would take at least ten minutes, probably more. I could still see the bottom of the trawler off to my right, and I had to find the *Halibut*.

I sheathed my dagger and swam over to the keel of the trawler, still wallowing in the swell. I could just barely make out the shadow of the *Halibut* below me. I struck out, kicking my way down with my right leg mostly. I knew I had lost a lot of blood, but I'd made it this far, and I wasn't about to quit now. I saw the light from the Can's open hatch when I reached about fifty feet, but as I continued to drop, the light disappeared. They had closed the hatch!

This wasn't good. Did they write me off? I couldn't believe that, so what was happening? Suddenly, the sub began to rise, and then I was on the deck. I was feeling pretty weak, but I needed to make some noise quickly. My knife was gone and my dagger wasn't massive enough. I backed up against the can and slammed my twin nineties against the hull. The sub stopped rising, and about a minute later the outer hatch opened again. A head wearing just a mask poked through the opening. I didn't recognize who it was, but he obviously was looking for me.

I could see him just fine, but it felt pretty comfortable lying there on the deck. I felt safe and secure where I was as a warm blackness overcame me. I vaguely remember being moved around, somebody stripping my gear off, being pulled through the hatch. But it's fuzzy, like a distant dream. Things got darker and then brighter, and I half wondered if I was going through a white-light-at-the-end-of-a-tunnel experience.

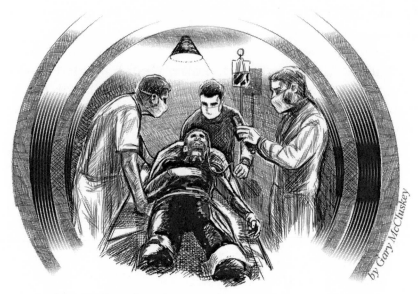

Mac undergoing an emergency operation in the Can

CHAPTER THIRTY-NINE

My suit was gone, but I didn't remember taking it off. I pressed my hands down against something soft and resilient – my left hand hurt like hell. I tried to roll over, but was restrained by something. Then I floated away again.

I felt something cool against my forehead, and a nagging, persistent voice calling my name. Maybe if I opened an eye the noise would go away. I worked at it for a while. A thousand minutes later I managed to pull my right eyelid apart. The noise stopped, but the bright light was pretty startling, and I snapped my lid shut. The noise droned on again. It was becoming irritating, so I forced both eyes open to take on my tormentor, but what I saw was the Skipper (without his cigar), Ski, Ham, and a stranger.

"Welcome back, Mac," the Skipper said. "We thought we lost you there for a while." He grinned at me and left my range of vision.

"Great to see ya, El-Tee," Ski said. "I got to go tell the guys. They'll want to know." He saluted haphazardly and left.

Ham smiled at me and presented the stranger. "Mac, this is Sergyi. He wants to tell you something."

Sergyi looked fully at me, straightened to attention, and said, "You damn fine brave guy, El-Tee. I much pleasure to know you. We play chess later, da?"

I managed a grin. "Spasibo, Sergyi," I said to the Ukrainian. "Maybe later."

He turned and left, accompanied by a crew member I couldn't see.

When he was gone I asked, "What happened, Ham? The last thing I remember is seeing the light disappear when the hatch closed."

Ham filled me in. When I didn't come back, they decided to isolate the outer hatch and bring the sub up to get me. Sergyi insisted on joining Jack and Jimmy in the outer lock. Since the excursion appeared to be within thirty feet, Ham authorized it, since he could think of nothing Sergyi might do that could jeopardize the rescue operation. Then they heard my banging, and the hatch cracked open, Sergyi grabbed a mask and thrust his head through the opening. That's why I didn't recognize his face. I didn't really know it, and I was practically unconscious from loss of blood by then. When he donned his mask and stuck his head through the hatch, he saw me in a prone position floating away. Although he was dressed only in a borrowed Nomex jumpsuit, he wasted no time coming back up to explain, but with the breath he already had he pulled himself through the hatch, swam about five feet to my position, grabbed my harness, and pulled me to the hatch. He stripped my gear off and wrestled me up into the lock where an astonished Jack and an incredulous Jimmy pulled me to safety. Then they hoisted the half-frozen Ukrainian back into the lock and sealed the hatch. They got a hot shower on Sergyi, and proceeded to remove my gloves. The obvious injury on my left hand made them change their tactics, and they cut the rest of my suit off.

The stab wound to my bicep appeared to be something that a bit of antibiotic and several sutures would fix. At first they didn't see the leg injury, but when they cut the suit away, the leg was filled with blood, and they quickly discovered that the Russian's knife had severed my femoral artery. Things happened pretty fast after that.

Sergyi strapped a tourniquet around my upper thigh, while Jack crashed the outer lock to the Can's depth, hoping he wouldn't rupture my eardrums in the process – a painful, but not life-threatening process. At the same time, Doctor Bollinger and Doc Branson were rushed to the Can where they pressed down in the entry lock. In three minutes, the doctor was examining my leg. He had no option. His only choice was to open the wound and attempt a repair to the artery. There was no time to decompress me – the job needed to be done immediately, or I was going to lose my leg or even my life.

Conditions for the operation were way less than ideal, but Doc sterilized my leg, and created a kind of clean space around the wound using sterilized cloths and alcohol wiped stainless wire that the guys rigged. Doctor Bollinger performed a miracle inside that cramped, overcrowded, pressurized tin can. A half-hour later, he and Doc removed their surgical masks and gave the camera a thumbs-up. A helium distorted cheer rose from the occupants of the Can.

Since we still had at least a half-day of decompression, the doctor decided to dress and suture my other stab wound. With that done, he attended my slashed left hand. Ham described his meticulous closure of the four-inch plus slash, and the thirteen careful stitches. During the entire procedure, Sergyi sat quietly out of the way, but paying close attention to everything that was happening. I found out later that the guys had told him the only reason he was alive was because of me, and the proud Ukrainian figured he owed me.

By the time the doctor had completed his third task, Jack had already locked back into the sub, going through a staged decompression, with a ten minute stop at fifty feet, a ten minute stop on pure oxygen at thirty feet, and a five-minute 02 stop at ten feet. Jimmy was none the worse for his experience, and locked out next. By the time Doctor Bollinger was ready to leave, the Can was at seventy feet, and he was able to leave with just a five-minute stop at fifty feet and ten minutes of 02 at ten feet. Doc stayed with me. The next day everybody surfaced, and they got me out.

In the meantime, the crippled *Whiskey* Skipper had panicked when his divers failed to return. Apparently the Soviet commander put his remaining diver in the water from the after deck on a tether. We knew this because our Skipper had initially deployed the Basketball to observe our activities. I didn't know about this because everything happened so fast that no one remembered to tell me, and once we were outside, there was no way to let us know, short of nudging one of us with the Basketball, and that just didn't seem like a good thing. So, from a distance through the Basketball the Skipper and everybody who could find a monitor watched our disabling of the *Whiskey*, saw Jimmy's predicament, observed my actions that ultimately saved his life, and then they watched in fascinated horror my silent pantomime – my death dance with the two Russian divers.

Once the divers were secure, including me, the Basketball returned to its observations for a few more minutes while we got ready to move back into our secure position underneath the trawler. We – that is everyone but me – watched the third diver discover the mess around the screws, and watched him pull the hawser out of the torpedo tube door. As for the blocked inlet, when the *Whiskey* shut down its diesels, the ragged patch must have fallen away. It would have floated for sure, and would have been easily spotted had it surfaced orange side up. Most likely it displayed the black side, because the *Whiskey* did nothing unusual to retrieve anything in the water.

Once I was safely inside the Can and it was clear that the *Whiskey* was disabled for a while at least, the Skipper retrieved the Basketball and maneuvered us back under the trawler, which had taken the opportunity presented by the disabled *Whiskey* to move away smartly at six knots. Within a few minutes we were back in place, with Sonar basically maintaining our position with the thruster controller while we made turns for six knots, or whatever the trawler was doing at any given moment.

As the trawler moved through the Fourth Kuril Straight, the U.S. Navy warships several miles to the north put up such a sonar racket that neither the *Victor* nor any of its fleet mates could hear themselves, let alone detect us creeping along beneath the Trawler. The Four-five-four apparently came to the aid of the *Whiskey*, but we learned later that the *Whiskey* had to dry dock at Petropavlovsk to have its shaft seals replaced. This meant the *Whiskey* had to be taken in tow by somebody up the island chain, along the outer coast, and ignominiously into the protected harbor at Petropavlovsk.

But that was all five days ago.

Ham happily informed me that we were somewhere in the vast North Pacific, trundling along at 600 feet, and making six and a half knots. Some higher-up had decided that we would bring our haul all the way back to Mare Island, which was fine by me, because that meant I would have a bit more time to get acquainted with our prisoner, and my personal savior.

I still was pretty weak, but I was healing, and Doctor Bollinger told me my femoral artery had knitted back together without a hitch. He wanted to keep me off my leg as long as possible to facilitate the healing process.

That afternoon, Sergyi showed up with a chessboard, and proceeded to teach me a thing or two about the intricacies of the game that I thought I already knew how to play. Over the next three weeks, he spent virtually every waking moment hovering near me, attentive to my every wish. At first it annoyed me a bit, but then I began to realize that he was profoundly grateful for having his life, and was trying to communicate this to me in the only way he knew how. When I tried to tell him that his actions on my behalf had evened the score, he would have none of it.

"If not Sergyi, then Jack or Jimmy," he said. "You no be lost. But if not El-Tee, Sergyi be lost for sure!"

There was no arguing with him. In his mind the picture was crystal clear.

As the days passed, Sergyi began to ask me about America and about my home. I told him general things, how I had come up through the ranks, and how we ran our military in a genuinely free and democratic society.

Sergyi expressed astonishment when I told him how I got my commission. "El-Tee sailor first, then officer... now Sergyi know why El-Tee damn good officer!"

It was a bit embarrassing, but I have to admit that I liked to hear things like that. Before the end of our transit, I was winning about half the chess games with Sergyi. Did he let me win? I couldn't tell you. But our friendship grew, and I knew that I wanted to keep in touch with this man, and perhaps even have some influence on what happened to him once we reached port.

#

Finally the day arrived when the Chief of the Watch announced on the 1MC: "Surface...surface...surface!"

Ballast tanks filled with rushing air, and we pierced the surface leaving our silent hunting grounds behind for a beautiful, fog shrouded passage under the Golden Gate, up the bay, to dock once again after so long at our Mare Island berth.

We were home at last.

Navy Cross Medal

EPILOG

The entire crew of the *USS Halibut* was assembled in the first few rows of the Rodman Theatre on Mare Island Naval Base. Behind them were their immediate families – wives, children, fathers and mothers, brothers and sisters – sworn to secrecy as a condition of being present at this occasion. In addition, a few specially invited guests were present, including one tall gentleman with short-cropped brown hair and slightly Slavic features that tended to disappear the moment you noticed them. He was accompanied by two nondescript men in dark civilian suits who never strayed more than a couple of feet from the guest's side.

The people in the theatre had been waiting for about fifteen minutes, when Master Chief Joe Thornton, *Halibut's* Chief of the Boat, called out, "Attention on Deck!"

The assembled crew came to attention in rigid silence. The guests straggled to their feet, looking at one another and around the room with curious interest. Only the man in the rear with the short-cropped hair stood like the crew members at stiff attention, eyes straight forward.

A moment later, the Secretary of Defense stepped onto the stage without fanfare or flurry. In a quiet voice that, nevertheless, carried to the back of the room, he asked the guests to be seated, and welcomed the officers and crew and the visitors. Then he opened a leather folder that he had brought with him. Without another word, he started reading from the folder:

By virtue of the authority vested in me as President of the United States and as Commander-in-Chief of the Armed Forces of the United States, I have today awarded THE PRESIDENTIAL UNIT CITATION (NAVY) FOR EXTRAORDINARY HEROISM TO *USS HALIBUT* (SSN-587)

For extraordinary heroism and outstanding performance of duty as a unit of the Submarine Force, United States Pacific Fleet. *USS HALIBUT* successfully accomplished two highly productive and complex submarine operations of immeasurable value to the Government of the United States. The superb professional competence, extremely effective teamwork and exemplary devotion to duty by the officers and men of *USS HALIBUT* reflected great credit upon themselves, the Submarine Force and the United States Naval Service.

Signed: The President of the United States

You could have heard a pin drop, the room was so silent. Here and there a tear rolled down a cheek. Several men gulped, working to control their emotions. The silence spoke louder than any applause.

Then Master Chief Thornton intoned: Lieutenant J. R. McDowell, front and center."

Immaculately dressed in his summer dress white uniform, and sporting a crutch under his left arm, Mac hobbled to the Secretary of Defense. Mac came to attention, supporting himself with the crutch, but managing to project a military bearing. Secretary Lehman opened another leather folder an aid handed him, and commenced reading:

The Navy Cross is presented to J.R McDowell, Lieutenant, U.S. Navy, for extraordinary heroism while serving as Officer in Charge, Test Operations Group, Submarine Development Group One. While leading the members of this team embarked on the *USS Halibut* (SSN 587), Lieutenant McDowell performed acts of extraordinary heroism and valor without regard for his own life or safety, thereby ensuring the success of the mission and preserving the lives of his entire team and the combined crew of the submarine. By his courage, aggressive leadership, and selfless devotion to duty, Lieutenant McDowell upheld the highest traditions of the Submarine Service and the United States Naval Service.

As the Secretary pinned the medal to Mac's chest, an audible wave of emotion swept through the assembled group.

Then Master Chief Thornton intoned: "Chief Petty Officer Jack Meredith, Petty Officer First Class William Fisher, Petty Officer First Class Harry Blackwell, Petty Officer Second Class James Tanner, Petty Officer Second Class Melvin Ford, Petty Officer Second Class Wlodek Cslauski, and Petty Officer Second Class Jeremy Romain, front and center."

The small group assembled before the Secretary, and came to attention.

The Secretary opened another leather folder an aide handed him, and announced that the identical citation was being presented to each of the individuals:

The Bronze Star is presented to each of the individuals standing before me, U.S. Navy, for extraordinary heroism while serving as a member of the Test Operations Group, Submarine Development Group One. While functioning as a member of this team embarked on the USS Halibut (SSN 587), each of the individuals before me performed acts of extraordinary heroism and valor without regard for his own life or safety, thereby ensuring the success of the mission and protecting the lives of the other team members. By his courage and selfless devotion to duty, each of the individuals standing before me upheld the highest traditions of the Submarine Service and the United States Naval Service.

One by one, the Secretary meticulously pinned the medal to each man's chest. You could hear audible sniffs from the audience. There wasn't a dry eye in the house.

Then Master Chief Thornton intoned: Master Chief Petty Officer Hamilton Comstock, front and center."

Ham strode forward, resplendent in his dress whites.

The Secretary opened another leather folder an aid handed him, and commenced reading:

The Navy Commendation Medal is presented to Hamilton Comstock, Master Chief Petty Officer, U.S. Navy, for distinguished heroism while serving as Unit Master Chief Petty Officer and Master Saturation Diver, Test Operations Group, Submarine Development Group One. While leading the members of this team under his Officer in Charge embarked on the *USS Halibut* (SSN 587), Master Chief Petty Officer Comstock performed acts of distinguished heroism and valor, thereby ensuring the success of the mission and preserving the lives of his entire team. By his courage, aggressive leadership, and selfless devotion to duty, Master Chief Petty Officer Comstock upheld the highest traditions of the Submarine Service and the United States Naval Service.

As the Secretary pinned the medal to Ham's chest, an audible "Yes!" could be heard from the onlookers.

And finally Master Chief Thornton intoned: "Lieutenant J.R. McDowell and Petty Officer Second Class Wlodek Cslauski, front and center."

Mac and Ski came forward, with Ski lending a steadying hand as Mac stumbled on the steps to the platform.

The Secretary opened a last leather folder, and announced that the identical citation was being presented to both individuals:

The United States of America, to all who shall see these presents, greeting: This is to certify that the President of the United States of America has awarded the Purple Heart established by General George Washington at Newberg, New York, August 7, 1782, to each of the individuals standing before me for wounds received in action. Given under my hand in the City of Washington on this date. Signed by the Chief of Naval Operations and the Secretary of the Navy.

As the Secretary pinned the heart-shaped medals on Mac and Ski, another wave of emotion swept the group. Several women were openly crying, and even some of the men were clearly working at keeping themselves in check.

There were no reporters at the ceremony. No photos were taken. No recordings were made, because as far as the outside world was concerned, it never happened. The generic language in the citations and the lack of specific dates only hinted at what had happened, and that was how it would be for the next twenty-five years or more.

Following the ceremony, the Secretary approached the Skipper and shook his hand. "I want to commend you on your persistence, Captain Jackson. If you had not persisted, if you had not refused the PUC unless family members could share in the ceremony, Sir, this day might never have happened. I salute you, Sir!"

Then he turned to Mac. "And you, Lieutenant Mc-Dowell. We could use more officers like you, across the board. I'm damn proud to have met you!"

With practiced political savvy, the Secretary quickly shook the hands of the other awardees, making sure he had missed no one. Then he left quietly by the side door.

Master Chief Thornton dismissed the *Halibut* crew, and the crew members mixed with the guests as they exited Rodman Theatre through the main door to the rear of the auditorium.

Mac hobbled to the back as quickly as he could, catching up with the former Soviet diver, proud ex-Ukrainian citizen, and newly accepted political refugee on a fast track to becoming an American.

"Good to see you, Sergyi Andreev," Mac said.

Sergyi popped to attention. "And you El-Tee." He paused for a moment, and then reached out and grabbed Mac's hand. "And my friend...Mac!"

And his escorts hustled him out the door.

by Gary McCluskey

Mac and the TOG divers celebration at the Horse & Cow

AFTERWORD – REYKJAVIK, ICELAND

Saturday, October 11, 1986

Höfði House, the former residence of John Greenway, British Ambassador to Iceland in the early 1950s, is a grim structure set on a bare plain facing the Atlantic just north of Reykjavik. Proclaimed haunted by the locals, the British had sold it in 1952 after pictures unaccountably fell off the walls. Memoirs of one of the earliest occupants of Höfði recount the presence of the spirit of a young woman who was either a suicide or drowning victim. The locals, however, insist that the house sits atop a Viking burial site, and that the liquor cabinet, therefore, is frequently raided by spirits.

Early on the morning of October 11, 1986, U.S. Secret Service and their Soviet counterparts checked their joint security set-ups and conducted their final joint rounds of Höfði House to ensure the safety of their respective country's leaders – President Ronald Reagan and Secretary General Mikhail Gorbachev.

For several days behind-the-scenes, hundreds of staffers on both sides had been frantically convening meetings, setting protocols, outlining proposals, arguing points...all the million-and-one preparations that make for a successful summit. A driving October rain set the scene for the President's Daily Brief, normally presented by an experienced CIA briefer to the President, the Vice President, the Secretary of State, the Secretary of Defense, and the National Security Adviser. On this still dark morning, speaking privately behind closed doors to the President and Secretary of State George Schultz, the briefer called attention to a veiled message the CIA had sent them. The briefer handed a large brown envelope to the President and said, "These are transcripts of the most recent submarine cable intercepts – a conversation between Marshal Sergei Akhromeyev and Fleet Admiral Vladimir Vasilyevich Sidoro..."

"That's their equivalent of our Chairman of the Joint Chiefs calling their Pacific Fleet Commander," Schultz interjected.

"I know, George," Reagan said with audible impatience.

"In the transcript Marshal Akhromeyev is briefing Admiral Sidoro on the Army's position, Sir. Apparently, the Soviet army is opposed to Gorbachev because he's open to making agreements with the United States. Soviet commanders are actually debating assassinating him. It looks like Marshal Akhromeyev is coordinating the effort. The CIA believes the only way Gorbachev will survive is for him to be perceived as successful at this summit."

Schultz raised his eyebrows.

"We do not believe Gorbachev is aware of these dealings," the briefer said quietly.

"And the rest?" The President indicated the remaining several pages, divided into two packs.

"These charts show the exact positions of the entire Soviet ballistic missile submarine fleet as of midnight, Sir. The photos," he pointed to a small stack of clipped photographs, "are the latest photos of the nosecone and components from the recent failed Soviet missile test, along with a CIA analysis of what caused the failure."

The President spread them out on the table in front of them.

"It's very unlikely that Gorbachev has seen any analysis of this failure," the briefer added, "because we have the failed parts."

#

Gorbachev and his party arrived at Höfði House at 10:30 a.m. sharp. After a brief photo-op with the press, the two most powerful men in the world settled down before a large fireplace on the ground floor, while the rest of both delegations moved to the second floor. The two leaders faced each other from identical overstuffed natural leather chairs set at an angle with the crackling fireplace over their shoulders and a small coffee table between the chairs to the President's left and the General Secretary's right. The President held the brown envelope loosely in his lap while they exchanges pleasantries.

"This may be our only opportunity, Mr. Secretary..."

"Please, Mr. President, call me Mikhail." The General Secretary smiled warmly.

"My friends call me Ron," The President reached out with a large, weathered hand, and the General Secretary took hold. They shook warmly.

"You obviously came prepared to show me something, Ron."

"I did, Mikhail." The President opened the envelope and handed the General Secretary the Russian-language transcript with the pertinent parts highlighted. He leaned back, crossing his left ankle over his knee.

Gorbachev crossed his ankles and read the transcript silently for several minutes. Then he looked up;

his face had paled, causing the birthmark in his right forehead to purple. "This is authentic?"

Reagan nodded.

"Am I to know how you got this?"

Reagan silently shook his head from side to side.

"You understand what this means for this Summit?" Gorbachev phrased the question firmly, leaning forward.

"I do, Mikhail, I do..." Reagan's voice trailed off. "I have more." He handed Gorbachev the packet of photos and the analysis. "This is..." he started to say.

"I know what it is, Ron." Gorbachev scanned the photos silently for a minute. "How did you possibly obtain these photographs?"

"You know that I cannot tell you that, my friend." Then Reagan handed Gorbachev the marked charts.

"But...but...even I do not know this information. Not even Sidoro knows this." Gorbachev sat quietly in his easy chair, obviously contemplating what he had just learned.

"You should understand, my friend, that I have a fast-attack sub within short-range shooting distance of every one of your boomers."

"Boomers?" Gorbachev's voice betrayed some stress.

"It's what we call ballistic missile submarines."

Gorbachev nodded.

"Open a missile launch door," Reagan added, "and..."

"But that means we have only our land-based missiles..."

"But we will never launch first," Reagan told him quietly, leaning forward. "We do not threaten you, Mikhail. Let's eliminate our mutual land-based threats, and then we both can significantly decrease our submarine launch capability." Reagan leaned back, placing his arms on the wide chair back. "We will continue to develop SDI, and invite you to every test. When it works, and it will, we will share the technology with you." Reagan smiled broadly. "I give you my word!"

#

Following the Summit, General Secretary Mikhail Gorbachev was not assassinated. The world began to see him in a new light. The Soviet Union began to change. Eight months later at the 750th anniversary of Berlin, at the Brandenburg Gate demarking the symbolic division between the free West and the enslaved Soviet Union, President Reagan challenged Gorbachev to "Tear down this wall!"

#

Halfway around the world, the Horse & Cow was crowded with noisy submariners. It was late, near closing time; many sailors had been there for hours. Nine men crowded around a table near a perpetually vacant World War II submarine-stern-planes-seat at one end of the polished oak bar. The men watched an overhead television with rapt attention as President Reagan issued his historic challenge.

Master Chief Comstock, unmistakable even in his civvies, glanced at the red-bearded Lieutenant McDowell.

"Whadya think, Mac?" He raised his mug.

McDowell stood, and the remaining seven raised their mugs in silent toast, while the roomful of raucous submariners cheered.

"Ivy Bells!" McDowell said with a grin.

Nine mugs clinked together.

###

Please post a review for
Operation Ivy Bells
on
Amazon.com and Goodreads.com

I really appreciate you posting a review on Amazon and Goodreads. Posting to Amazon.com is intuitive. To post a review on Goodreads.com, go to their website, and become a member if you are not already one. Search for *Operation Ivy Bells*, and click on the *Want to read* button under the image of *Operation Ivy Bells*. Indicate that you have read *Operation Ivy Bells,* and then you will be able to post a review. Thank you very much for going through this effort!

Excerpt from the First Chapter of
THE STARCHILD COMPACT
by
Robert G. Williscroft

Saeed Esmail prostrated himself toward Earth, nearly 400 million kilometers back in the direction of the Sun. He felt his stomach heave, and vomited blood on his prayer mat, and wondered aloud why Allah had abandoned him. At that moment he was hit with massive weight, several gees at least, and a twisting, wrenching, totally disorienting surge that made no mental or physical sense. In his weakened state, all Saeed could do was let his body be tossed from wall to wall inside his tent, and hope that he would not tear the airtight fabric. He heard somebody screaming, and then his stomach heaved again, and bloody vomit filled the space around him, flying this way and that, finally collecting on the tent walls. The lights went out, and someone still was screaming, but as the wild gyrations began to settle into a repeating pattern, Saeed realized that he was the one screaming...and he couldn't stop. He reached for his head, pulling out fistfuls of hair...and he screamed again. He retched, but his stomach was empty, and only a little bit of blood mixed with spittle left his mouth, flying at an odd angle to the tent wall...and he screamed, but quieter now, and screamed some more, but quieter still, until his screams morphed into a frightened whimper as he curled into a tight ball on his prayer mat.

#

A subdued bong captured Saeed's attention. A comforting female voice announced, "In five minutes we will pitch over and commence our arrival burn at El-four. Please make sure you are securely strapped into your seat, and that you have stowed any loose items you might have been using during the transit. Remain securely fastened in your seat until the arrival announcement tells you it is safe to unbuckle and move about."

Saeed checked his harness, and curiously looked out the port. He saw nothing but stars, more stars than he had ever seen, and off to the rear, the beautiful blue marble that the earth had become – *praise be to Allah.* Then the star field began to rotate, accompanied by a slightly higher pitch from the gyros that penetrated into Saeed's conscious perception. The blue marble moved with the star-studded sky until it was positioned above the capsule's port bow. While this happened, Saeed felt no movement. His only sense was that the sky had rotated, as if Allah had reached out and rotated the heavenly backdrop with His mighty hand. Weight returned with a popping hiss as the kick thruster ignited for a few seconds burn. As his weight vanished again, the gyros whined, and the sky began to move from right to left. In short order Saeed could see the Moon through the ports on the other side of the capsule. It appeared no larger than it did from the Earth, but the left side was one that Saeed had only seen before in holographs. He could not see the Mirs Complex, although he knew it had to lie off the starboard quarter. Weight returned again for about a minute as the restartable kick thruster slowed their velocity to match the orbital velocity of the Russian Federation built Mirs Complex as it circled the Earth in the Moon's orbit, 385,000 kilometers ahead of the Moon.

Several clanks and surges later, Saeed felt his normal weight gradually return as the capsule nestled into its berth in the capsule arrival bay of the main Mirs Ring, and picked up its rotational speed.

Bong. "Welcome to the Mirs Ring," a bright female voice announced. "It is now safe for you to unstrap and move about. You may disembark to the left side of the capsule. Lavatory facilities are located immediately to the left of the passageway. Your personal belongings will be available in fifteen minutes at the baggage handling dock down the passageway to the right. We know you have choices when traveling off-planet. We thank you for using

Slingshot, and hope you had a pleasant trip, and that you will think of us the next time you leave Planet Earth."

Saeed stepped out of the capsule and hurried to the men's room. Although the passengers had been warned about not drinking before the flight, and all the passengers had been issued absorbent diapers an hour before leaving Baker just in case, Saeed, as a faithful Muslim, abhorred fouling himself, and had held off, *by the grace of Allah,* until arrival.

While awaiting the baggage, Saeed checked the construction schedule for *Cassini II*, and then perused the poster-size diagram of the spaceship. *Cassini II* was a sixty-six meter long twelve-meter wide cylinder, divided into three modules – a twenty meter long crew module, called the Pullman, a twenty-three meter long equipment module, called the Box, and the twenty-three meter long power module and engine cluster, called the Caboose. The large Iapetus-bound spaceship had been constructed entirely at Mirs, about a hundred kilometers away on the opposite side of the main L-4 complex. All three modules had been built in place.

Over the next several days, Saeed mingled with the *Cassini II* provisioning crew that verified the final loadout of the Box and the provisions stored in the Pullman. Another, more technical crew completed the final installation and testing of the gas core reactor and the advanced VASIMR engines that would drive Cassini II to Saturn in record time.

On the final day, prior to the flight crew arrival, the transport tug that ferried the provisioning crew to and from the massive spaceship experienced a catastrophic seal failure where the tug attached to the Box. The entire crew was suited up except, apparently, one Saeed Esmail, the newest provisioning crew member. Searchers found bloody pieces of his suit and a few helmet shards on a trajectory that would ultimately have taken them to the Moon. They never could quite figure out what had actually happened to Saeed, but it was obvious that he had somehow managed to shatter his nearly unbreakable helmet, and rip himself and his tough suit to shreds as he depressurized. The conclusion was that an untracked small meteor, two or three millimeters in size, had gotten him, and somehow maybe even caused the catastrophic depressurization of the tug. Saeed Esmail was not the first casualty on the project, although the consensus was that he might have been the last.

#

After ejecting the bloody suit pieces and helmet shards from a trash lock in the outer bulkhead of the Box, Saeed worked his way into the hiding place that he had created during the loadout wedged against the outer wall at right angles to both lower level accesses. It was an airtight polymer tent of just over five cubic meters, with its own oxygen supply and scrubber. It would keep him alive during the transit to Iapetus. He had the freeze-dried food, water from the emergency supply, and he could dump waste out the waste lock. His Link with its collection of holofilms, books, and the Qur'an would keep his mind occupied for the projected four-month trip. He examined the four burst transmitters that had been included in his life pack. About the size of a softball, each was designed to be ejected through the waste lock, orient itself with the ship to its rear, extend a gossamer parabolic antenna, and do a circular search for Earth, using a very limited supply of compressed gas. Then, using a high-density charge, the device would transmit a series of encrypted bursts until the charge was consumed. Saeed was to deploy the first at the tether extension, the second following the Jupiter boost, the third when they arrived near Saturn, and the fourth was for whatever circumstance warranted a special transmission.

In his hideaway, Saeed prostrated himself facing Earth, he hoped, and recited his prayers, adding a personal thanks to Allah for keeping him safe thus far, and on line to accomplish His holy mission.

#

Jon Stock stepped out of the launch loop capsule at Mirs Ring and made a beeline for the men's room. "Those capsules need a latrine," he muttered to himself as he splashed water on his face. Steely blue eyes stared out at him from the mirror. His hair was gray and cropped short above a craggy, clean shaven face that testified to his fifty years. A lean, muscled 183-centimeter frame belied those same years. He wore the uniform of a U.S. Navy Captain, his left chest bedecked with ribbons. One stood out top center, jet black, framed in silver, with a golden image of Mars attached to the center – the Mars Expeditionary Medal. Jon was the second in command on that first expedition to the Red Planet. When Commander Evans was killed in a freak accident on the surface, he assumed command, saved the mission, and brought the crew back. Now he commanded the international crew of *Cassini II* on an expedition to Iapetus. They would travel five times further than any human had ever gone before. And what awaited them at their destination might very well change human history forever.

Iapetus... Jon reviewed what he knew about Saturn's iconic moon. In 2004, the *Cassini-Huygens* spacecraft flew by Iapetus. Iapetus proved to be unlike any other moon. The surface seemed to display an intersecting grid of geodesic sections, something not normally found in nature. A narrow mountainous wall extended around Iapetus at the equator, so that the moon looked something like a walnut. Iapetus' density was far too low for a moon that appeared solid, but if Iapetus were substantially hollow, then the numbers worked out just about right. Several of the "geodesic sections" appeared to have collapsed inward, revealing what could be interpreted as complex structures underneath the surface layer. A tall, very narrow structure extended from the surface at one point, like a towering spike a kilometer high. Like the "geodesic structure," this spike had no "natural" explanation.

In September 2007, the *Cassini-Huygens* spacecraft made another relatively close transit of Iapetus following the equatorial wall, revealing that the wall consisted of a series of mountains up to twenty kilometers high, following each other in series, none side-by-side. It also supplied further details on a series of equally spaced craters on a line parallel to the equatorial wall and halfway between the wall and the North Pole.

Iapetus had remained a mystery. It was very difficult to imagine that all the things discovered by Cassini-Huygens were natural. The implications of the discoveries being artificial were staggering. As more and more information was gathered by space telescopes in orbit around Earth, on the Moon, and at the Mirs Complex at L-4, the possibility that Iapetus could have an artificial origin became quite real. The initial concept for a human investigation of Iapetus had been put forward by Launch Loop International (LLI), the consortium that had built Slingshot as an entirely civilian operation, followed by several other launch loops around the world. While there was lots of pushing and shoving by the governments of the territories where the launch loops were located, in the final analysis, most people considered a launch loop as something akin to an airline company, and in the end, most of the loops were left in civilian hands, although governments exercised whatever control they wished.

Iapetus, however, was seen by the world's major players as a potential prize like none other. If Iapetus turned out to be an artifact, eloquent spokespersons from various governments argued, then it belonged to all the people, not just to the greedy corporations that found it. This argument fell on sympathetic ears of a world population that had grown used to being told what to do by benevolent governments. When LLI partnered with their former rival, Galaxy Ventures, to form Iapetus Quest, they found themselves faced with an unusually consolidated array of governments united in their opposition to a privately funded and operated Iapetus operation. The United States, in its still dominant position on the world stage, muscled itself into the leadership slot in the newly recast government owned and operated Iapetus Quest. The international debate had raged on how to structure the crew of *Cassini II*. Many had argued for a civilian crew, structured however they wanted. Eventually, by negotiated treaty, arm twisting, back-room dealing, and even outright bribery and coercion, an international crew was assembled that represented the interests of the participating nations.

You have just been reading from Chapter One of Robert Williscroft's exciting Science Fiction novel, The Starchild Compact.

Words of praise for
The Starchild Compact

In the not-too-distant future, a spacecraft heads toward Saturn's moon Iapetus to investigate whether it is an artifact, while a terrorist stows away on board hoping to destroy the science that contravenes the tenets of his religion. All this builds up the tension and suspense in this fascinating science fiction novel. Each part of this book solves and unfolds another mystery, making the book incredibly hard to put down. The research and science are impeccable. I marveled at Williscroft's imagination in conjuring up this story. I highly recommend this book!

– Marc Weitz, Past President
The Adventurers' Club of Los Angeles

Hard sci-fi reminiscent of Arthur C. Clarke or James P. Hogan, with a geopolitical twist worthy of Tom Clancy or Clive Cussler.

– Alastair Mayer
Author of the *Tspace Series*

The Starchild Compact *is a compelling read from the first page. Robert has written a fantastically engrossing space mystery that takes place in our own backyard. This book brought me moments of wonder that I had experienced when I originally read Clarke's* Rendezvous with Rama. *This does what science fiction is supposed to do: capture our attention, speculate about the wild possibilities, and take us just beyond our previous imaginings. But this book is not all spectacle. Robert tackles some of the more personal issues of space travel that often go overlooked, with a particular eye toward the role of religion in that exploration. It is a masterful hand that can manage the personal and cultural response to the wonders of space and still present those wonders as pure delight. Robert has done that in* The Starchild Compact. *From the beginning to the end, this is a must read.*

— Jason D. Batt
100 Year Starship
Author of *The Tales of Dreamside series*

In The Starchild Compact *Robert Williscroft has said in print what a lot of people (myself included) would like to do about present day threats to our democracy and way of life, but don't have the means or cojones to do it. He also courageously extrapolates tomorrow's mores and the religious direction our society is taking. Williscroft tackles these germane and "heavy" issues while crafting a fascinating novel that is hard to put down. I have to admit that I was moved to tears, because I could not be with the space travelers to come back and see Earth's future. I'm looking forward to both the prequel and sequel.*

— Myron R. Lewis, Co-author with
Ben Bova of several SF
stories including parts of
The Dueling Machine

OTHER BOOKS BY THIS AUTHOR

Please visit your favorite eBook retailer to discover other eBooks by Robert G. Williscroft and your favorite online bookseller for their paper versions:

Current events:
The Chicken Little Agenda – Debunking "Experts'" Lies

Children's books:
The Starman Jones Series:
Starman Jones: A Relativity Birthday Present
Starman Jones Goes to the Dogs
(scheduled for release in late 2014)

Novels:
The Starchild Compact

Novels in the pipeline:
Slingshot
(scheduled for release in early 2015)
The Iapetus Federation
(scheduled for release in mid 2015)

CONNECT WITH ROBERT G. WILLISCROFT

I really appreciate you reading my book! Here are my social media coordinates:

Friend me on Facebook: *https://www.facebook.com/ robert.williscroft*
Follow me on Twitter: *@RGWilliscroft*
Like my Amazon author page: *http://www.amazon. com/Robert-G.-Williscroft/e/B001JP52AS/ref=ntt_ dp_epwbk_0*
Subscribe to my blog: *http://ThrawnRickle*.com
Connect on LinkedIn: *http://www.linkedin.com/in/ argee/*
Visit my website: *http://www.robertwilliscroft.com*
Favorite my Smashwords author page: *https://www. smashwords.com/profile/view/RWilliscroft*

ABOUT THE AUTHOR

At the Adventurers' Club of Los Angeles

D r. Robert G. Williscroft served twenty-three years in the U.S. Navy and the National Oceanic and Atmospheric Administration (NOAA). He commenced his service as an enlisted nuclear Submarine Sonar Technician in 1961, was selected for the Navy Enlisted Scientific Education Program in 1966, and graduated from University of Washington in Marine Physics and Meteorology in 1969. He returned to nuclear submarines as the Navy's first Poseidon Weapons Officer. Subsequently, he served as Navigator and Diving Officer on both catamaran mother vessels for the *Deep Submergence Rescue Vehicle*. Then he joined the Submarine Development Group One out of San Diego as the Officer-in-Charge of the Test Operations Group, conducting "deep-ocean surveillance and data acquisition" – which forms the basis for this novel.

In NOAA Dr. Williscroft directed diving operations throughout the Pacific and Atlantic. As a certified diving instructor for both the National Association of Underwater Instructors (NAUI) and the Multinational Diving Educators Association (MDEA), he taught over 3,000 individuals both basic and advanced SCUBA diving. He authored four diving books, developed the first NAUI drysuit course, developed advanced curricula for mixed gas and other specialized diving modes, and developed and taught a NAUI course on the Math and Physics of Advanced Diving. His doctoral dissertation for California Coast University, *A System for Protecting SCUBA Divers from the Hazards of Contaminated Water* was published by the U.S. Department of Commerce and distributed to Port Captains World-wide. He also served three shipboard years in the high Arctic conducting scientific baseline studies, and thirteen months at the geographic South Pole in charge of National Science Foundation atmospheric projects.

Dr. Williscroft has written extensively on terrorism and related subjects. He is the author of a popular book on current events published by Pelican Publishing: *The Chicken Little Agenda – Debunking Experts' Lies*, now in its second edition as an eBook, and a new children's book series, *Starman Jones*, in collaboration with Dr. Frank Drake, world famous director of the Carl Sagan Center for the Study of Life in the Universe and the SETI Institute.

Dr. Williscroft's novel, *Slingshot*, was released in August, 2015, at the International Space Elevator Conference (ISEC) in Seattle. It tells the story of the construction of the World's first Space Launch Loop. A sequel, *The Starchild Compact*, is based on the discovery that Saturn's moon Iapetus is actually a derelict starship, and how Earth explorers eventually meet with the "Founders," who originally arrived on the starship and populated the Earth long ago. He is currently working on *The Iapetus Federation*, a sequel to *The Starchild Compact*, that tells the story of the World falling under the rule of a planet-wide Islamic Caliphate, where the Founders establish the Iapetus Federation, a loose federation of free off-world communities that operates under an updated model based on the U.S. Constitution, and carries out the traditions of the American Founding Fathers throughout the Solar System. These three books comprise *The Starchild Series*.

Dr. Williscroft is an active member of the venerable Adventurers' Club of Los Angeles, where he is the Editor of the Club's monthly magazine. He lives in Centennial, Colorado, with his wife, Jill, whom he met upon his return from the South Pole in 1982 and finally married in 2010, and their twin college boys.

1MC – Ship's announcing system.

Aquarium – The double-lock hull penetration in the Bat Cave used to deploy the Basketball, the fish, and to retrieve items from deployed divers.

ASR - Submarine Rescue Ship (Auxiliary Submarine Rescue) – Ships specially designed to rescue crews from downed submarines. They originally carried McCann Rescue Bells, later, two catamaran ASRs (the USS Ortolan and USS Pigeon) carried the DSRVs.

ASW – Anti-submarine Warfare

Baffles – The baffles is the area in the water directly behind a submarine or ship through which a hull-mounted sonar cannot hear. This blind spot is caused by the noise of the vessel's machinery, propulsion system, and propellers.

Basketball – A basketball-size, camera-carrying remotely operated vehicle (ROV) on a tether.

Bat Cave – The forward compartment on the Halibut used for special operations. Formerly the cruise missile launch location.

BCP – Ballast Control Panel; the console from which water is pumped into and out of a sub, and distributed fore and aft in the sub.. The Chief of the Watch occupies this position, under the control of the Diving Officer or the OOD.

Belay that – Countermands an order just given.

Bird – A helicopter, often using a dipping sonar.

Boomer – Ballistic Missile Submarine.

BOQ – Bachelor Officers' Quarters; hotel-like quarters for bachelor officers.

Bottom – Bottom of the ocean, the seafloor. As a verb as in "to bottom," putting the submarine on the sea floor.

Bow – Front of a ship or sub

Bridge – The place on a ship from which it is driven. On a sub, it is the conning station at the top of the sail, (See Conn.)

Brow – Gangway onto a vessel from the pier or another vessel.

Bubblehead – Submariner

Can – Slang term for the fake DSRV (Deep Submergence Rescue Vehicle) that was really the saturation DDC on the stern of Halibut.

Capstan – A revolving cylinder with a vertical axis used for hauling in a rope or cable.

Captain – The officer in command of the ship or sub. He is an absolute dictator, subject only to the Uniform Code of Military Justice, and the orders of his superiors in the chain-of-command.

Chopper – Helicopter.

Clear the baffles – A submarine tracking another submarine can take advantage of its quarry's baffles to follow at a close distance without being detected. Periodically, a submarine will perform a maneuver called clearing the baffles, in which the boat will turn left or right far enough to listen with the sonar for a few minutes in the area that was previously blocked by the baffles.

Cleat – A T-shaped piece of metal or wood, esp. on a boat or ship, to which ropes are attached.

COB – Chief of the Boat; the senior enlisted man on a submarine.

Column – (water column) All the water above and below.

Come-home bottle – A small gas bottle that gets a diver back to the PTC/DDC in an emergency.

COMSUBPAC – Commander, Submarine Force Pacific; the commander of all submarine forces in the Pacific.

Conn – The location from which the sub is controlled by the OOD (Officer-of-the-Deck) – also called Control. The Conning Officer (Conn), the watch position for the person who controls the sub's direction, speed, and depth. The OOD usually has both the Deck and Conn, but can pass off the Conn to another qualified officer. Sometimes the Captain will assume the Deck, leaving the Conn with the officer watchstander.

COW – Chief of the Watch; the enlisted watchstander (usually a Chief) who sits at the BCP and controls the ship's load of ballast water and its distribution throughout the submarine.

Coxcombing – A decorative knotwork performed by sailors to dress-up items and parts of ships and boats. Modern uses are to wrap boat tillers and ships' wheels with small diameter line to enhance the grip as well as the nautical appeal. Knots used in coxcombing include Turk's head knot, Flemish, French whipping, and others.

DDC – Deck Decompression Chamber; a pressure chamber on a ship's deck or just below the deck that contains a side lock for entrance and egress, a top lock to mate with the PTC, a small lock for passing in food or medical supplies, emergency equipment, and depending on how it is being used, bunks, lavatory facilities, etc.

Deck – The watch position of OOD (Officer of the Deck); the person in-charge of the sub when the Captain is not in the Control Room, or has not assumed the Deck while in the Control Room.

Dipping bird – A helicopter equipped with a dipping sonar.

Dipping sonar – A helicopter-carried sonar system that can be dipped to various depths by the chopper

Display Room – Located in the Bat Cave – a location with display monitors for following the Basketball or fish.

Dive Locker – A place where divers congregate and stow their gear.

Dive Manifold Complex – A console with gauges, valves and indicators from where a saturation dive is controlled.

Diving Officer – The officer or specially qualified Chief controlling the submarine depth. Works directly under the OOD. The COW works directly for the Diving Officer.

DIW – dead in the water; a ship that is not moving through the water.

Dolphins – The insignia worn by qualified submariners, silver for enlisted and gold for officers. It represents about a year of hard study to gain complete, detailed knowledge of the submarine.

Dry dock – A narrow basin or vessel that can be flooded to allow a ship to be floated in, then drained to allow that load to come to rest on a dry platform. Dry docks are used for the construction, maintenance, and repair of ships, boats, and other watercraft.

DSRV – Deep Submergence Rescue Vehicle; a specially designed mini-sub for rescuing crews from downed submarines. The DSRVs replaced the McCann Bells, and now, both DSRVs have been decommissioned. They have been replaced by the Submarine Rescue Diving and Recompression System.

EAB Mask – Emergency Air Breathing mask; an emergency mask that can be plugged into nearby pressurized air outlets throughout the submarine.

Executive Officer (XO) – Second in command of a ship or sub. Responsible for ship's administration and personnel.

Fast attack – See "Nuke fast attack."

Fast cruise – A one to two day period alongside the pier where all sub's systems are checked out just prior to deployment.

Fish – A towed, high resolution, side-scan sonar device that produces detailed images of the sea floor.

Fish – A torpedo.

Floating dry dock – A floating dry dock is a type of pontoon for dry docking ships, possessing floodable buoyancy chambers and a "U"-shaped cross-section. When valves are opened, the chambers fill with water, causing the dry dock to float lower in the water. The deck becomes submerged and this allows a ship to be moved into position inside. When the water is pumped out of the chambers, the dry dock rises and the ship is lifted out of the water on the rising deck, allowing work to proceed on the ship's hull.

Hawser – Heavy line used to moor subs and other vessels.

Helm – Ship's wheel and steering mechanisms. The person manning the helm.

Humboldt Squid – A large (5ft to 20+ft) squid found in the central pacific and along the Southwest coast of North America.

LOFAR – Low Frequency Analysis and Recording

Maneuvering Room – That part of a sub where the engines are directly controlled.

Maneuvering Watch – The special set of watch assignments for a sub or ship that is getting underway.

Mark 2 Mod 0 Deep Diving System – The original second version of the Deep Diving Saturation System.

McCann Rescue Bell – An old-fashioned type of submarine rescue system deployed from old ASRs; a bell-type of chamber that must be lowered directly to the sub's rescue hatch.

Messenger line – A light line, often with a monkey fist at one end, used to haul or support a larger cable.

Monkey fist – A monkey fist (or monkey paw) is a type of knot, so named because it looks somewhat like a small bunched fist/paw. It is tied at the end of a rope to serve as a weight, making it easier to throw, and also as an ornamental knot.

Nav – Depending on context, the ship's/sub's Navigator; or the navigation stand – typically near the Conn.

Nuke fast attack – A nuclear fast attack submarine – a hunter-killer submarine.

OIC – Officer-in-Charge; the Officer-in-Charge of a unit or operation. A lesser command responsibility than a Commanding Officer.

OOD – Officer-of-the-Deck; the individual in charge of the ship or submarine at any given moment. The OOD is responsible only to the Captain.

Operation Ivy Bells – A Top Secret Cold War plan to

retrieve Soviet missile parts and tap into their under-water communication cables.

Ops – The Operations Officer

Oxygen candle –Canisters containing a mixture of so-dium chlorate and iron pellets. When they are ignited, they produce about 150 man-hours of oxygen each.

Port – Left.

PTC – Personnel Transfer Capsule; a spherical bell that mates to the shipboard DDC and can transfer a max-imum of four divers to the underwater working site.

PUC – Presidential Unit Citation; a presidential award given to a ship or unit for exceptional performance (very rare).

R-C-H – Slang for a very small measurement.

Rope thimble – A loop of metal having a groove at its outer edge for a rope or cable, for lining the inside of an eye.

ROV – Remotely Operated Vehicle, an unmanned under-water vehicle that is remotely piloted either by wire or untethered, using sound.

Secure – Stop or finish a process, such as "Secure from Maneuvering Watch;" or when used as a verb, to make something safe, as in "secure the lines in the locker."

Secure the hover – Stop hover operations.

Secure the sidescan – Shut down the sidescan sonar.

Seizing – A length of cord or rope used for fastening or tying.

Sidescan sonar – A towed-fish sonar that looks to both sides to produce a high-definition of the ocean bottom.

SIOP – Single Integrated Operating Plan; the designated operating plan for nuclear war.

Sonar Shack – That part of a sub or surface ship that houses the sonar display equipment, where the So-nar Techs stand their watches. Usually close to the Bridge/Conn

Sonobuoys – A small (typically 5 inches by 3 feet) ex-pendable buoy equipped to detect underwater sounds and transmit them by radio.

SOSUS – Sound Surveillance System; a chain of underwater listening posts located around the world in places such as the Atlantic Ocean near Greenland, Iceland and the United Kingdom – the GIUK gap, and at various locations in the Pacific Ocean. The system was designed to track Soviet submarines.

Sound-powered phone – A shipboard communication system powered only by the sound of the speaker's voice.

SPCC – Strength-Power-Communications Cable; the umbilical that supports the PTC and supplies power and communications.

Starboard – Right.

Stern – Back of a ship or sub

SUBDEVGRUONE – Submarine Development Group One; the Navy command in charge of Operation Ivy Bells, where Mac had trained as a saturation diver.

SubSafe – A program instituted following the loss of the USS Thresher, to limit the number of openings to sea pressure in a submarine, and to make it safer in many different ways.

T-bar – A piece of metal that has a T-shape in cross-section. Used as a strength member.

TOG – Test Operations Group; a code name for the team that operated from the Halibut and Seawolf.

Topside – The outside deck of a submarine. Can also refer to the watch station at the top of the sail when a sub is underway.

Towed array sonar – A shipboard sonar system where hydrophones are attached to a towed cable about 50 yards apart. The size of the array enables the determination of the distance to contacts.

Turk's head – An ornamental knot resembling a turban in shape, made in the end of a rope to form a stopper.

Variable depth sonar – A shipboard sonar system on a telescoping shaft that can lower the sonar sensors to variable depths to get under shallow layers.

WRT – Water Round Torpedo Tank; a water tank used to flood a torpedo tube to allow a torpedo to swim out of the torpedo tube instead of being shot out with a burst of pressurized air.

XO – Executive Officer (See Executive Officer).

CPSIA information can be obtained at www.ICGtesting.com
Printed in the USA
LVOW06s2206171215

467075LV00003B/543/P